JOURNEY TO ZEMBEYLIA

A novel of exotic travel, sleazy doings, and murder.

THOMAS R. BRANSTEN

ISBN: 978-0-9969887-7-3

Printed in the United States of America by
Big Table Publishing Company, Boston, MA
www.bigtablepublishing.com

"Making other books jealous since 2004"

Also by Thomas R. Bransten:
A Slight Case of Guilt

To Bozenna, *pour toujours.*

"That corpse you planted last year in your garden,
Has it begun to sprout? Will it bloom this year?
Or has the sudden frost disturbed its bed?
O keep the Dog far hence, that's friend to man
or with his nails he'll dig it up again!"
T.S. Eliot, *The Wasteland*

PART ONE:
NOT OF THE LETTER!

Zembeylia, Southeast Africa, and New York, NY, U. S. A.
Monday, October 5, 1987 to Monday, November 30, 1987

"Not of the letter,
But the spirit.
For the letter killeth."
~ *2 Corinthians iii 6*

Chapter 1: Benefactor
The Uplands of Zembeylia, Monday, October 5

Baboons! Madame Félicité Briac jumps from her chair at the kitchen table. She is busy writing in her accounts book with a blue Mont-Blanc fountain pen. She must detail the sex of fifteen ostrich eggs by dangling a small silver pendulum over each one to see which way it twirls: right for males, left for hens.

But baboons…heading for her coffee plants? Lucky she spotted a shadow. Keep alert, no matter what. You have to be alert on this African plateau isolated from the world and, save for a handful of farming neighbors, so thoroughly on your own.

She rushes to the kitchen door, grabs her mop from a wall brace, charges into the yard, yarn ends flapping. "*Allez-vous en!*" she shouts, shaking the mop at the marauders. "Away! Out! Out!"

Three adults: a female, holding a baby to her breast, and two males. There's another large young male swinging down from the giant baobab tree at garden's end. The female turns tail, scampers to the tree for safety. The nearer males bark and bare teeth. Not daring to confront the mop, they slouch backwards, chattering.

The youngster just off the tree, lopes forward, picks up a stone, hurls it at Madame Briac. It skitters sideways into a bed of budding coca bushes. She ignores the counter-attack, advances towards the creatures shaking her mop and shouting.

The gang breaks, heads for the baobab's haven.

With handkerchief pulled from a sleeve, Madame wipes sweat off her face. She sighs and removes expensive American reading glasses: rhinestone decorated relic from more prosperous days. In the emergency, she didn't think to snatch them off.

Through the dusty windshield of his 1966 Chevrolet, S. K. Bharastri sees a parched hedgerow and above it moptails parading over a cascade of blonde curls that bob in the morning sun.

Blonde? Curls? Brakes squealing, he pulls up at Madame Briac's gate. Red dust boils from the rear of his vehicle. Dust obscures the dirt road that links a scattering of farms hereabouts. He ducks his white turban through the Chevy's open door, gives a push so khaki tunic and trousers won't touch the shiny red laterite layer that films his car's body.

Madame Briac stands at parade-rest, mop handle to earth, yarn ends dangling above her head. Mr. Bharastri experiences a flashback to the shakoed Horse-Guards of his Madras boyhood during the British *Raj*.

Giving a slight bow, he says in English, "Good morning, Missus. Troubles with monkey? Place meat poisons all around tree." He points to the baobab and grins. "No troubles then."

She turns to him, watching his eyes take in her perm, its golden color; he has only seen her gray, hair pulled back in a no-nonsense bun. Would he think her too coquettish for her age? No, his expression is admiring, flattering even.

Still, he's the postman. One must remember one's position.

She presses lips together to assume a severe look. "Poison? Too cruel." Gesturing toward the fenced-in coffee bushes, she says, "Monkeys like the red berries. When I don't watch, they climb across my fence. Unless they leave soon, I shall put up barbed wire."

Rains late this year. Threatening these past days, afternoon cumulus boils into the sky, clouds shot through with lightning flashes. Yet the downpour holds off. Severe drought has parched the earth. The baboons' normal habitat is due west, over the peaks of the Monogoro Range and down into the X'Ziloncado Valley's game preserve that borders Mozambique's frontier.

Riverbeds in the X'Ziloncado are dried up, water holes filled with dust, grasses withered. The great animal herds, predators dogging their heels, have moved north on the rolling prairie known as "The Veldt." They seek water and grazing grounds. The wily baboons trekked to this high mountain shelf, where Madame Briac and other ex-Breton farmers work modest holdings. The area's baobabs, dotting this upland meadow, now serve as the animals' sleeping-trees. Food they require, hence the attacks on Madame's coffee bushes and whatever else they can forage.

When the rains finally do arrive, her coca plantings will burst into bright yellow, the vegetable and flower gardens will bloom and, she fervently hopes, the baboon troupe will migrate back to its game preserve.

"Get watchdog. Get two watchdog. They are chasing all away. Even me." Mr. Bharastri's smile widens, showing teeth whiter than his snow-white turban. Their sparkle attests to hourly scrubbings with peeled green twigs that he and his fellow Tamils import from southern India.

"Well, Missus," the postman's smile turns into a frown of business. "Here we have most impressing document. Addressed to you." He holds up a large envelope. "We do not see such fine linen except in marriage announcement or funerary missive. Yes?"

Another bureaucratic demand? More money to pay? As if it will burn her, Madame Briac gingerly accepts the envelope. From a leather shoulder pouch, Mr. Bharastri pulls more mail bound with string, hands it over.

To receive this packet, she places mop under arm, eyes straying to the big envelope: postmarked Fulumbane, newly renamed capital city. Bretons here still think of the capital as Eugénieville, its name for a hundred and twenty years honoring Empress Eugénie of France, wife of Napoleon III.

In 1973, when France saw fit to abandon her children in East Africa by pulling out of Zembeylia, the place became Libertéville. Now this new monarch has changed the name again. To last for how long, *alors?*

Mr. Bharastri reaches into his tunic's pocket, removes a blue handkerchief, passes it over his face. "Most hot, Missus, most wery hot. Glass water?"

She nods. "Please step in. I shall give you something cool."

Leading the way, mop underarm, handle end pointing forward, an overlong version of the drill sergeant's swagger stick, her exotic letter, glasses and mail packet taking up both hands, Madame Briac grimaces. What possibly could...? The other mail she knows: bills, endless bills. With André in his grave, no matter what the farm brings, the bills keep ahead. How to survive without a man to help shoulder her burdens?

In the kitchen she snaps the mop into place, sets the ordinary mail, with her spectacles, on the table and this special envelope across the open page of her accounts ledger noting sex of ostrich eggs. From the fridge she takes a pitcher of iced coca-leaf tea, spiced by a touch of ginger. She pours the postman a tall glassful.

He nods thanks, drinks long and deep. The revitalizing brew washes down dust collected in his throat, as it collects everywhere in this dry season.

He looks frankly at her hair. "Wery glamouring. Missus to be married again?"

"*Mais non!* No!" Madame feels herself blushing. She presses her lips tighter. "Sunday we have our bazaar to raise money for the chapel's new tin roof. You will come with your family?"

A fortune it cost, this blondness. Five hours to get it done, with Permanent, at X'Ziromeu City's Le Salon Hollywood Chic. The bazaar does require one to look one's best, particularly when entrusted with overseeing the sale of ostrich eggs from all the farms of Nouveau Locronan, their tiny Breton community so far from Brittany itself.

12

And Pierre Dorland will be there. Will he notice her? She must make sure he does! At seventy he is older by six years, but handsome and fit.

Mr. Bharastri edges nearer to where the envelope lies. In a moment he'll be urging her to open it, read whatever is inside while he peers over her shoulder, remarking on every line. Then up and down the farms, gossip, gossip, gossip!

"Oh, this I already know." She gestures toward the alien object, stares him in the eyes, hoping her fib sounds offhand. "It is expected many weeks. No importance."

Taking his empty glass, she sets it in the sink, adds firmly, "You are needing to make your round. If rains come they will flood your automobile. We shall see you at the bazaar?" She practically pushes him out of the house, the image of his reproachful face lingering after the kitchen door closes, like the Cheshire Cat of *Alice In Wonderland.*

Madame Briac repositions the rhinestone glasses on her nose, resumes her seat at table, waits until she hears his car drive off.

Carefully, with an ivory paper knife, she slits the envelope's flap and pulls out two folded papers. She opens the first.

A money order? For her? *Mon Dieu!* Twenty-five thousand MUL? She shakes her head in amazement and disbelief. Her practical nature taking over, she tells herself she must immediately convert these MUL to U.S. dollars, only hard currency allowing exchange with Zembeylia's new money. Nobody trusts MULs, when they don't have to.

So, fifty MUL makes one dollar, meaning...Five hundred dollars! She takes off the spectacles rubs her eyes. Could it possibly be that the Good Lord in His Infinite Misericord has heeded a widow's prayers, comprehending how grim these times are for her?

She sighs, swallows hard. "*Du calme,*" she mutters. Her blood pressure won't stand such excitement. What does the other document say? A typed letter with French greeting followed by an English text. The French is translated too, as if the writer isn't sure

13

of what's written. Lips moving, Madame Briac settles to a serious read:

Chère Ame Soeur, Voué(e) à Notre Seigneur–Dear Kindred Spirit, Devoted To Our Savior: YOU may come to be CHOSEN for a <u>SACRED MISSION!</u> Here are MUL 25,000 to accomplish a FIRST TEST. Five more payments of MUL 25,000 each await you. EXTREME GOOD FORTUNE SHALL BE YOURS. <u>IF</u> you follow EXACT INSTRUCTIONS!!!

1. On Tuesday, October 6 at X'Ziromeu City rail station, find a reservation in your name aboard the ZEMBA ROYAL SILVERSPEAR EXPRESS. You will travel by FIRST CLASS PRIVATE CABIN to Fulumbane.

2. Upon arrival in the capital, proceed to CATHEDRAL OF OUR HOLY SAVIOR. Recite a complete ROSARY TO THE BLESSED VIRGIN. Light FIVE candles. Place PENANCE OFFERING of MUL 50–no less, no more– in Collection Box.

3. Walk two city blocks to ZEMBA ROYAL HOTEL METROPOLE, where a room has been prepaid for you, with vouchers for dinner and Continental breakfast. The *Concièrge* will give you an envelope containing ticket for First Class Private Cabin back to X'Ziromeu City aboard the SILVERSPEAR. Good ONLY for following day of Wednesday, October 7.

4. On the morning of the 7th, BEFORE you leave Fulumbane, RETURN to CATHEDRAL for early MASS. Pay <u>CLOSE ATTENTION</u> to FATHER YULBERT M'FASU. Note <u>ANY DEVIATIONS</u> from the <u>MASS</u> of which you become aware. A dangerous <u>HERESY</u> denying

the GODHEAD and exalting the MORTAL NATURE of CHRIST is loose in the land. BE ALERT! DO NOT TRY to understand. ALL will be explained, IF and WHEN you pass ALL your TESTS!

5. Exactly FOURTEEN days from today, ORDERS will come for similar DUTIES. And again, FOUR TIMES MORE after that. These TASKS must be executed FAITHFULLY!

6. Tell NO ONE, not even the Priest of the Confessional, else the LORD turn HIS face from you and EVIL engulf you, also your daughter and family in France! Do EXACTLY as you are told, QUESTIONING NOT and you MAY QUALIFY for a HIGHLY CONFIDENTIAL MISSION. Your name MIGHT become a GLORY unto OUR LORD!

Yours in the TRUE FAITH!
BENEFACTOR

P.S. The path of OBEDIENCE is the path to PROSPERITY!

Sacred mission? Heresy? A joke? Con-game? Think hard. Let good Breton peasant sense be the guide.

Takes her for a fool, most likely. She who alone must run this fifty-eight goat, forty-one ostrich farm with its coffee bushes and coca plantings.

Are they trying to panic her into drawing her painfully earned savings from the bank and handing them over to some stranger in the street? For "safekeeping"? The television has warned of such tricksters.

But…giving *her* money, not asking for it!

Again she reads the letter. Tomorrow she'll drive the Renault *estafette* pickup van to X'Ziromeu City. Instead of taking produce to the market square, as on Thursdays and Saturdays, she will go to the train station and see if they really do have a ticket in her name.

She can certainly consent to enjoy four hours of luxurious comfort aboard the Zemba Royal SilverSpear Express, and once in Fulumbane take the opportunity to pray at the Cathedral and attend Mass. If the letter isn't somebody's idea of a joke, she would be dining for free at a fine hotel, sleeping there too, all charges paid. Yes, she will keep her eyes open. Although, why pick a modest farm woman to detect heresy… ?

On her way to the station, she'll be sure to stop at the bank and get dollars for these MUL. Backed by an American-sponsored "Peace and Stabilization Program," MUL have replaced ZUL, underwritten by a Cubano-Chinese "Peoples' Friendship and Harmony Initiative," recently denounced by the King as "The False Friendship and Harmony Initiative."

The MUL money order bears a picture of M'Zumba I looking regal in his cheetah hat.

Madame Briac sighs. *Plus ça change*–The more things change…Since the end of colonial days nothing has been peaceful, stable, harmonious or even friendly in Zembeylia, especially not for the French here; they're mostly immigrants from the hardscrabble province of Brittany, its Cape jutting into the Atlantic. When France ruled, ah then it was a peaceful, prosperous place. Now those who had been elite are viewed as misfits, outcasts, eternal foreigners in an eternally upheaved land.

So, aside from this payment, five more are promised? That makes–*Ciel!*–three thousand United States dollars. In May she could visit France for little Louisette's First Communion. How satisfying to see her granddaughter all in white walk up the aisle with the other girls at Quimper Cathedral, just as she herself had done in 1937.

16

No! *Mais non!* One must be practical. With the money, if there really were $3,000, wiser to stay here, purchase sturdy dogs and send Louisette a lovely present from the capital. Most important, she would put savings by for her none-too-secure future.

The Lord's work? Once more she examines the letter. No signature, only the printed word: "BENEFACTOR." Suspicious? Or discreet? No return address, either. The paper is expensive. She holds it to the kitchen window: creamy off-white with watermark.

God or the Devil? *Voilà,* the question! Money, the Devil's commodity. Root of evil. Why the instruction to tell no one, not even Father Aubry at the chapel? The Devil giveth with one hand and destroyeth...If André, her poor husband, or more realistically Pierre Dorland, were here, would they know what to make of this?

Tomorrow early, on her way to bank and station, she'll stop at the cemetery yard of the Nouveau Locronan chapel to kneel before André's small headstone and pray.

Still, nobody can really help her in this moment of deciding whether to shun or to trust. How true the saying that alone you come into this life and journey through it, that in the big decisions you are always alone.

For her heart knows whichever way she makes up her mind right here, right now, she will hold to it, barring flagrant contradicting evidence.

She rises, goes to the stove, brews coffee with a good dose of chicory. She tops her cup by adding a dollop of fresh goat's cream from the fridge. Again, Madame Briac sits at the kitchen table to ponder the whole affair.

Here she is in Africa with her fellow immigrants, surviving as best they can in this southern exile, raising exotic animals and crops: ostriches, coffee, coca, corn, sisal, goats. Images of long ago come to mind. Silvery Atlantic foaming against Brittany cliffs under dark rain-filled clouds; an Easter pilgrimage by moonlight, up a mist-shrouded, tree-covered hill, its summit graced by a granite Celtic cross.

17

But…Now. Be practical! The money certainly, obviously, will come in handy. The letter says her mission will do the Lord's work. The Lord moves in mysterious ways. How can a good ex-*Bretonne* refuse such a call? Or such a reward!

She gets to her feet, goes into the bedroom. Gazing steadily at the crucified figure of Christ-in-agony on the wall above her bed, she makes the sign of the cross and kneels, as she does every morning and evening, to recite her prayers.

At length, rising stiffly, Madame allows herself a small smile. She has received no message to the contrary. Tomorrow, keeping a wary eye open and ready to retreat at the first sign of mischief, she will begin her strange assignment.

Chapter 2: Shangri-La
New York, NY, Monday November 30

"Your Multiflex Super-K flags you as thirty (30) days late on dues. If we do not receive payment by…" A burst of hail splatting against my storefront window has me peering at the climax of Manhattan's morning glut: hurrying pedestrians, a grid four vehicles wide of slowly moving buses, delivery vans, cabs and cars. Plus biker-messengers in black ponchos slaloming wrong way against traffic along this one-way thoroughfare: giant bats, scattering people as they try to cross the street.

Wind drives ice flecks, grit and paper against the plate-glass eye of my newly-acquired travel "boutique," as I like to think of it–Shangri-La: World Wide Journeys of Adventure.

The front door rattles as air whistles through its ill-fitting frame. I watch passers-by hunch under flapping coats and struggle with umbrellas that turn inside-out to become reverse parachutes threatening to whisk their owners up and away.

How many of those folks out there are ready for a real ride up and away? To enjoy a hula tour of Honolulu, a belly-dance jamboree through Baluchistan, a cha-cha fest in Camaroun or a tango expedition across the wilds of...where? Tierra del Fuego? Yeah, Tierra del Fuego.

What if someone does wander in, dripping puddles over our cracked linoleum floor? Will he-she-it actually purchase tickets at Shangri-La? No way! Some pay-over-the phone discounter will produce the whole trip with touch of a button. At a price I'd never match.

So, how in the @#$%^ Hell did I get myself into this "once in a lifetime business opportunity," as the ad in a trade magazine put it? Yeah, for anyone else it'd be once, only once and NEVER again. If some other idiot did happen to get conned into such an investment, he'd at least have brains enough to quick-hand it on to another lost soul while he himself raced for the far side of the world. Yes, anyone else.

An introduction. I'm Lincoln Goldstone, owner of this struggling business and one of the world's great *schlemiels*. *Schlemiel?* The American replacement for Yiddish is Sucker, of the kind P.T. Barnum said is born every minute. Not these days. Not here. Not any I can find. Nobody is sucker enough to swim into my welcoming trap and...GOTCHA!

Okay, already. I'll put Multiflex's late payment notice underneath the late rent "advice," mentioning eviction. I do need to pay the rent. And Internal Revenue is threatening a levy, so pay them as near to yesterday as I can manage. But these goddamn Multiflex bloodsuckers? They don't deserve more than a quarter of their invoice.

Damn rattletrap system, totally obsolete, breaks down every ten minutes...

Calm yourself! Yes, I admit it. Aside from a doom-and-gloom personality, I do like complaining, thus turning my various perceived catastrophes into dramas. We have *some* viable business and a string of commission checks trickling in any day now.

19

But lights, telephones, salaries, commission shares, garbage collection all demand to be paid. The garbage is Mafia sponsored, I've been told. "Pal, youse enjoy kneecaps? Youse oughtta consider payin'."

On and on for monies out, fed by, a much lesser stream in.

Heigh-ho for the life of a travel agent. A vision of bankruptcy and home a cardboard box in Grand Central's train tunnel looms. Not imminently, but if business volume doesn't improve some months from now, a predictable future.

Into this agency I've plunged all my savings from a news career and book royalties, plus my mother's legacy. Everything I possess after a long divorce, financial settlement and annuities for my kids. If I don't make things prosper here–

The door flies open, jangling a set of rusty chimes. Rahel Tefuri sweeps in.

"Morning," I say.

She gives a dry little nod, marches to the back to hang her coat. Spiked heels make her five foot-one. As she bustles about, I imagine she's thinking how overworked and unappreciated she is, especially since in Amharic, her last name, so she claims, means *Princess*. In my mind she grows to giant, intimidating, size.

When she settles at her desk, she begins a ritual of swabbing its top with rubbing alcohol, plus her telephone receiver and computer screen. She has a thing about germs. And a thing about men. And a thing about me, her boss: love-hate, the latter, I surmise, predominating.

Since she's third generation Harlem, from a doctor's family, brought up on a tree-lined side street and sent into the world with a Sociology B.A. from Hunter College–transmuted into ten underpaid years in travel–I figure Rahel sees me as "Whitey-The-Exploiter." At the same time, she seems to feel protective, like I'm the vulnerable idiot it's her mission to save from destitution Add this to another ambiguity, that she is casting *Moi* as Moses parting seas of

20

penury so together we'll sail Shangri-La into waters white with milk, sweet as honey...

No longer do I feel like Moses; I've become fixated on how to jump ship. Rahel senses this. It provokes a gamut of panicky emotions. I watch her scrubbing her desk. High cheekbones, a delicately flared nose slightly hooked, burnished skin of ebony. Proud-featured Ethiope: Queen of Sheba, pocket-edition. Yet she has the grinding, self-immolating masochism that my time in travel has shown me is the essence of a good agent's soul. Not sufficient to dedicate oneself to arranging other peoples' experiences, while having none or few of one's own. There has to be a special thirst for catering to clients who notice only when things go wrong, for becoming their vessel of blame when they miss connections in Calcutta, suffer bad weather in Walla-Walla, encounter surly service in Santiago. *Mea culpa, mea maxima culpa!* Exalted Highness or Princess she might imagine herself, but Rahel's personality seems wedded to a travel employee's whipping-post life.

She also understands agency nuts-and-bolts. Take her away, I can throw myself off the Queensborough Bridge.

The door jangles again, opening slowly this time. Schulz waddles onto the premises. To me he mumbles a greeting, ignores Rahel as he makes for the twisting passageway that holds a coat-rack and leads to the staff bathroom: leaky, hissing toilet and miniature cold water sink.

One more twist would confront the locked door of a back studio with its own bathroom, kitchenette and filth-encrusted window looking onto an air-shaft. I'm calling these quarters home. Temporary home, I keep telling myself.

Raincoat stowed, Schulz, favors us with views of his balloon belly and rumpled, dingy appearance. They clash with an insinuating, accusing manner, suitable to law-and-order types. He has a personality that inflicts, rather than allows itself to be inflicted upon. Definitely not a travel agent born, rather a mishmash of opposites, unpleasant ones. His manner is of a holier-than-thou

Gestapo interrogator, one you'd at least expect to be immaculately uniformed, with high-shine boots. Sartorially, Schulz gives the impression of a being at war with its aspirations. But inhalations, not aspirations, make his presence a daily trial. He favors some flowery perfume that, as the work day wears on, penetrates our office with an odor of roses in old sweat.

I want to tell him: "You need to steer clear of that..." can't bring myself to say perfume. How, euphemistically, to refer to...aftershave? But Schulz doesn't shave so you'd notice. At 9 A.M., five o'clock shadow. By nightfall the moonish, sallow face disappears behind a hairy cloud. Worst of all, the man has a smarmy, prying attitude to clients. And to me too. Towards Rahel he's catty, which never fails to drive her, catlike and screeching, up the wall.

Say anything, though, the guy could leave. If Rahel constitutes Shangri-La's spinal column, Schulz is keeper of its blood supply. As an ex-Austrian he has, on joining the agency, brought a dowry in the form of a personal client. This is Herr Gerhardt Amahdi, a Germano-Turkish rug importer who favors deluxe on overseas comings and goings. Herr Amahdi's business goes a long way to making the difference between my agency's life, or slow death from anemia.

"Ooh. That awful disinfectant stink!" Schulz sniffs loudly in Rahel's direction as he settles at his desk. *"Schatzi,* must you be so compulsive?"

She growls, pours more alcohol. And counterattacks. "Mrs. Potsdam!"

"What about her?"

"You put her on United's 2 P.M. to Cleveland. They changed the flight to 2:43. I had to phone her. Otherwise—"

"Otherwise, she'd arrive at La Guardia a few minutes early."

"Her relatives at Cleveland airport standing around forty-three extra minutes? Blaming us! Because our Mister Schulz is too lazy to—"

22

"Lazy? How dare you, you pint-sized, monomaniacal...! I had to deliver Herr Amahdi's *München* tickets: roundtrip First Class to London, with ongoing connections, also in First. Plus limos at arrival and departure. And then, a suite at *Hotel VierJahreszeiten*. Do you realize how much money this represents?" He turns to me. "Sir, my commissions are due on the fifteenth of the month. We are already the thirtieth and—"

"The Bensons with their five children," Rahel's, voice rises to a shriek. "ordering a Dodge Caravan at Phoenix Airport. And you get them a Mini. Where's your alibi there, Mister Big Shot?"

"I thought we'd agreed," I address Schultz in the measured tones I've practiced for staff confrontations. "You're to receive half of last month's commissions Friday, the other half at the end of next week. To make sure we pay only for trips proceeding as planned."

"This is most unfair. At my other job—"

"Where you were fired," Rahel again.

"Resigned," snaps Schulz. "Sir, it's not fair, given the small amount—"

"Fired!" shouts Rahel. "For carelessness. And something else..."

"Resigned! Sir—"

I slam my hand on my desk. "Schulz, you know I'll pay. Rahel, you've got four tickets to do. Start on them."

"Finished last night," she sniffs. "Fired!"

Schulz affects to be signing into his computer and not to hear, for which I'm thankful. Another day, another dollar. Out the window...

I turn from money matters to a second pile on my desk: unopened brochures describing the wonderful destinations none of our customers go to. A glossy folder features a new liner plying the Seychelles and African coastline. How I'd love to see Bird Island with its myriad flying creatures. Not to mention the lions and giraffes of East Africa's game reserves. And between exotic sights,

23

lolling on deck by the pool, feasting on advertised *nouvelle cuisine.* Maybe an heiress would spot me, fall madly in love. We'd marry, then in five months or so a divorce with golden handshake. Twenty million? After this venture into male prostitution, I could court my true love, Suzanne, and we'd live in the luxurious style I feel we both deserve. I see myself as the white-linen clad proprietor of a beach bar on Lamu Island, Kenya, drinking iced lager and duty free single-malt scotches smuggled across the Arabian Sea by *dhow.* My right shoulder would be graced with a marmoset, house-broken, wearing a diaper just in case: Trader Linc's trademark. And here come exotic curry creations, coconut sprinkled, borne by bare-breasted nymphs who, curtseying, hold them out...

My daydreaming reminds me how much I love travel; probably for the wrong reasons having to do with suspension between demands, obligations, responsibilities. Surely, the public shares my lust to go places, if for the more focused objective of arriving at them. I've never wanted to arrive, only ride comfortably on and on...deluxe, of course, like what some airlines designate "Luxury Sleeper Class," featuring seats, convertible by the press of a button to stretching out to almost the length of a bed; then via another button shrinking back to the delightfully comfortable chair, adjusted by more buttons to your every bodily contour.

I'm not a people lover, not even of those cosseted folks who can afford luxurious displacements. Let 'em all eat chocolate eclairs, or whatever Queen Marie-Antoinette said so disdainfully of the Paris mob. In revenge, it took off her head. That's the way the cookie sometimes crumbles for us types contemptuous of "The People," whom unfortunately one must occasionally reckon with.

I've certainly tried reckoning. When I started in this business, I'd gone up and down Manhattan skyscrapers visiting enterprises small and large, seeking out travel coordinators. Endlessly, I was told about a sister or aunt in travel, or about cheap deals on such and such a fly-by-night outfit. So, what kickbacks was I giving on commissions? Kickbacks!

My marketing lost momentum. I became resigned to vicarious voyaging, sending Mrs. Yablonski on a cruise that she declared she'd hated, owing to my putting her in a cabin directly under the dance floor. "All night, Mister Goldstone. All night long the ceiling over my head throbbing, pounding. How could I sleep?" And Dr. Fisk's honeymoon to Capri: days spent arranging it in loving detail, a travel agent's masturbatory dream task; unearthing obscure but charming hotels, sending overseas for Wagons-Lits sleeper accommodations and evolving a day-by-day itinerary. At the eleventh hour, when I happen to bump into the young resident in McDonald's, he tells me, "Oh, by the way, wedding's off…"

Once again the door jangles and opens. To let in the postman carrying a packet of mail. I note a long envelope lying on top, its face bears a photo: the narrow, mournful, lowering head of a gnu.

Chapter 3: Afric's Burning Shore
New York, NY, Monday, November 30

A gnu. Bush term for the creature white South African hunters call "wildebeest," humpbacked, spindle-shanked, silly-faced, often referred to, so I've read, as one of nature's bad jokes. Its greater antelope cousins, the eland and bongo, wear stately horns and dignified, if smug, expressions. Poor gnus have nothing to be smug about, except for breeding power managing to outdistance their many fatalities due to lack of brainpower.

When I see on the envelope where the gnu letter comes from, I almost deep-six it: The Zembeylian Tourist Bureau. Still resent my evening at its crummy office. Anyway, the country is in the middle of a civil war. Except, hasn't there been a settlement? "Peace break out in Zembeylia?" I ask Rahel.

"Nobody we know goes there." She glares at me. "Our clients feel Poughkeepsie's far enough."

"Yes, Sir. It has, Sir. For almost eight months now," Schulz sucking up to his boss. "The State Department has dropped all restrictions and advisories. Except on M'zu-m'zu, a wasting fever transmitted by scorpions. Eighty-seven percent fatal."

M'zu-m'zu? No wonder the tourism bureau is in a rundown SoHo loft instead of Midtown on Fifth or Madison Avenues where big-time destinations display their travel delights. Only reason I went to the "Evening of Discovery," featuring "Africa's Most Exotic Destination," as the invitation put it, was the promise of a "Fantastic Prize Drawing." A handful of us attendees stuck out a fuzzy slideshow and boring speeches in hopes…lucky winner got a canvas bag.

Sight of a new IRS notice causes my stomach to churn, my hands to tear open the gnu envelope. Whatever's inside surely is better than a message from Nemesis. Letter addressed personally to me, name spelled right for once:

Dear Mr. Lincoln Goldstone:

URGENT: FOR AGENCY OWNER'S EYES ONLY!

Now that peace shines again upon our shores, we want to show YOU, Mr. Lincoln Goldstone, the wonders of our diverse and many-faceted land. Come see for yourself!

For only $450, you can join a select group limited to twelve leading agency and airline owners specializing in African travel. Our partner, Eland Tours, officially representing in U.S.A. the tourism interests of our own Zemba Royal Corporation is making all arrangements.

Premier deluxe! Spend eight days–Saturday, December 12 through Saturday December 19 in a visit to our beautiful, newly democratized nation. You will fly First Class aboard Zemba Royal Airways sleek long-range jumbo jet...

Eland. Sheila Mondran's company. Really it belongs to her sister, Helen Farrar. Ah, Sheila! Belle of the Waldorf-Astoria's Travel Show. Such perfume! *Il Gattopardo.* Made exclusively for her by Francisco Mancini of Milan, she claims: Voluptuous, enveloping, unforgettable. The sister, Helen, is said to be a travel genius, and zillionairess. Aside from owning Eland, she controls a cruise line, plus one of those damn companies selling discount tickets by phone. And also Helenair, the charter airline that Club Med uses for its Caribbean resorts.

Evidently she has picked Zembeylia for a comer. Well, when the citizenry aren't cutting each other's throats, the place does have assets.

I look again at the letter: "...diamonds, tsavorites, gold mines, wild animals, beaches, resorts and fine wines from our very own vineyards."

Not to mention M'zu-m'zu...The itinerary sounds like out of my better daydreams. The group will spend a night at an Indian Ocean resort, visit vineyards, play with tame giraffes in a reserve, see a spice market, a gem exchange, then on to a tribal settlement whose lifestyle "hasn't changed in a thousand years!" Journey's climax will be two days of game-viewing at a camp that features living in luxury tents. To get to this bush camp, the tour will travel overnight aboard The Zemba Royal SilverSpear Express, "a train that features accommodations, cuisine and service so fabulous they far outshine any other rail transport on our Continent." Obvious snub to South Africa and its *Blue Train,* reputedly one of the world's most luxurious rail rides.

The two countries share a border across which, I remember reading in some newspaper, they'd spent sixteen years hurling threats and imprecations at each other without actually firing shots. Fugitives from the African National Congress (A.N.C.) have found haven in Zembeylia. There was also a story about a Zembeylian bank manager who'd been welcomed in South Africa when he skipped with $33 million plus a few hundred diamonds and tsavorite gems. The paper reported he was living comfortably in Capetown, no question of extradition.

"Once arrived at Zemba Royal Corporation's exclusive Tented Camp and Game Preserve," continues the letter, "you will see lions, hippos, elephants, rare rhinos, perhaps even a leopard or two in an unspoiled habitat, while enjoying every modern comfort and convenience."

My heart thumps, my mind raps out: You!...Only!...Live! ...Once! Lions and hippos in their habitat? I think of a poem by William Rhodes: *So I have heard on Afric's burning shore / A hungry lion give a grievous roar.* The poem goes on to say that another lion also gave a roar, whereupon, *The first lion thought the last a bore.*

Well, no lions for near-beggars. Taxes to pay. Here-and-now duties. Hands all but trembling, I open the IRS missive/missile. Turns out, it accepts my exemption claim. If I pay a $133.57 supplement, the jaws will loosen. And here are commission checks from Carnival Cruises, Pacific Tours, The Fairmont Hotel, even *l'Hôtel Georges V* in Paris. Reassurance? Temptation? How to get hold of $450? And how to appease Rahel? Could she and Schulz keep the peace in my absence? Damn it! What was owning an agency about if the owner can't enjoy one lousy spinoff trip?

"No!" say the business manuals, not during the early years of day-to-day nurturing. So when I was a hundred and three I could maybe take a bus jaunt to Atlantic City? Meanwhile, the rhinos would die out, Zembeylia would become a land of hi-rise timeshares and oil-slicked beaches studded, like our very own, with used hypodermic needles. And the only leopard I'd ever get to see was the plastic one on Central Park's merry-go-round.

Escape from here would itself be paradise. Galley slave freed from his oar. Only for a moment, sure; but for that blessed moment free!

28

Four hundred and fifty lousy dollars? I own an American Express card. *Don't leave home without it*, goes the ad; even if you never dare return home with it.

About 11 A.M. the phone rings. "Mr. Goldstone? Helen Farrar, Eland Tours. I'm told you received Zembeylia's invitation by mistake."

Mistake? Taking away what I've just been offered? "What do you mean?"

"Space is so limited. We can only allot nine out of the twelve first class aircraft seats to outsiders, since I'm bringing along both my husband, Mike Mahoney, and my sister, Sheila. She asked me to say 'Hi,' by the way. Unfortunately, Zembeylia was too ambitious with its invitations. Just one of those things…"

The fragrant Sheila Mondran saying Hi! Helen has a reputation for being a ruthless executive type. She certainly is living up to it. The nerve, trying to cheat me out of my once-in-a-lifetime experience.

"…a little mixup and such unfairly short notice, too. Thank you for your understanding. We appreciate—"

"No, I accept!" I blurt out. "Zembeylia sent its official invitation and I accept. Most kind to include me. By the way," —a little sand in the eyes— "how come a gnu on the envelope? Why not an eland?"

"Lionel Goldhammer," she ignores my question, "you know, vice-president of Abernathy and Scott's Safari Division? That's whom we meant to invite. A mixup. Similar names. Unfortunate—"

"The invitation clearly says Lincoln Goldstone and my agency, Shangri-La: WorldWide Journeys of Adventure. You sure you're not mixed up? This is from the Zembeylian government, not Eland Tours."

"Understand," Helen Farrar's voice takes an edge. "My company's the most significant outside investor that Zembeylian tourism has. We organized this trip for a single purpose: to show off the country's finest attractions to top U.S. travel executives specialized in Africa's tourist and safari markets. So they'll bring high-end customers to a new and excellent destination…"

Not letting me get a word in, she gives two dozen reasons to cancel my trip; and do I hear of compensatory payment? It dawns that she's begging, that she can't quite bring herself to renege on a written invitation. Maybe she doesn't have authority despite her boasts?

I start shuffling numbers, making $450 plus an extra $100, or better $200, for incidentals, presents, emergencies jibe with–

"…upscale business and I stress upscale. Our invitees are proven profit centers. Do you have clients for African tourism? Are you a safari profit center?"

Silence on the line, question hanging. Having no answer, I keep silent.

"Do you," she presses, "consider yourself a profit center?"

"Zembeylia must think so. It sent me its invitation. Mr. Goldhammer and I will just have to double up."

"Not the point!" Helen's voice goes hard as rocks. "Space is limited, we're spending a fortune on this tour and you're not in the league. So you'll have to cease and desist and–"

"I've been invited, formally and officially. I have my clientele." Yeah, trippers to the Catskills. I clear my throat. "I would hate to inform the entire U.S. travel industry that thanks to you, Zembeylia went back on–"

"Now you listen–"

Click-click on the line, another voice. "Helen, dear. You know Lionel Goldhammer refused and the Zembeylian Tourist Bureau, having Mr. Goldstone's name on–"

"Because you failed to clarify! It's your–"

"This has nothing to do with a mixup. Goldhammer simply didn't want to become involved with a rival company and was quite firm."

"Sheila! Don't be indiscreet. Especially not before this–"

"Now, now, now. As I told you, I'm impressed by Mr. Goldstone's sales know-how. Linc, do you remember me? It's Sheila Mondran. I–"

"Hello, Sheila. I certainly do re–"

"As I was saying, I know you'll put your sales talent to work and sell Zembeylia for us. Really, Helen, it's for the best."

"Just because you think he's a hunk–"

"Helen! You're embarrassing–"

"I'm most flattered," I manage to mumble. A hunk! A pulse beats at my temples. Not bad for forty-six. Just under six foot and reasonably trim. Dark hair nice and thick, almost no gray. Soulful brown eyes, straight nose, a chin that my orthodontist father has, through eight years of braces, helped make firm. And black-rimmed glasses giving me a serious, executive look. With sales talent to boot? What kind of line had I put out anyway?

"I realize you consider such short notice unsuitable," Helen staggering in for another whack at knocking me off fortune's wheel. "I certainly appreciate your wish to bow out of this trip for a more favorable–"

"No wish at all," I cut her off. "I promise to do my best to make Zembeylia a profit center for your–"

"Nevertheless," she insists, "I–"

"Helen," Sheila's voice is firm. "I hate to mention it, but you know we've practically been ordered to include him. Almost a necessity, if..."

Silence on the line. Ordered? Necessity? What's this new element about? Oh, well, never look a gift horse in the–

"You damn surely will help us make Zembeylia a profit center," Helen's tone, implying I was committed to proving a big-time Zembeylia promoter masks her capitulation.

Capitulation? I'm in!

"So why a gnu?" I ask again, to keep her off-balance.

"We had the photo. No time to go scrabbling for an eland. The secret of good business, Mr. Goldstone, is to use what's at hand. I won't keep you!" The crash of a receiver sounds in my ear.

"Well," I mutter, looking at the phone, "keep me or not, you've got me."

New worry: breaking the news to Suzanne. Without having to scrape her–or more likely myself–off the ceiling. Plus enlisting Rahel's active good will in keeping the business alive while I'm away.

Have to find money. I'd sworn not to touch my reserve fund; except for dire situations. Wouldn't not going and missing out be dire? No! Yes! Yes, dammit, yes! What did Helen Farrar say? Profit center. Upmarket business. That's what might come of this. When opportunity knocks…

"Nuts!" says Suzanne Carrington on her Thursday overnight from Washington D.C. She comes into town every week to appear Friday on a morning TV show "Plain nuts. But then your whole travel thing is."

I wince, pick at my vegetable korma. Can't afford tandoori chicken. We're at the Taj, splitting the bill. Nice place, taped sitar music softly twanging. Liquor license, so I can have a beer. Sane prices–for New York.

"I pleaded with you, begged you, went down on my knees telling you to stay a newsman. Stick with what you know, don't throw your money into a losing…So you do it, then come whining around saying I was right, that from now on you'll always listen to me. And I know, just know that whatever objection I make you're off to Zembeylia. Not hell, high water, revolution or, more likely, financial ruin can stop you. So why do you ask? What kick, seeing me upset?"

I spread my hands. "I keep hoping for understanding. Am I forever doomed to disappointment?"

"Understanding." She bites into a poppadum. It crackles. "I understand that shopkeepers mind their shops. Should've thought of it before you opened one."

"No shop, an agency."

"Quibble." She narrows her eyes. "As a reporter you could get to Zembeylia."

"They love each other now. Who wants to read–?"

"You'd do gorilla stories."

"You're thinking Rwanda. They're not into tourism these days, with all the ethnic massacres and starvation going on. Naturally, I'm hoping for a couple of travel articles out of this. To recoup what I pay. Anyway, Rahel knows her job. I was thinking, maybe you could drop in once and also give a call from D.C., just to let her know you're–"

Suzanne shakes her head vigorously. "I've no friendly feeling towards your enterprise. Where it's concerned, I'm not, never was, never shall be your helper. You run it, you make it viable. Then tell me how wrongheaded I–"

"Can't you act as a temporary guardian angel?" I take her hand.

She pulls it away. "Goldstone, when you opted out of a career that challenged your mind and kept you intellectually to the mark, you opted out of my taking you seriously. Now, you're an amusement, Thursday's distraction."

"Yeah, and I love you too." What an expert at turning the knife! Glumly I look at her. Maybe true that all I'd really wanted was to take it easy. A business providing food and a roof, allowing me to spend my days stretched on the balding, fur-lined backroom sofa-bed, as former owner Harley V. Stepanowitsch, Jr. used to do while others worked. Sofa day snoozes, larded with near-free trips. Definitely not the path my life-in-travel has taken.

"All the way to Africa and back in just a week? Dumb kind of journey."

"Travel agent's journey." I stare at the puddle of beer in my glass. "Quickies in this business. Nobody can afford to stay away long."

"So you lose the benefit of your obsession. As you take the walkway to the plane you practically meet yourself coming back. Crazy."

"Unfair. You can see a lot if you keep your eyes open." I signal for our double check.

We go to the studio apartment she uses when she stays over for the weekly live TV talk show. Thursday's man. For two years now. Ten years ago, in France, we had a passionate love affair. She'd left for Washington, where her career prospered and she'd married, had a kid, then divorced, the child being raised by the remarried husband. I'd divorced too, returned to New York, career lumping along so-so. Again we'd come together and then I bought the business, which is only killing our affair by half.

From the bed, I watch her at the dressing table as she unwinds her auburn hair from its coiled *chignon*. Does she touch it up? Can't tell. A deep burnished color full of shimmering lights, almost as it had been in Paris when we were in our twenties. Figure plumper now, at forty-two. Still, a magnificently womanly woman...

But, as she says, only Thursday's amusement.

Chapter 4: Following Orders
Uplands of Zembeylia, Monday Morning, November 30

From the kitchen window Madame Briac regards her new dogs with fondness. Yvon and Yvonne, good Breton Celtic names. The male, eighteen months—the female, a year old. Tough, sturdy, northern dogs, a cross between huskies and German shepherds. Bred here by the Breton community. They certainly keep the baboons away. Bright, playful, already growing as attached to her, as she to them.

She hopes they will love each other and have many puppies as time goes by.

Thank goodness for the much-needed money flow from "Benefactor." She doesn't comprehend its whys and wherefores; but who, *au fond,* understands the whys and wherefores of life on Earth? To serve the Higher Purpose is all one truly needs to know. Had Adam and Eve only served instead of eating of the forbidden fruit and then questioning, questioning, wouldn't we all still be enjoying immortality in Eden?

So here is the second-to-last installment that has come faithfully every second Monday. As with each of the other deliveries, Mr. Bharastri, through a deluge of questions, has shown his contamination with the curse of curiosity, if merely for the frivolous purpose of spreading word along his route regarding the mysterious envelopes' contents. She has successfully thwarted him, hoping he wouldn't resort to desperate measures, like steaming open the letters prior to delivery.

The thought makes her smile. He never would dare. Mr. Bharastri takes pride in getting the mail through. A Postal employee also serves.

Familiar shivers run through her as she sits down at the kitchen's large table, puts on her rhinestone glasses and slits open the latest of the cream envelopes so different in size, color, texture from all other letters she receives. This time will the message be different? Will she get an explanation?

The money order is here: another MUL 25,000. She hesitates to unfold the accompanying letter. Up to now, always the same instruction: the free trip to Fulumbane and back, with prayers and candles at the Cathedral, the prepaid room including dinner and Continental breakfast at the hotel.

Certainly, she doesn't object. Such easy tasks and so luxurious. Most enjoyable to visit the big city, pray, eat excellent food, window-shop, have money to buy basic necessities for the farm and little presents for herself, like the new hat for Sunday Mass.

But to what end? The question nags despite her attempts to suppress it. Pursing lips, she steels herself to read. Slowly, her expression brightens, a smile of joy and relief spreads over her face. She has passed her tests with honors. At last a mission is being revealed, if not in its details at least in its thrust. One more trip to the capital. And then!

What a significant mission it is! What a privilege to be chosen! Arduous and onerous it might at times become, but she will work to her last breath to obey and accomplish its demands.

She rises from her seat to kneel on the hard tiles of the kitchen floor and pray a prayer of thanksgiving.

Chapter 5: A Royal Ride On Posting Winds
New York and en route to Zembeylia, Saturday, December 12

"Visiting the continent of your forefathers," I say to Rahel on the morning of the day I'm leaving for Zembeylia. I give a nervous laugh.

She sniffs. "Zembeylians and Ethiopians are about as common-rooted as New Yorkers and Eskimos. Anyway, I'm a spoiled American requiring heat, air-conditioning, two showers daily. And no flies!"

"Okay, already. Are you going to keep things moving here without me?"

She shrugs. "They don't cut off the electricity, throw us out for not paying rent or in jail for not paying taxes, I'll do fine."

I sigh. "Things aren't that desperate. We just need business. This could produce upper-crust customers. We'll hold a 'Safari Night' when I'm back, invite our clients."

"All three of 'em?" Over half-rims Rahel gives me a look.

I take Schulz into the back hallway to lecture on keeping peace. "She's sensitive. Don't goad her."

"Goad? Sir, with due respect, I do not understand goad."

"Provoke, then."

"She is doing so to me. Always. Not five minutes am I left alone but–"

"Look!" I rap out the words parade-ground style. "I want team spirit around here. If she, the senior employee, complains, if receipts aren't up to par while I'm gone, I'll be on your case. Can't afford to keep a trouble maker."

Schulz sniffs and tries blackmail. "I and Herr Amahdi can go elsewhere."

"So you can." I keep my tone indifferent, leave it at that.

As the Kennedy Airport bus inches through unaccountable Saturday afternoon traffic bottling the Queens Midtown Tunnel, I tell myself, over and over, not to worry, the agency is positioned to hold its own for a week. One lousy week.

For me, a magnificent week, to be mulled over lovingly minute by minute, day by day during all the humdrum weeks and months and, God forbid, years when I'll be chained to this barely-afloat business. Ah, well, live the moment. I've paid Shangri-La's critical bills. All Rahel and Schulz have to do is keep the place on cruise-control.

Despite a slow ride, I arrive early. The reporter in me likes the idea of standing unnoticed at some out-of-the-way spot to size up my fellow travelers before the official meeting time. Our herd is due to gather at 5:00 P.M. in front of the American Airlines information counter. Zemba Royal Airways rents its single gate from American.

First, though, to celebrate the beckoning beaches of a far shore and my coming propinquity to lions, giraffes, elephants, I visit the bar. Double vodka martini: icy in the mouth, warm in the throat, massaging on brain and kneebacks. Freedom!

Important to give Suzanne a farewell call. When I reach her at *The New Republic's* bureau in Washington, she sounds sort of flattened. Not at all her usual bouncy self, if too often with sarcastic edge. Today she seems in a daze.

37

"What's wrong? I know there's something wrong. You still got your job?"

"Job? Oh, sure." Long silence. "Nothing you can fix. Listen, have a fine trip. Bring me back a giraffe. A small one to fit in my apartment."

"If you need me to cancel this—"

"No. Of course not. Love and kisses, okay?"

"Love and kisses." Worrisome. Despite the martini, butterflies roost in my stomach. But what can I do now?

I find my observation post by a pillar.

Sheila Mondran appears, standing alone. Mauve traveler's cape perfectly setting off those expressive dark eyes. And the ebony hair worn to her shoulders. How exquisitely it contrasts with her pale skin.

Yes exquisite, I decide. And give up my bystandership. Frangipani, patchouli, with the slightest tang of peppery cinnamon. Wonderful scent.

"Hi, there," she speaks first. "Welcome to our adventure." She takes my hand. "I'm so glad you could make it. We have a great sales program and you'll bring lots of clients."

I smile ruefully. "Helen doesn't—"

"I have faith." She lifts an eyebrow.

"Ah, the faith of a beautiful woman. How can I not succeed?" Suzanne calling me Thursday's man. Well, Fridays for Sheila? And maybe Tuesdays? Hey! A little steadfastness, *puh-leeze*.

"Helen, Mike and Barry are seeing to arrangements," she says "I have to play greeter. We board at 6:40 sharp."

"I'll keep you company."

She smiles but doesn't reply, busies herself with a clipboard holding the list of tour members. She does dress beautifully, the mauve fabrics of her jacket and skirt are subtly filagreed with silver. I know almost nothing about clothes, especially women's clothes, but everything Sheila wears that I've seen shows her off to stylish advantage. Suzanne looks neat, efficient, never this spectacularly elegant.

Mentally I shake myself.

Sheila fumbles in her handbag, pulls out a gold cigarette case adorned with a ring of colored stones, at its center a yellow tear-drop.

"Rubies, emeralds and some sort of sapphire?" I ask.

She shakes her head, laughing. "The reds are fire garnet, the green diopside and the yellow is a worthless beryl. Purely a trinket, but one I happen to love. Are you interested in gems?"

"They're pretty. I'm an ignoramus, though."

She offers a cigarette.

I decline. "None for five years now. Once in a while a cigar after some delicious, heavy meal, especially with a snifter of brandy."

"I smoke like a chimney. We have to sit together, since we're the only singles and First Class has just enough seats to go around. You'll be made to suffer."

"Mr. Mondran isn't coming?"

"Barry is our anchor here in New York, so it's the smoking row for you."

I make a slight bow. "If it were anyone else I'd yell my head off. But given the pleasure of your company..."

She smiles again. "Just for that, when we get to Diamantville you can help me choose a tsavorite. We'll be telling you all about Diamantville. Tsavorites, by the way, are green garnets. They've got more sparkle than emeralds and are becoming quite valuable. Zembeylia's a great producer. Diamonds, too, of course. Terrific bargains there."

I bow, feeling suave. Ought I beg to be allowed to offer a tsavorite? Only a hundred thou? What's such a trifling amount between friends?

Barry Mondran bustles up. "Michael's arranging for a baggage cart," he tells his wife. "I'm getting us a special checkin counter."

Puffy-faced fellow, about fifty. Fussy-manners and a flabby looking body, although big in the shoulders. He gives me a limp handshake. Fishwhite stubby fingers. I think of Schulz, except this guy's nails are cleaner. Whatever does Sheila see in him?

As Mondran hurries away, a man in a cowboy hat approaches. Following a few paces to the rear is a redhead, her high-piled orangy-red hairdo gleams under the bright terminal lights. She's wearing a gray-white fur jacket, which goes well with the hair and her green skirt.

The man in the hat sets down two expensive-looking suitcases, one in black crocodile. He doffs the ten-gallon off-on again, revealing silvery hair, thin on top but bobbed in back, Kit Carson style. "Waal, I dee-clay-aah," he says to Sheila. "Ev'y time I see ya, ye're even purtier than the la-yyst time." He turns to the lady, "Ain't thet ra'aght, Bitsy darlin'?"

Her sharply outlined pink lips make the pretense of a smile. "Honey," she tells Sheila in a brassy voice, "don't take what this boy from the Bronx-turned-Texan says too seriously. He's just practisin' our courtly Southern ways."

"Flattery I'm always partial to," says Sheila. She makes introductions: "N. Sherman Jamieson and his wife, Elizabeth."

"Oh, call me Bitsy. I don't answer to Elizabeth." She draws the name out, making it sound like an insult. "My friends've been callin' me Bitsy ever since I can remember. And bein' that we-all are travelin' to darkest Africa, well, we just have to be friends, right?" She blinks her eyes appealingly.

"Don' fergit'n call her 'Bitchy,' like I do sometimes." Jamieson lets out a guffaw.

She smiles a what-can-I-do-with-such-a-boor smile, glares at him.

He wipes his smile, assumes an expression of concentrated seriousness and shakes my hand. The grip is firm and frank, like the *shmo's* running for Mayor or about to sell me the Holland Tunnel. "Maaghty pleased, suh. Maaghty pleased."

40

Bitsy merely nods as though, despite her folksy protests, she's holding off until she decides whether a Goldstone is up to social speed. I note long red nails and fingers covered with rings. Under the lights, they flash.

Jamieson's clothes seem eclectic. The ten-gallon contrasts with a well-cut overcoat of herring-bone gray which, unbuttoned, reveals a Davy Crockett hide jacket that fails to jibe with a striped Guards tie, a button-down collared white shirt and charcoal flannel trousers. The flannels, though, are tucked into brown kid-leather boots shined so high they gleam almost as much as his lady's rings.

Two men join our group. One is blond, tall, bronzed and athletic-looking, a contrast to his companion's coffee-and-cream skinned chunkiness. Sheila presents them as Gordon Chandler and Alvaro Guitterez-Shaughnessy. The latter sports a bushy pirate's mustache. He gives a bow to the women, shakes hands with the men. His grip is hard, impersonal. He keeps his mouth shut.

From the trade press, I recognize Chandler as C.E.O of World-Trotters, an agency located on lower-Broadway, with Wall Street brokers and financiers for clients. Doesn't he also own or run an airline? Something about an airline got him into *Business Week* a while back. With his dark suit, silk tie in muted colors, the off-white shirt and shined black shoes, he appears every inch an investment banker en-route to his morning board meeting, instead of this all-night—and then some—sit-up flight. The other fellow seems more appropriately dressed. His tweed jacket and baggy tan trousers have a pre slept-in look.

Now a bulky individual in a double-breasted suit and an Asian woman present themselves as Gene and Miho Petroff. I'm impressed by the woman, svelte, with glowing saffron complexion and delicate features. Her raven hair, glossy, marvelously thick, flows to below her shoulders. It's enhancing for her nondescript partner to be in the company of so fine-looking a female.

Leading a uniformed Zemba Airways official pushing a baggage cart, a squared-off hulk of a fellow makes his way toward

41

our group. The bulky guy must be six foot four. He has the look of a pro-footballer, except for gray hair and bagginess in the jowels and under the eyes.

"My brother-in-law, Michael Mahoney," Sheila announces.

He puts an arm around her shoulders, gives a brief hug. "Hi, Sis, hi, folks. Welcome Aboard," he booms in a voice more suitable to a Madison Square Garden rally than in this place, where the click of high heels on tiled floor is the loudest noise around.

We all pile luggage onto the cart and proceed to the designated check-in counter, where suitcases are tagged, whisked away, our passports and tickets looked at, boarding passes given out.

Then Michael—*I answer to Mike, guys 'n gals*—leads us to an upper floor and the airline's V.I.P. lounge.

The New York manager offers champagne cocktails.

I pay my respects to Helen Farrar, whose platinum hair, over-shellacked and brittle-looking, doesn't go with her sallow complexion. No more than a few years Sheila's senior but none of her spicy sexiness. In fact, I don't see any resemblance. Maybe the hair color obliterates it.

Her mouth is a slash of lipstick, the crimson contributing to her skin's leathery cast. As does the green tweed suit with tiny orange dots. "Delighted," she mutters, her glare saying the opposite. "We'll talk on board." She turns her back on me.

A noisy group sweeps through the lounge door. Heading the crowd is a woman with a mink coat draped over her shoulders. I see a youngish face, more striking than beautiful. The fine-molded but hawkish nose and wide mouth, generously lipsticked, make it an actress's face: big features, easy for a theater audience to pick out or a movie camera to zoom in on. The woman's ebony hair, sweeping into a topknot, has a streak of silver. "Malvina Southgate," she proclaims in a loud voice. "These others," she looks at Helen and waves her hand imperiously, "my husband, Raphael, my partner, Giorgio D'Alessandro, his wife, Maria, and friends. They're here to see Giorgio and me off in style." It sounds as if she's daring Helen to bounce her gatecrashers. "Darlings," she continues in a bullhorn voice, "champagne cocktails and eats. Fall to! Fall—"

"Malvina, dear," shouts Helen, interrupting. "I knew you'd join us in some noisy way. But welcome."

"Shakespeare's lovely words, dear Helen," retorts Ms. Southgate. "All day they've been ringing in my mind. The ones that describe, she clears her throat, "...*What rides on the posting winds, and doth belie all corners of the world.* Marvelous impression of the sweep and wonder of jet travel. Pity, the old boy wasn't talking flying but tongue-wagging slander *that outvenoms all the worms of Nile.*" Her eyes, hard as black marbles, glisten. "Irrelevant to our happy band, of course."

Helen gives the new guest a long look, before joining a cluster consisting of husband Mahoney, the Jamiesons and Sheila.

Chattering noisily, the Southgate people pounce on drinks and plates of *hors d'ouvres* set out along the bar. The room seems to shrink to a crowded space on a subway train.

I approach the airline manager. "Can't help noticing that after flying on Zemba Royal Air, we stay at a Zemba Royal hotel, then move to Zemba Royal's ocean resort before entraining on the Zemba Royal SilverSpear Express to end up in Zemba Royal's tented camp. Your outfit certainly seems the one to reckon with in Zembeylia. Is it owned by the King?"

"Ah, but let me correct you, dear fellow." The manager is tall, thin, Savile Row attired, his ebony skin so shiny it looks as though he polishes it. He seems to speak perfect English, if with a French lilt. "Deluxe!" He taps the schedule he's holding. "You omit the word deluxe from your description. Everything about your journey is deluxe, so naturally royal."

"I appeciate it," say I, "believe me. But Zemba Royal–?"

"Is a private consortium backed by the government. King M'Zumba I is our honorary chairman and we are dedicated to promoting our newly pacified nation's international relations. Zemba Royal, as you will see, stands for the best."

43

I'm about to respond when suddenly the Southgate woman is standing too close, staring into my eyes. "You have to be Goldstone," she declares, nodding as in confirmation. "If things go our way, we'll talk."

"Well, I–"

A loud *whoosh-whoosh* interrupts. The woman at the lounge's reception desk is blowing into a mic, to prepare her meager line for our pageant of leave-taking. "The flight," she announces, "is ready to board. Please proceed to security."

At the special line, where our group will be speeded through formalities, contrasting to passengers traveling in what I mentally call "Cattle Class," Barry Mondran shakes hands all around. "Sorry to be missing out," he says. Looking more cheerful than sorry, he kisses Sheila on both cheeks with all the passion, it seems to me, of a French government official conferring the Palms of Academic Merit upon some research assistant.

Ms. Southgate's guests are boisterous. They stand by a large picture window, peering at and noisily discussing Zemba Royal Air's huge but stubby "Special Version," Boeing 747SP, designed for extreme long distances. Were these "Baby '47s," as safe as the full-size ones? They really should get aboard for a look-see and talk with the pilots. Two muscular-looking women and a man with a sidearm on his belt, firmly nix this idea.

Loud complaints, then a shift to passionate embraces, kisses, shouts of farewell, as if Southgate and D'Alessandro are embarking with Magellan, instead of a week's zigging away and zagging back again.

The emotionalism produces in me a jealous twinge. Why can't Suzanne be here to see me off with kisses and sweet words? Not that sweet words are her thing where I'm concerned.

The plane's interior is done up in African motifs. A warrior mask and shield hanging on the galley bulkhead greets us First Class passengers entering through a front doorway. We're in our own enclosed seating section. I wander to the rear of the cabin, pull the edge of a curtain, peer at an auditorium-like Economy Class, where milling *hoi-polloi* crowd one another. Amazing, the human mass you can squeeze into these aerial contraptions: a seething sea of humankind pushing, jostling, blocking aisles, arguing over seats, trying to stuff all manner of objects into not very large overhead bins.

A world of many attires: snowy Sudanese robes, the bearers sporting equally snowy turbans; striped Arab robes, not so flowing, and topped by red fezzes. Bobbing here, bobbing there, a group of old-style nuns, black garbed and cauled; three rabbis, two with wide-brimmed black cloth hats, the third sporting a distinctive brown fur number; as some unexpected bonus, a gaggle of shaven-headed Buddhist monks in saffron outfits.

Most people, though, are wearing Western clothes that range from designer jean outfits to pseudo-military fatigues dotted with camouflage spots.

"You want to sit back there, we certainly can arrange that," says Helen giving me a nasty look. Before I can respond she hurries back up the aisle to her seat.

I drop the curtain.

Our group, assisted and cosseted by crew members, is settling into spacious, armchair two-by-two seats, Already we're being offered champagne, along with dishes of salted *manous*, a Zembeylian nut looking like an oversized peanut and tasting like a macadamia. I note the male purser's fur turban, topped by the head of a catlike creature with golden, staring eyes and fangs open to a toothy yawn.

At my window seat, I'm joined on the aisle by my sexy companion for the next fifteen hours. Taking a deep inhaling breath I fill my nostrils with her delicious scent. Cigarette smoke doesn't destroy it, only darkens the effect to make it more sultry. We clink champagne glasses.

The plane trundles out to a runway. The engines howl, a shudder, a leap forward. I count off seconds: 45...46...47...I begin to wonder if we'll get airborne…a bounce, the nose lifts, the ground withdraws, we roar upward. The wing dips into a deep rightward turn and at my window appears a mini-Manhattan, complete with lit-up Empire State Building and, at the island's southern end, near Wall Street, the twin towers of the World Trade Center. Manhattan: set out like a toy town for kids to play with. I close my eyes, say farewell to New York, NY, U.S.A.

I open my eyes again when a lovely flight attendant in a chic uniform offers us caviar: *Sevruga* I note, cheapest grade. On the fishy side but approximating my fantasy of luxury travel.

"Not the best I've had," I remark to Sheila, "but one of the best occasions. In your company."

She smiles beguilingly. "I've got bad habits. I bet you'll get tired of smoke in your face. What are your bad habits?"

"*Smoke gets in your eyes,*" I croon. "Cigarettes used to be romantic and smokers worldly folks who seemed to know things unknowable to virtuous abstainers. I have lots of bad habits but I'll let you discover them. Now, please brief me on our travel companions. Chandler runs some airline?"

Sheila nods "A very significant charter outfit that competed with our Helenair for Club Med contracts in the Caribbean and Mexico." She smiles. "We got 'em."

"And the cowboy? Jamieson?"

"Fake cowboy, originally from the Bronx. Owns a chain of agencies, linked to an online wholesale travel center. Extends through the South from New Orleans to Los Angeles, with a big cluster in Texas: WideWorld Travel,Inc. Great potential for bringing Sunbelt clients to Zembeylia."

"Now, uhm, Mike Mahoney is Helen Farrar's husband, but she keeps her name…"

"An important one in tourism."

"It doesn't always seem to elicit joy. That Southgate woman sure didn't sound friendly to Helen. But what in the world does she want from me?"

"Oh, Helen and Malvina have known each other for ages. Friendly enemies, you might say. Or inimical friends. She and her partner, Giorgio D'Alessandro, are the East Coast's biggest producers of African safari customers. Like 'em or hate 'em, they're absolutely vital to our plans."

"On the phone, you said something about my being essential. Is this to do with Southgate? I get the feeling that—"

Wait and see," interrupts Sheila, smiling a smile of mystery.

We're served an elaborate meal. Still, the menu's "Stuffed Squab, Zembeylian Style" comes dry and crumbly, overcooked by microwave. Plenty of champagne, though, plus three kinds of wine and for me a finale of Irish coffee with double shot of whisky. Pie-eyed, I turn from my seatmate to peer at the stars. If only I could fly forever, drinking champagne, feasting on better-cooked squab, leaving down there and far behind all obligations, nagging doubts, uncertainties...

Our attendant comes by to offer a box of Turkish cigarettes, each wrapped in different colored paper encircled by a gold band.

"Compliments of Zemba Royal," she says.

Sheila eagerly selects a purple one, lights up. "Try them," she urges. "Filled with *Balkan-Sobranie* tobacco, I'm told. Anyway what's fine for the goose..."

I choose a crimson cigarette, savor a *cognac* chaser, roll out my footrest and cover myself with a blanket found on the seat. I close my eyes, puff on my coffin-nail, head spinning from booze.

Then Sheila's hand is squeezing mine. My God, I'm scoring and don't even know it!

I lean towards her. "A lovely evening," I whisper in the sexiest murmur I can muster. "I'll dream of you, smoky, beautiful Sheila."

"No dreams." Sheila whispers back. "Didn't you read your program? A meeting. Upstairs, in the lounge."

"No!" I groan.

"Come on now. You can't be as tired as I am. I flew in from Chicago this morning, spent yesterday at a travel show there and worked all day today. So, you see..." She stands up, turns, heads toward a circular staircase at our cabin's rear that leads to an upper deck.

I push buttons to make my chair straight, stagger out of it, follow her.

The stairs go to a bar-lounge whose focal point is a snarling lion's head stuck into the back bulkhead.

Chapter 6: Briefings and Welcomes
In flight and in Zembeylia, Saturday-Sunday, December 12-13

The lounge has tables with holders for cocktail glasses and zebra-striped chairs that swivel. The lion head, mouth agape in silent roar, is centered on its bulkhead. To the beast's left stand two slot machines, at its right a white electronic junior-size-piano. The purser is softly playing a medley from *My Fair Lady*. As the group gathers, he stands, goes behind a bar at the lounge's forward end to fill drink orders.

I set up my mini tape recorder, a Sony that Suzanne gave me.

"Why ever do you need that?" Bitsy Jamieson regards the little box with suspicion, especially its mike attachment that I clip to my shirt front.

"Handwriting's lousy. Can't read my own notes."

She sniffs, "I consider it an invasion of privacy."

"No privacy," I answer quickly. "A group event."

Malvina Southgate, in a shimmering greenish silk dress, stands by the slots feeding coins. It eats them, gives nothing in return. Sheila told me *La Southgate* is worth a few millions, so win or lose...

My eye is caught by Mike Mahoney. He's seated and keeps flexing his left hand, for a red ball, then a yellow one to appear and disappear between the fingers. With his other hand he pulls cards out of thin air. And a green bracelet.

"My bracelet!" cries the Southgate woman in shocked tones. "How did you get it?"

Mahoney, grinning, hands it to her.

"Well?" she demands, snapping the bracelet back on her wrist.

He puts forefinger to lips, stands, reaches out and from behind Bitsy Jamieson's ear, produces two shiny amber earrings. "Lucky you wear clip-ons and not those pierced-ear kind." He gives a chuckle as he sits down again.

"Really!" she exclaims.

With a nod, he gives her the earrings. "Finger magic. Used to put on shows. Packed 'em in at the Magic Center on Manhattan's East side. I was a poor boy then, but carefree as a—"

"Michael, stop your foolishness and hand everyone their pills," orders Helen Farrar coming up the stairs.

He rises once more, from a plastic sack dispenses medium-size triple bottle sets. Each set bears a label with a tour member's name on it, and the logo of a pharmacy.

When I'm handed my set, Mike winks. A wink? Twitch? Why would he wink? Is he communicating some secret message?

"Okay now," says Helen taking a seat in mid-lounge and swiveling sideways to inspect the group. "Listen up. Your medicine is a combination pill that's anti-malaria, anti-M'zu-m'zu." She stops to pull a cigarette pack from her purse, taps one out, sticks it in her mouth.

Mike leans over to light it with a flashy-looking lighter. Sheila, I note, is starting a new smoke from her previous butt. Sisters, indeed. The Nicotine Nymphs.

"We take two pills right now," Helen tells us between puffs. "Purser, glasses of water all around."

Quickly, the man pulls a bottle of mineral water from a small-fridge and fills glasses. He serves us from a silver tray.

"Here on out," Helen commands, "one pill at every breakfast, beginning right on the plane. And one at lunch. Then two more at bedtime 'til they're gone, which will be three days after we get home."

She looks at each face in turn. Malvina Southgate stops donating to the one-armed bandit, eases herself into a swivel chair. She buckles the seat-belt, as we've been told to do when sitting, folds her arms and stares at Helen with the fixed gaze of a cat looking at a bird in a cage.

"I realize," Helen continues, "that we've had a heavy meal, too much to drink and you want rest. But I remind you this is a working trip. We're going to keep mighty busy during the five and a half days real time we have in Zembeylia. Let's review our schedule. Sheila?"

"Tomorrow, Sunday, December 13," Sheila reads from the program, "we arrive early afternoon, local time. Met by Gowinda Lazuli, our guide for the duration. He—"

"Indian, Zembeylia's Indians are mainly Tamils from South India and Sri Lanka," interrupts Helen. "Only one and a half million out of Zembeylia's 12.6 million population, but they're an important element of the merchant and business classes. They hold a small share of Zemba Royal Corporation and 70% of its arch-rival, X'Zambili-Africa Tours, which is big in hotels, big in tourism throughout Africa and the world at large. Comparable to mainland India's Oberoi Hotel chain. But only secondary in Zembeylia, thanks to my company, Eland Tours and our coalition with Zemba Royal." She smiles sweetly at Malvina Southgate, who, stone-faced, stares back.

"In any case," Helen goes on, "for us in the travel industry, the Tamils, as skilled personnel in a variety of service disciplines, are a vital element."

She gestures to her sister, who continues: "We bus twenty-seven kilometers south—sixteen miles, that is, to Fulumbane, the capital, and check into our hotel. We rest for two hours before a reception and inspection of the hotel premises."

"Mandatory," Helen chimes in. "Boring, yes. You'll be tired and jetlagged, what with the time difference, but these are our hosts. They're wining, dining, squiring us around on buses they're chartering. So you're required to be there, bright-eyed and bushy-tailed. Oh, and pack up your heavy coats and clothes, then check them with the hotel staff. Useless in Zembeylia, given the tropic weather. They'll be delivered to the airport for our departure. Mike, you read on."

"Let's see," he looks for his place. "Monday, December 14, is for local sightseeing. In the evening we bus to the palace for another reception offered by His Royal Highness, King M'Zumba I. We also meet Prime Minister Léon-François X'Zirumba—with the X silent, right? So pronounced 'Zirumba' and His Excellency, Zecherias M'Bowé, Minister of Internal Security, Tourism and Culture."

"Mandatory again," puts in Helen. "Now we'll encounter the ruling 'cream-of-the-cream,' as the French say, especially M'Bowé. He's considered the man-behind-the-throne. Runs the police, including a newly formed elite corps called the Security Militia, or SM. No, not S and M," she gives a sour smile, "just SM. You'll spot them by their distinctive white tunics. Minister M'Bowé is a great promoter of tourism. Both he and the King are members of the M'Bélé tribe which, though a minority of 3.3 million, has pushed its rival of almost seven million X'Zambilis, into second rank."

"Hold on," says Gene Petroff. "I'm not sure what you're saying is accurate." He has a buzzing high-pitched voice. It makes me think of a revving-up turbine. "This X'Zirumba fellow is Prime Minister. And he's X'Zambili."

"Window-dressing to keep the crowd happy. Does what he's told. M'Bowé's the man to watch. Michael, move on."

"At least," puts in Petroff before Mike can speak, "you admit there's a crowd that has to be kept happy. Or else." He looks meaningfully at each of us.

"Tuesday," continues Mike Mahoney after a silence, "we spend the afternoon at Diamantville, government-sponsored community and shopping center near the site of Zembeylia's first diamond mine–"

"Wonderful buys," Helen interrupts again.

Stirrings. Her chimings-in and Petroff's hint of revolt are getting the group riled. I overhear Miho Petroff murmur to her husband, "She thinks we've never traveled here before?"

"Loose diamonds at Diamantville's gem exchange," Helen contiues, oblivious to the hostility she's causing. "I'm hoping to buy one for a pendant that Tiffany's is designing for me. Proceed."

So it goes through Wednesday and, at last, Thursday, December 17th, when we have a full day and a half in a tented game park for animal viewing. Friday evening, the 18th, a charter plane will fly us back to the international airport. We'll pick up our winter clothes and catch the flight home. Safe and exhausted we'll be at Kennedy by five A.M. Saturday, December 19th.

The so-called "eight-day tour," described in that letter I received counts our dawn ending as a full day, as well as tonight's evening departure. Standard travel agency rip-off, designed to make clients pay mostest for the leastest. Thank goodness this trip is so cheap. Almost a freebie, considering...

"Questions?" asks Helen.

"Well," says Gordon Chandler, "diamonds are fine but Alvaro and I want to see tsavorites. I'm disappointed we won't get to view the mines they're from."

On closer examination, Chandler isn't so great looking. His bronze complexion has a greenish tanning salon cast and his blond hair looks more bottled than real. I note crows' feet and droopy skin. A man in a race after youth with no bet he's gonna catch up.

"Time constraints," answers Helen. "We had to pick the most significantly touristic sights. Diamantville's a big attraction, layout inspired by Knott's Berry Farm: semi-authentic and catering to American and European visitors with its state-controlled gem

52

exchange and shops, a café, even a mine tour in a specially constructed replica."

"Fake!" Chandler shakes his head. "To travel all the way to Zembeylia for—"

"They can't have visitors running around the real thing, lousing up operations, getting hurt. Maybe stealing diamonds—" Helen responds in mouth-frothing mode to Chandler's mild objection.

"Alvaro and I," Chandler counters steel-voiced, his companion frowning, large, pirate's mustache making him look fierce. "On Wednesday we're renting a car and going off to see the tsavorite mines near X'Ziromeu City. I happen to know the train we're taking stops there while the dining car is still serving dinner. We'll climb aboard, get fed, no harm done."

Helen frowns. "We're a travel unit. We stick together."

"Wednesday's activities aren't what you're calling 'mandatory,'" argues Chandler.

"As a matter of fact, Helen darling," says Sheila, her voice low and almost contrite, "I was counting on Wednesday to get to the hospital run by Dr. Franz Hermann. You know, the Swiss doctor who's doing so much to battle A.I.D.S. in Zembeylia?" She looks around. "I'm on the board of a medical charity. We're interested in the doctor's pioneering work and—"

"You'll bring us back a barrel full of diseases?" Helen gives a snort. "A.I.D.S., we don't need."

"Not to worry," Sheila's voice sounds strained. "I'll take precautions. It does mean a lot—"

"As I say," Helen looks around the group. "This isn't *fun-in-the-sun*. We're on an expensive journey, paid mainly by my company. It has only one purpose: to get us rounding up hordes of tourists once we're home, tourists able to spend big bucks, who love adventure, safe adventure, that is. All of you will be sending them over to our hotels and resorts and game-viewing camps in Zembeylia. I've worked for three years to set up my company's exclusive tie-ins. I didn't invite you to indulge yourselves or slack off. Certainly not you, Sheila. Given time limits, I—"

"Oh, for God's sake let her go," says Mike. "Only once. For the rest she'll be on deck day and night. Right, Sheila?"

"You stick to your side of this, which I hope you can handle," Helen hisses at him. "It doesn't involve dictating my stepsister's schedule, or anything else for that matter."

She darts a glance at all of us, sees her temper display going over like an ice shower. "Oh well," her lips grimace into a smile at Sheila. "Do what you must that day. Just don't miss the train."

"Thank you," Sheila speaks meekly. "I won't. And I'm grateful."

The meeting ends. Some linger in the lounge, the purser goes back to tickling the ivories. Cozy atmosphere, but I want sleep.

I manage about an hour. Wake to pull down the shade when sun hits my face. Back in New York, only 2 A.M., or so. On arrival in Zembeylia we'll be a full eight hours ahead of the U.S. East Coast. I look over at Sheila, dead to the world. Stepsister? No wonder I can't see a family resemblance. Not my affair. I close my eyes.

We wing, bumpily, across Africa, sky thick with high clouds.

Sheila, once awake, spends her time writing reports and letters and emitting clouds of smoke; it stings my eyes, tickles my throat, makes me want to cough, not to mention keeping me awake. One little personality flaw, so less painful than Suzanne's nagging self-righteous intellectual snobbism.

From the seat pocket in front of me, I pull out the airline's magazine, study Zembeylia's map. Long and narrow, sort of like Chile. As Chile faces the Pacific, Zembeylia enjoys an extensive seafront with the Indian Ocean. Our tour will go north-to-south, with only a small jog west, since any great distance in that direction would push us into Mozambique and, lower down, to South Africa.

Fulumbane, Zembeylia's capital, is the country's main port. Everything from fishing vessels, *dhows* out of India or Sri Lanka, tramp steamers and the occasional cruise liner put in there. The country's second city, X'Ziromeu City, is where our luxury overnight train to the game camp will make a thirty minute stop—from 7:30 P.M. to 8:00 P.M. and hitch on an extra engine to ride over the country's highest mountains, the Monogoros, craggy and snowcapped. The camp is in the X'Ziloncado Basin's Game Reserve, which the magazine says is as big as Connecticut, Delaware and Rhode Island combined. At the southern tip, it's smack up against South Africa's equally vast Krueger National Game Park.

Sheila leans back, sighs. "Too much paperwork in the travel business. I'm glad I took calligraphy in college. Makes writing fun."

She lights one more cigarette, goes back to her task.

At length, we fly out over the Indian Ocean, curve back toward shore for landing. I note that my seat companion looks rosy and trim, as if she just had an eight hour beauty sleep, a health-food breakfast and morning run in Central Park. Half an hour in the lavatory evidently is almost as good. She must be pushing thirty-eight or nine, and with the eating, drinking, lack of sleep, the smoking as if she aspires to be Ms. Ablated-Lung-Of-The-Year, a wonder there are but hints of crows' feet around the eyes, plus a line or two at the corners of her mouth. Have to look close to spot these still attractive evidences of wear-and-tear.

Through a sudden torrent, the big plane settles low over a sapphire sea pebbled with raindrops. The shoreline comes up: a wide, tannish beach bordered by palm forest. Under the palms, the ground looks bright red. A gentle bump, the roar of thrust-reversers. We're in Zembeylia.

Just beyond Customs we find a small man with a sweaty face framed by black side-whiskers. He holds a sign: *WELCOME ZEMBA ROYAL-ELAND GUESTS*. Mr. Gowinda Lazuli wears a high-collared black coat and tight-fitting white cotton trousers, extending to natty white shoes. His head is adorned with a white turban decorated by a brilliant green stone.

55

"So pleased to meet you." He presses my hand between wettish palms. "So pleased. Welcome, welcome to our lovely country."

"See what I mean?" Sheila whispers in my ear, her head nodding towards the turban. "Tsavorite. Dig that sparkle."

Lazuli ushers us all to a bus, whose lower region is being loaded with bags. Fortunately, the downpour has stopped, the sun coming out hot and humid.

"They-ah's your'n, ain't it?" Jamieson, pointing to the suitcases, calls to his wife. "Ah mean the one in black crocodile."

"Yes, yes, yes. All is here," cries Lazuli. "All present and accounted for. Having no fears. Surely in your rooms you shall be receiving them safely. Now give me passports and climb aboard please. We must be getting on."

"Passports?" demands peroxide-blond Gordon Chandler. "What do you want with our passports? They've just been checked by Immigration."

"But not by our Security Militia, SM newly formed. From fourteen days ago, they are requiring by Royal Decree to inscribe particulars of all foreign passports for Exit Visa."

Lazuli holds up his hands, palms outward. "Having no fears," he says again. "All will be returned. Yes, surely, SM returns all."

"Why the hell do we need exit visas?" asks Petroff in his turbine whine. His exotic-looking wife nods anxiously. "We never had to do that before. Now look here, we came of our own free will and we'll leave anytime we damn please."

"Ah, ah, ah!" Lazuli holds up a forefinger. "Royal Decree, I am telling you. You shall leave when and if the Forces of Order, as we are calling SM, allow it. Of course, almost certainly they will allow, oh, yes indeedy. You are honored guests. But you must hand over passports and be complying with national regulations. Royal Decree."

"I'm not giving up my passport!" Chandler's face turns mottled red. He's supported by a chorus of groans. "How do I know I'll get

56

it back? How do I know I won't need it? How do I know I'll have a…a visa to leave this place? I never heard of such a thing!"

Helen climbs into the open bus door and entry step, claps her hands. "Calm down, everybody. It's the practice here for the Ministry of Internal Security, Tourism and Culture–our main sponsor, I remind you–to hold all foreign passports for checking during the first days of a visitor's stay. The exit visa is automatically stamped into the passports of legitimate tourists, such as ourselves. In three days or so you'll have your papers back. Then, at the airport, there's only the departure tax of $99.99 U.S. to pay and you're on your way home."

"$99.99?" Mavina Southgate's voice is a growl. "You never told us."

Helen opens her eyes wide. "Didn't your invitation letter mention it? Well, I suppose it was printed prior to the new regulat– Malvina darling, with the money your enterprises pull in I'm sure you can afford it. I'll be glad to lend–"

"Not the point," cuts in Chandler. "How many more tricks and hidden fees do we not know about?"

Helen tosses her head. "You've all been thoroughly briefed. We have to abide by the law of the land. When you need them, your passports will be there. Now we must get going."

More groans and mumblings. I'm in shock about the extra hundred dollars. I'll have to be more careful with money than I'd planned. Three hundred total cash for the trip. Now, already a hundred gone! Presents reduced, for sure.

Reluctantly, the passports are handed to Lazuli, who gives them over to an officer in a white tunic and gold epaulettes. The man salutes, walks away.

We board the bus and also leave, rolling southward through red-soiled country with western mountains making a blue shadow beyond the right-hand windows. The bus passes into a forest of coconut and banana palms succeeded by a spread of shacks across a wide plain.

What looks like an open river of sewage, all kinds of debris floating in it, borders the road. Listless appearing people sit in doorways or tend meager goats confined to small, wired-off yards. Skeletal children, some with swollen bellies, wave as the bus speeds by.

"Such poor souls," intones Mr. Lazuli through a microphone. "See over there," he points across the way to some barracks' buildings, whitewashed with a scattering of barred windows. "Our government wishes to build fine dee-welopment to house such people. But they do refuse to move." He sighs over the airwaves. "Terrible problem, Yes, most terrible problem."

More palm forest, Then clusters of comfortable-looking villas stretching up a slope separated from the road by a wall topped with barbed wire. On the hilltop I glimpse a number of extra-large, pink-stuccoed houses fronted by well-tended lawns and framed by bushes flowering in purples, crimsons, whites.

"Compound Number One," our guide's voice resonates with pride. "Most exclusively reserved for government officials, business executives, ambassadors and officers of the police, both SM and military, holding grade of Colonel or higher."

"You live there?" asks Guitterez-Shaughnessy.

"I am a resident of Compound Number Three," answers Lazuli. "For government and company employees having special skills. We are on city's south side."

"Houses as big as this?" presses Guitterez.

"Not quite so big." Lazuli looks uncomfortable. "But very nice quarters. Yes, yes, nice."

We pass the compound's entryway, guarded by sentries and a tank. The city proper appears a tangle of dusty, narrow streets glutted with people and traffic. It features hole-in-wall shops and wooden, rickety-looking multiple-unit buildings: tenements, in fact. A few open areas display goods spread helter-skelter over grass and pavement. We drive by a line of unfinished buildings whose upperworks are a lattice of piled up wood beams and rusty girders.

58

The bus creeps along, engulfed in floods of pedestrians and vehicles. Women bear produce baskets atop their heads. Many have veiled faces, dressed all in black from nose down; a few have their faces entirely masked, except for eye slits; another minority wear brighter garb and bare faces to the world. Men have on mainly dusty robes of striped blue or white. They often lead trains of donkeys and goats. People in rags, people on crutches, children darting here and there between oxcarts, rattletrap trucks, buses and cars that never stop honking. Everyone and everything appears focused on getting ahead of whatever is immediately in front of them.

Into this mix a smattering of motor scooters, reminiscent of the bike-messengers in Manhattan, race along the street. These scooters whip in and out even faster than in New York, putting the final touch on a chaos threatening gridlock. Stop-start, stop-start, we go, honking nonstop. Finally, the bus comes to a wide space with trees at its center and flanked on one side by massive French style stone buildings topped with mansard roofs. These, says Lazuli, house government ministries. Beyond the ministries, behind a blood red stone wall, stands the Royal Palace.

I'm almost beyond noticing. Too much food, liquor, travel, excitement. As the bus pulls into our hotel's driveway, I prepare for a dash through registration, a sprint to my room, a jump out of clothes for a hot-and-cold shower. And finally, the delicious crawl into bed.

"Photographs!" Helen Farrar says over the intercom. "We gather in the garden. Won't take more than half an hour."

Loud cries, a shout or two and a call from Miho Petroff, "Photographs? After our journey? Is she mad?"

All stifled by Helen's final word: "Mandatory! Vital for publicity at home." More groans from her business rivals.

The garden is beautiful, I have to admit: Frangipani, clusters of flame trees, bursts of pink and blue phallic-shaped lobelia and everywhere bougainvillea of a delicate apricot hue. A baobab,

Africa's biggest tree, its trunk a full fifteen feet in circumference, stands as centerpiece. The top is less impressive, tapering to a modest stump out of which twisting branches spring in profusion.

Using the baobab for backdrop, the photographer shifts us here, there, puts his head under an out-of-date camera hood. He emerges to shift us again. When at last he's finished snapping group pictures, he insists on organizing us in ones, twos and threes for more takes.

"Photos ready tomorrow in the lobby. Only $7.50 apiece, U.S. currency," shouts Helen as the camera clicks for a last time and we bolt to our rooms. When I get to mine, I take off my shoes, stagger to the bed and flop.

Chapter 7: A Royal Reception
Fulumbane, Zembeylia, Monday Evening, December 14

From Sunday through a busy sightseeing Monday, Helen Farrar keeps us on the run. That first evening, promptly at 6 P.M., the ringing telephone rouses me from an almost drugged sleep. I'm still in my New York clothes.

Sheila's voice says my presence is "mandatory" for the hotel reception. Quick shower, shave, change into lightweight suit, then downstairs for handshakes with Management. After introductions and a few minutes. chatting–accompanied by a glass of sweet local white wine–we're trotted off to inspect single bedrooms, double bedrooms, junior suites, deluxe suites, bridal suites, penthouse suites, government V.I.P suites, bathrooms with whirlpools, bathrooms without whirlpools...

A bed is a bed, a room a room, lesson driven home enthusiastically and relentlessly by Hotel Zemba Royal's staff.

Monday's climax occurs promptly at 8 P.M., when a bus deposits us at the palace for our reception with King M'Zumba I. His Royal Highness is on a gold throne perched so high it's like a tennis referee's seat. This in so-called Throne Hall, a long, narrow room with a glittery golden ceiling and two massive crystal chandeliers, all reminiscent of French sixteenth century grandeur. Utterly misplaced, I feel, in this late-blooming twentieth century nation of equatorial Africa.

The King, wearing a leopard robe and cheetah hat, sits on a pile of red plush cushions. He doesn't deign to rise but gives a speech of welcome, which he reads from a piece of paper held under his nose by an officer of the SM. The latter's dazzlingly white tunic jangles with medals.

From a speaker's podium to the monarch's right, the Prime Minister says a few words, after which His Excellency Zecherias M'Bowé, Minister of Security, Tourism and Culture, delivers a discourse the lengthiness of which more than makes up for his Sovereign's and nominally superior Minister's brevity. With the agility of a mountain goat leaping from outcropping to outcropping, M'Bowé springs from one mixed metaphor to the next on the order of nations joining hands and marching toward a sunrise of progress. His themes are cooperation, development and we want your money.

"Typical corrupt M'Benzi chatter," Malvina Southgate mutters into my ear. She has moved across the room to stand beside me. As guests of honor, our group is at the front of a crowd featuring military officers in eye-catching uniforms and a variety of diplomats wearing clothes ranging from dark business suits to colored robes complemented by fancy hats.

The Minister's sound and fury climaxes in a promise to recite a brand new patriotic ode composed for this occasion.

Modestly, M'Bowé reminds the audience of his authorship of Zembeylia's current national anthem. It has become, he announces, no less than his duty to bow to the clamor of public opinion and appoint himself Poet Laureate of the Nation.

"Allows him to lift an extra $750,000 a year from The Bank for African Restructuring and Funding." Ms. Southgate, standing on tiptoe, hisses into my ear. "Known by its acronym," she cackles, low-voiced. "Being the West's financial arm in Southeast Africa, it certainly B.A.R.F.s up lots of cash."

I raise an eyebrow but refrain from comment. *La Southgate*, as I am beginning to think of this peculiar woman, appears to have notions and habits definitely out of ordinary. She and her business partner, Giorgio D'Alessandro, pointedly did kiss their respective spouses goodbye. Here in Zembeylia she made a scene in the hotel about being assigned a room of her own. In fact, D'Alessandro also fussed, insisting they were rooming together; to Helen Farrar's obvious and smiling delight. "So sorry, my dears," she'd clucked. "I naturally assumed…but one never should. Assume, that is."

"This may be a working trip but it still gets us away from home," Mrs. Southgate pointed out.

The Minister rustles some papers. I strain to hear him before realizing the poem is on a printed sheet that an usher handed us at the hall's entry:

> *O varied Land that stretcheth wide*
> *From Sea to Mount and Valley fair.*
> *O Wilds sublime where leopards bide*
> *With elephants and fauna rare.*
> *A place where fierce M'Bélé roam*
> *And sage X'Zambili make their home.*
> *Now, Nation, raise a mighty tide*
> *Steadfast as one: Zembeylia's care*
> *Shall be our Fate, our finest pride.*

Clapping from the many glittering dignitaries. The King taps his knee with what looks like a silver flyswatter. He keeps it in his right hand, the local equivalent of a scepter?

Speeches over, everyone breaks into clusters. Footmen circulate through the crowd bearing glasses of mawkish local wine. I decide to question Ms. Southgate. "What do you mean, 'M'Benzi'?"

She puts finger to lips, again stretching herself to my ear. "I said the man is a corrupt 'M'Benzi' and his chatter typical."

"M'Benzi?"

"Kenyans say 'Wabenzi.' The language changes. Nothing else."

I allow myself to look mystified.

"Wheeler-dealers who, when they hit it rich, immediately buy a Mercedes to proclaim their affluence to the world."

"So I've learned a new word. Two new words." I nod. "Wabenzi and M'Benzi. Owners of Mercedes-Benz's."

"People of position, of power." Ms. Southgate gulps wine. "And corruption."

"You don't know that."

"I most certainly do," she glares at me. "The minority M'Bélés have quote-unquote 'pacified'" this country by starving and exterminating vast numbers of the majority X'Zambili tribe. Three million lording it over seven million? I ask you, is that viable?" Her tone is accusatory, as if all my fault. "Yes," she goes on, "persecution has more or less stopped with the establishment of this new monarchy, supposedly constitutional. Still, Parliament is a joke with the Council of Governance running things. The King is a former undertaker's assistant. He knows nothing about ruling. And the other groups, French, Indians but especially X'Zambilis, are totally on the outs. So they wait, just as a lioness waits for the wildebeest calf to lag too far behind its mother. Then what a power-grabbing dustup there'll be, let me tell you! A lot of hate, tribal and ethnic, goes on here under the smiling surface."

"From my reading this past week," I remark, "everyone seems to be enjoying peace and the notion of forthcoming prosperity. Zembeylians are hot to develop their tourist industry at the point where the French left off. This has to mean peace, doesn't it?"

Ms. Southgate tosses her head. "You and I better hope so. My own wagon's hitched to tourism's star. But something sinister's afoot, a helluva lot more sinister than most of our august company of travel-moochers can guess." She takes a fierce swallow of wine, gazes at her glass. "Foul stuff, eh?" A footman comes by and she grabs another glass. "Drink's drink," she mutters.

I help myself to *manou* nuts. I'm finding them addictive.

"Tourism, tourism," Ms. Southgate mumbles, looking drunk. I'd seen her at dinner in the hotel belting down wine as energetically as here. "Consider the way Zemba Royal Corporation beat out X'Zambili-Africa Tours for the best resort contracts and the overseas air concession. In which Helen—oops, I mean dear, dear Helen. Do you know we went to school together, in Switzerland? Anyway, dear, dear Helen connived to come up with a $450 million tourism and eco-development loan."

"Good for her! Somebody has to do it, I guess."

"First of all," Southgate waggles her finger, "she has only paid out $2.7 million of actual money. What the hell does that cover? Not even bribes to these fine gentlemen." Her hand sweeps across the room. "More importantly, X'Zambili-Africa Tours has a much better infrastructure, more hotel and resort management expertise than this upstart Zemba Royal Corporation." Again, she nods to herself, a habit she seems to have. "We know, Giorgio and I. We're heavily committed to X'Zambili-Africa with its Indian support. They're the commercial backbone of this society, the Indians."

"The French," I remind her. "Why shouldn't they get some credit?"

"Too tired. Spend their time feeling sorry for themselves, for having been abandoned by *Maman*. But," she draws herself up, dark brows knitted for battle, "the point is, if we'd had just a little more leeway we could've produced $800 million, almost double what Helen claims she can swing. And, if some folks in our group here were bright enough to back us like they promised and not play stupid games on their own, we'd make that over a billion in foreign loans."

"We?"

"Our corporation, Africa Wonderland Journeys, Inc. In coalition with other sources."

I regard her harsh but handsome face–the French phrase *une belle-laide*–an ugly beauty, perfectly describes it. The large nose and midnight brows, the latters' color matching eyes that spit rage, have a compelling allure, although individual features are too prominent to be alluring. Rage at what, I ask myself? The world? Life? Me? M'Bélés? Tourism? Or just general, unrelenting, unforgiving rage?

"Strange," I'm thinking of Lionel Goldhammer, who disdained this trip offered by a competitor, "that you'd come on such a tour."

"Oh, like the Petroffs. Helen ousted them from a lucrative Japanese golf connection in the Caribbean. She invited us here to get us to send business her way. But Petroff has a Japanese link through his wife, Miho. 'Eternal Beauty.' That's what the name Miho means. And not only is she a fine Mezzo-Soprano who's sung with the San Francisco Opera but she's also a Sakurai. The daughter of the head of Sakurai Electronics."

Malvina Southgate leans close. On her breath I smell the sour tang of half-digested wine. "This is in confidence," she goes on. "The Sakurai family promises to establish a world-class computer assembly plant here in Fulumbane, on condition the city will commit to building–with a Sakurai contribution–Africa's finest opera house, finer than Cairo's relatively new one. Miho Sakurai-Petroff shall be the star singer. And not Zemba Royal or Eland but a consortium including us and Chandler's airline will have the exclusive contract for transport to and from Japan and the arranging of accommodations here for all Sakurai personnel."

Ms. Southgate's voice rises in excitement. "We'll bring worldwide opera fans, as well as the safari and general vacation crowd, including golfers–the Japanese love golf–to a chain of deluxe hotels, tented camps and extravagant beach properties complete with casinos and top-rated golf courses that our consortium will build. And X'Zambili-Africa Tours will be in-country manager."

Too rich for me, such pie-in-the-sky speculations. Is the woman making it up as she goes along?

"Helen wants us to be humble," she continues relentlessly. "To give up any idea of investing and simply supply customers to her outfit for the commission she consents to pay. But just you wait!"

A footman passes with *hors d'oeuvres*. She grabs a sausage, wolfs it in a gulp. "We–"

"Come and meet the King, my dear," Giorgio D'Alessandro, nodding to me, links his arm with hers, sweeps her off to the foot of the throne, where His Royal Highness is leaning down to converse with Helen, Mike, and Chandler.

"You are enjoying your stay in my beautiful country?" I'm confronted by a short, large man with a round face, bulging eyes and prominent horn rims. Mister *Five-by-Five* in person: *Five feet tall and five feet wide,* as the old song goes.

The guy holds out his hand. "Antoine Bhulliwah-X'Zilone, one quarter French, one quarter Tamil-Indian and one half the son and heir of a X'Zambili tribal chief. I myself head Zembeylia's parliamentary opposition, as well as being X'Zambili-Africa Tours senior vice-president. And you?"

"Goldstone, New York travel executive," I answer, shaking the man's hand, finding his clasp languid. "I'm anxious to see your country but we've only just arrived."

Mr. Bhulliwah says, "I know New York: The Rainbow Room, the Four Seasons restaurant, The Sherry-Netherlands Hotel and, of course, Matilda's Parlor. Do you patronize her services?"

"Well, I've heard of her but–"

"One of the world's finest institutions of erotic massage." He lowers his voice. "*Screw* gives her its only six-cock rating. But I must tell you, right here in Fulumbane we have Madame Yvette's, an even more interesting venue. Thanks to the B.A.R.F."

I sip my wine.

"Nevertheless," the man goes on, "I know Los Angeles much better than New York. There, The Castle is perfect for sado-masochistic experiences." He sighs, perhaps caught up in nostalgia.

"Our esteemed Minister of Security Services and Tourism isn't much of a poet, is he? Do you know that I am his Shadow?" He looks mysterious. "Oh, yes. You should realize you are speaking to Minister M'Bowé's Shadow."

"I don't quite get it," I say.

"British Parliament, dear fellow. Shadow Cabinet. Do you take me for a mere backbencher? Oh, no, no, no!" Bhulliwah-X'Zilone shakes his head energetically. "Oh, no! I am the Shadow Minister of Security and thus and so, his other titles. Law, however, is my background, not poetry. I shall have to delegate poetic utterances to a speech-writer, like your Peggy Noonan of the Republicans. Now do you understand?"

"Most honored," I incline my head.

Bhulliwah beams. "Perhaps I can arrange to show you Madame Yvette's. An enlightening cultural experience."

"Thank you, I appreciate your hospitality. I have to tell you that I'm spoken for, as they say. I'd better keep away from temptation."

"Hmmph!" My new acquaintance seems to lose interest. Soon he moves off.

The party begins to feel as though it will drag on forever. Sheila is keeping busy with the government people, so I can't approach her. I chat with Jamieson, whose Texicanese, or whatever the hell his accent's supposed to be, grates. I even try striking up a conversation with Guitterez-Shaughnessy, get answered in monosyllables.

At length, Helen calls us out to the bus. Like obedient schoolchildren we pile in and are carted back to the hotel.

Chapter 8: A-Whoring We Will Go
Fulumbane, Zembeylia, Tuesday, December 15

"How can I be anything less than this nation's ultimate citizen?" rumbles Antoine Bhulliwah-X'Zilone in a voice of distant thunder. "How indeed? Given that the very blood in my veins represents the highest minglings of our heritage?"

"Whoa, Tony!" Dale Uppingham III holds up his hands. "Don't waste your golden tones on an old friend and ally."

Bhulliwah grins. "It becomes a habit, this rhetoric of Parliament. Hard to turn off the flow."

They're riding in Bhulliwah's government Mercedes limo, one result of a thirty-three million dollar "Special Development" grant that Uppingham arranged for Zembeylia. Bhulliwah leans forward to open a bar panel in the soundproof partition separating their rear compartment from the driver. Both men have already lit Davidoff *Château d'Yquem* cigars, reputedly Fidel Castro's finest. Now they taste Auld MacClatchie's thirty-year single malt, savoring its inner warmth while puffing out clouds of blue-tinged smoke as they luxuriate in the car's air-conditioned comfort.

"Birds of a feather." Uppingham settles into cushions of babysoft leather. "You, the black condor; I, the white albatross. Both elegant, both scavengers." He sips his drink. "I'm well-born, too, you know. What in the U.S. we call 'old money.' except my people's portion declined during the Great Depression. You crave power, I crave keeping up with the Rockefellers." He raises his glass. "Long live our symbiotic relationship."

Bhulliwah tips his glass to the toast. Dale has been good to Zembeylia. The Bank for African Restructuring and Funding (B.A.R.F.), of which Dale is Comptroller Africa, Southeastern Sector, recently allotted Zembeylia a further five hundred million U.S. for "Infrastructural Improvement." Of necessity, most of the money went to administrative expenses, a responsibility devolving on junior males of the nation's "Big Five," as Zembeylia's M'Bélé ruling families are known. Although not M'Bélés but of the X'Zambili tribe, the X'Zilones are "adoptive" or honorary members of the M'Bélé Peoples, accepted as part of the ruling upper-crust. In fact, Bhulliwah's younger brother holds a key position at the Fulumbane branch of a large New York bank. The lad spends his days at laundry-work: scrubbing, bleaching, spin-drying, starching and generally accomplishing squeaky-clean deliveries of monies to a variety of offshore accounts.

Among the beneficiaries are not merely the families and a few select associates, such as Bhulliwah-X'Zilone himself, but also Dale Uppingham. Only fair and just, given the man's hard work for their cause. Bhulliwah vows to let nothing change in the laundry and dry-cleaning operations of banking and government when he seizes power.

Uppingham blows a smoke ring. "How long's it been we've known each other? Thirty-two years?" He sighs. "Our fifty-fifth birthdays loom, old man. Time for realism." He looks over at Tony, remembering their first meeting in Fontainebleau. The young African, less paunchy in those days, was behind the wheel of a silver Lamborghini as it pulled into the courtyard of France's prestigious International Business Academy. A member of Zembeylia's new rich, Dale decided, and set about making Bhulliwah's acquaintance. They were both at the Academy for worldly polish as follow up to law school: he ex-Yale, Tony ex-Zembeylia's Freedom University. But the South-East African had money to burn, thanks to his father being Minister of Finance. Dale, on a tight budget, volunteered his know-how and connoisseurship, which allowed him to share in Bhulliwah's financial conflagration. Zooming up and down the "Autoroute of the Sun" on the stretch between Fontainebleau and Paris, enjoying life in a style they decided was their due, what great times they'd had. Yet, despite champagne nights and those trips to Deauville in the company of *danseuses* affiliated with the ultra-chic "Crazy Horse Saloon," they'd passed all their exams. Tribute to brainpower transcending hangover power.

With Africa his field of interest, Dale went first to the World Trade Organization for seasoning, then on to B.A.R.F., sponsored by the world's wealthiest multinational corporations. The bank's priority was to promote, in the name of the "global village," local cheap labor and the export of regional raw materials for finishing in the developed world. Its parallel mission was to block any homegrown manufacture that might lead to the training of skilled labor and demands for higher pay. These, in turn, could result in the passing of–God forbid!–traitorous, anti-global village laws clamping down on Africa's hemorrhage of raw materials.

For his part, Bhulliwah stayed on in Paris at an international law firm. Then a transfer to Los Angeles, the Lamborghini replaced by a red Thunderbird. Now he and Dale were reunited in Zembeylia, with Tony's feet firmly planted on the rungs of both the political and–thanks to his link with X'Zambili-Africa Tours–corporate ladders.

Dale is pleased that his friend has an eye for ladies. It makes entertaining him so easy. He proposed this little jaunt to Madame Yvette's as a thank you for services rendered to BriteStrider, Inc., a consortium of U.S. and Chinese shoe manufacturers. Bhulliwah should enjoy a reward for long and successful bouts of socio-political infighting, not to mention a respite from his nagging wife.

Once more Uppingham raises his glass. "Here's to BriteStrider. Going great guns, thanks to you."

Bhulliwah nods. Persuading the running-shoe conglomerate to build a factory in Zembeylia is a done deal, an exception to the B.A.R.F. ban on creating locally manufactured goods, due to a plum opportunity too good to miss. From the company itself, there were initial doubts, hesitations, objections. Finally, with the promise of a new law setting the hourly pay-ceiling at seventeen U.S. cents for locals and a ban on unions, contracts were signed.

"If BriteStrider has to face paying out salaries like those in the 'States and Europe, where unions keep insisting on a near-living wage," Dale points out again as in multiple times while terms were being negotiated, "what advantage coming to Zembeylia?"

Behind the scenes, Bhulliwah crafted and shepherded through Parliament "A Freedom To Work Act," enshrining every BriteStrider condition and demand, with a list of criminal sanctions for violations.

"You know at home," Dale puffs on his cigar, making it glow, "there were rumblings. The A.F.L-C.I.O. got bent out of shape at the closedowns in Illinois, Missouri, Maine and Connecticut. Laying off 48,350 workers at one go really caused a flurry. The company came near to facing a national boycott of its merchandise. When you're retailing glorified sneakers at $190 a pair, you need all the customers you can get. But now everything's A-okay. Our big public-relations campaign about how BriteStrider has heart and social conscience drowned out Labor's grumbling. Which is why we're going the extra mile on workers' benefits here in Zembeylia."

Indeed, BriteStrider was generously building barracks for its male and female laborers, whose desperation to find employment was causing many to leave their villages and walk hundreds of miles to the proposed factory site. These barracks, models of construction for Third World industries, house only 240 persons each, with every two buildings benefitting from a toilet. Shifts are being held to fifteen hours and the company has declared it would discourage employees under age nine from working more than eleven hours. On Sundays everyone is to get thirty minutes off, at full pay, for church.

Dale Uppingham pats Bhulliwah's shoulder. "You can count on the company's gratitude. Banque Pfister in Geneva, am I right?"

"Much obliged, *cher ami*." Bhulliwah sets his whisky glass into an armrest holder and glances out the window. Crowds of sweaty common folk, unwashed, clothes in tatters, many living in the roadway. Pah! Dogs, goats, oxen, mules and people pissing rivers, dropping dung. Thank God for lavish German soundproofing and air filters. Not a sound nor stink gets into the Mercedes. How

71

pleasant. How titillating too, the contemplation of an interlude—for free!—at Madame Yvette's.

"I understand there's a new girl, a genuine *Parisienne*," says Dale.

"Aha!" Ever since his Paris years, Bhulliwah has kept a special feeling about France, considering French almost his own language and France's tradition of refined pleasures civilization's highest expression. He would enjoy conversation, and more, with a *Parisienne*. He glances at his companion. Hair thinning, turning gray. But still collegiate in appearance. Tall to the point of being gangly, the pale blue eyes holding a boy's mischievous twinkle. An open face, mobile mouth quick to break into a predator's grin. So unmistakably American in his curt gestures, his let's-get-to-business mentality. Dale represents everything Bhulliwah admires about Americans: their energy, their salesmanship, their focus on the bottom line.

Half a block from its destination on *l'Avenue de la Volonté Populaire*—Avenue of the People's Will—the limo pulls to a stop. An SM roadblock guards Madame Yvette's. Allowed beyond this point are only senior government and business personnel, exclusively male. The driver flashes a pass through his side window. With a salute, the officer in white SM tunic, standing by a motorcycle, waves the limo on.

"Yvette serves an excellent buffet," says Dale. "I often lunch here. Fun to break bread with lovely women from all over Africa and Europe." He smiles. "For me there's no charge, including behind the red velvet curtains."

"Only fair you should have privileges." Bhulliwah can't be jealous. "You know, last year, when that crusading U.N. commissioner—quickly transferred, thanks to your intervention—accused us of questionable financial, accounting and banking practices, I thought who are we compared to that fellow in Zimbabwe, or the Indonesians and Russians?"

Dale nods thoughtfully. "Yes, I reckon that out of every hundred million dollars put in here through B.A.R.F., almost two and a half million go directly to improving Infrastructure. That's true tickle-down economics, positively lavish compared with what the Russians and Indonesians—not to mention your greedy African neighbor in Zimbabwe—release from their 'expenses.' Clearly our operation is a finer way for the West's 'little people,' salaried taxpayers who can't hide their assets, to contribute to foreign aid."

Bhulliwah has to chuckle, while raising an admonishing finger. "Careful, careful, *mon cher*. At Freedom University the other day, a student gave a speech in which he referred to the West 'throwing corrupting dollars down Zembeylia's bottomless toilet'. Under interrogation he said his tongue had slipped, that he didn't mean it. Poor fellow's doing a thirty-nine year re-education course at Disciplinary Camp One. Minus his fingernails."

"That place you built in the jungle?"

"Thanks to B.A.R.F.'s subsidy for road-and-bridge repair." Bhulliwah's brain is churning with geo-political concepts. "Yes," he says, "your Robin Hood-In-Reverse policy, milking the poor to feed the rich, is indeed powerful."

"Damn straight," Dale grins approval. "It's up to us to intervene decisively and uphold free-market values. Only way to secure a social order benefitting the right people."

The Mercedes stops in an enclosure protected by whitewashed walls. The chauffeur and a doorman rush to open both rear doors for the passengers. Bhulliwah and Dale step up to an imposingly carved wooden entrance. Above their heads, in a recessed niche, a closed-circuit television camera scans the Zembeylian's five feet four inches, his 238 pounds of well-nourished flesh and the American's six foot three, near-paunchless body.

A buzz, a click, the entryway swings open. A tall, ebony goddess of a woman bows her head in greeting. From the waist up she's modestly dressed, bosom chastely covered. Her nether regions, contrary to tribal tradition, are clothed only by minimalist

73

see-thru panties that don't leave much to male imaginations. Bhulliwah allows himself a discreet shudder, thinking of the reaction village elders would have to this flaunt of custom and modesty. Fortunately, no village elder will ever be allowed on these premises.

The hostess shows them to a softly-lit lounge. Furniture consists of oversized sofas, where numbers of women chat with male visitors, or decorously recline while sipping drinks and awaiting the call to duty. All are dressed in the same style as the hostess-greeter, with panties of red, yellow green and even spangled silver.

"I'll leave you now," says Dale. "Fatima has me scheduled for a double sensuality massage. Make yourself comfortable. Eat anything, caviar included. They serve genuine, unwatered champaign here, real *Dom Pérignon*. Have as many women as you desire, all on me." He gives Bhulliwah's back a fraternal thump, disappears through Madame Yvette's notorious red velvet curtains.

Bhulliwah settles himself on a sofa. Should he ask about the *Parisienne?* Or submit to Zulala, the dominatrix from Senegal? So elegantly coiffed with a large, floppy hat of magenta velvet, the kind he imagines high-society Frenchwomen wear to horse races at the Longchamps track. Her hair—not on her head, which he can't see—is dyed a rakish blonde. He wonders what's under that hat.

Or perhaps, given the pressures of life just now, might it not be wiser to massage his ego by forcing submission from virginal Missy? Madame Yvette insists she's a legal thirteen, although with her just-budding breasts, she looks more like eleven. Perhaps Zulala and Missy together...?

The hostess approaches. She bears champagne in an ice bucket and opens the bottle with a fine cork-pop. *Dom Pérignon*, indeed! Pristine, unwatered, just as Dale said. Expertly, she pours splashes of pale gold bubbly liquid into a fluted glass, waiting between pours for the foam to fizzle down.

He takes a sip. *Ahhh!* Truly exquisite. She gives a nod, withdraws. Moments later she's back, bearing a telephone.

"For Monsieur," she murmurs as she sets the phone on a side table by the champagne glass, plugs it in.

Damnation! Now what? Reluctantly, Bhulliwah picks up the receiver. It crackles with static.

"Tony, is that you?"

Bon Dieu! Why were rich white women so brassy? So demanding? If the money these travel agents were promising wasn't so good he'd tell this busybody troublemaker to go stuff it up her— "My dear Madame Southgate, how may I help you?"

"It's how we're helping you that counts. Right? There's a machination going on and you'd better head it off at the pass. Otherwise—"

Pass? Trouble in the Monogoro Mountains? What would she know about...? Always talking riddles, this one! Ah, for the clarity, the preciseness of the tongue of Voltaire, of Victor Hugo, of Anatole France... "Calm yourself, chère Madame, and tell me exactly what it is that has you so, how do you say it? So perturbed. But wait, wait." He presses the scrambler button embedded in his phone. "Are you scrambling?"

"What? Scrambled eggs? No, I had pancakes. Anyway, the waiter's cleared away room serv— Oh, this red button you mean. Can you hear me now?"

"Yes, yes." The crackling stops. She has activated her own scrambler, thoughtfully provided by the hotel. Presumably anyone listening would hear gibberish. Presumably. You could never be sure. "Please, Madame, be discreet in what you are saying. One cannot tell—"

"There's danger to our cause," bellows Malvina Southgate, as though he's in a boat a mile out to sea and she standing on a cliff trying frantically to communicate. Bhulliwah holds the receive away from his ear. "Eugene Petroff is plotting against us. In cahoots with

Chandler and that Colombian companion of his. They're betraying us, cozying up to your arch-enemy, M'Bowé and—"

"No names, Madame. I implore you, no names." Can't have the Minister mentioned in a subversive conversation. Disciplinary Camp One beckons.

"In the Uplands, they want to grow poppies, coca bushes, hemp for marijuana and other drugs. My source says the climate and soil are ideal for raising all sorts of illegal substances. Do you—"

"Illegal? Not here, Madame. Not here." Poppies! My God! Fields teeming with red poppies, their vista bordered by a line of refineries churning out white powders…Yes, of course! Why hadn't he thought of…? Zembeylia could become a world hub for—

"Do you realize what it would do to our entire resort and tourism industry?" Ms. Southgate's tone is anguished and rising. "Everything we've worked so hard to achieve? Killed dead! I'm telling you—"

"Coexistence," murmurs Bhulliwah. If push came to shove, profits from drugs far outweigh what tourism can bring. Truly a most exciting concept!

"Americans and the whole developed world would shun us. They'd make it so tough for anyone coming from their countries, or returning home, that no respectable person would dare visit Zembeylia."

Riches beyond imagining! What were tourists gawping at hippos, giraffes and a few mangy lions in comparison? "Madame, dear lady, calm yourself." Bhulliwah utilizes the basso-profundo tones of sincerity that he reserves for his finest legislative utterances. "No one," he intones, "shall be allowed to interfere with Zembeylia's glorious natural patrimony." Coca plantations could be touted as a natural patrimony.

"Our carefully-laid plans," wails Ms. Southgate. "I helped Chandler make headway with his Air X'Zambili project. Now he has betrayed! I thought I had both him and Petroff sewn up. Japanese golfers. This whole business of the opera house and—"

"What opera house?"

She ignores Bhulliwah's query. "The important thing. Do you know who Petroff is?" She doesn't wait for an answer. "A Fenster, that's what! The nephew, no less!" She pauses for effect. "A Fenster! Here to thwart all our plans."

Opera houses? Japanese? *Fensters?* Bhulliwah-X'Zilone is totally at sea. This Southgate woman, so full of surprises, few of which make sense. *"Man kann unmöglich bei offenem Fenster schlafen—*It is not recommended to sleep by an open window," phrase from college German and on European sleeper train notices: *Fenster?* Meaning *fenêtre?* Meaning window? He sighs. "You'll have to explain."

"My God, Tony, you're the original innocent. *Fenster.* Harlan Fenster. He just happens to control the Jeffrey B. Ace Corporation. You know what that is, I hope."

"The American takeover company?"

"The global takeover company, you mean. Sometimes it seems there's hardly a corporate entity that Ace hasn't got fingers into. Through Fenster, Ace's evil genius. If he backs a narcotics development deal—and he's quite capable of doing so—it'll have unlimited resources for start-up costs. Ace's own participation will be so hidden, so unproveable he'll be immune from scandal."

Poppies and powders. Bhulliwah blinks his eyes dreamily. Barrels of Swiss francs spilling into his Geneva account....

"With that kind of wealth," continues Ms. Southgate implacably "the present régime here will be unshakable."

Point and match! He's doomed to play the ecology card, at least for now. Suddenly, it comes to him: John Wayne on late-night television in Santa Monica. "We will, as you say Madame, head them off at the pass." He eyes a voluptuous white woman entering the parlor. She detours to saunter by his armchair, eyeing him back. The *Parisienne?* "I must go. Important affairs to attend to. Let me work on it."

"You'd better and damn fast. If Petroff and Chandler...Those traitors! And that snake Guitterez-Shaughnessy. Guess where he's

77

from: Cali, Colombia! I knew he was bad news soon as I laid eyes on him. A Drug Kingpin if there ever was one, mark my words!"

"But," says Bhulliwah soothingly, "surely Helen Farrar's involvement in our tourist industry is such that—"

"Are you kidding?" Ms. Southgate's voice rises to a near howl. "That betrayer of the whole concept of ecological tourism. What does she care for animals? What does she care for nature? Sherman Jamieson—not an important player, he only has agencies and a travel discount phone service, but he's loyal—told me that at the government reception last night he overheard her comment to Minister M'Bowé. Both laughing away about 'the little white powders.' Some joke! On us! It's no longer her money riding on Zembeylia's development as the only source of private funding. With Petroff's support, meaning Ace, plus Chandler's charter planes consolidated with Helen's own airline, she'll be at the center of a global spider's web, holding all the strings to power and drug distribution while she disposes of unlimited funds."

From *La Southgate* Bhulliwah needs calm until he can figure what's what. "Ms. Farrar is American, her company, Eland, is anchored there. Any dealing with drugs would compromise—"

"Oh, she won't do it through Eland. I hear she already has a Liechtenstein entity to handle everything: Traumgestalt International."

"How do you know this?"

"Jamieson has connections. He may talk in that phony accent of his but he keeps his ears open where business is concerned. A true professional."

Silence. Bhulliwah scratches his chin. "Terrible," he finally murmurs. If such an alliance between the M'Bélé's and Americans comes to be, the X'Zambili cause, and his own career, will—

"They'll have every M'Bélé who's anyone dancing to their beck and call," Ms. Southgate echos his thoughts. "So you'd better hop to and—"

"Hop, Madame? Hop?" She has gone too far. The X'Zambili-Africa Tours vice-president's complexion suffuses an apoplectic magenta. "Rabbits hop. I am a corporate executive, a Minister-In-Waiting and—"

"Tony, I hate to tell you, but you're a future bum living on the streets from garbage cans. Unless we both get damn busy damn quick. Put 'Plan B' into action. Not 'Plan A,' Emergency 'Plan B,' you hear? Farrar and Chandler and that goddam Fenster. Gotta beat 'em to the punch or we're screwed. Life-and-death!"

Plan B? If only he *had* a Plan B! Despite the cool of Madame Yvette's air-conditioned lounge, Antoine Bhulliwah-X'Zilone fishes in his jacket pocket for a silk handkerchief, wipes sweat off his neck and under a too tight collar.. He breathes in-out, manages to speak calmly over the phone. "But of course, Madame. Be assured when Bhulliwah moves it is with the swiftness, silence and deadly accuracy of the leopard that strikes its prey. I guarantee it."

He hangs up. Hesitates a long moment. Finally, slowly, he dials again: this time to just a block away, where he knows a certain someone will be taking his postprandial ablutions and massage. Has to wait an eternity before the hoarse, sarcastic voice with its singsong accent growls in English "What now?"

"We must meet," says Bhulliwah. "Emergency."

"I am meeting no one until after my napping. You are realizing this. How are you daring to disturb me?"

"Sir, it's important. A plot."

Raspy chuckle. "Plot? Of course, many plots. We are aware of plots. We are making them." The chuckle wheezes into a cough. Long silence. "Well," says the voice at length, "for a stoutish fellow such as yourself a good steaming is certainly doing wonders. All the too-rich food and drink you are so liking. You may come. I am giving orders to Mustafa."

"Most kind," says Bhulliwah hastily, "But I won't waste your time. We—"

"I will be seeing you only after you are taking full treatment. Once you have been finishing by immersing in ice bath six full minutes, no less, you may repair to private lounge for mint tea and powdered 'fingers of young virgins.'"

"But it's urgently nece—"

"This is my condition."

Bhulliwah sighs. He knows that to argue is futile. Tea and the sugarcoated, cigar-shaped cookies known as "virgins' fingers" he might enjoy; but having to submit to a sweaty steambath, at the *Hammam Sidi ben-Gezirah*–Authentic Turkish Baths–then a poking, prodding, slapping, pummeling, perhaps even a walk on his back by the beefy Mustafa, with, finally, a forced plunge into the freezing waters of an ice pool, these so-called 'healthful' activities he positively dreads.

Sexual exertion aside, Bhulliwah has always hated life's physical demands; especially since grammar school when his sports-minded father had insisted he take up boxing. In the first round of his first bout the opponent, beanpole, squint-eyed Zecherias M'Bowé, had landed a lucky punch and broken his nose. Once the bleeding stopped and his face dressed in that humiliating splint, the instructor forced him to shake hands with M'Bowé and declare bygones to be bygones. Which they'd never been.

Sighing hugely he snaps his fingers at the sinuous-buxom hostess, tells her to inform Monsieur Uppingham that he'll have to take a rain check. "Obligations," he murmurs, casting a wistful look at the champagne bottle in its bucket and the women lolling on couches. "One is ever called to the struggle."

Chapter 9: M'Goma's Finger
Traveling in Zembeylia, Wednesday, December 16

Red. The earth an unyielding red, at once setting off and sucking up other colors of the landscape, even in the city where red dust dominates over pastel yellows, blues, pinks of street-front shops and villa walls. Here on the shore, a curved headland of red cliffs leaves its stain not only on beach sand but also by reflection on the sea.

In bed, I prop head on elbow to stare out an open doorway and, beyond the bedroom's balcony, watching sunrise light those cliffs even redder; the color envelopes in incandescent glow the green palms at their summit.

Suzanne was right. Days passing too quickly. Today, already day five–counting Saturday's departure from New York–and things are beginning to blur. Soon I'll be back in Shangri-La's jangling maw. I'm doing everything to freeze time: keeping notes, talking into my tape recorder, snapping photos, writing long descriptive letters to Suzanne and sending short, exhortatory cables to Rahel. Still, the minutes, hours, days flee, losing their boundaries.

I shut my eyes tight, trying to savor every moment from leaving the office, single suitcase plus cabin tote-bag in hand, riding the subway and airport bus to all that followed. Only a scene here, a conversation there remain vivid. The subway: all those people hurrying on hum-drum journeys. And I off to Zembeylia! How I wish I could freeze-frame the specialness of such a moment.

I scrunch up my pillow. Jet lag has me awake at dawn. The pounding surf beyond my window is lulling but I can't manage more sleep. Shifting onto my back, I stare at the ceiling fan slowly turning. If I were to walk the beach in the sunrise I'd surely meet a giraffe. Gentle, friendly creatures bending their long necks to see if you have something for them. They roam freely all over the property of Royal Zemba Luxury Oceanside Resort And Giraffe Reserve. Only problem: lumps of dung in the sand. Too much to ask the huge stately creatures not to soil pristine sands as they wander.

Dung between the toes? Unenticing.

I jump from bed, do my daily set of twelve push-ups and fifteen knee-bends to get the blood circulating. Busy day, with this

M'Bélé native village to see and later another mandatory briefing aboard the train.

Despite the "mandatories," it really has been a magical time, every bit as interesting as I'd told Suzanne it would be. The Indian Spice Market was a huge covered area redolent of curries, coconut, sandalwood, exotic perfumes and offering a lot more than spices. I bought Suzanne a magnificent blue silk sari shot with gold. And for Rahel a set of sandalwood perfumed candles. The whole caboodle set me back only forty bucks. Prices great in this land, where the U.S. Dollar is still almighty. But I have to save that $99.99 to get out of here.

Diamantville? On the *kitschy* side, refined *kitsch*. The gem shops, featuring diamonds and tsavorites, are genuine enough, with government-controlled prices and local certified gemologists to pass judgment on the goods, all adding up to wonderful buys. For Suzanne I found a tsavorite necklace at just over thirty dollars; and a pink tourmaline bracelet for Rahel, costing eleven. That finished their presents.

Schulz? Bottle of Zembeylian wine. Could get it on the way home for about $2.50 at the airport's duty-free shop. Maybe instead, a wallet of elephant hide—about $4 or $5.00? Tour Manager Lazuli has explained that each year the game reserve "culls" its elephant population because the X'Ziloncado Reserve, vast though it be, can support only a limited number of the inadvertently destructive beasts. They plow through trees and bushes, devastating everything in their path and devouring huge amounts of leaves and grasses. Then they rub against tree trunks to scratch their tough hides, splintering the bark, causing denuded trees to rot.

At Diamantville the great buy is Helen's. It takes the whole afternoon of her picking, pawing and haggling but she comes away with a 65.7 carat near-flawless diamond, which she intends to have re-faceted in New York for the Tiffany pendant she mentioned on the plane.

82

"Only $539,000, she'd announced over the loudspeaker on our charter bus back to town. "Do you realize I can sell it at home for over two million? Talk about a steal…" After a pause she declares, "I hereby name it 'The Eland Diamond.'"

Everyone applauds, including Malvina Southgate and her consort. I wonder how many of those clapping have reason to hate the guts of this bossy, self-congratulating woman who, when anyone stands in her way, must show all the compassion of a Sherman tank.

And me? Doesn't she expect me to produce Zembeylia customers from clients who make a big deal out of a trip to Buffalo? No cause for hate but certainly concern.

I could try falling back on *Herr Amahdi*. "Animals, Mister Goldstone?" In my mind I hear the man. "What makes you believe I am wanting to look at animals?" Not the safari type, Amahdi. Might go for cheap diamonds. Nah! Given his connections, he'd know ways to get ones cheaper.

I watch the sun's huge ball, coppery gold, rise over the sea, tinting it crimson. Beautiful place. I should win the lottery, marry Suzanne and bring her here for a honeymoon.

A large verandah overlooking the beach serves as breakfast area. Sheila is there, cigarette smoke curling from behind a copy of *Royal Zembeylian Nation*, the national English-language paper whose subhead is *Royal Democracy and Progress in Unity*.

"Look at this," she says as I sit across from her at our group breakfast table She points to a front-page photo of us all flanking a beaming enthroned King, with the Prime Minister and Minister of Internal Security, Tourism and Culture standing to one side. She rises. "Excuse me a second. I have to get my things. Be right back."

Warm Welcome to Overseas Friends is the headline of the paper's lead story, an unenlightening description of our reception. On the second page I find my name featured in the guest roster as "Lincaline Stonengold" and my agency "Shan's Grilling Adventure." Not quite *New York Times* precision.

Sheila returning, pulls the paper away. "You can read the rest when I'm gone. Right now, talk to me."

"Gone? Oh yes. You're off to see this hospital in the bushes. No wonder you're up early."

She nods. "Chandler and that strange guy with him left ten minutes ago for the tsavorite mines. I'm joining them at X'Ziromeu City for a pre-train drink."

"Hey, why don't I come with you? I was an army medic and—"

She puts her hand on my arm. "I'd love nothing better. But Dr. Hermann hates entertaining visitors. He only consented to see me after several letters back and forth. He thinks Helen might contribute…Anyway, I believe he has prepared a meal and it would be unfair to impose an extra person. Besides, you wouldn't want to miss the native village." She giggles. "A treat, wait and see." She signs her breakfast chit, stands up.

"Did you get good wheels?" I stand too.

"A little Renault Five. What we call *Le Car* back home. Fine for what I have to do. Only 59 miles, then another 70 miles to X'Ziromeu City and the road all the way is supposed to be good. No cross-country. We'll get plenty of that up in the game park."

"Well, have fun."

Sheila smiles brightly, bends to pick up a long sausage bag, stylish looking in red velvety material. Giving a wave, off she goes.

The waiter brings a basket of croissants with butter and jam, along with a casserole of poached eggs. They swim in cream mixed with chewy melted *gruyère* cheese. One thing about a former French colony, the chefs around here know how to prepare rich, fattening, delicious food. What's a plugged artery or two when confronted by such gastronomic experiences?

I'm buttering a croissant when my shoulder gets a hard nudge. A head pokes over the verandah rail and a raspy blackish tongue comes out to claim the croissant. I look into the velvet eye of an Oppenheim Giraffe, endangered species, distinctive for six horns in a diamond-shape atop the cranium.

"I'm hungry, too," I tell the animal, but give over the croissant. The giraffe chomps away, jaws moving side to side. Elderly lady or gentleman? Probably the latter since males are loners. The darkened skin indicates age. How old? Some are said to live thirty or forty years. I hope a croissant diet won't cut this one's lifespan.

By the time I've shared the last one, half and half with, for me, a little plum jam from Alsace, the table has filled with our other tour members, At two tables adjacent to ours, there's a contingent of Asians: men in round-necked, grayish suits, ladies sporting pajama-like outfits of blue or green cotton. Many greetings there, loud and hearty, with choruses of giggles and furious clickings in all directions of boxy-looking cameras.

Lazuli beckons the Eland people to a minibus; the Asians pile into a full-sized bus right behind us. I sit alone, ruminating about Sheila.

Not that I'm in love with her. Only Suzanne has my love, irritating as she too often is. But Sheila...So damned attractive. Sheila as a person? Hardly know her, only that she's adept at keeping herself to herself. I'd been attentive at Diamantville, helping her choose a tsavorite ring. Most of the afternoon she spent with Helen, who was fussing about her diamond. At least she'd had the good sense to trust Sheila's judgment and pick from three possibles: a round very faceted gem, another called a marquise, shaped like a boat with prows fore and aft, and the one finally decided upon, a delicate, colorless almost unfaceted pear.

To me it looked perfect. The resident gemologist said its colorlessness almost put it in the perfect category, but the trained eye could see the tiniest of inclusons deep within. So it has an F/G classification, instead of the perfect D. "Which," said the gemologist, "would make it worth more than a million, even here."

Last night I danced with Sheila at the hotel disco. Bodies close, sending messages back and forth; but only a hug and quick brush of lips at her bedroom door. Hate the idea of being unfaithful. Maybe she does too. Still, you only get one turn on life's merry-go-round.

Suzanne with her damned labeling. *Shopkeeper! Thursday's amusement!* What would she care?

Our two buses leave the coast, cross a river and enter the "Sacred Zone," a reserve of some nine hundred square miles, where the villages, customs and culture of the M'Bélé warriors and herds-people are kept "pure, removed from all modern corruptions." So says the government pamphlet that Lazuli distributes at journey's start.

The first blow against modernism is an end to pavement. A red dirt track winds up and down hills that grow higher. Looking through the bus's rear window, I witness a crimson dust storm boiling up and blanketing the vehicle carrying the Asians. Gradually, red grit seeps through our window frames. I feel it between the teeth, on my tongue, at the back of my throat. It puts a shiny cinnamon colored powder over my shoulder-strap bag.

I concentrate on the scenery. A land of cattle: meager grasses covering gravely soil, with straggling cane fields, plus row upon row of corn and other grains, here and there some rice swamps. I'm intrigued by the houses, beehive shaped, made of thatch with pointy roofs and clustering on hillsides to constitute villages.

Lazuli blows into the microphone attached to his shirt front. He reads from a paper: "The Southern M'Bélé's are culturally linked to Zulus across the frontier in South Africa. Like Zulus, they practice polygamy and measure riches in cattle. Each marriage must be based not only on a woman's dowry but a spouse's family wealth of ten cattle minimum. A single beast's worth is set at MUL 15,000, or $300 in U.S. currency. If you live outside the 'Sacred Zone,' say in the city and have no cattle, you must find the equivalent of $3,000. In our present economy, this does encourage single, not multiple marriages."

There are questions about cattle, money and why not goats as units of wealth? We're seeing plenty of goats along the road.

"Custom," answers Lazuli, opening wide his large eyes. "Oh yes, custom. Who is to be arguing with that?"

The buses take a long rise. At its top the road ends in a circle surrounded by bushes and spiky thorn trees.

The door opens, we hear singing. In a line are twenty or so bare-breasted young women, each of their faces streaked in green, white, yellow, red, with necks garlanded by flowers and beads. Bells hem hide skirts. More bells are fixed to circlets around their ankles. Every time they move they jingle-jangle. A horde of children, chanting too, flank the girls. The kids are jumping up and down with excitement.

As I exit the bus, an attractive female, face daubed in green, her breasts dark upstanding calabashes, removes her own wreath of bright yellow flowers from her neck, places it around mine. All the girls choose a member of our tour or one of the Asians.

This welcoming committee leads us along a narrow path cutting through thick bushes and trees. My young lady has taken my arm and sings loudly. Very exotic, very romantic except the garland attracts flies. They buzz, land on my lips, eyes, ears. Rahel, in her fastidiousness, would not love this. I spend a lot of time flapping my free hand.

"What is your name?—*Comment vous appelez-vous?*" I have to shout over the singing.

The girl answers with a dazzling smile showing strong, healthy teeth but doesn't break her chant.

We emerge from the bush into a large clearing set off by rows of the beehive-shaped huts ranged in semicircles on a slope, one row above another. On a hide throne sits the village Headman. At either side are other elderly-looking men, all clad, so I later learn, in warrior dress. They wear boat-like fur hats.

The Headman himself is distinguished by a jackal hat and bandolier. He has black cow hair bracelets on wrists and ankles, attesting to his cattle-wealth, according to Lazuli's briefing on the bus. His belt holds a dagger. In his left hand he grasps a hide shield like the one we saw aboard the plane; in the right hand he holds a long evil-looking spear tipped with red.

Mike Mahoney steps forward, bows deeply, recites a few words in M'Bélé. His Asian counterpart, a short, gray-haired man, steps forward and bows. He speaks in what sounds to me like Chinese. A man and woman come up behind him, unfurl a long red banner bearing characters in gold. Almost definitely Chinese, I decide.

My escort abandons me to stand with the group of females. Again they burst into song, this time accompanied by a strange instrument: a hide affair shaped like a drum but with a hole in the middle through which a stick is pushed, pulled and twisted to make various groaning sounds.

"A M'Gungo," says Lazuli standing next to me and doing his job as guide.

The women begin to dance. I note that the older ones have their breasts covered; some with blouses made from hides, others with cheap-looking white bras.

"The married ladies," murmurs Lazuli following my glance. "And those wearing black hats are widows."

"Ah," I nod meaningfully.

The morning wears on, the sun getting hotter and hotter, the ceremonies becoming more and more—ceremonious. Hard not to feel bored, sleepy, eyelids heavy. Funny how a sea of naked breasts comes to seem ordinary, even dull. It's the mystery, the fuss, the *peek-a-boo now you see 'em, now you* don't attitude of us in the West—and, for all I know, in Asia too—that make the mammary appendages of half the human race so exciting and…Damn flies! Only things keeping me awake. A real challenge, fending them off. I take photos, tape record a couple of chants, the recorder hooked to my belt. I wish this was over…

Interest livens with the appearance of a Shaman: a woman. Among the M'Bélé peoples holders of mystic powers most often are women, so Lazuli whispers. As a child, he says, this one would have been picked for her spiritual aptitude, schooled for several years in the accumulated lore and oral traditions of the tribe, then

88

apprenticed to a senior before achieving full *M'Goma*, or Shaman, status.

Formidable looking, her headdress bearing goat bladders that mingle with plaited bead-strung hair. Severe features, covered bosom. A no-nonsense type. Back in the States she'd be head of a university Sociology department or chief matron in a women's prison. Her job here is to put herself into a trance, then point at anyone whose spirituality harbors a potential for sin, guilt or tragedy.

When she accuses someone of a crime, the Council of Elders decides on a course of action. She herself rules in matters affecting the psyche and individual problems: a cross between Dr. Freud, Houdini and the F.B.I., with a whiff of Savanarola thrown in.

She gives us a demonstration. Slow drum beats, female chorus wailing, a cry that reminds me of Arab women in North Africa: "YOO-YOO-YOO-YOO…" Eerie yodel with tongue like a snakehead vibrating back and forth.

The M'Goma circles and circles in front of the Headman, kneels down, bends forehead to ground. Suddenly she lets out a piercing cry, rises, stretches her right arm and forefinger. She revolves slowly round and round and round…And stops eyes closed tight. Tears course down her face, her arm rigid but shaking. She moans. Her finger remains pointing.

"See here!" Mike steps forward. "What kind of joke is this? Pretty bad taste, I'd say."

She opens her eyes, stands nodding her head, arm still outstretched, finger pointing straight at Helen Farrar.

PART TWO:
CORPOREAL CATASTROPHES

"Oh don't the days seem lank and long
When all goes right and nothing goes wrong…"
~ Gilbert and Sullivan, *The Mikado*

Chapter 10: Delights of the Feast
M'Bélé Sacred Quarter to Zemba Royal Silverspear Express,
Wednesday, December 16

Our group files into a beehive hut, called the Beer Hut. The Asians
are led to another hut. Central attraction in our place is a huge pot
of beer brewed from corn. A young woman, giggling, ladles the
frothy liquor into bowls of wood fibers lacquered in black. She
hands the bowls to Lazuli who, assisted by Bitsy Jamieson–
managing to give the impression she's dispensing alms–serves the
rest of us as we sit in a circle on sisal floor mats.

The incident with the M'Goma has left tension. The shaman,
confronted by Mike, claims to have been in a trance. All she would
say is that she sensed "a great sadness" surrounding Helen.

"Like an aura, I suppose," Bitsy murmurs, and smirks.

"Result of having fingers in too many pies," I hear Malvina
Southgate comment to D'Alessandro. When he remains impassive,
she says, "Fingers poking all over the place get chopped off."

He pats her arm, a calm-down gesture. She gives a sniff.

Helen, when she became aware of being singled out, shrank
back, put her fist to mouth and berated Mike for allowing it to
happen. Now she's trying to be vivacious, talking loudly, life of the
party; obviously shaken. She takes up her beer bowl, hand
trembling, has to grab it with the other hand not to spill. I suppose
that like many driving, overly self-assured people, Helen's Achilles
heel is superstition.

In earlier times she would have had her own shaman, or maybe
a soothsayer. Didn't Hitler employ an astrologer? Packed him off to
a concentration camp when the predictions got gloomy.

Mike slowly circles the group, playing host. When he squats down beside me, he nods toward the various trees whose trunks and branches rise through the hut's floor into the ceiling. "Floor of cement mixed with cow dung," Lazuli has kindly informed us. Which does nothing for the appetite, although the heavy mats overlay whatever is underneath.

"These trees hold the place up," says Mike. "When the trunks grow old and start bending, a younger one gets added in. After awhile, you can't see the trees for the forest." He chuckles.

I take a sip of beer: sour-bitter but with a tang giving it affinity to "real" beer. Not bad.

"You know the makeup on their faces?" Mike lowers his voice and gestures towards the women at one side of the hut, bending over a line of cooking pots. "Furniture polish. Ordered in bulk from the *Bon Marché* department store in the capital. Only wear it for special events, like our being here." When he sits down by Helen, she frowns at him. He holds up his bowl, bends his head to hers and says, "Drink up and forget your troubles."

"Sweet Michael, I don't think. So concerned for your meal ticket."

"Darling, hush. Mustn't take on so. All nonsense. Now drink, it'll calm you."

She glares at him, but takes a long swallow.

"See? Pretty tasty. And the food's healthy."

Each of us receives a long boat-like plate. Very light. The vessel seems to be of parchment. A spoon of the same material comes with the plate.

We all rise, line up and the M'Bélé women dish food from their pots: rice, sorghum, corn cakes, red beans. No meat. The M'Bélé tribesfolk are vegetarians.

"Eat like this every day and you'll live forever," says Giorgio D'Alessandro.

"I'm looking forward to tonight's meal on the train," replies Helen. "French-trained chef, plenty of champagne and goose-liver *pâté*. That's for me!"

Mike says, "May this meal be a guarantee of good cheer and good fortune for the rest of our journey." He spreads his arms. "This beer is actually great for you. Hardly any alcohol."

During the meal, Malvina Southgate–my self-appointed political mentor–sits down beside me and talks my ear off about how the Chinese are playing the X'Zambili-Indian-French card here in a big way, with the idea of beating out the M'Bélé rulers and, through them, the West. "Or at least, giving Minister M'Bowé and the B.A.R.F. apoplexy. Making the bastards *barf* that is." She chuckles at her own wit.

After lunch, we all bow in turn to the Headman to say goodbye. So do the Chinese: civil service workers from Shanghai, Lazuli informs us. The village maidens, singing again, escort us back up the hill to our buses. We leave with chants of farewell ringing in our ears.

And I begin to feel sick.

No, can't be, I tell myself. No, damn it! My stomach rumbles and roils The jouncing bus doesn't help.

Anybody else sick? Doesn't look it. Mike is talking into the intercom, telling a M'Bélé tale about a little boy on a sunny spring day fishing in the river.

Concentrate, I order myself. It'll go away.

"…And the kid's fairy M'Goma suddenly appears, saying: "I'll grant you three wishes. Now wish well because no more wishes after. "So the boy wishes for great wealth. Suddenly a mountain of gold appears on the riverbank. All his. Or maybe he gets a notice from a Swiss bank, I dunno."

Chuckles all around. I have to swallow to keep from vomiting. I'm also beginning to suspect–more than suspect–a case of trots. Can I hold till we get somewhere, like the train?

"The M'Goma says, "Wish again, lad. And this time the kid looks at his reflection in the river and says, "I wish to be white. Instantly, he turns white. Rich and white. What could be better? He's come a long way since a minute ago."

Hold tight, I'm barely listening, scrunching my bowels.

"Now it's his third and last wish. 'Think deep,' says the M'Goma, 'because this is forever.' The boy thinks and thinks. Finally he says, 'I wish to be truly happy.' The fairy M'Goma waves her wand and what do you know? He's transformed right back into a little M'Bélé boy fishing on the riverbank."

Applause.

"Ain't it beautiful?" says Mike. "Really teaches people to keep their place."

"Michael!" croaks Helen. "Michael, help! I'm going to be sick."

He rushes to her. "Darling, what's the matter? A little car dizzy?"

She shakes her head. "Oh God, that food. Stop the bus. I'm ill."

The bus halts. She stumbles out, Mike holding her. She retches onto the roadside grass. I stumble after. Nobody holds me but I retch too.

"Shall we try to get a doctor?" Mike asks when we're underway again.

Helen shakes her head. "Have to keep to schedule. I'll be all right on the train."

"I'm sure it will pass," he mutters.

God, I tell myself, I hope so. I close my eyes, praying I won't mess my pants.

The Zemba Royal SilverSpear Express, pride-of-Zembeyla's rails, is due to stop just for us and the Chinese at a small country station beyond the "Sacred Zone." The train left the capital at 3:00 P.M. and will arrive here exactly at 4:13. By which time I have made three trips to an outhouse thoughtfully provided at the far end of a red gravel platform. I lean back on a bench against the wall of a shack serving as terminal building. My stomach twists and turns, my bowels cramp, my head pounds. I'm miserable, exhausted.

Helen, looking as green as I feel, is stretched on another bench, everyone hovering around her. Nobody but us two seem affected. What had we taken that was different? The others drank the beer, had eaten a little of everything on offer. It had tasted pretty good...

A light shines in the distance, bells start clanging, the train is arriving. As it never usually stops in this place, today's pause is an event. Children and dogs—both seem ubiquitous in Zembeylia—are hopping around shouting, barking. Despite my condition I'm excited too. I've always loved trains. As a kid I traveled back and forth across the U.S. continent between a divorced mother in San Francisco and a father with a new family in Connecticut. The two never seemed able to get closer, peaceably at least, than 3,000 miles. The strains of moving from one family to another, and being used as a guided-missile in both directions, to denounce each parent in turn as to how wicked the other was, had been offset by delicious independence aboard the cocooning, train slowly making its way across America's great land-ocean. A shrink from more prosperous days, had helped me understand why I was so hooked on travel. Fat lot of good the insight has done. I've still thrown my money into the goddamn agency...

Clutching my stomach, I rise to get a photo of an impressive purple and silver diesel engine, whose front bears the green, gold and black flag of Zembeylia. The locomotive roars by. A flash of recognition. Must be American. The cars, too. Sleek and silver, like some of the ones I used to ride out West.

"All is righty-right now?" asks Lazuli sidling up. "We meet this evening, yes? In observation lounge back of train: 6:15 P.M. sharply. I will tell rundown on game camp. I must be saying to you of ticks and other importances. Then we shall be dining. Excellent dining." He rubs his hands. "Most enjoyable."

"I'll try," I answer weakly. "Tell me, this train is American?"

"Originally coming from your Santa Fe and other lines. From, I think, expresses named Super Chief and California Zephyr. Being, of course, totally refurbished by our own Tamil-X'Zambili consortium known as X'Zambili-Africa Tours. They who, with French and my own Tamil peoples are rebuilding railroad."

The cars halt.

"We hurry to be on board," shouts Lazuli, belaboring the obvious. "Hurry, hurry to be boarding Sleeper B, not to be forgetting your baggages."

I summon every ounce of strength to grab my suitcase and bag, climb up the train steps. Almost don't make it to the corridor.

Fortunately my sleeper cabin is the first one. I put my case on the rack, close and lock the door, pull down a folding sink, stand over it heaving great dry heaves. "Christ!" I mutter, tearing off shoes and stretching out on a long couch that reaches to the window I close my eyes.

My dreams are tormented. Sheila laughing at me, her perfume all-enveloping. Knocks wake me. The door? I open my eyes, try to get up. Oh, what the hell! "Go away," I mutter, again close my eyes.

More knocking.

With supreme effort I lift myself halfway off the couch, flip open the lock.

"What now?" I groan, hoisting myself to my feet.

"Aren't you wanting your passport?" Lazuli asks brightly. He hands over a little booklet, which has turned from navy blue to bright red. On its first page is the picture of a smiling woman, middle-aged, Asian.

"This isn't me." I shake my head. "Not mine."

"Now, now," says Lazuli. "Our Security Militia are making efficiency their byword. They leave no stones unturned." He raises an admonishing finger. "You must not always be complaining so."

"For God's sake!" I rap the red booklet's cover with my fist, stomach protesting the movement. "Do I look, like this? Are you telling me I'm an Asian woman? Haven't you eyes?" I thrust the thing into Lazuli's hand.

The guide takes a step backward, turns his head away, disdaining to regard the object. "I shall have to be reporting your stubbornness. Oh, yes. Lack of good faith. Refusing of your travel document. The SM shall not be taking it lightly, I am telling you."

I'm about to reply when Eugene Petroff, breathing hard, jerks the cabin door wide and thrusts another red passport under Lazuli's nose.

"I ask you," whirring in his peculiar voice, "where in hell is my passport? I see I'm being required to demand it."

"My goodness gracious," says Lazuli. "You Yankee-Doodles are so difficult. So fussing over trivia details. Our Chinese friends appreciate what we do for them. You complain, complain, complain!" He throws up his hands, one bearing the passport I've refused.

Petroff stiffens, takes the hand, opens the fingers, puts the Chinese passport alongside my other one. He closes the fingers. "Now," he says quietly, "if you do not wish war to exist between our two nations, a war in which I remind you that our nuclear capability would pulverize your miniscule monarchy, then take these passports and do whatever you want with them. But," his voice rises to a turbine roar, "you will get both our passports, and my wife's as well. Be so kind as to produce them expeditiously, no ifs, ands, buts or mistakes. Am I clear about this?" He lets out a deep breath. the turbine winds down.

Sullenly, Lazuli nods and slips away towards destinations unknown. Petroff gives me a nod too, closes the door.

I stagger to the pull-down sink for a long vomit. Then go back to the couch, close my eyes. Passport, shmassport. Do I care? I fall down a funnel, twisting, twisting into dark sleep.

When I wake, about two hours later according to my watch, I feel a little better. The passport begins to nag. I hope Lazuli will come through with the right one, resentful though he might be at making a search. Petroff certainly didn't try the diplomatic approach tailored to keep existing friends and influence Lazuli to tread a path toward righteousness.At least he didn't until the end, when he seemed to regain his turbinesque stately calm. Then he was firm.

I should have been milder too, instead of jumping all over our poor if infuriating guide.

The Petroff approach could convert the obnoxious little man into more of an enemy than circumstance requires. How not to gain the affection of indigenous populations!

Dinner? Ohh! The very thought brings a stomach spasm. Never would make it, and if I did...

Shakily, I get to my feet, fish in my suitcase for pajamas and robe. Compact cubicle this, but well appointed with an accordion door hiding a fold-down sink and beneath it a pullout toilet. The mirrored medicine chest on the wall above bears a bottle of real French Perrier fizzy water.

I open the door to the corridor, peer up and down. No sign of Lazuli. No sign of anybody. Sheila's perfume? I sniff deep. Merest trace. Imagination? Lovesickness? My stomach lurches. No, probably her baggage loaded into the cabin she'll occupy when she comes aboard at the X'Ziromeu City stop. I'd seen her suitcases on the platform: two Gucci canvas-plus-leather jobs costing a mere eight hundred or so dollars apiece. No plastic and cardboard for our Sheila. They'd be impregnated with *Il Gattopardo*, spreading the scent everywhere. Even though I feel like hell, thoughts of her were causing a more traditional metabolic reaction.

I close the door and ring the porter's bell. Almost immediately, a knock. I ask to have the bed made up and some tea and dry biscuits.

"Please give my regrets to the group but I'm going to keep to my room tonight."

"Very well, sir." The porter nods.

I sleep, wake, empty my bowels for what seems the fortieth time, sleep again, finally sit up. Blanket around shoulders, I watch a dramatic sunset. The train has crossed a first low range of mountains. After X'Ziromeu City, there will be much higher ones.

Now we're in a huge bowl covered by spiky grasses, green blades and gold ones, all growing higher than a man. From a map I've studied, I identify this area as the "M'Zélé Wilderness." Here and there are groves of erythrina trees, recognizable by their tortured bare branches from which bloom flowers of brilliant red. The grasses are becoming sparser. Bare ground is dotted with termite mounds: skull-white, smooth cones atop twisty sides reminding me of Gaudi's architecture, the strangely skewed spires of Barcelona's *Cathedral of The Holy Family*.

The train passes a herd of grayish-brown kudu, one of the largest antelopes, bucks identifiable by U-shaped spiraled horns curving backward. The herd pounds parallel to the tracks, raising clouds of crimson dust. Blood red as at dawn, the sun hangs over distant, western hills. It gives a last illumination to red soil, yellowing grasses, great dome of azure sky unspotted by a single cloud.

Suddenly, incongruously, there's a boy in a tattered-looking blue robe, leading three goats. He waves frantically at the train. Feebly, I wave back. When darkness takes over, about 6:45 by my watch, I sip cold tea, lie down, drop into gentle, dreamless sleep.

Which is how the police find me when they snap the door's inner chain and burst into my cabin.

Chapter 11: The Blessings of Obedience
X.Ziromeu City, Wednesday Evening, December 16, 1987

At last following orders is about to pay off. As she sits in her Renault *estaffette* at the X'Ziromeu railway station's parking lot–dark and remote northeast corner, exactly as specified by "Benefactor"–

Madame Briac congratulates herself on having decided to take her mysterious letter writer's demands as emanating from a Higher Order and to comply with every one of them.

In a few minutes she hopes to learn more of what her true task will be. Already she knows that tomorrow she'll fly to Rome to confer with Cardinal Lannec–a Cardinal of France, also a true son of Brittany, born in the Atlantic deep-sea fishing port of Douarnenez and formerly the Archbishop of Rennes, Brittany's regional capital. He was promoted Cardinal when assigned to the Roman *Curia*. No lesser personage than His Eminence shall be Madame Briac's mentor with regard to steps she must take in combating the dangerous heresy that threatens Mother Church in all of Southeast Africa but especially Zembeylia.

These facts have been laid out by the letters, also instructions for tonight's encounter with "Benefactor." She glances at the illuminated dashboard dial: 7:34. The Keepers' emissary is due now.

Madame Briac closes her eyes, blanking excitement from her mind. She reaches into her purse for the rosary. Touching beads, she recites prayers.

At 7:36, a tap on the window, the passenger door opens. A figure cloaked in black slips into the front passenger seat. Wearing a face mask, chalk white, with almost no features: a bump for the nose and grimacing garish red lips. But a mask, after all.

"Benefactor?" she asks.

Her visitor puts finger to lips. Speaking quickly–in whispered French–the emissary details Madame Briac's mission. A wallet is handed over, containing, she is told, tickets and papers for Rome. Dollar bills show from its top.

"Your passport is in order?"

Madame Briac nods. The accent? Definitely not French. A sing-song tonic lilt. Could be German. But the pronunciation of "R"s sound British. Or American?

"Give me your last letter, please." A gloved hand reaches out. "You have destroyed all our communications? Everything?"

Madame Briac nods again. "I burnt the papers this morning. At the hotel."

It was, of course, the tiniest of untruths. How could she not guard a fragment from her life's most extraordinary happening?

"Good. Now you must take this." From a pocket, her interlocutor pulls a silver box and opens it. Large pill inside, the kind, thinks Madame, that her vet might prescribe for a sick goat.

"You know the cholera epidemic in Italy?" With a gloved hand, the emissary unscrews the top of a small bottle of mineral water, hands it over.

"Cholera!" exclaims Madame Briac.

"Cardinal Lannec was adamant. You must take this pill now and he will supply you with more upon arrival. He is very concerned that you be fully immunized."

"I didn't know. The papers here have written nothing."

"The authorities don't want to cause panic, so they hush it up. But not to worry. We Bretons can trust in the wisdom of our very own Cardinal."

"Breton? Surely you are not Breton. Your accent, is perhaps foreign?" Madame Briac puts a hand to her mouth. "Oh, *pardon*," she murmurs. "I don't mean to be indiscreet."

The visitor pats her arm. "You must learn to weigh every word, if you are to serve. Now drink your pill."

Madame puts the large pill on her tongue. She requires several gulps of water to wash it down.

Removing the bottle from her hand, the emissary screws on its top, shoves it into a pocket of the cloak and regards the dashboard clock. "7:45. Follow your instructions in the wallet. I wish you a fruitful encounter with our Cardinal. I will keep watch here. We'll meet upon your return. May God go with you!"

It—Madame Briac has no idea whether this whispering individual is man or woman—steps out of the car, vanishes into darkness.

Slowly, the ex-Brittany woman drives home, mind grappling with the idea that of all persons she has been chosen to go to Rome, to meet with a Cardinal and discuss great issues of the day.

As Jesus Himself has said, the meek, the humble, the obscure shall be chosen to keep Faith. Thus proving themselves worthy of the Kingdom of Heaven.

Chapter 12: Train of Woes
Aboard The SilverSpear Express.
Late Wednesday, early Thursday, December 16-17

Two large men tower over my bed. All cabin lights are on.

"You are Mister Lincoln Goldstone, member of Zemba V.I.P. Tour?" one man asks in English. "Your papers?"

"What?" I sit up, blinking. Head hollow. Stomach also hollow, but cramps?...Gone? Thank God for that! I look at the two: a grizzled older guy in a suit and a young giant in a police uniform. "What?" I say again.

"Papers." The giant holds out his hand. "Passport, tickets, all."

"Oh, sure." From under my pillow I take the body pouch, where I keep money and tickets, hand it over. "No passport. You police have it. At least I hope so." A pause. "Why all this?"

"We ask the questions," says the older man. From his suit pocket he pulls a dark blue booklet with silver legend. "U. S. Passport," it proclaims. Carefully, he looks at the document, looks at me, looks back at the passport. "You wear spectacles?"

I nod

"Put them on. As in passport."

Where? Can't remember...Oh, yes. Behind that door masking sink and toilet. The mirrored medicine chest, on a shelf.

I get up, brush past the huge fellow. Glancing at the mirror, my face looks pale and green. Lighting? Reality? "At least you've discovered I'm not a Chinese woman," I mutter.

"What is that?" asks the grizzled man.

"Oh, nothing. Nothing." I put on my glasses.

After checking the passport photo again, the man gestures for me to remain standing. Giant pats down my pajamas, takes my bathrobe from the wall hook, turns it inside-out, fishes in the pockets which, aside from a Kleenex tissue, are empty. They allow me to put on the robe, along with–after peering into them one by one–my slippers. They open the cabin door, indicating I should step into the aisle.

I stand in the passage way, watch my cabin being taken apart, systematically, totally. The men go through my suitcase and carry-on bag, dump everything onto the bed, check the case's lining, pat my lightweight suit, turning out pockets, examine each shirt, my socks, underpants, the bedding, even the mattress. All this done, they stuff everything back into my case, helter-skelter, except for dirty laundry and the small plastic bag I keep it in. They leave these items scattered on the bed.

In the bathroom area they pore over the contents of my toilet case, which the airline gave to all First Class passengers. It bears the imprint of Zemba Royal Airway's Flying Gazelle.

"Ha!" exclaims the big guy. He holds up a small medicine bottle, fished from the case after he has set toothbrush, toothpaste, razor, soap and the bigger, three-pack anti malaria-anti *M'zu-m'zu* pill bottles on a shelf above the sink. He confers with grizzled plainclothes, who steps forward holding the little bottle. "What is this?"

I reach for it, the man snatches it away.

"Can't tell what it is if I don't see it."

Plainclothes thrusts the little bottle towards me again.

Not the anti M'zu-m'zu medicine. "Not mine." I shrug.

Plainclothes opens the bottle, shakes out some small white pills.

"Not mine," I say again. A thought strikes. Before I can stop I blurt, "Hey, you sure your guy there didn't plant it?"

Plainclothes gives me a sour look. He nods at his companion who says, "You come with us."

"In my pajamas?"

"Come."

Uniform leading, Plainclothes trailing, and me as sandwich-filler, we hike all of four steps along the corridor to the next cabin. On its closed door is a large gilded number '2,' just as my cabin bears the number '1.' Uniform raps twice. Plainclothes pushes past us both, opens the door, gesturing for me to follow.

Blood! Blood everywhere. On the walls, smeared over the upper berth's casing, on the mirror where a grinning face is drawn in blood. I shrink back, not before glimpsing the lower berth. Helen lies there, body arched, throat jaggedly cut, the top of her head all smashed and soaking in blood, a meat-like substance, brain-matter? spilling out…wrists cut, too, I note, as I shove hand against mouth not to start vomiting again.

Blood has flooded onto sheets and blanket, cascaded to the carpet where my gaze takes in a smashed blue-and-white ceramic teapot minus spout, several other pieces lying on the floor. On the carpet, in soggy patches of blood, I see a broken cup, a broken plate, an upended tray and a cracked woman's watch, all mixed with spilt tea dotted by yellow biscuit crumbs.

"Jesus H. Christ!" My stomach heaves. I hit the side of my head. Is this some ghastly nightmare? I turn away. Plainclothes, uniform and another uniformed cop standing by the window stare at me. Eyes closed, I lean my head against the unbloodied wall by the door, breathe slow panting breaths, searching for anchor. Carefully I open my eyes. The men are watching me like crouching lions watch a luscious baby antelope headed their way.

I shake my head. "What happened?"

No answer. At length, Plainclothes says: "You do not know?" He gestures to the uniformed cop standing by the window. The cop goes to the cabin's far wall, which I see is a panel that connects this space with somewhere else. He opens the panel. It folds inward like an accordion. Sheila and Mike sit on a made-up bed holding each other. Mike is bent into her shoulder, his body shaking. Tears run down Sheila's cheeks. She, too, stares at me.

"Now we shall go to your place," says plainclothes closing the door. The giant nudges me. In a trance I allow myself to be shepherded back to my cabin. Plainclothes shuts the door, gestures for me to sit on the bed.

I sit, brushing the dirty laundry back into its bag, pushing bag toward bed's window end. For the first time I notice the train isn't moving. Out the window I see a lighted sign: *X'Ziromeu-Ville*. We're in the station at X'Ziromeu City.

Plainclothes joins me on the bed. Uniform stands by the window. Plainclothes pulls out a wallet, showing I.D. "I am Captain-Detective Matthias X'Zimbalwa, Central Services, posted to X'Ziromeu City. This is Police Senior Sergeant X'Zvnanda X'Zntuxz X'Zmbulu." He pulls out a cigarette case, offers it. I take a cigarette, inhale deeply. Steadying.

The questioning begins. What was I doing on the tour, my knowledge of the others, my whereabouts since getting on the train? I tell them of being sick and immobilized.

"You see," says the Sergeant with the unpronounceable name, "all others, they be accounted for at time Madame Farrar she die. They in observation lounge, then dining car. But you here. Alone."

"I never left my cabin. The porter will tell you."

"Sadly," says the Captain-Detective, "the porter has been busy making beds while passengers are away for dinner, so he has not been all the time watching corridor."

I put my head in my hands. "Why would I want to kill Helen Farrar? I hardly knew her."

"She has diamond, very large. Now she has it not!"

"Well, you can't take it with...You mean missing?"

Both policemen nod.

I gesture at the cabin. "You tore this place apart. You sure didn't find it."

"But this we find," Captain X'Zimbalwa holds up the medicine vial. He takes one pill, very lightly and gingerly touches it to his tongue. "We shall be having this analyzed. My feeling tells me it is emetine compound, what you call Ipecac. Make people very sick. Vomitus, dizzy, cramp. She," he points towards the murder cabin, "she have all these symptom, so cannot come to dinner. You say you have symptom, so too cannot come to dinner. You and she only tour people on train not come to dinner when she is being murdered." He pauses, draws on the cigarette he has lit for himself. "Also, it is being said, you are here because you wish to take away Zemba interest of Madame Farrar. Very good for you if Madame Farrar die. Not so?"

"Me? Who's saying that? Take over Eland's multimillion dollar interests? With what?" I sigh heavily. "It's all I can do to keep my own business going. Look at my bank account. This is silly."

"Ah yes." The Captain squints at me. "But may you be working on behalf of other? 'Man of Thatch,' we say in my language."

"We say 'straw man.' What is your language?"

"X'Zilantu is official language of X'Zambili peoples. I and the Sergeant are X'Zambili. We speak together in X'Zilantu. Also French. You speak French?"

I nod vigorously. *'Mais oui, Messieurs, que je parle français*—Yes, gentlemen, I speak French. And I assure you," I continue in that language, "I have committed no crime."

After staying in Paris for twenty-three years, having had a whole career as a news reporter there, and also an extremely messy divorce, one thing I do know is French. I remind myself, it's Zembeylia's second language, as this was France's easternmost African colony. Decolonization had been more or less friendly, France largely escaping blame for the ensuing civil wars. So the French have continued to work on the country's infrastructure, like financing and helping build this railroad down its length to the South African border.

A thought strikes. Insanity? Night-Stalker? I shiver. Had I risen in my poisoned sleep, opened the cabin door and, Frankenstein-like, marched into Cabin 2…No! For Chrissakes NO! Haven't lived forty-six years being Goldstone to…No! End of story.

"Look," I switch back to English, as my eyes lock onto the Captain's. "You're not going to believe me but I swear by all that's holy, on the heads of my children—*mes enfants*—I didn't do this. I didn't do anything." I thrust out my jaw, raise my chin. "I don't think you can prove I did!"

The cop drops his eyes. "We have now certain inquiry to make, including to analyze your medicine…"

"Not MY medicine. I wish to go on record that I never saw this bottle before in my life. Maybe it was left in the cabin…"

The detective raises his hand. "I say we are removing body, which we are flying to capital for autopsy at Freedom University Hospital. Tour shall proceed on this train with Sergeant here." The Sergeant scowls evilly. "No one shall leave. Not even husband, not even sister. Everybody go to Zemba Royal Tented Camp as your schedule say. There my superior, Colonel-Chief Detective Félix M'Bazi, who is flying from capital, will take over. We shall keep you all under our eyes. And you will remain in camp until case resolution. *Tu comprends?*—Understand?"

My God! Using the familiar *tu* form, not the decently polite *vous*? French police do this when addressing a convicted criminal. Like American cops calling you by your first name when issuing a speeding ticket.

I shiver. "*Capitaine*, I would appreciate basic courtesy. I demand it! Funeral arrangements? Surely the husband and the sister have the right…I don't think any of us will want to continue this trip under the circum—"

"When we are ready," interrupts the Captain, "we fly you all to capital, then home. Except for guilty one. The family can provide funeral here, in the United States, wherever they wish."

"So," I say slowly, "you're not accusing only me."

109

The detective spreads his large hands. He smiles showing regular teeth and two steel fillings. "I accuse no person yet. I now gather all fact. We put fact together and come to truth, whole truth, nothing but truth. Is not what you say in English?"

"Yes, but I! Am! Not! It!" I rap out each word.

"Then find me truth," says the Captain beaming. "Yes, Monsieur. Find me truth." He laughs a rich belly chuckle. "Oh," he continues in French, "I use the *tu* form because this is how the French colonialists always addressed us, as in France they address children. And dogs. You will find the form commonly used throughout French-speaking Africa. We're most familiar with it."

As if I didn't know, with all the time spent in French-speaking Africa. Why didn't I think-remember this fact of colonial life? Too hot under the collar for my own good. And too recently sick-as-the-proverbial-dog. I sigh and they leave. Without giving me back my passport, though I ask for it. I sit frozen. Gut okay. Lightheaded with hunger and flu-like aches all over, but...My God, poor Sheila. What do I mean, poor Sheila? Poor me! And Helen! Poor driving-driven woman. The Shaman's trance sure was prophetic. My God!

Find the truth? Damn well better. But what on earth happened? I look at my watch: 9:47 P.M. Quickly I put on my suit, no necktie.. Buttonhole the others. Since I didn't do it, somehow I have to come up with a line on who the hell did!

Captain X'Zimbalwa doesn't get to Madame Briac's farmhouse until 11:05 P.M. He has learned of her presence on the train from Sleeping Car 'B's porter and wants to drive out to interview her. He's glad to see the Renault pickup in the driveway, indicating she's home.

The house is dark. Quietly he and two aides climb steps to the front porch. A growl, then furious barking from behind the main door. Two large dogs barrel out of double flaps built into the door's lower panel. The cops scramble back down the porch steps. The dogs stand snarling, teeth bared.

110

At a nearby farm, other dogs begin to bark. Beyond a scattering of houses, a chorus of hyenas growl and some unidentified animal loudly moans. Goats ma-aa, roosters crow, a litter of puppies yip-yap. No lights go on, no stirrings in the house.

"Shall I shoot?" a cop has his pistol trained on the dogs.

"No!" shouts the Captain over a chorus of barks, hyena howls, groans, moans, yips, maa-ing, growls, yaps and a cock-a-doodle-doo.

After several moments of enough noise to rouse the dead, let alone anyone alive, Captain X'Zimbalwa takes a reluctant decision. He sends a man to his car to fetch equipment out of the trunk: a net and lengths of rope.

The Captain ties rope to the net. He whirls it, lasso style, above his head, as he approaches the steps. The dogs move forward, barking. A second cop makes flapping motions with his arms, taking several paces toward the steps' far side. One dog moves to cover him. The Captain lets fly the net, lands it neatly over the dog standing center ground. The animal thrashes and yowls, further entangling itself.

The other dog turns to its companion—and the second cop charges. He grabs the animal—twisting, snapping, snarling—by its wide leather collar, holds on for dear life. Other cops rush up the steps, loop ropes around the beast's legs and neck, drag it howling on its back to a porch pillar, where they bind it firm. With one mutt struggling in the net, now strapped around with rope, and its partner securely tied, a skinny policeman—handgun at the ready—crawls through a dog-flap into the house. He unlocks the front door. The Captain and men rush into the premises, turning on lights as they go. They open doors, peer into rooms, shout Madame Briac's name. Entering a large bedroom, they find her curled up on the bed, knees to chin, no covers, body rigid, lips, ears, face, neck purplish.

Convulsed? Dead? As the Captain runs back into the hall to grab a phone on a table there and call for medics, one of his men tries for a pulse. Can't tell if she's breathing. Or if they need only the coroner.

Chapter 13: Blues in the Night
Aboard the SilverSpear, early Thursday, December 17

A uniformed cop stands by Sleeper B's front exit, just beyond my cabin door. The man is talking to the porter, who looks shocked, his dark skin drained and ashen.

"I'm going to the dining car," I say. The policeman nods. I turn to the porter. "Would you remake my bed, please? They really tore the place up."

"Yes sir, I shall." The man appears relieved to be doing something.

The next car, Sleeper A, is quiet. Two Chinese men stand by a corridor window smoking and talking in low tones. I continue to a car with a long passageway that passes by crew cabins and a galley kitchen separated from the corridor by a wall. After the kitchen, with no door between, is the dining car. Lights are dimmed. A couple of waiters set silverware for breakfast.

The chief steward sits at an end table doing paperwork. I approach him. "Any chance of my getting something to eat? And coffee?" I ask in French. I'm horribly hungry, on top of everything else. Knees and hands trembling. Need food to steady up.

The steward smiles. "We are closed, chef's asleep. Maybe you can find a snack in the observation lounge. They have coffee, I know."

"Guess I'll have to try there. I missed dinner. What time's breakfast?"

"Seven A.M. to nine, sir. No reservation necessary."

I nod, turn and again pass through the kitchen car and Sleeper A, where the Chinese men are still smoking and talking; then through my own car, acknowledging the policemen on guard at the front and rear doors and noting the porter tidying my ripped-apart cabin.

I arrive at the rear car, whose stainless steel entryway is labeled *Observation Lounge.* The train jerks, causing me nearly to stumble. What's happened to the ride's "legendary smoothness" as touted by the invitation letter? Is everybody losing it?

We start to move. The brakeman leans out the upper half of a doorway. Over his shoulder, as we travel along the platform, I see a covered stretcher being loaded into a boxy looking ambulance. A red light flashes from its roof.

The brakeman gives a wave, slams the door shut.

Entry to the Observation Lounge is electronic. I step between lights on the doorposts and the door slides open.

Quite a car. Stairs to the so-called *Vista-Dome,* which after dark turns into a nightclub complete with small dance floor. I hear a band: *The M'Zimba Boys–Three Piece Ensemble,* says a notice by the stairs. They're belting out Sinatra's "Singin' The Blues."

The corridor slopes down below the dome section. This low-ceilinged area holds an intimate bar with soft lights and music piped from the band. Its three tables are occupied by Chinese couples in dark Mao suits, the womens' studded with spangles. Elegant evening attire *à la* Comrade Mao.

But no one here from our group.

The floor slopes up again. I've reached the lounge's rear section, with the far outer walls curving together to embrace a wraparound end window. Comfortable, well lit lounge–on wheels that includes sofas, armchairs, two writing desks and its own bar along a partition at the forward end. Clustered on a sofa with surrounding chairs pulled close are almost our whole group. Everyone except the directly bereaved and the Southgate-D'Alessandro pair. Are the latter consummating their illicit relationship? Plotting more kills?

I acknowledge those present, go to the bar, negotiate a selection of cheeses and smoked trout *canapés* left over from cocktail hour. A pot of black coffee, too. I hope food won't start another run of trots. For now, nothing left to trot.

With sustenance and caffeine promised, I approach my travel companions, take an armchair. Despite its substantial weight, the runners slide easily over the carpet. I pull up to the group, receive stony glances.

"What happened? How did it happen?" Silence. "I was out for the count," I add lamely.

More silence.

Mrs. Jamieson gives a harsh chuckle. "You see, Bubba? If not him, it had to be the hand of God. Strange Our Lord would make such a mess. You'd expect a more tasteful demise."

"Now, Bitsy!" says her husband, still in his ten gallon. Does he take it off in bed?

"Look," I say. "Why me? The police know I have no axe to grind with the woman. Not like what I hear about most of you. In any case, I was deathly ill after that meal. Wouldn't have had the strength to cut my own throat, let alone hers."

"Your exquisite sensitivity does you honor. Thanks for speaking with such tenderness and understanding about our newly departed friend." Gordon Chandler's voice sounds as hoarse as his words are sarcastic. "No axe to grind? No motive? What's a mere two million dollar diamond to the owner of a hole-in-wall agency with an overhead fifty percent higher than its income?"

"Thirty percent." I'm stung. "Our income's climbing."

Chandler gives a laugh. From a side table, he picks up *The International Herald Tribune*, holds it to eye level, nose buried in the inner pages.

My order appears, carried over by the barman. I gulp coffee, devour *canapés*. "Will somebody please say what happened? The police aren't accusing anyone. You should give me the benefit of the doubt. Just assume, for the sake of argument, that I slept through the whole thing. Which I did. Now what in blazes went on?"

"We all came to the meeting here, except for those off the train and waiting for it at X'Ziromeu City. Didn't we, Gowinda? So how should we know?" Bitsy Jamieson jangles bracelets and spreads ring-loaded fingers.

"This is true, Mister Goldstone. This is being very true, yes." Lazuli nods judiciously.

"Lazuli, just tell me the sequence. When, what, how?"

"Well," the Indian clears his throat. "We are all showing up exactly as we plan, right here in this lounge at 6:15 P.M. To learn from me about the game park and significations."

"Such as the red *metastigmata*, or, to you, ticks. You'll be digging them out of your skin every time you walk in the bush," says Gene Petroff in his high whine. "And the green *genus scorpionida* indigenous to the area. Leave your tent, stroll into surrounding vegetation, turn up a rock or two and you'll see a whole collection of beautiful, juicy scorpions. Carriers of M'zu-m'zu, according to Gowinda here. Fascinating, really. I actually look forward to finding 'em. But be sure to shake out your shoes and socks every time you get dressed. And look in your bed before settling down to a nice sleep. Otherwise, it could be your last. Linc, old man, you really missed a very informative briefing."

Calling me, Linc? A guy with whom I've barely exchanged a word? The nerve!

Lazuli waves his arms. "Oh, Mr. Petroff, you are exaggerating. Tents have wire mesh all around, so scorpion and snake cannot crawl there. Inside, you are all being perfectly safe."

"Oh, yes?" God, that turbine voice makes my head ache all over again. "We still better shake-and-look before putting on shoes or lying down."

I want to get to business, "All this was at 6:15. Helen here?"

A shaking of heads all around.

"You and she were absent," says Miho Petroff, ignoring a glance from her husband.

Her voice, smooth as velvet, makes me think of rich milk chocolate. How did this singer with her sensitive ear get involved with the unmelodious Petroff? Money? Surely not, given her rich industrialist father. She has all the family money she'll ever need.

"Then Michael did come at 6:30," she continues, "and say to us Helen still is sick, so she possibly will not be at dinner."

"Sheila, Mr. Chandler and Mr.Guitterez-Shaughnessy obviously weren't present," I remark, "since the train hadn't yet arrived at X'Ziromeu City. When was it due? Around 7:00 P.M.?"

"7:30 on the dot," says Sherman Jamieson. "Most always is on the dot." He frowns, shakes his head. "Y'all kin set yer watch by it, thet's whut they keep a-tellin' you here. In any case, *amigo*, yo're correct. Them three wuz out of it."

"Okay, so you and Mrs. Jamieson, the Petroffs, D'Alessandro, Ms. Southgate and Mr. Lazuli plus Mike, making eight, were all here in the observation lounge at 6:15 P.M."

"And then Helen come about 6:40." Jamieson again.

"What? I thought you said she didn't."

"She did—and she did not. Miho Petroff looks mysterious.

"Now listen—" I begin.

"She came there, by the bar," whines Petroff waving his arm towards this area's front end. "Mike got up, went over to her. They talked for about a minute. She left and Mike rejoined us."

"But only for a second or two," chimes in the bejeweled Bitsy Jamieson.

"I understand that he made some remark about Helen feeling really bad and sticking to her cabin. But, of course, this is hearsay since I wasn't present." Guitterez-Shaughnessy puts in his two cents, sounding like the take-charge guy I figure he is. You have to be in the drug racket, I guess. And maybe he's a Colombian, but his American English is perfect. His voice, a moderate baritone, sounds civilized, not in keeping with the piratical looks. Or his alleged

116

profession. "Michael, so I'm told, decided to arrange for a tray. He left shortly after she did and later joined us at dinner. Isn't that right, people?" The alleged drug lord looks around at the others who nod agreement.

"Dinner started at 7:15 P.M., very prompt," says Lazuli. "Precisely as planned."

I stand. "Excuse me." And hurry back to the dining car.

Dark now, except for a small beam from a reading light where the chief steward is deep in a paperback.

The man looks up. "Is it true," I ask "that you served Mrs. Farrar in her room? Cabin Two, Sleeping Car B?"

"Yes," the steward says. "This is true."

"What did you serve?"

"What her husband ordered: dry biscuits, a pot of tea, an apple."

"Did you take it to her?"

The man shakes his head. "A waiter. Rajhni Kemoth."

"Indian?"

The steward nods again. "Not really a waiter. He is in an apprentice program as part of executive training."

"That's a very American method. Beginning at the bottom."

"Americans designed our business course."

"May I talk to Mr. Kemoth?"

"He is sleeping now in our dormitory section. You may talk to him tomorrow. At breakfast."

"Fine, that's what I'll do. You're not ready to sleep?"

"I sleep next to the kitchen. But I read here. My cabin has too much of the kitchen odor."

"Well, thank you for the information. I wish you goodnight."

The steward acquiesces, yawns and stretches, goes back to his book. I return to my car and find the porter sitting on a jump seat at its front end.

"Your room is all clean now, sir," the man says.

"Oh, fine," I say in French. "I'm grateful for your trouble." I give him a MUL 500 note. Ten dollars worth of goodwill? Would a murderer be so generous? A murderer who has just stolen a two million dollar sparkler possibly could spare ten bucks. "Tell me, did you see Mrs. Farrar get her dinner tray?"

The porter nods. "I was there. Monsieur, her husband, and a waiter came from the dining car. I pressed the door buzzer. Madame Farrar got up and unlocked her door. Monsieur opened it. Madame got back in bed. Her husband took the tray, put it on her lap."

"You saw all this?"

"Also earlier, when she left the compartment to go to the observation lounge and find her husband. Then I saw both of them come back. She came first alone; a couple of minutes later, he came through this car on his way to the diner. He didn't stop. In about ten minutes, he returns with a waiter holding a tray."

"And you actually saw her in bed."

"Yes. I stood like this," the porter indicates with his hands. "I saw the lady inside her cabin in bed. She has yellow hair, no?"

I acknowledge that fact. "Everything looked normal?"

"Yes, normal." The porter sighs. "Not like later. Terrible. Just terrible."

"I know. You say the door was locked?"

"The door? Yes. And when the husband left–he left with the waiter to go back to the dining car for his own dinner–she again locked up. I heard the sound, the slip-sound of the chain being attached."

"So the husband was there only a minute or two and then went to dinner."

The porter nods.

I stroke my chin, hoping for inspiration. "There's a communicating door from Cabin 2 to Cabin 3. Was that open?"

"No, no. Locked."

"Number 3's a single cabin, like mine. Right?"

118

"Yes. The door between the two is kept locked. I tested it before we left the capital, then again at X'Ziromeu City."

"When again?"

"When I made up the bed for Madame Mondran, who came aboard at X'Ziromeu City."

"And the food tray for Mrs. Farrar arrived at what time?"

"About seven P.M."

"So you see her alive at seven. Then everyone leaves, she locks her door. The train pulls into X'Ziromeu City at 7:30 and Chandler, Guitterez-Shaughnessy and Ms. Mondran get on sometime before departure at 8:00, say about 7:40 or 50? You check the communicating Cabin Three, which is locked, just as when you checked it earlier before the train's departure from the capital. When this sleeping car was empty of passengers. Yes?"

The porter acquiesces. He says, "There was another person in Cabin 3 from Fulumbane, our departure point, to X'Ziromeu City. A Madame Briac."

"Well, at, say, 7:45, when the train was standing in the X'Ziromeu City station, was Cabin 3's door into the corridor locked?"

"Yes," says the porter. "Madame Mondran got on. I unlocked Cabin 3's door to the outside corridor, she put her small bag in, opened the lavatory section to wash her hands—she didn't even close the door when she did this—and then went directly to the diner. By that time, we were underway. I made up the bed, tested the partition to make sure it was locked, and locked up the cabin. 'After dinner, when she returns,' I say to myself, 'I'll give her the outer door key.' But by that time..." He sighs again, looks out at darkness rushing by.

"And the inner communicating partition to Cabin 2 stays locked?"

"Yes."

"No other doors anywhere?"

"No."

119

"The window. It opens?"

"Train's air conditioned. All windows are sealed."

"Did the train stop between where we got on and X'Ziromeu City?"

The porter shakes his head.

"Is there a way to get from the roof into Cabin 3?"

He shakes his head again.

"From under the train? Through the toilet or sink, maybe?"

He grins. "No, no, no!"

"So Mrs. Farrar was totally locked in. Nobody could have got to her. Maybe it was suicide."

"She smashes the back of her own head? Struggles? Throws food all around? Makes that blood picture on the mirror? Why doesn't she stab a knife into her heart or shoot herself in the temple like ordinary suicides? She has a gun in her purse. A small pistol. Why not use that?" The porter pauses for a second. "Does she steal her own diamond?"

"Well, how could I have done it? That's what the police and the other tour people think. But you're proving to me I couldn't. Nobody could."

"Maybe you came through the sink?" The porter chuckles. Remembering the situation, he becomes solemn, frowns. "Someone did it," he mutters.

I snap my fingers in frustration. "How many people stayed in this car during dinner?"

"You. In Cabin 1, a single, no upper berth. You stayed. Madame Mondran arrived at X'Ziromeu City, went into Cabin 3, left her bag, went to dinner, as I said. Cabin 4, on the other side is one of our deluxe compartments with king-size lower bed and a bathroom featuring a jacuzzi, which Monsieur and Madame Petroff occupy. They went to the observation car meeting, then straight through to dinner without stopping in this car. Cabin 5 is an ordinary double having washing arrangements like yours, but with upper berth. Madame Southgate and Monsieur D'Alessandro are there and they complained about the accommodation when they came aboard. They went with the others to the meeting and dinner. Monsieur and Madame Jamieson have our other luxury double in 6. They went to the meeting and straight to dinner. Messieurs Chandler and Guitterez-Shaughnessy in 7, an ordinary double cabin, with upper berth, got on the train at X'Ziromeu City and went to dinner. Monsieur Lazuli in Cabin 8, a single like yours, no upper berth, went to the meeting and dinner. And Cabin 2, a double with upper berth, is the one belonging to the lady who was killed. We've already talked about her and her husband's movements. So that's all."

"Well, what about Cabin 3 before X'Ziromeu City?"

"Madame Briac was there. She's from a farm and doesn't know any of you."

"Madame Briac didn't go to dinner?"

"Her ticket doesn't allow dinner. She only traveled from the capital to X'Ziromeu City."

"And she stayed there in her cabin the whole trip, until the train got to X'Ziromeu City?"

The porter nods. "I served her a tray with *cognac*, mineral water, a pot of coffee, some cheese, biscuits, fruit. I put the tray in her cabin before we left the capital. She closed her door, stayed where she was. When she got off at X'Ziromeu City, I cleared the dirty dishes, spruced things up. Then Madame Mondran arrives, stows her bag, washes hands, goes to dinner and I make her bed."

"You say she stowed her bag. One bag? She has more than one bag. Two big suitcases." I'm grasping at straws.

"The luggage for Madame Mondran and Messieurs Chandler and Guitterez-Shaughnessy, I put in empty Cabin 7 when all of you came onboard at the special stop we made for you. When we got to X'Ziromeu City, Messieurs Jamieson and Guitterez-Shaughnessy took over that cabin and I moved Madame Mondran's suitcases down to Cabin 3. But she came aboard carrying a red bag. Velvet. Very elegant."

"So when all the tour people went to dinner, was Ms. Farrar discovered yet?"

"I told you. Everyone but you and the dead lady went to dinner, including the new arrivals as soon as they boarded. They hurried to get to the dining car before it closed."

"I can check on their presence in the diner with the steward."

"We left at 8:00 P.M.," continues the porter. "At about 8:40–I know because we were crossing the X'Zirambabwe River Bridge and I look at my watch to check if we're exactly on time, which we were–Monsieur, the husband, returned to his wife. He knocks on the cabin door, no answer. He tries the door. Locked. He calls to his wife, shakes the door. No answer. He calls to me. I use my passkey to open the door. But the chain is on. He peers inside, says, 'There's something strange. We must break the door.' We snap the chain and find..." The porter passes a hand over his face. "You know what we find."

"Yeah." I let out a deep breath. "This was about 8:40 P.M. or so. What then?"

"I go to the train chief. He has an office in the observation car. He comes back with me, takes a look, phones the engineer to halt the train. He radios X'Ziromeu City, and we back up all the way to the station. The police are waiting there."

"Thank you for the information," I say. "At least I have an idea of what happened, blow-by-blow. By the way, what tribe are you from?"

The man draws himself up. "X'Zambili-X'Zilantu. I'm X'Zambili. But we're all one people now. Or try to be. Not so easy. We try." He smiles ruefully.

We shake hands. I make my way back to the observation lounge, where I manage to buttonhole the train chief before asking a few more questions of the group members. They seem to be making a night of it, grim, sort of a wake fueled by plenty of drink. I get confirmations on much of what I have learned. Nobody contradicts the information that, so far as I can see, adds up to:

1) A sleeping cabin locked on all sides into which
   no one can enter.
2) Into which, by all accounts, no one did enter.
3) Yet where a murder–not by any stretch of
   the imagination suicide but murder–
   stern murder in the direst degree, as
   Shakespeare's King Richard III puts it in a
   self-excoriating soliloquy–takes place.

In a nutshell, one impossible crime.

Chapter 14: "Monsieur l'Assassin!"
Aboard the SilverSpear Express
Thursday Morning–Early Afternoon, December 17

I sleep the sleep of exhaustion. Nightmarish, full of bare-breasted voodoo females pointing fingers at people who vomit rivers of blood. Then I wake as dawn is touching the sky. The train twists and winds through a hilly pass, these hills dark and bare, slope eastward to a panoramic sea lighted both by the moon and, at the horizon, orange streaks of sun.

The SilverSpear's general course, as I know, is south, with a western veer away from the Indian Ocean over mountains and into the X'Ziloncado, a vast stretch of woodland and savanna country, some of it covered by grasses growing ten feet high. Given last night's delay we won't arrive at our stop there before noon.

In the sky, quickly lightening, I see a cloud of large dark birds wheeling round and round. Vultures? The train leans into a curve and there are two lions, a male and female. They lie in grass companionably chewing on a four legged creature: the headless remnant of an antelope? In a wide ring around the two, on nearby ground, are more of the dark birds–vultures? For sure vultures, hop-hopping, flapping long wings, waiting their turn.

The train rounds another bend, the creatures disappear except for those in the sky wheeling, wheeling. Over me? Invisible wings bat above my head. Better cultivate a predatory sense if I want to get to the bottom of this business, and keep my own bottom off the electric chair, or whatever they use in these parts.

More curves. On a meadowy upland ringed with low trees stand elephants. I spot a couple of small ones under their mothers. Then come giraffes and a herd of zebras. A few giraffes are munching leaves from high branches; others, forelegs awkwardly splayed, bend heads to graze. None of the animals seem to give the train notice. I regret not having my camera in hand. Have to remember what I'm in Zembeylia for, never mind human violence and stupidity.

I open the accordion door to the sink, take camera off inner hook, manage to get shots of a field of enormous twisted red rocks, one a mini-replica of the mushroom cloud in photos of the Hiroshima bombing. An image to underscore my mood: combination of disgust and plain old panic.

In a flower-studded valley, all whites and purples, I snap a small herd of ostriches racing away from the train. Their bare necks, their tiny bald heads contrast with the full black featherdness of their bodies and yellow-bustled rears.

Breakfast at seven. Hungry as hell. Getting to the diner early means a chance to question waiter/executive-to-be Rajhni Kemoth before he gets busy. Tall, slim, with a mane of blue-black hair, chiseled features and flashing teeth: great poster-boy for whatever company he works for. Yes, he carried the tray and followed Mike Mahoney to Cabin Two, Sleeping Car B. Mahoney knocked on the door. Everyone present heard the inside lock being turned, the chain slipping out of its holder and the lady call, "Come in!" Rajhni glimpses her sitting up in bed before her husband takes the tray, places it on his wife's knees. The waiter hears him say she should try to eat and ask if there is anything else she needs. Kemoth sees her shake her head. "You'd better get back to the group," she tells Mahoney, or words to that effect. Her husband nods, closes the door. Again, Kemoth hears the lock turn. But no, not the chain slip into place. "I am needing to leave in a hurry to get back to dining car," he says. "For dinner service."

"Did Mr. Mahoney come with you?" I ask in English. The Indians of Zembeylia tend to make it, not French, their *lingua franca*.

The waiter nods. "He come to join his party. They are already at table."

"And when was this?"

"Maybe 7:12-7:15 P.M. Not later, since passengers are still entering into the car and we serve very prompt. Mr. Mahoney's party is having two tables of four places. Already full, except for Mister who is coming right behind."

"So now, including him, there are eight people of the Eland group?"

Kemoth nods.

"Did you serve them?"

"Yes. I am serving these people and then the three who are getting on at X'Ziromeu City."

"Where do they sit?"

"At table of four, right behind others."

"Was there anyone else at their table? Another passenger from another sleeping car or one of the Chinese, finishing his or her dinner?"

"No. We are holding that table empty. We are holding thirteen places for Eland, so two tables is making eight plus third table is making twelve, plus one place free at two person table on other side. But only eleven come, including tour guide. We are putting last three at table of four places."

I glance down the car's length and note that, facing forward, it features tables for four on its right and smaller tables for two left of a center aisle. Inviting looking car, decorated art déco style with reddish tinted mirrors separating the windows. Choose between watching nature's magnificence or your own apoplectically tinted face stuffing itself.

"You aren't a waiter by profession?" I ask Kemoth, who serves half a marvelously fragrant, pinkish melon.

"I am hoping to enter management. I am preparing for that. More coffee, sir?"

I nod. "Zemba Royal's management?"

Kemoth shrugs. "I am staying with the train service. Government is considering to give train and game camp administration to X'Zambili-Africa Tours."

"Why is that?"

"Government and King M'Zumba own fifty-nine percent of Zemba Royal but other company, X'Zambili-Africa is representing powerful private and population interests in nation. Political people in Parliament do not wish to be accused of favoring one over other."

"I have heard the government does strongly favor Zemba Royal, especially your Minister of Internal Security, Tourism and Culture who's very powerful because of controlling Zembeylia's great potential moneymakers: us tourists." I drink black coffee. The meal is giving me ballast. Beginning to feel human again.

Kemoth smiles, showing splendid teeth. "Yes, what you say is true and so everyone is knowing. But government do not wish to appear too much favoring Zemba Royal because of accusations in Parliament and trouble from X'Zambili and Indian and settler-French population."

"I get it," I say. I order eggs mimosa. Might as well have some enjoyment from all this, I tell my vermilion self.

As I'm finishing, the rest of the group and our three-man police escort straggles in. The sergeant, whose mile-long name none of us has tried to remember—let alone pronounce—sits down at my table, as do Lazuli and, a little later, Sheila. She looks pale, barely acknowledges our presence. Mike isn't to be seen. Sheila picks at her melon while staring out the window. Her presence stifles talk.

At length, I lean across the table "I'm just terribly sorry. Despite what anyone thinks or says you must know I had absolutely nothing…that is…if there's anything I can do," I mumble and excuse myself.

Instead of returning to my cabin, I head for the observation lounge and take a seat upstairs in the dome. Watching the panorama of the train's descent into the X'Ziloncado Basin, I try once more to piece events together.

"We have news," says the sergeant, slipping into a swivel armchair across from me and speaking in French. "Early this morning I got a radio message that Madame Farrar's wallet, travelers. checks and jewelry–without the diamond, of course–were found by a police-supervised crew investigating along the track. In U.S. money we recovered about five thousand dollars in travelers' checks and dumped goods. We can calculate exactly when the train passed this spot, since it was right on schedule, having made up time lost when it stopped to pick up your group plus the Chinese tour. The loot must have been dropped from a tilt-up wash-sink at between 7:20 to 7:23 P.M., no earlier, no later. Just before the *SilverSpear* started to slow for X'Ziromeu City." The sergeant pauses swiveling in his chair to gaze out a window.

Finding the game inside more interesting than what he can spot beyond the glass, he turns back to me. "We fitted this information with hands of the victim's smashed watch showing 7:19 P.M. So we have evidence as to when the crime occurred." He smiles. "That, of course, is when only you and she of your group are in Sleeping Car B, the others either being off the train or together for a meeting in this car, the observation lounge. Then at dinner all tour members, except you and the lady, are present and accounted for by the dining car staff. *Tu comprends?*"

The smile grows broader. "The murderer-robber grabbed every valuable item he could, then decided the wallet and minor stuff

127

were too incriminating, too hard to hide from a thorough search. So he dumps them. He keeps the diamond, leaves the cabin, goes back to his lair."

"He?" I say. "Our group? You assume it's a he and a member of the tour. Why? Since the stakes are a hugely valuable diamond, why not one of the other passengers, or even train personnel? Why not a woman, for God's sake?"

"*Voyons, Monsieur,*" the Sergeant is chuckling now. He leans across and with a great paw gives my shoulder a pat. "We both know who 'It' is, *n'est-ce-pas?* Only those in the group knew about the jewel. Had to be an inside job. And, of necessity it needed to be the single individual who is unaccounted for, not away from the train at the very moment this *crime affreux*–this horrible crime takes place. *Non?* I mean, why look further when things are so obvious? In other words…"

"How the hell did I get into her cabin, since you're so convinced I did it? Which I didn't, damn it! And where's the fucking diamond? You certainly took my room apart, took me apart, too. Did you find it? Goddamn it to hell, did you?" I realize I'm displaying a lack of my never very profound cool.

"Patience, patience, *Monsieur l'assass*in." The sergeant heaves himself off the seat, stands towering over me. "Remember, we are trained by the methods of the French *Police Judiciare.* We of the Zembeylian detective force take pride in always getting our man. *Bonne continuation*–Have a great day." He leaves, chuckling.

Suddenly I feel very tired, decide to go to my cabin, lie down. I find the porter stripping the bed and stuffing blankets, sheets, pillows into a large space underneath. He flips the mattress, strapped to a revolving baseboard, other-side-up, revealing the day sofa.

"Tell me," I say, "this Madame Briac. Do you know anything about her? Does she ride the train, murder a passenger or two and then get off?"

128

The porter smiles. "No murders. She takes the train often, these last two-three months. She's a widow with an ostrich and coffee farm in the uplands near X'Ziromeu City. When she goes to the capital, she likes to travel comfortably. We make it in four hours and thirty minutes between Fulumbane and X'Ziromeu City."

"Last night she got off when you arrived there. At 7:30?"

"Yes, she was waiting in the corridor. Stepped off as soon as we stopped."

"Did she have many suitcases?"

The porter shakes his head. "Only a green bag. Overnight bag."

"And then the two men and Ms. Mondran boarded, right?"

The porter nods, giving the room a final flick with his duster. "As I told you last night." He withdraws to the corridor.

I'm about to close my door and sit on the sofa when the sergeant comes striding by.

"Sergeant," I stick my head out the door. He stops, turns. "This Briac woman. You've questioned her? She, like me, was here in this car at the fateful hour. Not so?"

"All is being taken care of. Not to worry," he says and continues on his way. Stopping, I note, to knock at Cabin 3. Sheila's cabin.

"Massive heart attack, maybe," the doctor shakes his head. He speaks in French.

"Will she live?" asks Captain-Detective X'Zimbalwa.

"Too early to tell. Farm work has given her a strong constitution and she looks in good shape, for a woman her age."

They're standing by the door to Madame Briac's private room in the heavily guarded police sector of X'Ziromeu Municipal Hospital. She lies on the bed, the upper part of her body encased in a respirator to help breathing. Her arms are stuck with needles attached to tubes and bottles that hang from three portable stands.

A monitoring screen displays her vital signs. A nurse stands close by.

The doctor, a slim, very dark-skinned man with gray hair matching a gray goatee, again shakes his head. "Even if she does survive, she may never come out of her coma. Or, if so, she could be unable to speak or function normally. You can't tell with these seizures, or whatever…Especially not in the early stages."

"You're sure it was a seizure? A natural cause?" asks the Captain.

"A seizure, yes. But *non, Capitaine, non*! I have no certainty of the cause. In fact, it might very well be poison. An Aconite preparation? An overdose of Trifluoperazine? I don't have proof one way or the other. We've had to be cautious in administering medicine. Last night we gave what anti-poison treatment we could without causing more strain to the heart, respiratory and circulatory systems. We did have her inhaling Amyl nitrate—0.3 ml. for fifteen seconds per minute—and also dosed her with Naloxone, then Benadryl to relax face and neck muscles. Not forgetting Phenytoin for ventricular arrhythmia. So you see, we've been a bit shotgun in our approach, working to counteract a range of poisons that she might have absorbed. On the other hand, we've had to go gently, since we didn't want to kill her with our treatments." He pauses, shaking his head some more. "Lucky you came along when you did. Another few minutes and she'd surely have been unsaveable." He smiles grimly. "Of course, in that case we could have done an autopsy, although even then the only signs of poisoning would be indirect and inconclusive. In any event, we've had to proceed symptomatically."

The captain turns to go. "If there's the slightest sign of her waking up, being coherent or even speaking at all, I need to know immediately. We must communicate with her. A lot is at stake."

The doctor strokes his goatee. "Her well being comes first. I'll let you at her only if and when I feel it doesn't endanger her further."

Madame Briac gives a loud sigh-groan. The nurse leans over her, both men stop to listen. As the doctor approaches the bed, peering at the monitor, his patient murmurs something like, "Pierre.Ohhrr... *Pierre.Ohhrr...*" She moves her head side to side, agitated.

The doctor gestures to the nurse. Slowly and carefully she squirts a solution into one of the intravenous tubes.

"This will calm her," he tells the Captain. "She needs rest."

"*Pierre*, was that what she said?" asks the Captain, pulling out a small pad and making a note. "Maybe *Pierre d'Or?* In English that would translate to Goldstone. Which would confirm our hypothesis. I'm pretty sure she said *Pierre d'Or*, aren't you?"

"Sounded like it."

"And you think it was poison?"

The doctor shrugs. "At least an even chance. So simple to make it look like a heart attack. But with certain suspicious anomalies. Unless, of course, I'm mistaken, which I could be."

"In any event," says the Captain, "we're going to spread word of her death."

"Death?" The doctor looks aghast.

"If someone out there wishes her dead and that someone is connected with the other crimes we have on our hands—the train murder of a prominent American investor in our tourism industry and a missing diamond of great value— then we certainly don't want such a person alerted as to the possible failure of the machination, insofar as poor Madame Briac is concerned."

The Captain opens the door to the hospital hallway. "Tell your staff to keep silent about this."

"But her family, her friends," exclaims the doctor. "We can't inform them she has died if she hasn't."

"I understand the practicalities," says the Captain. "Just refer anyone who asks about her to me. My service will put up the right sort of bureaucratic barrier."

And talking more to himself than to the doctor, he adds, "God knows if the French taught us anything, they certainly taught us how to set up bureaucratic barriers!"

PART THREE:
ROUND AND VARNISHED TALES
Zembeylia and New York City, Thursday-Friday, December 17-18

"Meet me by moonlight alone
And then I will tell you a tale…"
J.A. Wade, "Meet Me by Moonlight"

Chapter 15: Into The X'Ziloncado
X'Ziloncado Basin, Thursday afternoon, and
Washington D.C., early Thursday morning, December 17

The rest of the morning our train travels through landscapes of forests and high grass. For about forty minutes, we're in jungle. Dark, gloomy, vine-entwined trees weave a leafy canopy making the sun and sky all but invisible.

I stay in my cabin. No more stomach for hostile policemen calling me "Mister Assassin," or equally hostile, if slightly more circumspect tour members.

From my window I see elephants feasting on leaves, plenty of the antelope-like creatures that South Africans call springbok plus a zebra herd. Trotting beside the tracks, tails held stiffly high, a line of warthogs comes into, then passes from view. Tuskered, mustachioed, they look like a band of self-important military officers on significant maneuvers. In this restrictive environment the world outside seems remote.

Beyond my door murder and gathering suspicions have me hemmed into a cabin—refuge from fear and accusation. I look out again and can almost believe I'm traveling through a super-zoo on the outskirts of a town like San Diego, where animal-minded taxpayers have shelled out tons of money for a game reserve.

Need to keep prodding my mind to realize this is Africa, real Africa. How I long to get off the train, go for a game walk—protected, of course, by rifle-bearing guides—and experience the animals as a two-footed animal in my own right.

A little after 12:15 PM, the *SilverSpear* slows. Creaking, as trains seem to do at the end of journeys, it pulls up beside a red gravel mound forming a platform. A gray-painted school bus and two open Land Rovers are parked close by. No station shack here. Nothing but a sign in French and English: "Game Preserve."

As I step from the sleeper, heat comes at me as from a blast furnace, seeming to fold me into itself. Dry heat, more tolerable than New York's sticky kind, but a helluva lot hotter. The sky is deep blue, with high-piled blackish clouds, menace-looking. Yet, it's so hot!

The Chinese emerge from Sleeper A, snapping photos and chatting to one another in raised voices. I wonder how many have become overnight Americans, thanks to passport mixups. I watch their minders form them into a line in front of the school bus.

I turn my attention to a grinning young man and woman, who hold up signs saying, *WELCOME ELAND!* They wear identical khaki tunics and shorts. Their heads are protected from sun by tan, stiff jungle helmets of the type Teddy Roosevelt made famous when he shot big game and went around saying "Bully! Bully!" I resolve to buy a hat. Jamieson has the right idea with his Texas ten-gallon.

The twelve of our company—ah yes, should have been thirteen but one of the little band of sisters and brothers— honored leader in fact, is no doubt this very moment being de-gutted in a hospital basement—we remaining twelve climb into the Land Rovers. A woman greeter escorts our sergeant-with-the-unpronounceable-Name and his men to a jeep marked *POLICE*. It takes the rear of the caravan as we jounce along a red dirt track that winds up, down and around through forest intermixed with grassland. Uphill, downhill, turning tight corners hemmed with trees.

After forty minutes of this, some of the group start groaning. I take it stoically, until my bladder tells me that enough is enough and if we don't arrive soon at a destination with sanitary facilities, I'll have to demand a halt by a tree trunk.

Arrive we do. The trees clear. We go up a hill and the lead driver jumps out to open a tall steel gate flanked by equally tall fencing. We pass through. Back of us, the police jeep stops so its driver can swing the gate shut.

Below us, beyond a downhill slope, is a gathering of pavilion tents, green-and-white striped. Each stands isolated in clumps of trees and bushes that ring a wide, manicured lawn on one side and a large brackish-looking pond on the other. At the edge of the lawn, close to the road, is a sprawling wooden lodge.

Just at the lodge, the road ends in a looped driveway widening to a tarmac-covered parking area. Beside jeeps and Land Rovers stands a black helicopter. From my days as a correspondent in France and Algeria, I recognize a French-built *Alouette*: small job holding two, maybe four persons. Like our following jeep, the word *POLICE* is stenciled in white on its side.

We pull up before the lodge and two khaki-clad women with clipboards, wave a welcome. A few paces to the rear stands a tall, thin fellow in a dark business suit. He, too, holds a clipboard but looks a city slicker in the midst of this jungle.

The police jeep roars ahead of us, the big sergeant jumps out and salutes the tall man, who sticks out a hand. A second's hesitation and the sergeant shakes it. Here, obviously, is the big-shot detective from the capital: Sherlock Holmes, Zembeylian style. No doubt the sergeant will puff up his chest and proclaim that he has solved the case, that, of course, the hideous assassin is none other than *moi*, a "Man of Thatch," whose motive is taking over Eland's millions with my tender offer based on the $8.23 that the I.R.S may have left in the agency bank account. Plus Donald Trump's billions? Not funny. Better get to a telephone.

The women with clipboards begin organizing tent accommodations. The man in the suit steps forward, raises his hand. Talk stops, everyone looks at him.

"Hi, people," he says in perfect American English with a New York tinge. "I'm Colonel-Detective Félix M'Bazi of Central Services. You met my boss, Minister M'Bowé, the government official responsible not only for tourism but also for police and

137

national security. I'm here because of the tragic death—a murder, we have now confirmed—of Mrs. Helen Farrar-Mahoney. It is my sad duty to inform you there has been another death, that of a lady who traveled with you on the train. She isn't known to you, not as far as we can gather: Madame Félicité Briac from a farm near X'Ziromeu City. She died of an apparent heart attack shortly after leaving your train, on which she had traveled from the capital in Cabin 3 of the sleeping car mainly reserved for your group." He pauses, his gaze catching each of us in turn. "I shall be interviewing you individually, and also possibly together, during your stay here. My job is to get to the bottom of Mrs. Farrar's murder and, if relevant, the death of Madame Félicité Briac. I am counting on the cooperation of those who have nothing to hide and who are as anxious as we police to clear matters up, so free themselves from the taint of suspicion. Before going to your rooms, please identify yourselves to me. Then, after you have settled in and had a late lunch, I'll begin interviews in the reading lounge off this lodge's main lobby. I hope to be finished with a first round before late afternoon, when you'll probably want to participate in a game-run aboard the Land Rovers. I'll try not to interfere with your tour here any more than necessary. Thank you."

When I present myself, M'Bazi gves a broad grin and makes a slight nod of his head. "I'm specially pleased to meet you. We have lots to talk about."

"I don't think so," I say firmly. "You guys are barking up the wrong tree. What reason did I have to kill that woman?" I square my shoulders. "I demand to make a phone call."

M'Bazi's grin grows broader. "Would I prevent you from telephoning? We Zembeylians use the old French-and-British formula: 'Assisting the police with their inquiries.' The more you 'assist' us, the more we'll know. The telephone is at your entire disposition, *mon cher*. Entirely yours."

Less than reassured, I repair to my rather luxurious tent, complete with mosquito-netted canopied bed and private bathroom. Don't they, in these parts, call the toilet a "thunder-box?" It certainly produces a roar of cascading water when flushed. Also, of course, it makes a counter-clockwise whirlpool, since Zembeylia is below the Equator.

I return to the lodge, where I'm served a good lunch at a solitary table. The condemned man and tour-pariah eats hearty.

I go back to my tent to get on the phone. Sure, M'Bazi's men will be listening to every word and whatever I say will be used against me. But what can I do but try to get help?

Suzanne. Due overnight in New York for her ridiculous TV talk show led by that pompous fat-faced man who hardly lets anyone else speak before sounding off with his opinions. He styles them "prophecies."

She admits it's hot air, not even her hot air; but persists in having faith about her presence opening a door to prime time. She's sure she'll get noticed by talent scouts, if ever she says more than three consecutive words. Delusional, as far as I'm concerned. Her purpose on the show seems the same as the plastic potted plants placed near the Big Man's chair. Pure *décor*.

At least the delusion keeps her coming to New York.

By my watch, 2:40 P.M., with the East Coast eight hours earlier. At 6:40 A.M? Should still be in her Washington apartment catching up on beauty sleep. Unless, she's found another man to— God! Sickening! Don't want to know!

After a lot of clicking and waiting, she's on the line. Sounding sleepy and irritable. In condensed form I fill her in.

"Well, did you?"

"Did I what?"

"Murder the woman. You told me she was impossible and I know you lust for her sister. Don't try to deny it. I could hear it in your voice when you spoke—"

"For Chrissakes, Suzanne. I'm a suspect in a murder case. I may be arrested, tried, electrocuted, gassed, hanged!"

"*Guillotined.* French tradition, remember?"

"You've got to help me." Pause on the line. "Of course I didn't do it. You really think I'm a murderer?"

"Remember that execution we went to in France? I promise to come to yours. With a camera crew and—"

I bang down the phone. Godammit to hell! I'd been a fool ever to think....

I throw back the netting, lie on the bed. Betrayal! Jezebel! The phone rings.

"All right, I'm sorry," says Suzanne. "I have lots of resentment over your lifestyle. Your irresponsible, intellectually betraying, financially ridiculous lifestyle. Lots of resentment! And it comes out in funny ways. What do you need?"

"I need you to be the investigative reporter. Murders don't just happen, they have backgrounds. This background has to be at least partly in New York. Find out about Helen Farrar, who, what, why, where. Get Rahel, even Schulz involved. They can help their boss beat a murder rap. We've got to understand what's going on. And most of all, who the hell benefits? Can you do it? I mean this really may be life-or-death. No kidding!"

"'The Fifty-Ninth Street Irregulars.' Like Sherlock's Baker Street ones?"

"Yeah, exactly. With you sifting, analyzing, using your *paparazza* experience to get at the real honest-to-God truth. And prove it!"

"Background's one thing but the murder is your end. And the missing diamond? Someone over there's going to profit. Surely, it's up to you to find clues."

"I'm trying my damnedest, believe me. Please Suzanne!"

"Linc, you don't have to beg. Of course."

I let out a sigh, feeling suddenly weary. "Thanks."

"I'll be in touch. They owe me vacation days at *The New Republic*. And, after all, if there's a story it'll be exclusive."

"Yeah, we can do a joint byline and maybe—"

"No way! I'm the reporter, you're the travel agent. And murder suspect. Guess I'll hold things until you're chopped, then go with: *Wrongful Execution–True Story Revealed!* Only kidding. I'll call as soon as I have something. Be good, or at least stay out of more trouble." She hangs up.

Oy veh! is all I can think. I stretch back on the bed, then jump up, go to a table in the clearing outside my tent, sit on a wooden chair there.

I did think to bring my Olivetti portable typewriter. I set up this light, compact, eminently practical machine that fits so easily in my tote bag. With a pack of paper I've also brought along, I start pounding away on the keyboard, creating a detailed chronology of all that has happened. Maybe it will help reveal the truth. At least I can phone reports back to Suzanne, fill her in on happenings here.

About an hour later, one of the clipboard women appears and tells me it's time to see M'Bazi.

Chapter 16: A Deal Proposed
X'Zilancado Game Lodge, Thursday Afternoon, December 17

The reading lounge is a comfortable medium-size room with mahogany paneled walls and leather-padded double doors, to shut out noise from the lodge's nearby bar.

Colonel-Detective M'Bazi sits behind a gilded imitation Louis XV writing desk that looks too dainty for the room, or to accommodate his tall frame. He rises when I enter and once again gives me a not unfriendly nod. I feel like an animal being lured into a cage, or a dog into an elevator. I resolve to resist as if I have four feet, instead of my vulnerable two. Splay them, tug back on the leash. "C'mon, Roscoe, ol' pooch, into the elevator. For your own good." Like Hell!

I decide on the General Patton defense: attack first. "How come you speak such good English?" I demand. "Or I should say colloquial American."

M'Bazi sits back down, stretching his legs to the side of the desk. "My mother was Haitian, my father of the M'Bele tribe. After my father, died, my mother settled in New York City, Queens to be exact. So I went over to finish my studies there instead of to Paris, where most of our senior bureaucrats-to-be and aspiring politicians go. You've heard of the John Jay College of Criminal Justice in New York? I graduated and for eight years worked as a Manhattan cop. Made Lieutenant, later Captain Of Detectives before returning here to Zembeylia. So, I come by my English honestly." He leans forward. *"Mais on me dit, Monsieur, que vous connaissez le français*–They tell me you speak French. How so?"

"Well, I studied at the Sorbonne, spent many years in Paris as a reporter. Was married to a Frenchwoman. Not anymore."

M'Bazi strokes his chin. He reaches into a folder lying on the desk, pulls out a rumpled paper. "In Madame Briac's affairs we found this letter fragment. Written in French, her language. The instructions were to burn it but she disobeyed. It's signed *Gardiens de la Sainte Foi*, which to me translates as 'Keepers of the Holy Faith.'" His tone hardens. "When did you write it?"

"Here we go again. I don't know what you're talking about." I hold out my hand. "Let's see."

M'Bazi holds the letter back. "I'm sure you remember the contents. Funny thing, just before she died, Madame Briac kept murmuring the same word: *Pierre. Pierre.* And then *Pierre d'Or...Pierre d'Or.* Now, how should we translate that?"

"Look here! I deeply resent–"

M'Bazi ignores my expostulations. *"Pierre,* in English is, of course, 'Stone'. And then we have *d'Or,.* meaning 'of gold.' Wouldn't you say? Thus, we arrive at the strange phrase 'Stone-of-gold.' Now what could that possibly signify? My, my, such mystifications! 'Stone-of-Gold?' Can we think of something–or, yes, someone–we could designate as Stonegold?" He snaps his fingers. "I've got it, my dear Watson! Translate French word sequence into English sequence and what have we? Why, none other than Goldstone! Could she have been trying to say 'Goldstone.' in French, but too far gone to pronounce the whole word? It's what we of the police conclude." He rises from his seat, goes over to a wall phone, lifts the receiver, speaks some words, then turns back. "Look, fella, I've ordered us coffee and some good French brandy. You like *armagnac?* I love the stuff, the best sits in your throat nice and warming. We'll drink up while you give me your full confession. Tell me what gives, what this machination's all about. I'll do my very best to get you off with life. You can all but forget the guillotine. Deal?"

He pauses. "By the way, when I say life I mean only eighteen or so years. And *presto!* You're out on good behavior. The national prison at Fulumbane isn't half bad. Oh, not as nice as what you're used to," he waves his hand around the room, "all this luxury living. But for a jail, absolutely A-1. Almost better than *The Tombs* in New York, I can tell you."

My fingers and toes feel icy, my mouth stiff. "Confess to what I didn't do?" I can hardly get out the words. "Go to jail for...for..."

M'Bazi gives a big sigh. "I see you're going to be difficult. I took you for smarter than you are. Do you really want me as an enemy? Egging on the prosecution to demand death, instead of allowing for, even urging attenuating circumstances? Arranging, while you await the blade, to have you put in Disciplinary Camp One, a hellhole like you wouldn't believe?" He pauses before saying softly, "That's the other side of the coin, fella. Make my life hard, I make yours a living Hell. *N'est-ce-pas*, Mister Murderer?"

"I want a lawyer."

M'Bazi laughs, rumbling like Zeus in one of his testier moods, like when he swallowed his ladyfriend, Metis. "We'll get you the best, the most ruinously expensive lawyer in all Zembeylia. Won't help you a bit, But he'll send you a bill…" The Colonel-Detective's big hands spread up-and-down, illustrating a bill a thousand miles long.

"I'll take the coffee and the drink," I say. "Need 'em. But I didn't do it, I swear to you I didn't. I have no motive, no reason. And how could I have done it anyway?"

"We believe that Madame Briac's so-called 'Holy Faith Guardian'–what a joke! Damn nasty joke that gets my blood boiling–slipped her a pill or liquid, some sort of delayed action poison, either on the train or at the X'Ziromeu City station. We don't know the details yet but we will."

"What about the murder in the sleeping cabin? How could I have done that, since it was locked on all sides?"

M'Bazi stares me in the eyes. "That's what I want you to tell me."

I shrug. "I simply didn't do it, I wasn't there. So I can't tell you, can I? And you can't prove a damned thing."

"Not yet. But it happened, therefore it can be unraveled."

"You won't get too far if you go for solutions, apparent though they may be, that have no sense or logic to them. Unless, of course, what you really want to do is hang someone, just anyone, innocent or guilty, for the credit of solving your case."

"*Guillotine, mon cher.* In Zembeylia we *guillotine.* Time-honored method of dealing with murderers here, *à la française.* Anyway, I have this crazy respect for truth and won't be satisfied by convicting any person, male-female, horse or hyena we can pin these crimes on. But I remind you that the theft of a multimillion dollar diamond makes a helluva lot of sense from where I sit. As do you as murderer-thief, since you and the victim were the sole occupants of Sleeping Car B at the time of her death. And that is a fact we've already proven beyond the shadow of a doubt, as the saying goes. *N'est-ce pas?*"

Coffee and *armagnac* arrive. M'Bazi signs the bill. I nod my thanks. When the waiter leaves, I raise my snifter of *armagnac.* "Just

144

for fun, why don't you pretend you don't think you know who the killer is and start from scratch? Step-by-step-by-step from the beginning. Investigate me, but also everybody else. Without prejudice. You may stumble on, or deduce, the real affair. I'll help any way I can."

"That, of course, is what we're doing," says M'Bazi. "You're not arrested, just close, very close. No one else is. I'll give you rope, fella. Find me a better candidate and I'll be more than happy to apologize for my mistake. Fair enough?" He lifts his *armagnac*. "To solutions." He tosses back the drink as though it's vodka, then takes a gulp of coffee.

Before sipping this fine variation of French brandy I say, "I'll drink to truth. To truthful solutions, not just any old solution that gets you cops off the hook with a fast arrest. To truth. And it will proclaim my innocence!"

We leave it at that.

Chapter 17: A Warning Snarl
X'Zilancado Game Reserve, Thursday, December 17
Late Afternoon to Friday, Early Morning, December 18

When I get back to my tent, the telephone is ringing. Suzanne? No, Sheila's voice, husky and seductive. "Please, I'm so upset." A pause. Then, "Come to me now. Tent Nine."

Blood pounding in my ears, stomach cramped with guilt, I hurry to Tent Nine.

Twice as big as my own. Sheila's bed is a king-sized four poster, with mosquito-netting forming a canopy that gracefully cascades down to surround the sleeper. The netting is up. Decorously, curvaceously she lies upon the bed's leopard skin cover. A harem princess!

Her hand stretches out to grip mine. "Tell me you didn't do it. Tell me you didn't murder my stepsister." Tears start from her eyes; she drops my hand to hold out both of hers in supplication.

I sit on the bed, not quite daring, wanting–not wanting to put my arms around her. "Of course, I didn't. As I told those crazy policemen. I mean, why would I?"

"It doesn't make any sense. Does it? But then how? I can't make head or tail…Poor Helen, why did she have to die?"

I shake my head…"I'll do everything I can to find the truth. I'll help any way you wish me to." I lean towards her. Ah, the perfume. "Just say the word, I'm yours to command."

She throws her arms around me, buries her face in my shoulder. Her body shakes with sobs.

Over the intercom an electronic gong sounds, summoning guests to the late-afternoon game drive. "I'm too upset to go," she murmurs into my shoulder.

"I'll stay with you," I whisper. Zebras, elephants, lions, the Call of Africa? Suzanne? What are they versus this sexual imperative?

"No, no!" She shakes her head. "You must be with the others, talk to them, find out everything you can, some sign, some clue We've got to get to the bottom of this and clear your name." She blinks her eyes. When all this is over…"

Suzanne. How can I even think…? I rise from the bed, muttering the line I used too many times in bachelor days about parting being sweet sorrow. And leave.

Two open Land Rovers are lined up on the circular drive by the lodge. Seven passenger seats come in tiers: two next to the driver, two on a raised second row bench, two on a bench a step higher, then a single seat on a highest step, fourth level in back of the others.

Camera at the ready, I make for this top. "Best seat in the house," I say to Southgate and D'Alessandro, who sit directly in front of me. I look down over everybody's head, spot a rifle clamped to the dashboard in front of the empty driver's seat.

Mike, appearing subdued, a black armband around the upper left sleeve of his khaki shirt–climbs into the front. He slumps over the dashboard, hand covering eyes. The Jamiesons take the second row. The remainder of our group, Sheila excepted, board the other vehicle.

Finally the driver gets in, takes the wheel and off we go with the second Land Rover leading, then stopping to open the gate at the camp's fenced boundary. Our vehicle drives through, driver halting us to close the gate again. The two Land Rovers now head in opposite directions straight into the *bundu*, as Rhodesian bush-colonials of the last generation called the vast, if these days shrinking, African wilderness.

We crash and bump through forest thorn tangles and across meadow clearings. The two drivers communicate by radio-telephone. In the clearings are springbok, zebras, giraffes. The animals pay us little attention.

Our driver, a young, clean-cut looking M'Bélé, tells us he's a graduate student of Animal Ethology, getting his PhD at a university in Kenya. He comments that the animals here are so used to these vehicles tht they consider them part of the natural fauna. "Just another beast and a non-threatening one. Except for elephants; they take Land Rovers as rivals and don't like us at all." His name, he says, is M'Zeki. "You English speakers can call me Zeke."

We come to a meadow. At its edge under a tree are cheetahs: a mother with three cubs. The animals don't stir as the vehicle draws close and stops. Much clicking of photo equipment.

"This, of course, means the animals' behavior is perverted by the

presence of humans," D'Alessandro speaks in low tones. "Under such conditions, how can you claim to study the creatures in their natural habitat?"

"We can't totally," responds Zeke in excellent British English. "We intrude as little as possible. After all, studying anything means some intrusion. We're rather successful keeping our interference with animal life to a minimum."

Just then, the mother cheetah stands up, sniffs the air, head twitching slightly as she searches the tall grass before her. She must spot a movement, imperceptible to us watchers. Suddenly she whizzes through the meadow, a streak of yellow.

Mike straightens. "By God! Look at her go!" he exclaims. "Fastest land animal in the world, I've read. What's she after?"

"Something small," says Zeke. "A hyrax or the mini-antelope we call dik-dik. Maybe even a gerenuk, although it's big enough that we'd probably see the whole herd of them; they hunt in groups."

Now the cubs race after Mom, one of them stumbling and falling, stumbling and falling, its right hind leg bloodstained, scabby, curled under the body.

"See how thin it is?" says Zeke pointing. "Starving to death. The mother won't let it feed until she and her other cubs have their fill. Soon dead."

"Medical facilities?" asks Malvina Southgate indignantly. "Don't you have vets? An animal clinic? Can't you call for help on that radio of yours?"

"It would be interfering with nature in a big way," Zeke explains, a little glibly it seems to me. "Exactly what Monsieur," he nods towards D'Alessandro, "was objecting to."

"But it's so cruel," Southgate responds. "Surely they could splint that leg, fatten the animal up. Release it when fit. Like in the old television series *Daktari,* about an African bush doctor who cares for the animals."

"Law of the jungle, Madame. Survival of the fittest." Zeke shrugs, gallic style. "The way of nature is the way we leave it, to the best of our ability." He re-starts the engine, we drive on.

Crackles over the radiophone. Zeke bends to his receiver, listens intently, then swings the Land Rover in a semicircle, heading for a line of trees. "Lions," he says. "We'll see if we can get close."

Lions! I feel a tingle of excitement. Dream of the bush come true!

The Land Rover turns straight into thorn thickets, plowing through what looks like an impenetrable gray-green wall. We arrive at a small clearing. Parked on its opposite side is the other Land Rover with the rest of our group aboard.

Once more, Zeke kills the engine. He puts finger to lips, points towards a wide clump of undergrowth. "In there, a male, a female and cubs," he whispers "Be very quiet."

We hear a companionable *basso* grunt, probably the male. After a time, rustlings. The lioness emerges, two cubs trot behind her. I stand up, aim my camera.

"Pour l'amour de Dieu!" silently mouths Zeke. He motions with his hand indicating I should sit. Fast!

The lioness stops, gives the Land Rover a sideways glance, emits a snarl, sniffs the air. And stalks on. Zeke, looking as gray as his dark skin allows, waits a couple of minutes, then turns on me.

"Do you realize," he asks, "how close you came to getting us mauled?" He shakes his head. "One more sound and she would have been on us, jumping onto one of us, raking us all with those claws. She'd have taken us out before I even could grab my weapon. Not one of us would have escaped."

"I–I'm sorry," I mumble. "I didn't—"

"A lioness with cubs is merciless. Ah," he adds without lowering his voice, "here's the male."

More rustling and a magnificently-maned animal emerges from the hideaway. Preening himself, shoulder muscles rippling, he marches around the Land Rover.

"Er, kin we take pitchas?" whispers Sherman Jamieson.

"Certainly, Monsieur," Zeke speaks in a normal voice. "Stand up if you like. He won't do any harm."

149

As if on cue, the lion stops, faces our Land Rover, emits if not a mighty roar at least a respectable one. Then he stalks off to the other vehicle for a repeat performance.

As we approach the camp gate, back on a dirt path-like road leading to the airport, half a mile away at the South African border, Zeke stops our vehicle some yards from a mountainous elephant. Its tusks, like curved scimitars, sweep inward almost meeting before the face. The beast stands square in the road, reaching with its trunk into bordering trees. With a snap a branch comes away. It tucks the branch into its jaws, tongue rasping off leaves.

"That's old M'Kawi-X'Zamba," Again Zeke speaks in a near whisper. "A male bull. We'll wait until he's done."

After several minutes, Bitsy asks, "Why not shoo him away with the horn? I want to get back, have a bath before dinner."

"No, Madame. We must wait."

A few more minutes and her husband says, "Boy, we'all ain't accomplishin' nuttin'. Whyn't you stawt up, toot youwah horn, git him outta heah?"

Zeke shakes his head. "As I said, elephants, especially this bull, don't like Land Rovers. They consider themselves kings of the bush and see our vehicles as rivals, since for them lions are too small to count. If we challenge him, he'll get very angry. Best to wait. He'll move in awhile."

"We have to sit here while he holds us prisoner?" sniffs Southgate. "I thought humans were boss. Mrs. Jamieson and I need to get to our rooms."

Again Zeke gives his French-inherited shrug. Cautiously he restarts the engine, inches the Land Rover forward. M'Kawi-X'Zamba stops munching, turns toward our vehicle, head lowered, ears stretched out like sails, trunk swaying side-to-side.

Zeke stops the Land Rover, slowly backs away. The elephant gives a satisfied rumble. He stands for a moment, then, appearing to my imagination like some great, gray vessel sailing majestically down a seaway, ambles off the road into the bush.

"You see," says Zeke. "You have to show him he's big boss. Then he'll be generous and let you by."

On the way to my tent, I stop short, hearing terrible screeches followed by shouts. I run toward the noise, coming from a tent that bears the number 7.

The sergeant sprints ahead of me. I stand at the door-flaps, shocked at what I see. Clothes, torn, scattered all around; feathers from ripped pillows floating in the air, coming down like snow. Face cream jars smashed, contents gobbed onto white Berber carpet that covers the tent's flooring; powders dumped all over the dressing table, jewelry sparkling from the room's every corner, perfume bottles rolling on the floor, shaving cream and toothpaste from tubes squirted on the bedspread, even on the canopy of mosquito-netting.

A policeman with Corporal's stripes shoves me aside, gesturing I should stand away from the tent by a clump of trees.

The colonel comes loping up the walkway.

"I didn't do this," I shout to get the man's attention. "I was on a game drive. You can't frame me with this one."

He dismisses this with a gesture. With another gesture, the police corporal indicates I should shove off.

Dinner on what was supposed to be our only night here—until the murder and diamond theft—is around a bonfire. We sit in a circle of tables. I note that Bitsy Jamieson looks as though she's been crying: no make-up, red-eyed. And still in her safari clothes. Unlike her, not to have changed for dinner. Jamieson, too, looks unkempt, his expression grim.

Colonel M'Bazi enters the dining area, a large enclosure lined by trees, its perimeter a tall wooden picket fence. He's accompanied by a smallish man in a business suit.

The man holds up his hand. "Ladies and gentlemen," he says in good English, "I am Pierre M'Falumba, the manager here. We had a bit of trouble this afternoon because of an electricity breakdown in the barrier that surrounds our tented camp. A gang of baboons managed to penetrate the compound. One tent, whose flap was left unbuttoned, got broken into and a mess was made. Fortunately, our staff quickly became aware of the invasion. They shooed the baboons away before the animals caused too much damage, except to some bed pillows and the tent itself. Clothing, it is true, was thrown about and some torn. A few pieces of costume jewelry were also scattered. These items have all been recovered and returned to their owner. We regret that three cosmetic jars were smashed. The Zemba Royal Corporation will endeavor to replace these and the damaged clothing or pay appropriate compensation, at the earliest possible time. We're sincerely sorry for this occurrence, which has never happened before. We particularly apologize to Mr. and Mrs. Jamieson for the inconvenience caused. We are moving you to a fresh tent."

"Y'all l'be a-hearin' fum me, I kin promise you thet. Them baboons should be esterminated!" Jamieson glowers under his ten gallon. His wife, nodding fiercely, puts her hand on his arm.

"Please understand, ladies and gentlemen," says the manager, his forehead glistening with sweat, "when one comes to see the wild animals, it is perhaps understandable that they, the wild animals, are also curious to see their visitors and to experience, in turn, how these strange creatures called human tourists choose to live. This is not to excuse the deficiency in security, which we are correcting as I speak. But it is to remind you that circumstances here in the protected animal reserve of the X'Ziloncado Basin are exceptional."

"Damn nig…natives," Jamieson mutters "Cain't git nuttin' raaght."

We dine on barbecued springbok, filet of zebra and, yes, elephant brochettes.

"My God!" exclaims Giorgio D'Alessandro, "to eat the very animals we have come so far to see. There's something wrong about this."

"Not so," says Zeke, who acts as spokesperson for his fellow guides. "If we don't from time to time 'cull' the populations you're chewing on, they'd overwhelm the limited space we have for them, given the spread of human settlements and farmland."

"But you've got a reserve big as three small states of the United States," says D'Alessandro.

Zeke nods. "An elephant herd needs tremendous space. Too many elephants will destroy a habitat, upset the ecological balance and starve the other animals quicker than you would believe possible. In five years we'd no longer have a balanced population, due to rotting trees, decimated landscapes. We must keep elephants to a certain number or other whole species will disappear. As for zebras and springbok, they're also an ecological danger because of numbers. So eat up and consider you're doing a good deed."

Of the three meats, I find zebra and springbok stringy, tasteless. Reluctantly, I have to admit that elephant shish-kebab, marinated and barbecued, is delicious. One of the sweetest, most tender, tastiest meats I've ever had. Still, I hate the idea of shooting down magnificent, intelligent, fundamentally decent beasts like old M'Kawi-X'Zamba, who stepped aside to let us pass once his authority was acknowledged.

The evening ends in music. Several of the guides play African instruments, one, a wooden box with metal keys I recognize as a *Marimba*. Another is a flute-like object. Zeke has an electric guitar, complete with boom-box.

The sing-along goes from African chants to French songs to American ones like Bob Dillon's "Blowin' In The Wind." The sergeant-with-the-unpronounceable-name proves to be a harmonica virtuoso having a flair for Caribbean numbers, notably Harry Belafonte's "Matilda," about the woman who *take all me money and run Venezuela.*

He also plays a Calypso song about a man plotting revenge because his friend, Johnny, came to dinner, partaking of the man's hospitality and then made off with the guy's wife. Detective-Colonel M'Bazi belts out the words in a ringing baritone.

The evening's final song does nothing to reassure me. M'Bazi again, looking unwaveringly in my direction, sings, with great conviction, Sinatra's "I Did it My Way."

Like a hyena chased from dead meat by bigger marauders, I slink to my tent, stomach in knots. Bone tired, too, after this long, over-eventful day.

What a fool I'd made of myself with the lioness. Why couldn't I learn to think first and act in consequence instead of always vice-versa? An Epimethean, that's what I am. His brother, Prometheus, stealer of fire, defier of the gods, sees things before they happen. Poor Epimetheus has wisdom by hindsight. So he eggs on his girlfriend Pandora to open that damned box. "Go ahead," he urges when she hesitates. "Let's see what's inside." Welcome malaria, leprosy, cancer, plague syphilis, war, pestilence, *M'zu-m'zu*, the works. Good ol' Epimetheus!

I lie on my bed, put out the light, mentally determined to review the whole miserable business of Helen's death and my implication in it. Instead, I listen to the rustle of animals, the moan of a hyena, the grunts carried on still air of unnamed beasts. And somewhere, out there in the *bundu*, under a scimitar of Moon, the muted roar of a nearby lion. My eyes close…

The ringing phone startles me awake. I scrabble for it, other hand reaching for the night-table lamp. "Yes?" I say. "Yes?"

"I need you." Sheila's voice, low and husky.

Jeezus! What to do? I look at the bedside clock. 2:05 A.M? My God! Yes, but…

"Need you. Now."

"Be right there," I say.

Chapter 18: Steamy Sessions
X'Ziloncado Camp, Friday, December 19, 2 A.M.
& New York, Thursday, 6 P.M. December 18

To enter, or not to? Even here in the African night redolent of jungle fragrances I think I can sniff the lascivious perfume emanating from Sheila's tent, drawing me in. I stretch out my hand for the flap–

"*Goldstone! How can you?*" Suzanne's voice.

Furtively, guiltily, hand returns to side.

"*So far away,*" my own inner voice. "*How will she know?*"

"*It's you who will know,*" persists Suzanne. "*And I will sense your guilt.*"

"*To possess this luscious, envelopingly sensual...*" The other eight thousand miles distant..."*Come on, man. Be a man!*"

"*A manly man resists temptation. Loyal and true to his helpmeet, his life's love.*"

"*Oh, yeah? My denigrator, saying my only purpose in her life is to be Thursday's amusement.*" God, that rankles! Her fault, damn it! Would I be attracted elsewhere, if...?

I step forward, throw open the tent flap, ready to be received in shadowy, sensual, conscience-numbing embrace...

Center light on. Harshly shining. Sheila, in a black-net negligee sprawls backward across her bed, head and shoulders hanging over the far side.

I rush to her, kneel, gently lift her onto the pillows. Her mouth is a grimace, her lips blue. A smell of bitter almonds. My God! Cyanide?

"Sheila," I say softly. Her eyelids flutter. Alive! I take her wrist, feel for a pulse.

The sergeant-with-the-unpronounceable-name bursts into the tent. "*Voilà!*" he cries.

Two police follow. Quickly, the sergeant takes over at the bed, sniffs Sheila's blue lips. "Get the nurse. Get the Colonel-Detective," he shouts to his cohorts. "You!" He points at me. "Away from her! Over there in the corner! Don't move!"

The sergeant's men scurry off.

Three minutes later a Land Rover screeches to a halt on the lawn outside. A gray-haired Indian woman in her bathrobe and Detective M'Bazi enter. They rush to Sheila. Quickly the woman checks for vital signs.

"Pulse strong," she says in French. "We need to pump her out at the infirmary. Not a moment to lose!"

Sheila groans, suddenly vomits, stench of vomit overpowering the almond smell, also the lingering fumes of *Il Gattopardo*.

"Good," says the nurse. "Elimination is ground gained." Reaching into her robe pocket she brings out a large gauze pad, wipes her patient's mouth. She then motions the men to lift Sheila gently and carry her to the vehicle. Through the open flap I see them lay her on a three-seat bench of the Land Rover's second row. The nurse clambers in beside her, puts Sheila's head on her lap. The sergeant takes the driver's seat. Engine roaring, they lurch across the grass.

M'Bazi reaches down to replace the phone receiver from the floor back onto its hook. He motions me outside, away from vomit stench. "So the murderer has struck a third time," he says pulling out a cigarette packet and lighting one. He doesn't offer a smoke. "You get your jollies bumping people off, or what?"

I clear my throat. Hard to talk. "You won't believe I'm a bystander—"

"Some bystander!" interrupts the Colonel-Detective. "Where you stand, the bodies tumble."

"But I—what can I say? Not my fault!"

"You mean you're sort of a Typhoid Mary, unwitting carrier of death? That's what you want us to think?"

I find myself getting angry. "I don't give a good goddamn what you think!" I pass a hand over my face. "Well, I guess I do, since you can throw me in jail."

"Oh, I can do better than that," rumbles M'Bazi. "Have you forgotten *Madame Guillotine?*"

"Look," I say, "let's be logical for once. Do you really believe I'm so stupid as to keep putting myself into compromising situations with corpses? Doesn't it make more sense to think someone wants to make me a goat?"

"Why were you in that tent?"

"She called me on the phone. Said 'Come to me.' I shouldn't have, but I did."

"You're lovers?"

I shake my head. "There's a woman at home. But I'm attracted to Sheila. When she called me in the middle of the night, I thought... "

"And when she refused your advances, you poured cyanide down her throat."

"Hell, no! I...I'm not the type to hurt a fly."

"For flies you have compassion, it's just people get you riled." M'Bazi takes a long puff of his cigarette making the end glow fiercely. "I'm confining you to your tent. After we search it, of course. You'll be under guard, your meals will be served there. House arrest."

"Can I telephone?"

"I told you, phone all you like. On your nickel. But save your money. You may need that expensive lawyer after all." He snaps his fingers, motions for one of his policemen to follow. The three of us walk across the lawn to my tent.

The sergeant is already there with his two men. Taking the place apart.

"Talk of *déjà vu*," I mutter, seeing my possessions dumped all over the bed and floor.

"Duty is duty," says M'Bazi.

Then a corporal bends down, snaps an electronic bracelet on my ankle. It beeps.

"Oh, my God!" You're making me into some sort of slave."

157

"White slavery." M'Bazi gives a sour grin.

The corporal withdraws to the edge of my tent's allotted terrain.

From a canvas bag he takes out two steel stakes with a wire between them, pulls a large hammer from the bag, starts tapping the stakes into the earth.

Holding another small plastic bag, the sergeant approaches his chief. *"Très intéressant,"* he says. "I have put some very significant items here in this bag. Discovered under his shirts." He hands the bag over.

"Monsieur Goldstone," snaps M'Bazi in military tone, "is confined to his tent and immediate outside area. The ankle-bracelet will let us know if he violates this condition of non-incarceration into Disciplinary Camp One, a not desirable alternative. His meals are to be served here. Put a one man around-the-clock guard on him." The colonel pauses. "Oh, yes. He can use his telephone. And, Sergeant, leave him be. Only I will question him."

"A vos ordres, mon Colonel." The sergeant salutes, turns on his heel and is about to leave when a cop, whom I don't recognize, bursts through the flap opening. "Sir! Sir!" he shouts at M'Bazi. "Come quick! Another killing!"

The policemen all run out. I start to follow, get to the edge of my little compound and the ankle bracelet, flashing red, lets out ear-piercing whistles. "Oh, my Lord!" I groan and turn back to the tent to sit on the bed. "Where will it end?"

The phone rings. I snatch it up. Suzanne's voice. "What in hell's name have you been up to?" she shouts across the Atlantic, the Equator and the African continent. "Now you've gone and gotten ME accused of committing murder!"

PART FOUR:
MURDER, SHE SAYS

U. S. A.–Zembeylia, Small Hours Thursday, December 17
to Friday Early Morning And Later, December 18

"'Murder', she says…
'Is that the way to make love?'"
~ Old time popular song

Chapter 19: "O Sheep of State!
New York, NY and Zembeylia, Thursday, December 17
to Friday Morning, December 18

That damn Goldstone! Suzanne grinds her teeth. Whatever has she seen in him? All he's brought her over their years together is anguish, trouble and more anguish. A fundamentally irresponsible person. Oh, with great bouts of pseudo-responsibility that only serve to attach his fortunes to disaster. A good newsman, because a rolling stone without anchor, just a peeker of insatiable curiosity. A socio-politico-*voyeur* into other people's lives. And totally lacking in luck; which negative attributes, she has to admit, go hand in hand with a respect for telling things like they are.

So what does he do with his one talent? Throws it in the garbage can for a business he knows nothing about and for which he has less than no capacity. As a businessman, Suzanne has an abiding sense that Goldstone is King Midas inside out. He touches gold, it doesn't even turn to stone. Only dust!

"And now," she shouts at him over the phone, "You've gotten me suspected of murdering a man I never even heard of until this evening, when the police came to my door!" She takes a long swig of tea laced with Drambuie. Crazy drink, she knows. A concession to her life's current craziness.

"Explain!" Goldstone shouts back through the 8,000 miles. "For God's sakes, explain!" Over the distance, his shout sounds tinny.

"Who the hell is Barry Mondran?" retorts Suzannne. "As his murderess, I demand to know!"

"Mondran dead?" Goldstone's voice comes over shocked, taken aback.

Et tu, Mondran? Suzanne thinks. And continues with "I'm supposed to have fed him marijuana cigarettes that really were angel dust laced with some poison called Chloramine-T."

"Jesus! You?" The voice still sounds taken aback, as if she, Suzanne, could be the cause of all his troubles? No, just her normal paranoia sounding off. She decides on a reprimand.

"Not funny, Goldstone. Not funny! I never told you about last Friday. Felt you were too idiot-busy transmuting into fake 'Doctor Livingstone-I-Presume,' to give any attention to a vicious practical joke played on your supposed love. What do you think I am?" she shouts. "A piece of furniture to be moved around at whim?"

"*Du calme,* Honey. *Du calme,*" comes the voice, by implication blaming her again. A murderess should at least keep her cool when confronted. "Why are you ranting, anyway? I've got plenty of troubles here. People dying like flies."

"You should all die, after what you put me through!" She hears Goldstone take a long breath.

"You'd better explain," he says.

"Okay, listen to this! Last Friday morning in New York, just after you left the apartment for work, I get a call. A man claiming he's none other than Hector Weintraub phoning from Los Angeles. You know who he is? Only Johnny Carson's scheduling manager, that's all. Says he wants me to fly out right then and there to be on that night's show, along with this year's Pulitzer prize winners. Carson has chosen me as a rising star of the media, this man tells me." Suzanne brushes a fist across her eyes, clearing away tears. "You can imagine how thrilled I was. I called my office in D.C., rearranged my life, raced out to Kennedy Airport, grabbed the first nonstop for L.A. and showed up at Carson's office on the dot of five P.M., their time."

"You should've called me," says Goldstone long-distance, probably isolated from a radio or television. "I'd have loved watching you give Johnny Carson hell. Or possibly vice-versa."

"There wasn't any show!" Suzanne's voice rises to a wail. "That's what I'm trying to tell you. Some lousy pervert's idea of a joke. You, maybe?"

"Suzanne! You know better." The voice sounds reproving.

"I go rushing in there full of excitement about my Big Break. And they've never even heard of me. Hector Weintraub, they say, is in Amsterdam. They were very polite but you could tell they thought I was some nutcase off the street. I slunk away, took the red-eye back to D.C."

"No wonder you were so grumpy when I called from the airport in New York to say goodbye."

"At least then," says Suzanne, "I didn't connect you with my troubles. This evening, an hour ago, two detectives show up at my door here in New York. They start grilling me about Barry Mondran, deceased. Not naturally deceased, mind you. Bumped off by a poison-dipped pot smoke from an L.A. package. With my name as sender!"

"Oh my God!"

"Well, I know he's the husband of that woman who's half the reason you're on your trip–"

"Not true! She may be dead as well. From cyanide!"

"You *have* gotten yourself into a mess, haven't you? And me with it."

"Suzanne, you've got to investigate, as I said. Sooner than soon. Then tell me everything so I can put the pieces together. They have me under tent arrest, but I can communicate and I can still think. Get me information. And for God's sake utilize Rahel and Schulz. Make 'em pull as a team for once."

She gulps Drambuie. "I'm way ahead of you. As soon as I got the police off my neck, anyway temporarily, since they've sort of bought my story of being totally unconnected with this Mondran character–except for you, of course–I called Rahel. She's heading out to L.A. in the morning to try and find out how I'm involved in your dung heap. She'll be back next morning, our time. Then we may learn what my alleged role is all about."

"You're paying for her, I hope? Rahel doesn't have much money." Goldstone sounds worried; probably wondering if he'll end up having to foot Rahel's bill.

"I'm sure her pay's mingy, working for you. Don't worry, it's mostly for free, thanks to her travel privileges. I'm picking up the rest. I just couldn't go back there myself. Too damn painful having those Carson people look at me as if I'm a freak. Rahel was very nice about it. God, you're so lucky to have–"

"I know, I know," he interrupts; clearly doesn't want to suffer her next remark about Rahel being the only normal and efficient human-being at Shangri-La. Implying that her boss isn't normal, efficient or even a human-being. "So you've got Schulz holding down the store on his own, eh?"

Suzanne detects a shudder in Goldstone's voice. "Yeah, Schulz. I don't know what I can do with him. He's so...so fundamentally the sort of helper you'd choose to–"

"I'd appreciate your not knocking my carefully-selected personnel," Goldstone sounds defensive. "His client, Amahdi, is our best customer. I'm very grateful to Schulz."

Suzanne lets a significant pause go by before saying, reluctantly, "I suppose we're an unholy alliance, you, me, Rahel...even Schulz. My guess is you didn't murder anybody. I don't see you as a murderer, Goldstone. But then I never saw you as a travel agent."

"Oh, hell!" he says, exasperated. "Did you murder Mondran?"

"How in blazes can anybody think I've murdered somebody I don't even...Okay, okay. You didn't murder, I didn't murder, we're both pure as driven snow and I'll go to my lethal injection and you to your *guillotine* all fuzzy and warm inside 'cause we know we're innocent." She takes several deep breaths. "No way a desirable scenario. I'll call when I have something to tell." Before the trans-

164

ocean, trans-continental reply can come, she hangs up, pours herself another drink and reaches for a yellow pad.

The story behind the story is key. How to pry it out?

The phone rings at 5 A.M. Southgate again! How did he ever, Bhulliwah wonders, get mixed up with such an impossible individual?

He sits in his baby blue, Chinese silk pajamas–especially tailored for him in Shanghai–on the edge of his bed, listening with one ear to Southgate's telephonic tirade. With the other, he's hearing his wife complain of sleep-deprivation, thus his being emotionally cruel. She'll make him pay, he knows. Financially, through the nose, her one and only talent. Why in blazes does she need a psychoanalyst? You'd think he beat her or something, when all he's ever done is try to escape her eternal whinings and reproaches. Fifty dollars U.S. per hour and a fifty minute hour at that! A U.S. dollar a minute at an unfavorable exchange rate with MUL, for lying on a couch? What do they do on that couch, the fifty dollar pimp-shrink and the wife? His own sleep! Did any of these females consider him? He who was giving his strength and energies to national uplift, as well as to securing the financial future of his family? So that wifey dear could continue her voice lessons and *macramé* lessons and go on and on about needing a bigger house and a second butler, as well as that bloody shopping trip to, of all places, Beverly Hills! Paris no longer good enough for her?

"…and now this guy, Goldstone. The cops are doing their best to pin the murder on him, since politically it suits their goddamn boss, M'Bowé."

"Yes, dear Madame Southgate, yes. But couldn't all this wait until after breakf–"

"I want the pinning on Petroff or Chandler! Both of 'em, dammit! Bloody backstabbing bastards!" Southgate is shrieking again. "Sheila Mondran is out of the picture. She's gone and fallen

165

foul of the murderer's clutches, ha ha. Another ten points for our side!"

Did the woman think she was watching a tennis match?

"Trouble is," she goes on, "Petroff with the Ace-Fenster coalition and Guiterrez with his Cali drug lords will destroy us. What're you doing about it?"

"If you don't hang up on that bitch," hisses his wife, "I'm going to sue for divorce and it won't just make scandal. It'll bring a nice alimony!"

Surrounded by enemies! With his free hand, Bhulliwah takes a tissue from the night table, wipes his face. His stomach heaves.

"I'm telling you," Southgate's hoarse voice falls and rises, rises and falls, making him positively seasick. "This is our one and only golden chance. Utilize Helen Farrar's murder to bring down the régime. It's your window of opportunity for putting the X'Zambili People back in the saddle. Why, Tony, you could even be King!"

Agitated though he is, Bhulliwah deliciously shivers to hear out loud the unspoken thought always hovering in his mind. If that stupid undertaker's assistant could get the crown, why not he? A true ruler, with no puppet-master like M'Bowé behind the throne. He'd send M'Bowé to live with Baby Doc. In France, already? Didn't deserve so luxurious an exile. No, give him to the Chinese, admonishing that they provide a cold-water "maid's room" atop a twelve floor walkup building in the factory section of Hangchow. Then let anyone beware who presumes to defy Bhulliwah The Magnificent!

As the proud lion rules the jungle–lions' days, of course, are numbered, since trees would be eliminated and poppies planted–so, lionlike, he'll rule New X'Zambilia: a suitably revitalized name for the nation that hails him as savior. And he'll own lock, stock and ton after ton of joy-bringing powders.

"Oui, mon vieux. Très bien. Formidable, même–Yes, old man, Terrific, in fact." At 10 A.M., His Excellency Zecherias M'Bowé,

166

Minister of Security, Tourism and Culture listens to Colonel-Detective Félix M'Bazi's report from the X'Ziloncado Tented Camp. He hangs up the phone well pleased. He had doubts about the colonel-detective. Even when they were schoolmates, back in the days of French rule, he was always shocked by Félix's audacity in defying authority and his contempt for those, like himself, who preferred to work mole-like inside the existing order.

Too much the maverick, M'Bazi, with his independence of mind that was sure to have been encouraged by those years in the States. No reverence for the time-honored, well-regulated French approach to administrative goals, based unswervingly on the principle of hierarchy knowing best, the system being the system, the rules the rules and truth a flexible instrument to accomplish whatever was decreed from on high by those in command.

In sum, no waves. The colonel-detective, M'Bowé has always suspected, is potentially a wavemaker. Still and all, this time the man has accomplished excellent damage control. Hope for him yet. Might, in due course, send him to Paris for a little bureaucratic polishing. Disconcerting, Helen Farrar's murder. Tragic, of course. But more to the point, highly inconvenient at this delicate time, given the leverage it provides X'Zambilis and their so-called "Democratist Party" to raise hell in Parliament. Provoking even "His Royal Dimwit," the King, to ask questions.

In his penthouse suite at the Ministry–imposing mansarded structure on Fulumbane's Government Square, blood-red, since built of local stone–His Excellency sighs deeply, rings for a servant and orders a pot of coffee. Think of it! Helen Farrar, Zemba Royal Corporation's mainstay, its best money provider–as well as substantial potential feeder of his ever-hungry personal accounts in Liechtenstein, the Bahamas and Guernsey–so horribly bumped off. Provoking all sorts of reverberations emphatically unneeded! Especially now, with his ongoing highly delicate secret negotiations that promise to outstrip all earlier attempts at winning true wealth and power.

He gestures to the white-jacketed valet, who places a tray with its silver pot, its basket of croissants and porcelain cup with saucer on the right hand side of the desk.

Waving the man away, M'Bowé pours his own coffee. Very egalitarian. That's how he feels these days, an attitude the Americans encourage. Big they are on the trappings of equality, if not equality itself. A bit of back-slapping pseudo-democracy is a small price to pay for the millions they, through B.A.R.F. and the other international aid organizations, are supplying him. And, of course King M'Zumba. The two of them never neglect to throw a penny to the Zembeylian people. Trickle, trickle, trickle down. And speaking of trickle, From a lower drawer he pulls a bottle of *cognac*, pours a sizeable trickle into his steaming coffee cup.

The warmth! Much needed after such horrible happenings. One has to hang tough, hoping every day that the tempest finally has blown itself out. With a murderer safely arrested, why doubt that peace and discretion once again will settle on the land? And on Zemba Royal's affairs. Colonel-Detective M'Bazi certainly has put his hand on the only little fish, genuine minnow among a school of big-time barracudas. Ideal, under the circumstances, this Goldstone fellow. No embarrassing corporate howls to be raised at his trial. Perfectly cast as a villain bent on sabotaging Zembeylia's prosperity and political stability.

The Minister can hear the *guillotine*'s snick-snack; satisfying sound of blade sliding from on high, cutting cleanly through the neck of a man he could publicize as the nation's arch-enemy, whose disconnected head, bearing a grimace of horror, the world's news cameramen would photograph from all appropriate angles. The media could then characterize the head's expression as a telltale rictus of guilt. Justice will be seen to be served and Zembeylia will gain new respect in the eyes of the international community; while his own business interests stay rock-steady.

He'll turn then to overthrowing these enviro-Nazi animal-lovers and get to exploiting the X'Ziloncado Basin's true wealth, its

168

abundant reserves of oil, natural gas and uranium. And he'll start a modest cocaine venture on the side. All in all, he can look forward to a most prosperous future.

Yes, the Ship of State has suffered a torpedo, a salvo of torpedoes, given the other, lesser deaths. But its watertight doors are holding firm. A ragged hole in the hull is now being shored up; the indomitable vessel is righting herself. No *Titanic* here!

Allowing a touch of poetic license—fitting for Zembeylia's Poet Laureate as helmsman—and ably assisted by his subordinate M'Bazi, all will soon again be serene aboard the mighty, if figurative, liner, *SS Nation*.

Shipshape, you might say.

He'll give Félix a medal. This will help him fit into the scheme of things. "The Royal Order of National Security": blue-orange-magenta ribbon with silver-plate oval and embossed gold-plate palm leaf will do.

Awarded by the King in a courtyard ceremony at the palace.

Plus, of course, a cashier's check for 310.59 MUL

Excellent photo-opportunity, since he himself will pin the medal.

Minister M'Bowé dips a croissant into his coffee-*cognac* brew. He thinks of the line from Longfellow that Winston Churchill used when up against it.

In French-accented English he intones "Sail on, O *Sheep* of State, Sail on!"

Chapter 20: Conversational Interlude
X'Zloncado Tented Camp, Friday Morning, December 18

I'm sitting at a small iron table on the wooden duckboard verandah in front of my tent. As I finish my breakfast coffee, poured from a metal pitcher, I watch a pensive mother monkey suckle her largish baby. The two perch on the thin, swaying branch of a thorn tree.

The infant, furred and round-headed, buries its face into her breast, turning every now and then to stare in my direction with huge, sad-looking eyes. Somehow, it makes me think of photos of children in the concentration camps of World War Two: shaven-heads, eyes enormous, faces gaunt from starvation.

The mother, most of the time, seems barely to notice her baby. She keeps looking every which way, reaching out a long arm to pick succulent young leaves from the tree branches. Then, as if suddenly remembering, she bends her dark green shiny face to the young one and spreads the hairs on top of its head to pick for bugs. The greenness of her face set off by a snowy fringe, makes her quite the handsomest monkey I have ever seen. Vervets, our guide yesterday called them. More green-faced vervets scamper and swing across the trees of the grove forming an enclave around my quarters. Trees partially screen the large muddy pond on one side, while opening to carefully manicured lawn on the other.

The monkeys hoot and chatter, jump and catch one another in complicated games of tag; their ruffs look dazzlingly laundered in the yet cool rays of morning sun.

A small black-and-white bird zooms onto the branch of an acacia at the bank of the fenced pond, in which huge hippo heads–hippopotamuses? Hippopotami? Just hippos, I decide–bob and blow continuously. The bird has a little crown of whitish feathers atop its tiny cranium and a long yellow beak slender as a hypodermic needle.

"Black-and-white kingfisher," says Colonel-Detective M'Bazi, pushing through the short path from lawn to grove. He settles himself into the only other chair at the table. Today, I note, he wears khakis, same as the guides. The small golden insignia of an elephant, upcurved trunk curled around a packet of lightning bolts, is pinned to one shirt collar. From the in-flight magazine aboard Zemba Royal Airways, I know this to be the mark of a colonel here. "Great water hunter birds, rare to spot," he goes on. "They usually keep themselves well hidden." As he speaks, the bird dives for the water, comes up with a silver minnow impaled and wriggling on its beak. It flies off.

"You an amateur naturalist?" I ask.

"This country's survival as anything but a waste dump depends on our people's ability to appreciate and coexist with nature. Destroy her animal and vegetation splendors, we destroy ourselves. May I?"

Without waiting for an answer, the colonel-detective pours coffee. From the pot into an empty water glass, takes a sip. He turns his gaze on me. "You've been busy destroying a goodly crop of what a handful of mothers, fathers, spouses and loved ones consider their very own human splendors. How many folks have you taken out? Four, plus a possible? Damn good for a guy who keeps telling us how innocent he is."

I slam my cup on the table. "Round and round we go! I really don't know why the hell you're picking on me." I let out an irritated sigh.

"Let's see. Mrs. Farrar on the train: dead." M'Bazi spreads the fingers of his left hand, folds the thumb in. "You did that one quite brilliantly, I have to admit." He smiles. "We sure know who, but we don't know how. You'll tell us eventually, don't worry. Then the poor French lady, Madame Briac, also a traveler on the train and also dead," he folds in his forefinger. "Barry Mondran in New York, with the help of your loving fiancée, Ms. Suzanne Carrington. Another dead." Index finger in. "Now Michael Mahoney's dead as a doornail, with Sheila Mondran so sick to her stomach and bowels she probably wishes she was dead, although she may live." The hand closes to a fist.

"Thank God!" I exclaim. "Hey! Did you say Mike Mahoney?"

M'Bazi gives a Mephistophelean chuckle. "As if you don't know. The cause of our rushing off last night just as we'd brought you back here. Found by one of my men when I gave orders to get him for more questioning. You see?" M'Bazi smiles. "I'm trying to

171

follow your advice of not neglecting the others." He frowns. "But they keep checking out on me."

I rub a hand over my face. "God! God!"

"Don't blame Her. She lets us run our own disasters." M'Bazi takes a swallow of coffee. "Yeah, there was Mike, lying on the floor of his tent, dead at least four hours. He's currently residing in the lodge's walk-in refrigerator. Until we can fly him to Fulumbane for a reunion with his beloved spouse in Freedom University Hospital's autopsy chamber. Unless, of course, the kitchen staff mistake him for an eland and serve him, broiled, to their hungry guests. Yum-yum."

"C'mon," I say, shaking my head. "You don't have to be ghoulish. It's all bad enough."

"You should know," M'Bazi shows his teeth in a grin. He leans over the table, pours the last of the coffee into his glass. "Here's hoping you've run out of cyanide."

I picture The Big Bad Wolf, pouring himself an *apéritif* prior to eating up defenseless Little Red Riding Hood. Again I sigh, feeling the *guillotine* blade plunge toward my outstretched neck.

A rustling in the bushes make us both turn. Giorgio D'Alessandro squats near the pond's edge, a glass jar in one hand, the other carefully upending rocks. He senses our watching, straightens in a hurry, smiles embarrassedly. "Amateur naturalist at work," he calls to us "Don't mind me."

"Oh, but I will," mutters M'Bazi. He gives a casual wave, and D'Alessandro retreats through a strand of bamboo.

"Yeah, you're quite the cyanide kid," says M'Bazi turning back to me, "the 'A-One' prime suspect. Which brings up our interesting discoveries made while rummaging through your second bureau drawer and other possessions, during the duly warranted search of your quarters. Warrant, I should mention, faxed to us yesterday afternoon from the capital. As a precautionary measure."

"Discoveries? What possible discoveries?" I almost shout. "Not planted by you, that is!"

172

"Now, now!" the colonel-detective holds up an admonishing finger. "My job is to find the truth. Nothing but the truth, as we used to swear in court back in the 'Old Country,' I mean New York."

From his shirt pocket he takes a pack of cigarettes, tears it open and holds it out. I shake my head; M'Bazi selects one, lights up. "For starters, your shirts hid an unlabeled bottle containing five red-and-green capsules, the very kind your group takes against malaria and *M'zu-m'zu*. Even here at camp we were able to identify the powder within these capsules and in your possession as potassium cyanide."

He blows a cloud of smoke. "You see, we have a portable poison-detecting kit that can flag such obvious substances. The kit has a fluid that poured on solids such as powder will, in case of cyanide's presence, turn blue. Which it did."

He puffs on his cigarette. "Of course, we're sending everything to our central police lab at Fulumbane for confirmation. But rest assured, just a formality." He settles back in his seat, stretches his long legs to the table's side. Look!" He points at a thorn shrub on which sits another lovely bird, body orangy-red with a round head of metallic blue. The blue appears again in its long tapering tail-feathers. "Carmine bee-eater. Opening its beak. If we shut up, maybe it'll give us a song."

We stay silent. Sure enough, the bird warbles a long call, before beating its wings and speeding out of sight behind tangles of bushes.

"So, where were we?" continues M'Bazi. "Oh, yes. In your same drawer we also found a pack of cigarettes, each one dipped in enough cyanide to turn the testing liquid of our portable analysis kit a dark, dark blue; so strong as to kill off ten Sheila Mondrans and Michael Mahoneys. Again, we'll send these marvels to the Central Lab to confirm."

"How convenient to find such incriminating evidence casually stuffed in my bureau drawer," I say. "Can't I get you to consider the

173

possibility of a plant?"

"But of course, *cher ami*. Only–" M'Bazi fishes in the pocket of his tunic, brings out a paper that he carefully unfolds. "How do you explain this? Discovered inside the lining of your suitcase, cut and re-sewn; which we, regrettably, had to rip open for our search." He holds the paper so I can see. Clearing his throat theatrically, he intones: "Printout of a letter. Addressed to Mr. Harlan Fenster, Senior Vice-President, International Acquisitions, Jeffrey B. Ace Inc." M'Bazi looks up. "Famous corporate takeover shark, no?" He nods, answering his own question. "Dated Saturday, December 12th, the very day of your group's departure from New York to Zembeylia. I won't read what you already know, the gist being that Eland Inc., profitable though it currently is, will become so weakened by the deaths afflicting its executives that a buyout should be possible at a firesale price."

He refolds the paper, looks me up and down. "Did you or did you not write this on your typewriter in New York, with a carbon copy or two, as is standard procedure in most offices?" He gives a long pull on his cigarette, blows out more smoke. "Now for a question I don't know the answer to. How much do you make for playing Judas–a hands-on murdering Judas–for Ace Incorporated?"

Once more I pass a hand over my face. "I tell you I'm being framed," I speak slowly. "Whether by you and your people or the tour members, I don't know. But there's almost too much evidence against me. Isn't there?"

M'Bazi laughs a loud booming laugh and leans back in his seat. "Oh, that's a good one. What a defense! The too-much-evidence-against-me plea. That'll float like a ton of cement in the East River. I strongly urge you to use it at your trial."

He leans forward again, stabs his finger at my chest. "Know what I discovered in my years as a New York cop? A detective cop, mind you. That, just like you, ninety-nine point nine, nine, nine percent of criminals leave an evidence trail a mile wide and ten feet deep. Especially your garden variety murderer. They're one-time amateurs playing against us professionals with our years of training, our experience and specialized equipment. Most murderers are stupid in the execution of their crimes. For instance, once you mailed that letter to Ace, why bother to bring a carbon copy with you and hide it in your suitcase? You didn't need it here, surely. Why not leave the carbon hidden at home, where it would be far less likely to surface than under a badly sewn patch in your suitcase? When your excrement hit the fan, if you'll excuse my opinion of your crimes." He strokes his chin. "It's almost as if you're crying out, through ingrained feelings of guilt maybe, to get caught and punished? If that's the case, I'm happy to oblige." He looks at me quizzically.

I stare back, eyeball-to-eyeball. M'Bazi is first to shift his gaze.

I speak, as calmly as I can, "I never did do any of this. Naturally you won't believe me but it's the truth." I turn to stare through the trees at the pond with its hippos. A mother and two little ones are waddling up the far bank. Slowly they disappear into thick ferns and brush. "Jeez," I mutter "Mike Mahoney dead too. I liked the guy."

"Not enough not to kill him," says the colonel. "After all, coordinating with Ace was going to net a fat pay-off for your most unworthy self."

"Absolutely no!" I cast another glance at the hippos in their pond. "I came all the way to Zembeylia mainly for the experience of game-viewing. And here I am, bound in this little space by your goddamn ankle bracelet, missing the whole purpose of my journey."

"I'd call four murders and a three-quarters successful one that may go your way any minute, a pretty decent accomplishment for one quick trip. And let's not forget your *heure de voluptée*—your hour of sensuality with the so-attractive Sheila. These things are better said in French, don't you agree? Yes, quite a successful trip, all told. Pity you've been caught dead to rights."

Once more I shake my head. "I was feeling bad enough about betraying Suzanne just by being attracted. So I, uhm, sort of resisted. At least yesterday afternoon. With Sheila's help, I admit. She kept insisting I had to go on the game-viewing drive. To check-up on the others. She at least believed in my innocence."

"Later, of course, it was necessary to eliminate the lady, since your assignment was to destroy all Eland's movers and shakers. You must have shed a tear. Especially, as she believed you were Mister Purity. If she did, which I somehow doubt."

I throw up my hands helplessly "You've got it wrong. I tell you I'm being framed. A Judas? I'm the goat being led by some Judas goat to slaughter! What can I say? I'm just not a murderer. Or a machinator. Neither is Suzanne. Much too sensible, much too in control of her life and career. Give us time, we'll prove it, somehow. The truth has got to come out."

Something hits me. "Hey, if I sent Ace a letter from my office in New York, why would I hide a carbon copy afterwards in my suitcase? That doesn't sound logical. If the letter was sent, I'd have that carbon copy from my office typewriter available, if necessary, several times over through our photocopy machine. Taking the second copy and hiding it in my suitcase destined for Zembeylia seems nutty, extremely stupid too. Unless, of course, someone else wrote that letter and planted the carbon on me as one more piece of damning evidence against me. What do you say to that?"

M'Bazi stares down at the table. "As I stated before," he speaks slowly, "I'm only interested in truth. But these deaths have national and international significance."

"You mean that aside from you deciding I'm guilty or not, I'm politically convenient?"

M'Bazi smiles, not so broadly as before; a little wanly, it seems. "Got it in one. You're presumed guilty, thanks to a stack of damning evidence plus your presence alone in the sleeping car when the first victim, Helen Farrar was murdered. And also because you're a little-shot compared to the big-shot others in your group; you're convenient. Then again, maybe you planted your own letter in your suitcase for two reasons: One, because a record of your doings on behalf of the Ace people might be necessary if they 'forgot' to be suitably grateful. Blackmail material, in other words. Two, to claim somebody had it in for you if we confronted you with the document, as I've done and as you're hollering even as I accuse Y-O-U! Mind," again he points his finger at me, "like I just got through telling you, most guilty parties make things very convenient, given the trails they leave."

"You don't sound quite so sure I'm it."

The colonel-detective shakes his head. "I'm only desirous of tying up the few–the very few–loose ends, to make our case airtight. As per my official instructions."

"Can't you let me circulate, do some snooping and questioning on my own? So I can try to vindicate myself?"

M'Bazi shakes his head. "Thus giving me notice as to whom you're going to murder next: Lazuli, the guide? Finish off Sheila? No way." He sighs. "As it is I'm cutting you a helluva lot more slack than strictly authorized. Letting you stay here in this tent, instead of helicoptering you to our Disciplinary Camp One in a swamp area, which you really would not enjoy. Plus allowing you to telephone anywhere you like."

"So there's where we're at," I take a deep breath, hold it awhile before letting it out.

Now a nod. "But," he says, "I'll listen to anything reasonable you have to tell me. And if you can convince me you're innocent, I'll back you a hundred percent. I'm only a detective. My job–as well as my professional pride–is to put my finger on facts, whatever they are and whomever they implicate." He finishes his coffee, stands. "Just be assured," he continues, "that as of now, all evidence and implications point directly to you."

Chapter 21: Pink Horizons
Los Angeles, CA, Thursday, December 17

Rahel Tefuri's first stop in L.A. is the Johnny Carson office, where she has an appointment with Hector Weinberg's secretary. Secretary to the Great Man, not the Great-Great Carson. Weinberg, through reflected glory, is important enough to make Hollywood's single "Greatness" category.

Again, he's out of town, this time in Honolulu. Interviewing, says the secretary, a homegrown sumo wrestler currently making it big in Japan. If the guy's verbal skills are a quarter as impressive as his weight, he'll qualify for The Show.

Ms. Wilensky, blonde and comfortably plump, brews coffee on a hot plate. "The least I can do, you coming all this way. Especially after our brush-off of your friend," she says, offering cookies. "I still feel guilty about it."

She sits beside Rahel on a comfortable love seat, obviously ready for a gossip. "Poor woman came here all excited about being on The Show. Claimed she'd talked to Hecky. She hadn't, of course. We all thought she was a lunatic. We get occasional starstruck crazies wandering in, as you can imagine." Ms. Wilensky pauses to sip coffee. "We giggled at her delusion of grandeur, sent her on her way. Then I got to thinking. She looked so crushed, poor thing, after I assured her we never had either her or the program she mentioned on our schedule." She shakes her head. "I finally realized she was the victim of a cruel hoax. Now who could be so heartless as to have her fly all the way across the country only to face such a let-down. And the cost!"

"It's what I'm trying to find out," murmurs Rahel. "The whys and wherefores. We think it has to do with murder."

Ms. Wilensky's eyes grow wide.

Rahel nods. "Part of a plot in which Suzanne Carrington was set up as target."

"Well, now," the Great Man's secretary sets down her cup, all business. "If that's so and you solve the mystery–and your friend is innocent, like she claims–then we might get her on the show after all. Keep me posted."

"I certainly will," says Rahel, and hurries to her next appointment.

As a travel professional, she has access to free air, a discounted car rental and, if she needs it, a night's accommodation at one of several Sheratons. "God knows you don't get much travel out of the travel biz, judging from Goldstone, who claims he's too busy and too poor for a moonlight ride on the Staten Island ferry," Suzanne has commented. "So please take the freebies and save me from having to face those Carson people again." She promised to pay any balance due on the rental car, as well as for meals, incidentals and all costs not covered by free offerings.

It takes Rahel an hour of bumper-to-bumper traffic on a smog-choked freeway to cross the Coast Range and guide her loaded Lincoln Continental–at the price of a Compact–into the San Fernando Valley.

The police station seems Encino's most imposing building, aside from a mini-skyscraper Hilton. Sergeant Ed Ramirez, in charge of local investigations, sports a long drooping black mustache. He looks more like a *bandito* out of the *Sierra Madre*–measuring Humphrey Bogart with his eyes, while twirling a silver pistol and saying "Sorry, meestah, now I gotta keel you"–than the suburban cop he is. He also seems more interested in manhandling a toothpick to dig out the remains of lunch from his molars than in anything Rahel has to say. He rummages through teeth and with his free hand scrabbles among some papers piled at the edge of his desk. The phone rings. Long conversation in Spanish. He ignores Rahel's throat clearings, rustles and other noises aimed at getting him back to her. At long last, he pulls a manila folder from the paper pile, opens it, leafs through some documents, hands her a rumpled one.

More Spanish palaver...finally, he hangs up. "Not much to tell you," he says, nodding towards the paper. "U.P.S. waybill, marked 'gift package for third business day delivery.' Addressed to the deceased and signed by a Suzanne Carrington as sender. That's all we know. Except she was in L.A. that day. Plenty of proof." He gives a final ream to his left molar, removes the toothpick, breaks it in two, drops the pieces into a tin ashtray filled with broken sticks and butts. "Go see Bill Murphy," he tells Rahel. "Owns and runs the place where she sent the package. Maybe he can tell you something."

The little storefront on the main drag bears a large sign: *Photocopies, mail boxes, Fedex, UPS.*

"What, again?" says Murphy, when Rahel tells him her mission. He gets up from a folding chair to stand behind his counter. "You another cop? I've had 'em up the ying-yang, even FBI. Which're you, CIA? KGB? Woman mailed a package is all I know."

"You remember her?" asks Rahel.

He spreads his hands. "How can I forget? Ditzy redhead, right?"

"Auburn-haired but no ditz. Very down-to-earth."

"This one—believe me, lady, when I tell you—she was a ditz. She come flouncing in here about 6:25, just when I'm getting ready for the last pickup, then close shop and go home at 6:30. And she spends more'n ten minutes tryin' to decide if she should send her damn package Fedex or UPS? If her boss needs to get it there overnight, or how much would two day delivery cost, as against three days? And on and on. Near drove me and the UPS guy crazy. She made him late on his route. I was three-quarters of an hour late gettin' to my dinner, which didn't please my wife none." He shakes his head. "Not likely I'd forget her."

"Her boss?" asks Rahel. "What was that about?"

"Here," says Murphy. He pulls open a file cabinet, looks through some folders. "Here's the Waybill. I gave a copy to the cops. See? Address is c/o Pink Horizons Travel, 10650 Encino Boulevard."

"Yes, I've got that. The police let me have a copy." Rahel pulls her own Waybill from her purse.

"Well, you see." Murphy stabs a finger at the signature box. "Signed Suzanne Carrington."

"Yes, but she doesn't work for…You say this woman had red hair?"

"Yeah, bright red. Tall, slim, good looker, uhm, for her age."

"Hmm. Suzanne's getting a bit stout. Not fat, mind you. A touch voluptuous. How old?"

"Fussy, though." Mr. Murphy is on his own orbit. "Like I say, Couldn't make up her mind. By the time she left I was tellin' myself 'Lord protect me from ever gettin' involved with such a broad,' er sorry, female!" He pauses to scratch his chin. "Oh, about thirty-eight, I'd say. Maybe just the wrong side of forty. Not by much, though."

"This travel agency," asks Rahel. "Far from here?"

"About ten blocks that way," Murphy points westward. "Fella named Clive owns the joint. Seems they cater to 'special' clients." He leers. "If you know what I mean."

Rahel purses her lips. "Thank you, Mr. Murphy, you've been helpful." Her voice is prim. "I won't keep you." Turning on her heel, she marches out.

Fortunately, Pink Horizon's address is clearly marked. Otherwise, she might have missed the place, or joint. Joint is more exact. A joint bathed in pink, with rose-tinted display window featuring the Eiffel Tower colored salmon by a setting sun; plus a Taj Mahal suffused in Dawn's early light. All this and the carmine sands of a Bermuda beach, as gazed upon from the deck of an ocean liner by two men, arms entwined around each other's waists, with the legend on a life preserver: *S.S. Pink Rose of Spring*.

181

Inside the walls are pink, the typewriters and a lone computer pink, even a pink carpet, featuring here and there large brown-blackish coffee stains. Otherwise, the look of the place and the lone, overweight individual behind a terminal, give her a strong feeling of *déjà vu*. Absent the stains, this dump could pass for Shangri-La West.

The agent, to be sure, is dressed more informally than by New York standards. His half-buttoned green and yellow Hawaiian shirt sporting red-eyed dragons, barely covers a belly pregnant, if not with meaning or child, with junk food. Same early five o'clock shadow as Schulz. Aside from niceties of attire, he looks like Schulz's *Doppelgänger*. Slowly, he lifts his eyes from a rosy typewriter to scan her up and down, before pronouncing "Ye-es?" redolent with hostility.

"Are you Clive, the owner?"

The man titters. "Goodness, no! Whatever would you want with Clive?"

"I need to speak to him. It's quite urgent."

The man shakes his head, presses a button on an intercom. "Clive," he shouts into the machine, while smirking at Rahel. "There's a woman here, says she has to see you. Urgently."

Quacking noise from the intercom.

"Yes, female. Urgent."

Rahel nods vigorously.

"He'll be right down, dear," says the agent. "Just sit over there. You can look at the brochures." He bends his head to the typing keys, fingers trilling over them, a veritable virtuoso.

Rahel, is damned if she'll read a travel brochure on this day off from her own computer some three thousand miles distant. She fishes into her large plastic bag, pulls out a free copy of *Time* from the plane.

Clump-clump of feet down a stairway beyond the far wall. Front door opening–same tinkling of chimes as at Shangri-La–and a tallish man enters. His executive stride attests to ownership.

182

Rahel, rises from her seat.

"Clive Lawrence," he says. "You wish to see me?"

Fifty or so. Face running to jowls. Fastidiously dressed in a lightweight pinstripe featuring pointy Yves St. Laurent shoulders and tightness at the hips. Complexion carefully bronzed, with his black hair looking not quite right? Weave job, she decides. Far cry from her boss whose appearance, always hastily put together, reveals rumpled absent-mindedness, somehow conveying an unconscious gentlemanly quality that this overdone tableau of fashion will never attain. Which is why, she supposes, she sticks it out at Shangri-La, reluctant to abandon reincarnated Captain Smith, the *Titanic*'s incompetent but for no definable reason, endearing master, to his deserving fate. She shakes the hand that Lawrence sticks out. "Rahel Tefuri," she murmurs, 'Shangri-La Travel, New York."

Clive Lawrence raises a well-manicured eyebrow.

"I've come about the package you sent to Barry Mondran."

He shakes his head. "I never did." He hesitates. "Let's go to my office. We'll have coffee and a chat."

She follows him out the agency's front door and through an adjacent one leading to a staircase. At the top, they enter an outer office, where an elderly gray-haired woman sits listening to dictation earphones and typing. She nods to Rahel, who follows her host into his own office, walls lined with photos of himself and celebrities: Jerry Lewis, Michael Jackson, ex-President Ford in a golf cart.

Lawrence bustles about, offers coffee, which she declines saying she's all coffee'd-out. He goes to a side cabinet, opens it, reveals an array of bottles. Again, she declines. He pours himself a scotch, sips it neat as they talk. "Yes, I knew Barry and liked him. I mourn his passing. We met at a travel show in Phoenix about eighteen months ago. We became...close. No, I didn't send him poison cigarettes. I don't send marijuana through the mail. Not even by Federal Express, or was it UPS?" He pauses to swallow whisky. "I've explained all this to the police and, wonder of wonders, they seem to believe me. Now what do you want?"

"Nothing much," says Rahel. "Perhaps information you don't know you possess. If you didn't do it somebody did. Who?"

"What do you care? You a detective? Hired by his awful sister-in-law?"

"She's dead, too."

Lawrence pales. "I didn't know. How ghastly." He rises, refills his whisky glass.

Rahel nods. "Happened while on tour in Zembeylia where the authorities have so far managed to keep it out of the media. You'll be reading and hearing about it in a day or so."

He takes a handkerchief from his pocket, passes it over his face, rises to pour more drink. "Sure I can't offer you one?"

Rahel shakes her head. "The woman out there. Your secretary?"

"Mrs. Galeota? She comes in three times a week. That's all I can afford right now, business the way it is."

"Mrs. Galeota is your only secretary?"

He laughs bitterly. "Absolutely, as I just indicated. I know nothing about this Ms. Carroway or whoever the sexy redhead the police mentioned."

"Carrington. Suzanne Carrington. A friend. She seems to have been the butt of a sinister machination."

"Yes, well in any case, I was in Honolulu on that particular day and can prove it. Attending the 'Gems of the Pacific Travel Fair,' where I had a booth promoting Gay and Lesbian travel. Upwards to three hundred people can testify to my presence. I helped arrange a showcase breakfast, gave an evening lecture, stayed two nights at The Waikiki Towers and socialized constantly. I couldn't possibly have been anywhere near here when that package was mailed."

"Which doesn't mean you didn't order it done."

"But why?" Clive Lawrence leans forward, fixes Rahel with a frown. "I had absolutely everything to lose and nothing to gain,

184

believe me. Not only have I lost a friend–I do mourn him, if no one else does–but I've lost the possibility of retiring very, very wealthy." He finishes off his drink. "Barry was on to something. He expected it to bring so much money that we could retire to Fiji and live like kings." He pours more whisky, drinks a quick gulp. "Maybe it was just a dream. I dunno. Neither of us had money in our own right. If anything, my net worth–nothing to brag about–is greater than was Barry's."

"There's always Eland," murmurs Rahel.

Again Lawrence shakes his head. "This had nothing to do with Eland. I don't run in that league, never shall, alas. But Barry was convinced..." He pauses.

Rahel looks at him expectantly.

"Ah, what does it matter now?" He shakes his head sadly. "Look, I just know hearsay. Through Barry. Nothing else, mind you. But he talked, very guardedly, about an initiative to take over a big swatch of land in Zembeylia. Some sort of a huge valley, or natural basin. To clear it for oil, gas and mineral exploration. He was by-passing Eland with a deal directly counter to everything Helen was working for, her developing tourism, especially ecological tourism."

"But," says Rahel, "without Helen Farrar and her contacts–"

"Barry had his own links to a top man in the Zembeylian government, so he claimed. And Barry himself was facilitating negotiations with a certain third party and carving out a fifteen percent commission plus ongoing royalties for both of us." Lawrence pauses, gazes out his dusty window at a McDonald's parking lot. "You know, he was a pretty smart guy, a C.P.A. He got into some legal difficulty that Helen Farrar quashed or resolved for him. It put him in her pocket; he was always complaining about the short financial leash she kept him on. Said he felt like a house-slave."

He finishes his whisky, makes a show of looking at his watch, a thin, gold, Swiss job. "I don't mean to be rude but I have to get

185

going. If I can help, I will. But I'm really for naught in this whole affair." He stands.

They shake hands and he ushers her out the door.

By the time she boards the red-eye for New York, Rahel is exhausted. Thank goodness they again put her in First. She sinks into a comfortable seat, closes her eyes and doesn't open them until it's time to deplane at Kennedy.

PART FIVE:
SLEUTHINGS AND MACHINATIONS
Zembeylia–U. S. A., Thursday to Sunday, December 17–20

"My sleuthing left Sherlock Holmes green with envy.
Or maybe it was because we left him
out in the rain too long."
~Attributed to Groucho Marx.

Chapter 22: Rumblings
X'Ziloncado Camp, Friday, Late Morning December 18
and Fulumbane, Zemebylia's Capital

"Hey, people! Cool it! Murder is murder. Yeah, I'm sorry, you're gonna hafta abide by our rules." In the lodge's lobby, Colonel-Detective Félix M'Bazi, sounding anything but sorry, faces a gathering of outraged Americans. Rhinos and lions are all very well, but today is Friday and this very night, the travelers–depleted lot but still capable of making noise–are due to be whisked from the African jungle back to their own prime jungles: New York City and Dallas, wild, woolly, asphalted but familiar and remunerative.

Slight problem: no sign the murder inquiry is going anywhere. With new disasters happening almost by the hour and detention in the game reserve clearly not ending as per schedule, panic has set in.

"Listen, y'all cain't do this," shouts Sherman Jamieson. "We got bidnesses to operate!"

"We're not going to sit in these godforsaken boonies to get bumped off one by one," chimes in Bitsy, bracelets clinking with outrage.

"Shaddap, fa Chrissake," Jamieson's accent slipping with stress. He grabs his wife's arm. "You let the men handle this."

"Men!" she snorts, pulling her arm away. From a new giraffe-skin handbag, bought at the lodge's variety shop, she produces a lipstick and mirror, begins reinvigorating heat-faded lips. "Wasn't me left that tent flap open," she mutters between swipes of *Rosa Romantika*. "Trust men to louse things up six ways to Sunday! Men and baboons!" She grimaces as she pushes her lips in-out, in-out for moisturizing.

"I don't wanna have to do this," M'Bazi's stentorian cop tone and New York accent have the desired subduing effect, "but if you won't calm down I'm going to confine all of you to your tents, put guards on you, maybe even ankle-bracelets like I've done to our number one suspect." He waits some seconds, savoring the silence. "Now, stay loose and we'll leave you free to roam here, enjoy the amenities, even go on game drives. But you wanna play rough, we'll play rough." He clears his throat loudly. "Get it through your heads, you're here for the duration. Until we solve this case. Understand?"

"Youse've already got the criminal, goddammit to hell!" shouts Jamieson. "What's this bullshit, anyway?"

"You'd like to think so," retorts M'Bazi. "But until we have definitive proof, no one is above suspicion. And you're not," he can't stop a slight smirk, "going anywhere!"

Under his breath, Gene Petroff mutters "We'll just see what Minister M'Bowé has to say about this."

It has happened again. Bhulliwah has allowed himself to be battered, walked on, frozen for six full minutes in that wretched ice-bath, all for the privilege of being condescended to as he sits in a canvas chair, shivering, dressed in a thin beach robe, hands around a glass of mint tea to try and get some warmth back into his bones.

The liquid is soothing as it goes down. *Parbleu!* He can order mint tea anywhere, anytime! Doesn't have to endure such discomfort, such indignities to–

"Our pleasures, my dear Antoine, are being all the more appreciated when they are compensating for life's discomforts," murmurs the elderly man as if reading his guest's thoughts. He snaps his fingers. A servant proffers a plate of sugar-powdered "virgins' fingers."

Bhulliwah, frowning, takes one. Shouldn't acquiesce to the bastard's whims but quite peckish after all the unpleasantness. "We must get to business." His voice sounds hoarse.

190

"My experience is that getting to business is putting oneself at a disadvantage. Let the business be getting to you, I say."

"What are we going to do about this terrible scheme of M'Bowé's: to make himself and his government untouchable by—"

"Do not be talking to me of Untouchable!" Hand upraised, Y. Sanjeev Sandaram's glittering eye stops Bhulliwah in mid-sentence.

So sensitive? He's careful to keep his face blank and innocent-looking. Could it be that back in India those years ago…? Was Sandaram not always Sandaram? Could he possibly have emigrated, slyly changed his name because…? "I am merely noting," Bhulliwah's tone is soothingly smooth, "that with the riches brought in by covering Zembeylia with illicit vegetations, the present régime will become impregnable. And our tourism blighted. How disastrous, how vulnerable for X'Zambili-Africa Tours. To avoid being compromised, the corporation will have to leave Zembeylia and stay far away from home."

Sandaram chuckles. "You are regretting not having your own hands on those seductive plants and powders. I am seeing you dreaming of shifting X'Zambili-Africa Tour's interests from traveling to trafficking."

"Not at all, sir, not at all," protests Bhulliwah. "I play the ecology card."

"You are forced to be playing the ecology-environmental-tourism card, this is what you are meaning." His interlocutor and corporate boss waggles a finger. "I am telling you it is a good card. There's staying power in it. Are you believing that our Uncle Sam will be tolerating Zembeylia's sudden arriving on the drug scene? What about the Colombians, the Afghanis and Pakistanis, the Soviet Russians, who are using western contributions to their national treasury to be carving out a big slice of the drug and prostitution markets worldwide?"

"Well, a little healthy competition…" says Bhulliwah. "Take Russia, with its doddering Communism heading to collapse. For so-called 'stimulus and redevelopment,' the more western funds flow into the hands of a few gangsters-capitalists, as opposed to Communist ones, and thus not to the population as a whole–the better everyone, the Supreme Soviet included, seems to like it. You can control the few; the many are prone to get stubborn ideas and act on them. Like a desire for real, as contrasted to cosmetic democracy, a philosophy favored by both East and West. Quite a state of affairs, when an observer can discern not a jot of difference between two ostensibly opposing sides and government systems"

"Yes, yes." Sandaram waves a hand. "All the big boys are profiting, so long as there is no scandal. When scandal is striking, and sooner or later it is always striking, then you will be seeing fuss. Probably quashed with a few lesser pigeons roasted; the great birds shall be excused, as in corporate and mortgage cheatings that the West pretends to be horrified at even as we speak. Nevertheless, a fuss can be causing some great birds to fly low awhile. Who is needing such troubles?" In a grandfatherly way, eighty-five year old Sandaram gives the arm of his guest a friendly, parental-like pinch. It leaves a welt. "No, no. We are sticking, gladly so, to golf, sightseeing, animal viewing, hotel bedrooms with-and-without verandahs, luxury excursions of all types plus exotic incentive trips for tip-top sellers of detergents and lawnmowers. Slow but steady income. We all are making money in the long run. And keeping out of exile."

"Doesn't have to be just tourism," grumbles Bhulliwah, "if you play your cards right."

His host's expression sharpens, voice sounding anything but grandfatherly. "This environmentalism is your card today. Play it and quick! The time is now."

Bhulliwah nods. He will denounce wicked, deceitful, self-seeking M'Bowé. The people are ready to be roused. At least, he hopes they are. All is in place for a *coup*. And "Bhulliwah-The-Deliverer" will seize the reins of power. "The matter of these inconvenient murders," he remarks. "The government is preparing to accuse this Goldstone person, an insignificant individual in

Eland's tour group. He will be put on trial and eventually *guillotined.* Well and good. It will encourage other tourists to refrain from abominable crimes while visiting Zembeylia. Nevertheless, this leaves free the ever-dangerous Petroff, representing Jeffrey B. Ace Corporation. And Petroff's cohorts, Norman Chandler along with Guitterez-Shaughnessy, who has direct links to the Cali drug cartel. I have information they are negotiating with M'Bowé."

"Petroff is being the danger," murmurs Sandaram. "Forget Chandler and the other fellow. I know for a fact they are loyal to our cause. Bring down Petroff and you are bringing down M'Bowé." And saving me from further outside competition, he could have added. As always, he thinks it wiser to keep his mouth shut, a policy that over the years has paid off." Under his breath he murmurs, "Need to know."

"What's that?" Bhulliwah eyes him suspiciously.

"You must go. Go and be starting your revolution"

"Our mutual revolution, surely." Bhulliwah heaves himself out of the canvas chair and stands before his boss and mentor.

"Yes, yes, go, my boy. Work to bring about our good fortunes." Sandaram remains seated at the round metal table with its umbrella canopy that stands in a small windowless room especially set aside for his use. A languidness of tone, those hooded eyes, his too-casual wave of hand fail to underscore the encouraging words.

Upon Bhulliwah's departure, the old man picks up a telephone, presses the red scrambler button and dials a familiar number. "Zecherias, you really must be learning discretion. I am—"

A torrent of words from M'Bowé's end of the line.

"Well, our negotiations shall be coming to naught if you are allowing visions of poppy-fields to be inflaming you-know-who."

Sandaram frowns at protestations that go on and on. Fellow thinks he's addressing The Council of Unity? Or declaiming a poem? The point is to play both ends against the middle. Let enemies attack Ace from all sides, devour him as they maul each other. Then X'Zambili-Africa Tours will pick up the pieces.

His interlocutor talks interminably. From the table, Y. Sanjeev Sandaram picks up a copy of *Paris-Match*, thumbs through the photos. Thoughtfully, he regards Brigitte Bardot shaking her finger at the camera as she cries out against the plight of persecuted pigeons. He decides it's time to interrupt. "There is no use making a political speech at me, dear boy. I am not being one of your constituents. Only an ally of convenience, yes? So do be stopping your preachings."

Subdued noises from the receiver.

Sandaram leans back in his chair. "This Goldstone fellow—"

Another flood of words.

"Yes, yes, I am understanding all that. The one personage we can discount as too weak to make trouble for us in U.S.A. Very good, diplomatically speaking, using him for both show-trial and execution. Except—"

The man would keep interrupting.

"Except, as I am saying, what does Goldstone accomplish?"

Long silence. Followed by small noises.

"Now, if instead you are nailing this Ace fellow, this Eugene Petroff, then you are truly spiking the cannon, so to speak, of a serious rival ready to be betraying us both."

Thunderous noises. Sandaram lays the receiver on the table. He re-examines Brigitte. Still a handsome woman, if not the sex bomb of her late 1940's-early 1950's blockbuster, *And God Created Woman*. Ah, youth!

At last, silence on the line. Sandaram picks up where he left off. "The opera house? I, too, am believing in culture. I am loving great music. Just because you *guillotine* Madame Petroff's husband is not meaning that Sakurai Corporation shall be denied building electronics plant here. Or that she is not being given beautiful opera building. She is no criminal, only the husband. Think of this as compensation, as therapy, the feeling of being wanted that an opera house will be giving the poor lady, once her misguided spouse is disposed of." He nods at the comments emanating from the phone. "As you say, a sad end to marriage is becoming blessing in disguise. So Zembeylia may be having all her cakes in hand and eating them too." He allows a small giggle.

They hang up in perfect accord.

The moving finger is turning from Goldstone to Petroff; but Sandaram, eager to muster as much insurance as prudence dictates, places one more call: to a Dr. Fang Shi Wu, ostensible Second Secretary at the embassy of the People's Republic of China.

Chapter 23: Whodunit?
X'Ziromeu City, Late Morning Friday, December 18

"Of course, Monsieur. Yes, Monsieur, I know but…The facts. Interpretations? Yes, our cause…" Captain-Detective Matthias X'Zimbalwa sighs as he puts down the receiver. Antoine Bhulliwah-X'Zilone shouting at him to pin Madame Briac's impending death-by-murder on a man he'd barely noticed aboard that accursed train. And Minister M'Bowé resolutely demanding—four times a day—that he make the case against Goldstone airtight. That, at least, seems sensible, given what a centimeter-by-centimeter search of Madame Briac's farm and belongings have revealed.

He touches his pointy goatee, styled after Patrice Lumumba. Marie keeps nagging to shave it off. She claims it tickles. No mere statement of manliness, so far as he's concerned; an outright defiance of his semi-bureaucratic condition. Defiance small enough to avoid hurting chances for advancement. He considers it an essential element of his personality. She doesn't like it? Should've married someone else. A hairless eunuch, maybe? Twinge in his stomach. Can't square with his conscience that he's informed a mere civilian about Madame Briac not being, in fact, dead. No official right or reason for Bhulliwah-X'Zilone to know.

195

And Bhulliwah is Minister M'Bowé's arch-enemy. The enemy of my boss is, or should be… still, Bhulliwah stands as the X'Zambili tribe's best hope for power. And, therefore, his own personal hope for elevation to the highest pinnacles of…

If the Goldstone fellow proves to be IT, as in the child's game of tag, then the whole affair could become business-as-usual. He'll be lucky to retire a Captain here in the provinces. Well, not a bad life. At least relatively safe, only the occasional shoot-out with criminals or revolutionaries to worry about. Family secure; Marie and the kids content with their lot here. She certainly is a wonder at managing the modest family income.

But, damn it! Isn't a man born to reach for the stars? How challenging to move to the capital as a bigtime wheeler-dealer in the hub of intrigue, while at the same time serving the X'Zambilis, his people, his tribe; X'Zambili hands–his hands–will grasp the throttles of power. A sky's-the-limit future hangs on his ability to fit the facts in this one wretched case so as to implicate…What's his name? Ah, yes, Petroff.

The Captain reaches for a manila folder holding Madame Briac's file. Let's see: Elderly widow. She and her husband among the 28,553 farming families emigrating here from Brittany after World War Two. Arrives in '46, when France offers its own war-ravaged, near-bankrupt farmers tracts of land in Zembeylia's fertile uplands at rock-bottom subsidized prices. The French needed to swell their presence in southeast Africa far more than they required legions of subsistence Breton potato-growers at home.

Prosperity eludes the Briacs, as with most of their kind. A few French manage to buy or consolidate large holdings and are now wealthy. But the Briac family works only four hectares. Their produce is subject to bouts of abundance and meagerness, due to fluctuations in market prices and the myriad vicissitudes of weather besetting farmers everywhere. So, while they're able to keep the hyena away from the door, that ravening beast is never far. With her husband three years dead and her grown daughter returned to

France, married in Qumper, Brittany, what a struggle it must be for Madame Briac to run the farm all on her own.

X'Zimbalwa turns to the next page of the history that he and his men have compiled painstakingly. Suddenly, *La Briac* starts throwing money around. Lavish contribution to her community chapel's new roof fund; a whole series of trips in deluxe accommodations aboard the Zemba Royal SilverSpear Express; overnight stays at Fulumbane's finest hotel. What is she fabricating out there on her farm? Hashish? Heroin? Crystal Meth? Crack? This has to be some sort of drug event; the hypothesis jumps out at you!

How else to account for such a change in lifestyle? True, she doesn't appear the drug-dealer type; most successful criminals don't look to be what they are. Or they wouldn't be successful, eh? Q.E.D.

The search of her farm hasn't revealed drug evidence, as such. Yes, a few coca bushes, a can of leaves and a half-full pitcher of coca tea in the fridge. That sort of brew is merely calming to the nerves and here in Zembeylia perfectly legal. Still, the scrap of letter buried under a loose floorboard in her bedroom is one sure indication: top burnt, bottom burnt, readable only for a fifth of a page. Eloquent though, this legible bit. He opens his desk's center drawer, reaches for the scrap, holds it gingerly between thumb and forefinger. Don't want any crumbling. Photocopies he has, but the original is precious. He can hear the public prosecutor intoning, "Mesdames, Messieurs of the jury, let this compromising piece be recorded as Exhibit A!"

From the pencil tray on his desk he lifts a magnifying glass, trying for the umpteenth time to make out print. In English, just visible under a coat of carbon. Something, something "...once in a lifetime CALLING..."

Well, drug lords don't give their minions or couriers second chances if they slip up, as Madame Briac must have done. These few tantalizing words are all he's able to make out in the burnt part.

Putting glass aside, he re-scans the clear portion of print: "...so here, as before, is a money order of MUL 25,000. One more journey to accomplish and you will be ready to set out on your TRUE ASSIGNMENT. Remember, discretion is the WATCHWORD! However, we can now reveal to you WONDERFUL news. Your MISSION will involve contact with our very own highly placed representative in Rome, a TRUE SON OF BRITTANY! I refer to His Eminence, CARDINAL JEAN LANNEC, former ARCHBISHOP of RENNES and present member of the CURIA. His concern for Africa, notably ZEMBEYLIA, where so many Bretons have found a new home, is great indeed. But he feels religion must be based on PRACTICAL CONSIDERATIONS!!! And also on a BUDGET worthy of the name. For this very reason he requires an energetic, believing—and believable—lay AGENT to carry out his work for strong MUTUAL BENEFIT in the cultivation of willing SOULS. Therefore, you must prepare a journey to ROME to meet PERSONALLY with Cardinal Lannec and receive from HIS HANDS..."

Here again the burn takes over. Try as he will, the rest remains illegible. He closes the folder, closes his eyes in yet another attempt to marshal ideas. Certainly mystifying, the whole thing, though he knows the facts by heart. How do they add up? Cardinal Lannec involved in drug trafficking? Oh, stranger things have happened.

Perhaps the Prelate tells himself that the cause of Church prosperity in this region of Africa counts for more than a few spaced-out junkies, who, if he didn't sell them the stuff, would acquire it from sources less virtuous in ultimate goals. Certainly sale of drugs is the conclusion to draw from the words "practical considerations" and "a budget worthy of the name."

The Cardinal, of course, denies everything, even knowing about poor Madame Briac. He says he'll pray for her soul, misguided though she may have been. As for her coming to see him or having contact with him, he declares to Interpol, through

Vatican Security, that he's never heard of any of it, certainly not of the lady, nor of a supposed mission.

The guy's tracks are covered. Nothing but mention of his name to implicate him, along with a few vague words in the letter. Whichever way this thing develops, Lannec is likely to be in the clear. Therefore, not in itself a fruitful line of inquiry. X'Zimbalwa lets out a small groan.

So, start with the train murder, a step-by-step chronology of the tour group. Re-apply–as if he hasn't done so a hundred times–the deductive process from there onward. Had to have missed something crucial. The Missing Link–.

He reaches for a clean sheet of typing paper from the stack atop his file cabinet, lays the sheet on a hard plastic desk pad in front of him.

That fatal day, last Wednesday, December 16, the group started out at the Zemba Royal Oceanside And Giraffe Preserve. He scribbles a note. They were thirteen, counting the local guide. Another note.

But three, Sheila Mondran and Chandler with his cohort, the Colombian Guitterez-Shaughnessy, obviously a professional drug-dealer, go on their own to X'Ziromeu City, where in the evening they catch the SilverSpear train.

What were they doing out there? Collecting drug samples from Madame Briac's farm? Had Guitterez-Shaughnessy met previously with Madame to arrange things? Is the plan to co-opt her farm for growing drug-producing plants? As the site of a refinery?

The movements and contacts of all three–the woman, Chandler, but especially Guitterez–are being traced. Tomorrow at this time he hopes to have a full report.

Nevertheless, the smashed watch and Ms. Farrar's personal effects found on the track point to Helen Farrar being killed *prior* to the train's arrival at X'Ziromeu City's station. These members of the group are exempt from suspicion of direct participation in her murder.

Any one of them, or all of them together, could have ordered the Farrar killing. But they didn't carry it out.

For committing the crime, evidence continues to point to Goldstone, perhaps the human equivalent of a guided-missile. Commissioned by remote sources?

Guitterez-Shaughnessy of Colombia. How fitting to cast him as mastermind. Has he, in cahoots with Petroff, orchestrated the double coup of killing the Farrar woman in her compartment and slipping slow-acting poison to Madame Briac? How?

How indeed? Always, of course, through Goldstone, surely Helen Farrar's physical killer.

The Captain gazes up at the ceiling. Not very efficient, Goldstone, as a murderer. Three victims out of five with Barry Mondran dead in New York, through Goldstone's girlfriend, Suzanne Carrington.

Let's see, the Captain spreads fingers of his left hand while holding pen to paper with his right. Helen Farrar, dead directly through Goldstone; Sheila, Mondran, near death, once more through Goldstone but bungled; Madame Briac, hovering between life and death, another Goldstone bungle. And, oh yes, this Michael Mahoney fellow stone dead, thanks to Goldstone.

So, with the Sheila woman and *La Briac* considered still alive, though both liable to pop off any minute, The murderer, Goldstone, has botched two killings out of five, with one success handled by proxy.

An assassin having any pretension to competence is bound to make sure *all* his targets are eliminated. Unless—

Are there two separate murderers and two separate agendas? A competent killer and a sloppy, incompetent one?

Petroff, the efficient, manipulating Goldstone? Plus Guitterez-Shaughnessy, a slob, too used to delegating efficient hit-men for his crimes back in Columbia?

Or Goldstone and Guitterez-Shaughnessy the efficient ones and Petroff—jealous of Guitterez's masterminding the creation of an illicit drug industry through Madame Briac–a slob who tries to kill her with an inefficient poison and then goes after Sheila Mondran with equal inefficiency.

Or is Goldstone, efficient the first time, sloppy the second...? X'Zimbalwa beats his fists against his head. This will drive him mad! Deep breaths. All right, somebody, "X," not always efficient. But clever, undeniably clever. How the devil did he/they...Or yes, yes, maybe a she? Mustn't jump to conclusions...

All the same, pretty obvious. Goldstone has to be it, Old fatso Bhulliwah-X'Zilone and X'Zambili political maneuverings be damned. Truth is truth!

So how does Goldstone get into that cabin? And out again? All doors locked, only a communicating partition, between the cabins occupied by victim Farrar and the one housing Madame Briac...

Now that partition was locked too, by the porter from departure through the murder time and the stop at X'Ziromeu City station, all the way to discovery of the crime, when the train is far up the track from X'Ziromeu. When she gets off at X'Ziromeu City, Madame Briac seems to the porter perfectly healthy, certainly of sound mind. Would she have let Goldstone, or Petroff, go creeping around her space, forcing her to drink poison and then watch as they broke down the locked partition to Ms. Farrar's compartment? Without screaming her head off? That makes no sense. And no door or partition was broken, anyway.

Unless...Could she have *willingly* signaled Goldstone or Petroff. Or Guitterez?

No, no, Guitterez was off the train, she couldn't have signaled him. But might she have gestured to the person–again call this person "X"–that the coast is clear, that the porter has his back turned, or is in a cabin making up beds and that he or she or IT, damnation to Hell, can come into her cabin, so conveniently communicating with the victim's?

The porter has the only key to open the partition between cabins, a special round, serrated railroad key that he claims stays on his watch chain at all times.

So the porter MUST be the killer! He poisons Madame Briac's *cognac* with a slow-acting concoction, not wanting her to be found dead on the train, then enters Ms. Farrar's cabin by unlocking the connecting partition. He kills her and lies about *La Briac's* condition when she gets off at X'Ziromeu City.

The Captain visualizes this poor woman staggering down the platform, just managing to make it home in her van before collapsing onto her bed, thanks to the sinister porter's ministration to her brandy...

Were they accomplices, the treacherous porter and Madame Briac in a plot to steal Ms. Farrar's diamond? Were they partners in the drug trade, until the porter got greedy and tried to eliminate Briac to keep the gem and all drug profits for himself?

But what about the other murders when the porter is far away on his train, or back home in Fulumbane? Besides, he's a known, entity of respectability. Twenty-nine years with the railroad, a year from retirement. With zero complaints, in twenty-nine years, about his services or a light-fingered approach to passengers sporting expensive goods. He's also a family man who owns a house, has been married thirty-two years, is a grandfather. Doesn't seem plausible. Just as Madame Briac doesn't seem like Queen of the Druggies...

Round and round and round. Man, get the cobwebs out! Facts. Stick to the facts!

Captain X'Zimbalwa jumps from his desk, paces back and forth in frustration. Guitterez? Petroff? No, the facts all point in the same direction: Goldstone, only killer who makes sense.

"*Messieurs les jurés*–Members of the jury," he sees himself elegantly expounding his Killer-Equals-Goldstone-the-culprit.

Alas! The Colonel-Detective, damn his M'Bélé blood, will take the limelight in court. Ah, well, Goldstone obviously killed the

Farrar woman and stole her diamond, which he hid most cleverly. How? Swallowed? Given its transparency, doubtful even an X-ray would reveal presence in the digestive tract. By this time, it must have emerged. Disgustingly.

How Goldstone got into the victim's cabin remains a mystery. And how Madame Briac fits into the scheme of things, if in fact she does, is also unclear.

Well, Colonel M'Bazi can solve those problems. After all, he's supposed to be the great big-shot sleuth. Let him earn his reputation.

The Captain looks at the paper in front of him, now covered with scribblings. Sad that his ratiocinations prove he'll have to pass up his chance of a lifetime, his golden opportunity to be of service to the X'Zambili people, to Bhulliwah-X'Zilone, to emerge from this a hero, toppler of governments, a man owed a scintillating future by the highest powers-that-be. But Petroff and Guitterez-Shaughnessy as suspects? They just don't cut it.

He'll end a Captain. With lots of luck—and a ton of servile kowtowing to the right people, always assuming they'd still be the right people and not the very wrong people a week, a month, a year down the road, it might barely be possible to make Assistant Departmental Commissioner with the rank of Major and a semi-comfortable retirement.

Not a bad goal, really. But from one minute to the next in Zembeylia you never know where things are going.

Still, best to serve Minister M'Bowé faithfully, while kidding Bhulliwah-X'Zilone along, just in case. If Bhulliwah wants the murderer to be Petroff, tell him that evidence is gathering…

How can the man have done it under the eyes of everyone on board? White magic? The Captain chuckles. Whites, when you've seen through their posturings and maneuvers, aren't so impressive. Like all tricksters, they dazzle when viewed briefly from a distance. Up close, you see the mechanisms and they become as mundane, greedy, and sordid as Zembeylians. Maybe more so.

His telephone rings. He picks up the receiver. Minister M'Bowé. "Captain, it is now clear that Eugene Petroff is our chief suspect. Not Goldstone, but Petroff. It would be most desirable, yes most desirable, if you found evidence to implicate him in these murders. Perhaps in concert with Monsieur Goldstone? I leave that to you. But we have become convinced, here in the capital, that Petroff is the architect of these evil doings. We urge you to substantiate this in the quickest possible time. Am I clear?"

"Yes, Sir. I do understand, Sir."

"Excellent. I await your report. This case can be a great opportunity, Captain. On the other hand…" Minister M'Bowé hangs up.

Captain X'Zimbalwa cradles his head in his hands.

And the phone rings again. "Get your ass up here double quick," says Colonel-Detective M'Bazi. "There are developments and I need help."

Chapter 24: Lionheart
X'Ziloncado Game Preserve and Fulumbane,
Friday Afternoon, December 18

Roaring across the skies in a police helicopter makes Captain X'Zimbalwa feel important, though he had to fill out a dozen forms with explanations and justifications as to why he couldn't hop a train or drive or, at best, take the daily DC-3 flight to M'Bukusa's international airport, only three-quarters of a mile from the game resort-reserve.

That Colonel-Detective M'Bazi's clout is the deciding factor in commandeering this elderly *Alouette* chopper also doesn't help his feeling of being vital to the scheme of things.

Still, the colonel considers him a significant enough ally to whisk him aloft, even if on the telephone he referred to the captain's posterior in language usually reserved for addressing privates.

X'Zimbalwa looks down on Mount Adrienne, with its snowy peak, the snow dry, patchy, brown with mud. On the mountain's western flank, he sees red rocks and grasses, the lushness of tropical Savanna. As he peers through Plexiglas, the mountain falls away and the whirlybird descends to skim over miles of trees and grasslands. He sees giraffes and zebras and herds of wildebeest. At a bend in the X'Zulongo River–Zembeylia's answer to Kipling's "Great Gray Green Greasy Limpopo"–they come upon a troop of elephants bathing. Four large cows stand guard, two on each bank, while the others cavort in the water, splashing mud over themselves against the day's heat and stinging flies. He sees mothers blowing water at their babies, always watching they don't wander too far from shore or out of their depths.

None of the creatures so much as raise heads as they roar above. The pilot keeps high enough so the sky-beast won't be considered a threat, despite its noise.

Do they know who we are? Do they have a concept for human being? wonders the Captain. He dismisses these questions as idle, tells himself to concentrate on the case.

They land in a fine cataclysm of sound and swirl of dust. Gratifying to see small figures on the ground, grow large and put hands over ears as their craft settles onto its runners in the circular drive before the game lodge.

M'Bazi and the captain's own sergeant, the one the Americans have baptized "He-With-The-Unpronounceable-Name"–are there to greet him.

X'Zimbalwa ducks under the still turning rotor blade, straightens to salute his superior and receives return salutes from both men. Then they all shake hands.

"We'll sit on the verandah and have tea," says M'Bazi. "Sergeant, check on our prisoner." The non-com clicks his heels, salutes again, takes himself off.

Settled on the flagstoned terrace, shaded by an umbrella, with tea and some shortbread cakes before them, the colonel gets to business. "Our guests are dying like flies and I'm not satisfied we have the killer."

A ray of hope shoots through Captain X'Zimbalwa. Can it be, uhm, Petroff, ah, yes, Petroff, after all? How pleased that would make Bhulliwah! And, of course, the Minister!

Again he allows a vision of himself, gleaming General's stars on his uniform shoulder-boards, riding around the capital in a luxurious staff car and rapping out orders to obsequious subordinates. "Yes, General of Detectives X'Zimbalwa, Sir!"

Whether or not there was a god in the sky, he would be almost a god on the ground in a X'Zambili-dominated X'Zembeylia. One day he might even be telling M'Bazi–still and forever a colonel? Alas for him!–to "Get Your Ass Here On The Double!" Sweet revenge. Oh not really, just a deserved comeuppance.

But there are others whose snubs and sneers he has suffered. As the saying goes, revenge is a dish tasting better for being savored cold. "I have always found Petroff suspicious," he murmurs. "Can we truly account for his movements?"

Immediately upon leaving Sandaram in the Turkish Baths, Bhulliwah speeds to his Parliamentary office. Provided he works with dispatch, the moment is ideal. At least he hopes so.

Inspired by Britain's Parliament, on Fridays at 4 P.M. the government, through its Prime Minister, has to answer questions from, in Zembeylia's case, the Not-So-Loyal Opposition.

Prime Minister Léon-François X'Zirumba isn't the quickest mouth in the African southeast but he has the Council of Unity and Governance behind him, with its veto rights over any Parliamentary initiative slipping by his vigilance. He also is beneficiary of the "Defense of Freedom of Speech Act (D.F.S.A.)," guaranteeing his government's freedom to arrest any Parliamentarian, "…who by an ill-considered use of words, abuses the People's right to express its Will through exercise of the Legitimate Authority."

So far, D.F.S.A. has been effective in curbing over-exuberance by the Opposition at question-time. Especially after the shadow-Minister of Postal and Welfare Services had been dragged screaming from Parliament House to a sedan with curtained windows. Plainclothesmen–"Surveillance Guards?"–had done the dragging, at least it's assumed so. These are official government employees and the poor ex-Minister hasn't been seen these past eight months.

Minister M'Bowé went on national television to explain what he termed "A sad but necessary procedure in defense of Zembeylian democracy." A U.S. State Department bulletin fully supported what it called "This demonstration of Enlightened Authoritarianism by a régime devoted to its own form of democratic endeavor."

And B.A.R.F. promptly donated another $300 million of U.S., British, French, German and Japanese taxpayer funds to a "Defense of Democracy" initiative launched by King M'Zumba I.

In any event, Zembeylia, according to *Newsweek*, is "…enjoying what government spokespersons and international community specialists describe as 'A wave of economic resurgence.'"

The withholding of paychecks to salaried personnel has, in fact, allowed official unemployment figures to be reduced, in statistical reckoning, from 88.3% to less than 20.1%, with fewer than 500 people per month reportedly dying of starvation.

Infant mortality, too, has benefitted from new statistical methodology to shrink from 57% to a low, low 44.5%.

Bhulliwah-X.Zilone looks at his golden Rolex. Before Parliament's session, he has just time to make all-important phone calls putting the machinery of revolution in motion. This is the hour he has toiled for. He can only hope it isn't premature.

Not without misgivings does he stand up in the House and thunderously demand to know what sinister machination is being perpetrated against the Zembeylian nation by the murderous maneuverings of one Eugene Petroff and his lackey, Lincoln Goldstone. Their connection to the Jeffrey B. Ace Corporation have just been revealed to him.

"And what is this Ace Corporation?" Bhulliwah demands rhetorically. "I will tell you what. A corrupter! A scheming underminer of our nation's great patrimony: our wondrous natural glory, our beaches, our forests and rivers, our X'Ziloncado Basin and Game Preserve. These attractions are the key to wealth, untold wealth. They shall bring world-class resorts, tourists, opera houses to our shore. Through *trickle-down* economics, they shall benefit all. I repeat ALL! But Ace, vicious, unprincipled schemer, seeks to lay waste our mountain climes and unspoiled shores for the purpose of entering into a totally illegal trade: the sale of poisonous drugs, condemned by every civilized nation." Bhulliwah pounds the lectern with his fist. "Zembeylians! X'Zambilis! We must stop this rape and perversion of our cherished land." Impromptu, he utters the words that Y. Sanjeev Sandaram had spoken to him, words that in the ensuing hours will become his slogan and the slogan of X'Zambilis everywhere: "The Time Is Now!"

"The Time Is Now!" echo *Democratists*. Whistles and foot stampings drown out protests from government loyalists.

The Prime Minister reaches for a telephone at his desk to call in the SM guards. The instrument is ripped from his hands. Several Bhulliwahites run to the doors to barricade them.

"I call on the nation," their leader continues, "I call on all X'Zambilis, all Tamil-Indian peoples, all French and minorities and, yes, M'Bélés of goodwill, to go on STRIKE! I have given necessary orders to accomplish this. The revolution is at hand! Not a streetlight shall burn, not a telephone shall ring, not a truck nor train shall run, nor a ship sail, nor a plane fly. Shops and schools shall not open, factories shall shut down, markets shall close. No longer are we to be crushed into the dust by an unscrupulous minority that treats with such as the Ace Corporation. Down with the oppressor! Down with the Council of Unity and Governance, stiflers of democracy! And down with those who would pervert our beautiful natural environment for sordid personal profiteering! Let true democracy and X'Zambili Nationhood prevail!"

"Arrest that man! Arrest him!" manages to cry the Prime Minister, "D.F.S.A.! D.F.S.–" a hand goes over his mouth, he's toppled backward off his seat and pushed onto a bench. Three *Democratists,* awaiting further instructions, sit on him.

Bhulliwah strikes a Napoleonic pose. "Arrest me if you dare," he cries. "You cannot arrest all the people. My only word is this: Forward to Victory! The Time Is Now!"

My ankle-bracelet chafes, itches. Every time I walk to the edge of my little compound it starts to bleat and a rifle-toting guard jumps out of the bushes to point his damned weapon at my stomach.

Where is Suzanne? Is anyone doing anything to get to the bottom of this mess? Or are all those I love and count on sitting back, partying, laughing, proceeding with life's routines and agendas while waiting for my head to roll? What a relief for them all when it does! One less thing to feel conscience stricken about. And what a conversation-piece!

I chew my nails.

I even miss the colonel-detective. At least I can carry on an intelligent discussion with the man. And they won't let me go see animals, the reason I came here in the first place.

Yeah? Why was I in a position to come? Why invited? Oh, obviously because of my agency's brilliant record in sending money-soaked clients on African safaris, I don't think. Or is it because of the number of bus tickets to the Catskills that Shangri-La has sold? Better stop griping and try, yes try to figure things out.

Beyond the fence, beyond the hippo pond and trees, something catches my eye: a tawny blur. Leopard leaping from a branch onto the back of an antelope calf, dragging it into tall grass.

209

As fast as ankle-bracelet allows, I limp into my tent for the camera. Then I brush through trees, start down the pond's embankment for a clearer view.

The alarm goes off; the soldier appears brandishing his rifle. Damnation to HELL! Can't see much anyway. Grasses too high. I gesture to the guard, point towards waving sheaves through which the leopard is dragging the kill to its tree.

The guard shakes his head, motions with the weapon to get back to the clearing.

With a sigh, I sit down at my outdoor table, where I take the typewriter from its case. The guard goes back to his station. I return to my chronology, painstaking markdown of everything I can remember about my troubles.

"There is nothing that says Petroff couldn't be involved," says Captain X'Zimbalwa hopefully.

"There's nothing that says your great aunt's cousin's mother-in-law isn't the murderer, at least as far as the train is concerned," responds M'Bazi. "Except she wasn't on it. There's not a shred of evidence indicating Petroff. Without evidence, what have we got? A politically desirable subject on whom we'd both love to pin the murder to please our boss. In my book, not good enough."

"I suppose not," says X'Zimbalwa glumly. He brightens. "Unless we help the evidence along?"

M'Bazi waves a finger at his subordinate. "Once you start playing those games you travel down a slippery slope. I'm no saint, but I have this lingering respect for truth. So will you, as long as you're working for me."

"I guess," says the Captain reluctantly. "It means we're stuck with Goldstone."

"Yeah, buckets of evidence pointing towards him. Trouble is, too much evidence for my liking. I'm finding it harder and harder to believe he's the one."

"Aren't you overreaching, Sir? Making this more complicated than it is?"

From his shirt pocket, M'Bazi takes a rumpled pack, shakes out a slightly bent cigarette, offers it. X'Zimbalwa declines. The colonel-detective sticks it in his own mouth, lights up. "You can put it to my New York experience but I'm just not interested in railroading, no matter how useful. Plenty of guys over there on the take and guys who cut corners; but we had honest cops too. Their satisfaction came from getting the case right, whether it pleased the powers-that-be or not. They're the ones I admire. You can find worse models in this world."

X'Zimbalwa mumbles something.

"What did you say? Go on, spit it out."

"I said you're a bloody idealist. So court martial me!"

"Naw. You're right. But in this crazy place where who's up, who's down can change in a flash, just plodding along chasing truth could be the safest career-move for us both. Think on it, pal."

The captain stays silent.

One of the women guides approaches. "Colonel, a phone call for you. From *Monsieur le Ministre* M'Bowé. Urgent, he says."

M'Bazi hurries inside the lodge, to his "consulting room," as he likes to think of the library. He picks up the desk telephone.

After some crackling and buzzing, Minister M'Bowé comes on the line. "Revolution!" he shouts. "That monster Bhulliwah has called a general strike. This whole place is being shut down. I've mobilized troops but they're useless; except for the SM, whom we pay. The phones may be cut anytime."

"What can I do from here, Excellency?"

"The Chinese are getting into the act. Should've realized those goddam *Democratists* are Commies. Bastards! So the Chinese are broadcasting worldwide denunciations of what they call our government's connivance with, and I quote: 'Imperial Goldstonism, conceived and carried out by the American-backed lackey-puppet who heads an international capitalist conspiracy to make Zembeylia

211

a leading narcotics pusher, thus an outcast among nations...'
Wordy, these fucking Chinese, aren't they? Poetry can be so much
more succinct, if not in the epic form I favor. Anyway, they're
threatening to send paratroops from Beijing and Cuba to bring
about, I quote again, 'A government, healthy and pure of spirit,
reflecting the people's true will...' What a load of lionshit!"

"Do you want me back in the capital?"

Loud laugh. "Try and get here, *cher ami*. The place is ringed
with X'Zambili marauders secretly armed by guess who? Must've
been the Chinese—unless the C.I.A. is operating some devious
double...No, impossible. You'd better stay put. A helicopter's out
front here waiting to take us—my family, the Minister of Finance
and a few necessary items he's bringing—as far as Komati-Poort in
South Africa. From there we'll fly commercially to New York so I
can address the United Nations, and then on to Washington D.C.
We'll urge our own re-invasion and counter-revolution. Meanwhile,
you defend our interests here. Make the Tented Camp your
command post. I appoint you 'Acting-Generalissimo-in-Chief Of
Zembeylian Military, Police and Security Services (SM)' under my
authority. You have my full backing. The King and his wives are en
route to Beverly Hills and I—Ah, here's the Finance Minister."

Background shuffling and the thump-thump of heavy objects.
Mutterings. "Damned cases weigh a ton."

"No, dear. You and the children must carry one each. Do you
want us to starve?"

Then, "Colonel, I mean Generalissimo," Minister M'Bowé is
back on the line. "I leave the national interests in your hands. Be
worthy of the trust!"

Silence. M'Bowé has hung up.

What to do? M'Bazi summons X'Zimbalwa and the whole
police detail, except for the man guarding me. In terse words he
explains the situation.

The ensuing hours are hard to endure. The telephones go dead.
Police and resort staff worry about loved ones far away, especially

those in the cities. Fulumbane is in Bhulliwah's hands. National Radio has been rechristened "Radio Freedom." It is broadcasting propaganda lauding Bhulliwah as "The Nation's new leader." His cohorts and a so-called "Popular Front Coalition" is spearheaded by the "X'Zambili Peoples' Party."

Moreover, Zembeylia is no longer Zembeylia but "New X'Zambilia," in honor, says the broadcaster, "Of the X'Zambili ethnic majority."

At 8 P.M., another announcement from "Radio Freedom." It has changed its name again to "Radio New X'Zambilia," The announcer says that Minister M'Bowé., his family and the Finance Minister, have fled. Three-quarters of the national treasury's gold reserve has fled with them.

However, Dr. Fang Shi Wu, official representative of the Chinese Communist Party in New X'Zambilia, is said to have given assurances that emergency aid is coming for "National rehabilitation as a free Popular Democracy liberated from international capitalist greed."

Generalissimo M'Bazi can't think of anything for himself and his men to do. He decides their most effective initiative is to take no initiative and see where the chips fall.

So police, the resort staff plus the American enforced guests from Eland, minus my pariah self, sit down at a verandah table to tense, subdued dinner.

The Chinese tourists have long since departed, presumably for home. Or parachute-muster?

One of the camp staffers comes running out. "The telephone's back," she cries. "We have service! And there's a call for you, *Mon Généralissime.*"

M'Bazi hastens inside again. X'Ziromeu City on the line: an SM lieutenant at the Municipal Hospital. He announces that Madame Félicité Briac has regained consciousness.

213

Chapter 25: Bhulliwah Rules
Tented Camp, Friday Evening, December 18

Madame Briac! The colonel, or rather the newly-promoted Generalissimo, had almost forgotten her. Not really, but he'd written her off as a lost cause, no practical benefit. Now she's conscious and coherent, according to her doctor; although weak and at any moment liable to slip away into near-comatose sleep.

"Can we meet with her?" he asks the physician.

"So long as she's awake and willing. But her sleep takes priority. It's the best therapy we can give her just now, especially today with…" the medical man, realizes he's speaking to a political person, decides not to finish his sentence.

"How's the situation?"

"We believe she's on her way to recov–"

"I mean the streets, man. What's happening?"

"Well, a few hours ago there was shooting and yelling and you could hear glass breaking. Looting the shops, you know. No one came in here, except a few battered people to the emergency room. Pretty tame, for a revolution."

"Safe for us to come to the hospital? We have a helicopter."

"Oh, I wouldn't tonight. The lights keep flickering on and off. Of course, there's our own emergency generator, so we're not too worried. The hospital compound does have a helipad. In the rear courtyard."

"I know, I know." The Generalissimo makes a decision. "We'll try in the morning. By that time a lot of smoke should've cleared."

He hangs up, calls X'Ziromeu City's police headquarters. After a wait he gets through to the desk sergeant (SM), who reports there has been a flurry of violence and looting, with some soldiers breaking ranks and joining the revolutionaries to make off with TVs, VCRs, computers, video game apparatuses and, for some reason, bathroom fixtures. "Lots of bathtubs and bidets reported missing," says the sergeant, adding "The ordinary troops here haven't been paid in several weeks..." He lets the sentence hang.

As abruptly as the disorder occurred, calm has returned to the streets, so the sergeant says. The municipal police have come out of hiding. A deputy minister, sent by the Central Government in X'Fulumbane, as the capital is now re-named, flew in to reconfirm a hierarchy of order.

Military commanders were summoned to police headquarters and told to gather up their troops with a promise of no sanctions plus this month's pay to be disbursed tomorrow; provided, of course, they return immediately to barracks and don't agitate for six month back salaries. Such won't be honored. Only a single month.

"Given the circumstances, sacrifices just have to be made," the deputy minister delivers his power-elite mantra in weighty tone before climbing into his private airplane and heading back to a 6,000 hectare plantation-estate near the capital.

A trickle-down boon to common folk, if not to shopkeepers, comes with Bhulliwah's Emergency Decree #9, that loot needn't be returned if all marauding stops. Now! The new "Government-of-the-People," as self-appointed Prime Minister Bhulliwah's régime styles itself, declares a general amnesty for "irregularities" occurring in the context of what is officially referred to in Emergency Decree #11 as "The Glorious-Almost-Without-Bloodshed Revolution."

Emergency Decree #15 states that from now on all military, including the SM, would be styled "The People's Military" and police "The People's Police." It is ordered that every citizen must address every other citizen as "Friend," and put this meaningful sign of general equality before all titles. So Bhulliwah himself is now "Friend Prime Minister." And X'Ziromeu City's Police Chief is "Friend People's Police Chief."

"A little less than Brother and more than Comrade," is M'Bazi's cynical paraphrase of Hamlet's pun on kin and kind.

215

"Oh, and you M'Bélé's," says the Friend Sergeant, "are to put an 'X' before your names, so you are now X'M'Bazi Friend Generalissimo, Sir."

Friend X'M'Bazi, and, suddenly of the X'M'Bélé tribe, finds himself at a loss for words. Gently he hangs up the receiver. He manages to get through to his family. They're safe in a walled Big Five housing development ringed by loyal SM troops paid out of B.A.R.F. funds. His wife sounds calm. She says they have food for a long siege, the kids are fine, her father and X'M'Bazi's brother are armed and coordinating with the SM.

Aside from a radio announcement that schools will be closed all day Saturday, instead of open for the usual morning half-day session—as modeled on a former French system—things seem pretty normal.

"Nobody really has the stomach for war these days," says Friend Mrs. X'M'Bazi. "In a way it's sad, given our M'Bélé tradition of always ready for a good fight."

Pensively, the Generalissimo makes his way back to the verandah. Yes, his people have been herdsmen, wanderers, warriors up to as little as fifty years ago and for thousands of years before that. They're proud to be an offshoot of the tribes-folk of the Upper Nile: highlanders from near its source in Burundi and lakes.

Tall, with well-defined features, skilled at war and the ways of animals, almost at one with nature. Very different from X'Zambili lowland farming and fisherfolk, whom they're condemned to live with.

Oh, X'Zambilis are said to have superior brainpower, an Old Wives Tale. But the M'Bélés have a monopoly on glamour and poise, with their self-contained wildness, their ability to settle wherever they wander: at home in the heights, at home in the grasslands, at home in Africa's vast middle.

His grandfather, dead these ten years, had still known a thing or two about organizing, building and defending a *kraal* of mud huts. The Generalissimo remembers as a boy how the old man took

216

him to the stream near their house to teach him to fish with his bare hands. He'd caught a few, although he's never been a handy type. Too civilized. Too many traditions lost...

X'M'Bazi sighs. Now Zembeylians or New X'Zambilians, or whatever the hell they'll be called day-after-tomorrow, need to learn to catch hold of and hang onto the twists and turns of this so-called modern world.

Twisting towards what? Survival? Annihilation? Of course annihilation, humanity and all the major animals with it is inevitable, given human talent and inventiveness for polluting the environment and developing such "boons to civilization" as the Hydrogen Bomb, Disease Warfare, etc. etc.

Such annihilation potential, coupled with human greed for the immediate advantage and no attention to long-term consequences will end our existence pretty quick. X'M'Bazi chews over this idea, as though he hasn't chewed on it thousands of times. What a blight we humans are on Earth, our Mother. The Friend Generalissimo sighs in sadness.

Best thing any of us endowed with a grain of good will is to struggle, thus stave off inevitability. One hopes, too, that humans are merely transitional to a better, more careful, less brutalized race of beings, who will treasure what they have and strive to keep peace among themselves and among all children of nature, including the birds, the bees, all the fine and wondrous animals whose presence still bless New X'Zambilia or whatever its name-to-come.

No way to tell locally if we Africans can be good temporary guardians of this patrimony. Certain things have to change, like the corruption infecting every aspect of national life. Corruption! A long agony, though he is one of the few top-dog types benefitting from its privileges.

What must be protected at all costs, so to endure, is the X'Ziloncado Basin with its glorious abundance of plants and animals living in accordance with nature's laws and Darwinian theory. Yes, harsh and unforgiving to species unfit to survive,

217

humankind being a prime candidate. Harsh, but always favorable to those advancing the cause of selection through adaptation. Sometimes brutal and unforgiving, sometimes gentle. But uncompromising in the cause of Earth, of Nature herself

X'M'Bazi's brow lightens. Space. Maybe humanity's enlightenment will come from a spaceship landing here with creatures so advanced they'll take over as wiser, more creative, more far-seeing rulers of our world and its treasures: like elephants and porpoises and the other advanced animals of proven intelligence. There's an idea to make a man smile; to soldier on in hope, eternal hope—

As he comes back to the table, Captain X'Zimbalwa looks at him anxiously.

"Madame Briac's awake and coherent," X'M'Bazi reports "Now go call your family. I'm sure they're safe. Things sound okay, especially in X'Ziromeu City."

Hastily, the captain leaves for the lodge's telephone.

The Generalissimo decides not to sit down again, saying, "I'm off to check on our patient and our prisoner."

At the infirmary, he finds Sheila looking pale but relatively perky. Her hospital bed is tilted up and she's reading. They chat for a minute or two. He doesn't think it an opportune moment to inform her of changes: Zembeylia becoming New X'Zambilia, or his own, uhm, dazzling (?) promotion. He'll be lucky to retain the rank of colonel, or even yardbird once this new régime settles in.

Disquieting. Oh for "The Sidewalks of New York!" Pensively, he walks down the infirmary hallway.

The nurse catches up with him, plucks at his sleeve. "I am being deeply disturbed," she says. The Generalissimo opens the double swing doors of the infirmary's lighted entry. He gestures for her to step through.

They stand outside and he produces his cigarette pack, offers it. She shakes her head. He lights one for himself. "So what's the story?" he asks.

"Well, you see, sir, I–"

The lights go out. From Sheila's room, a bloodcurdling scream.

Chapter 26: Dinner For Two
Manhattan, Friday Evening, December 18

"I'm really so grateful," says Suzanne, once they've ordered filet of sole shirred in cream and garnished with bananas for herself; vegetarian organic brown rice with *azuki* beans ringed by macerated kale for Rahel. "I just couldn't have faced the kindly contempt of Carson's acolytes, not to mention going to 'The Valley' and having to explain everything to those seedy, uncaring…" She takes a gulp of vodka martini.

Rahel waves her hand dismissively. "But what did we find out? Okay, that somebody's impersonating you with the idea of sticking you for a murder." She sips Mother Nature's Organically Grown Sarsaparilla. "Who it is, we don't know. I may have found a clue as to why."

"Well, a woman did it. That eliminates half the human race."

"Less than half," Rahel smiles a schoolmistressy smile. "There's a good chance she's a puppet, perhaps the unwitting one, of a man, since women so often are. Or was it a man dressed as a woman?"

Suzanne shakes her head. "She stayed too long at the mail drop and talked too much. The guys there, the owner and U.P.S. driver, would've cottoned to a female impersonator." She leans forward. "Has to be someone connected with Goldstone and his stupid trip to Africa. I mean, that's where we need to look for motives."

Food arrives, served with a flourish by a red-jacketed waiter. He sweeps away chafing covers to reveal their orders, each topped by a radish shaped like a rose and borders sporting mint sprigs, mark of this brand new half-gastronomic, half-organic eatery on the Upper East Side: Amandine. Totally "in" these days, as attested by a quick look around. Two tables to the north, Woody Allen and his party consume sliced duck. Three tables to the east, Congressman A. "Snakebite" D'Annunzio (R-New Jersey) is holding forth, napkin tied around neck, fork waving in air.

At Amandine, Manhattan prices are at their most flamboyant. The least she can do, Suzanne feels, is to invite Rahel to a really splashy place after her tiring cross-country journeys back and forth. The restaurant is the only one she can think of that combines Manhattan *chic* with the demands of her guest's restrictive health food diet.

A wine waiter, bow tied and dressed in black, uncorks a half bottle of *Chablis*, sniffs the cork, gives a sage nod, pours a splash into a glass on a side table. He sips it with a susurrating gargle, nods again.

At last, almost grudgingly, he fills Suzanne's glass to the quarter mark and sets the bottle in an ice bucket. He opens a fresh bottle of sarsaparilla for Rahel.

Suzanne sips wine; with her fish knife she carves a luscious slice of delicately browned sole, well marinated in its sauce. She feasts and gazes somewhat guiltily at Rahel delicately sampling her slim-worthy, organic vegetarian dish. "Sure," Suzanne opines, "stealing the diamond is a motive for Helen Farrar's murder. But the other murders? They've all got to be connected, don't you think?" she chews meditatively. Really delicious. Fattening, but…

"Seems clear," responds Rahel. She essays another swallow of sarsaparilla. "We can't ignore Helen Farrar's professional position as king-pin, I mean queen-pin, of her dominant, and domineered-over, empire. The others, her husband, the sister, that Barry fellow you're supposed to have murdered, any one of them could have run things after her death." She takes a forkful of rice and beans. "If they had to be bumped off as well, for the murderer's purpose, then this mess goes beyond the diamond. Helen's business ventures have to be key."

"Okay, who benefits, as the lawyers say?" Suzanne nods to the waiter; he pours more wine.

Rahel shrugs.

"Well," says Suzanne, looking over her raised glass at her guest, "it's what we need to find out. And I've made a start." She pulls two sets of papers from her handbag. "One for you, one for me. A list of tour members, their companies, their addresses, closest associates, near and dear ones, as far as I can determine from what we know already; also from searching their names on the Internet and public records. Somewhere in here has to be a lead. In fact, I believe I've developed a couple of leads." Looking mysterious, she takes a final bite of fish.

When both have finished their respective main courses, the waiter pounces on the empty plates, makes them vanish at near-magic speed. He serves two portions of frizzy salad garnished with croutons. "Will the ladies take dessert?" he asks." Coffee? Liqueurs?"

"Have you herbal teas?" asks Rahel.

"Mint, verbena, calendula, camomile, willow–"

"Calendula," interrupts Rahel. "Flower tea. That would be fine."

"And Madame?" the waiter turns to Suzanne.

"The tiramisu." She looked apologetically at Rahel and murmurs, "Can't resist. Also espresso."

The waiter bows, withdraws.

"Now," Suzanne continues, "These tour people, other than her direct associates, and Goldstone, of course, they're all Helen's business rivals. They want to grab her place in the sun." She shakes her head. "Can't imagine why she'd invite them. Or why they'd go on a trip celebrating her company's supremacy in an up-and-coming area they'd all like to control." She studies Rahel. "As someone in travel, why do you think this particular group of rivals would journey as guests of Helen Farrar and her Eland Tours, the very person and company that muscled them out of what looks to be a potentially lucrative market?"

"Let's begin at the beginning," answers Rahel, "Helen herself. Her motive is clear. All these folks are big-time suppliers of tourists. She wants them to recognize her dominant position in Zembeylia and help her make money by supplying warm bodies to her company. They'll get commissions; but she controls the infrastructure, so is positioned to make the big money, not those glorified tips they'll make." Rahel ponders. "So, maybe, all her surviving guests are in this together? A collective murder gang? Again, excluding poor Goldstone."

Suzanne reaches over, lifts her bottle of *Chablis* from its bucket, pours the last of fragrant golden wine into her glass. "Hmm. No dregs," she murmurs. "Know what the French say? Drink the dregs, you'll marry within a year." She takes a swallow. "Collective murder wouldn't make sense. The interests are too conflicting. Sure, the survivors, Goldstone, excepted, poor idiot, were jealous of Helen and wished bad things for her company; well, I've discovered some very strange items about a few of the tour group."

Dessert and Rahel's tea arrive. The waiter holds a silver pot high over a porcelain cup. The liquid makes a downward geyser. With a spoon he scoops a dried yellow flower from a plate, plops it into the brew. The petals, seem to bloom.

Suzanne eyes her generous portion of tiramisu. "How about sharing?" she asks "Too much for me."

Rahel shakes her head. "Cake soaked in liquor makes me ill."

"Well," Suzanne takes a bite. "Absolutely delicious." The waiter beams at her, places the espresso cup by her plate. "Now, Helen aside, let's go down the tour list," she continues briskly. "Who've we got, other than Goldstone and Helen's own people, her poor, dead husband, her almost dead sister and, here in New York, the sister's dead husband? There's eight left. The Jamiesons and the Petroffs—" Suzanne ticks off her fingers, "Chandler with Guitterez-Shaughnessy, the Southgate-D'Alessandro couple, very exotic, according to Goldstone. Anyway, they all have to be our suspects, okay?" She pauses for a mouthful of dessert.

"You forget the guide they picked up," says Rahel. "We don't know anything about him, but he counts as a suspect."

"Oh, okay. He's Suspect Number Nine, since he's traveling with the group. I'll get his name and information on him from Goldstone. But I have something to tell you about Gene Petroff. Through, his wife, Miho, he's extremely well connected in Japan. His specialty is golf tours and the Japanese are big on golf, particularly abroad since they don't have much space for courses at home."

Rahel nods agreement. "A year's membership at a top Japanese golf club can come to the equivalent of a million dollars in Yen. So it's much cheaper to travel and play elsewhere. The Japanese also have the reputation of being travel enthusiasts. Despite their recent economic troubles, a lot of them are still loaded."

"Zembeylia," says Suzanne, "has plans to develop some world-class courses, along with new luxury resorts. That's what my research turned up. Question is, who will do the developing? Helen Farrar's Eland Corporation, in partnership with local Zemba Royal Company? Eland certainly has an in with the government. But there's X'Zambili-Africa Tours, with much more resort expertise in several countries and excellent connections worldwide."

"I know about the Southgate-D'Alessandro couple." Rahel, pours herself more tea, sipping it delicately. "As the biggest packagers of safari tours here on the U.S. East Coast, how galling the prospect of having to go through Eland to get into Zembeylia. My understanding is they're trying to organize a major money consortium. In fact, I saw in *Travel Agent Weekly* that this consortium, called Olympia Projects, Inc., plans to build Africa's most upscale resort-casino complex right on the Zembeylian coast and that a Southgate-D'Alessandro X'Zambili-Africa Tours partnership will run it, supply it with tourists."

"So those two travel on an Eland-sponsored trip?" Suzanne shakes her head. "There's got to be a catch." The tiramisu has disappeared from her plate. She takes a good swig of coffee.

"There's something else I found out, Chandler and this Guitterez-Shaughnessy guy. Do you know where he comes from? Cali, Colombia!"

Rahel frowns. "So?"

"Don't you see? The Cali connection. Drugs. Cocaine. They say the climate and conditions near the mountain spine running north-south along Zembeylia's western side are ideal for growing coca plants. Looks like Guitterez-Shaughnessy is a conduit for some world-class drug-producing and smuggling scheme. I bet he's from a Cartel family. I'm certainly going to find out, even if I have to go to Cali to do it!"

"For God's sake, don't you get killed," says Rahel. "But you're way off base."

"Don't worry," responds Suzanne somewhat huffily. "I'm a good reporter. I know how to take care of myself. What do you mean, off base?" Without waiting for an answer, she asks, "Would you like a brandy or something sweet, like *crème de cacao*?"

Rahel shakes her head. "You go ahead."

"Only live once. And since I'm not getting married, judging from the wine…" She gestures to the wine-waiter, who hastens over. "Do you have *armagnac*?"

He smiles suavely. "We have a twenty-three year old Maillac. Truly superb and it bears the gold 'Medallion, *l'Aquit d'Or*,' an official symbol of quality. As a poet said, it has *a scent of wood violets that softly exhales through mingled aromas of ripe quinces, greengages and burnt hazel nuts.*"

"How can I refuse?"

The wine waiter hurries off.

"What do you mean off base?" Suzanne asks again.

Rahel smiles. "Chandler runs Astra Air Intercontinental, or AAI, a large, respectable charter airline. In the Caribbean, he was

224

beaten out by Helen Farrar's Helenair, for the lucrative Club Med. contract, a real windfall for her. But elsewhere, AAI is a major player as far as tourist destinations are concerned: Europe, Hawaii, Australia and New Zealand, Malaysia, South Africa, Mauritius, all sorts of premium tourist places. Except, of course, Zembeylia, where Helen again beat Chandler." Rahel pauses to drink tea. "Guitterez-Shaughnessy is Chandler's son-in-law. And chief pilot. He may be Colombian-born, but he has an American mother and he's been here for something like thirty-four years. He has a U.S. Air Force background, holds the rank of Brigadier-General in the reserves. He flew for Continental until he joined AAI. His flying credentials are impressive. So are his personal ones."

"Well, don't you see?" exclaims Suzanne excitedly. "There's a great motive for murder. Excluded by Helen Farrar for the up-and-coming Zembeylian air routes, the two of them, Chandler and Guitterez, blow away all the Farrars and Mondrans so that Eland becomes a headless snake. And they take over. Not only the air routes to Zembeylia but Helenair's Caribbean trade into the bargain."

Rahel looks doubtful. "As I said, their reputation is up-and-up."

"So was Macbeth's, loyal companion to kings. Until he decided to murder his way to becoming king himself."

The waiter returns bearing an oversized snifter and venerable looking bottle. With a careful, precise twist of the wrist he pours a splash of sultry golden liquid, tinged slightly with green, into the glass. He stands back as Suzanne, swishes the brandy, breathes its woodsy aroma, as emanating from a cavernous, tulip-shaped vessel. She takes a small mouthful, looks up at the waiter. "Quinces, apples, hazel nuts and wood violets? Waverley Root, our magnificent American gastronomic writer, has written that the characteristic taste of *armagnac* suggests peaches." She nods her head. "I'll accept the wood violets, the hazel nuts and, yes, a touch of peach along the way. And chocolate, maybe? Truly fine." She turns to Rahel. "Too bad Goldstone isn't here to enjoy this. He'd be in seventh heaven. Sure you won't join me?"

"I really can't."

Suzanne raises her glass. "Well, to our Goldstone. One of life's great blunderers. But, on occasion, lovable."

Solemnly Rahel raises her teacup. "I'll certainly drink to him," she murmurs.

"The other thing I learned," continues Suzanne, "is that we're dealing here with Ace. Know about him?"

"The Jeffrey B. Ace Corporation?"

Suzanne nods. "Got its mitts on Pacific World Airways, a very successful operation. And they have something to do with South African mining. In any case, I came across the name while looking through our archives at *The New Republic*." She lowers her voice. "About a month and a half ago, the Ace company sent a representative to Zembeylia. He toured the country, met with the highest government officials. The articles I read didn't say what was agreed on, except that when the Ace man was leaving Zembeylia, he made an airport statement. I copied it down." She opens her bag, brings out a rumpled paper. It says, 'Investment in Zembeylia is an investment in Africa's future. Ace certainly is interested.'" She takes another sip of *armagnac*, savoring its warmth in the mouth and throat. "Now here's the kicker. Know who the Ace man in Zembeylia was?"

Rahel raises an eyebrow.

"None other," announces Suzanne, "than Eugene Petroff. He just happens to be the nephew of Harlan Fenster, the company's chief operating officer. What do you think of that?"

Rahel's surprised expression is gratifying. She leans toward Suzanne, also lowering her voice, "*The Wall Street Journal* had a short article a month or two ago about a squabble between the Ace people and Helen Farrar. It was over Helenair in the Caribbean. Jeffrey Ace lives in Mexico, in Cuernavaca. He's semi-retired and Fenster, runs things these days. Because of Helenair's exclusive rights to Club Med traffic, Ace was accusing the airline of monopoly practices and threatening an antitrust lawsuit. Then the story disappeared."

"I missed it," said Suzanne. "You read *The Journal?*"

"Daily," says Rahel. "Especially everything to do with travel."

"You're much too good to be working in Goldstone's rat hole."

Rahel shrugs. "A living."

"Yeah, but not a life. So, who has a life?" Suzanne takes another swallow of *armagnac*.

Rahel gazes down at her teacup, brow furrowed. "There's one thing I found out in L.A." Her voice is hesitant.

Suzanne looks expectant. She's learning that her dinner guest doesn't make thoughtless remarks.

"Clive Lawrence, the owner of Pink Horizons, an agency out there that promotes gay and lesbian travel—and from what he implied he was Barry Mondran's lover—he told me Mondran was onto an oil, gas and mining deal involving Zembeylia." Rahel sips tea. "When I got back, I called a contact at Exxon, a friend from college. I found out two things. One, that Zembeylia looks a likely place for oil, natural gas, uranium and other metals that you strip-mine, like copper. All the goodies are concentrated in the X'Ziloncado Basin, where most of the animals live. And second, that Richmond Oil And Mineral Explorations, a company headquartered in Bermuda but with offices in Dallas, has been to the X'Ziloncado to do a preliminary study of the terrain. Richmond is a surveyor and contractor that hires out to the big oil, gas and mining firms. My source tells me there's a report from Richmond. It recommends clearing the X'Ziloncado to develop open-pit mining, drilling and frakking for oil and gas. A sizable investment would be needed but the outcome is probably a bonanza."

"What about the trees, the animals, the ecology of the place?"

Rahel shakes her head. "There would have to be a wholesale 'culling,' as they call animal slaughter over there. The animals that couldn't be taken into South Africa's Krueger Park or placed in small zoos near Zembeylia's coast for tourists to look at, would have to disappear. And the trees would go. A land of forests and tall grass, with patches of jungle and swamp, would become something different. A moonscape, maybe?"

"Horrible," says Suzanne. "I bet Ace is the link. The investor with his finger in every pie, the mover and shaker, the catalyst who'll say to big oil, big gas, big mining: 'Go to Zembeylia. Here's a fistful of cash to get started. Bastard! And Barry Mondran mixed up with them? And this Petroff character?"

"You may be jumping to conclusions."

"All I know is Goldstone–and myself too–are victims in this. We need to get to the bottom of it but fast. Ace, now. He lives in Mexico? You know what the French say: 'For results, go directly to God, don't bother with His saints. I'm off to Mexico!' She gulps the last of her *armagnac*, signals the waiter.

He comes bearing a silver platter, on which lies a leather folder.

"Ah!" exclaims Suzanne. "Moment of truth. Or, as the French say, 'The bad news!'"

And what a moment! Five years' rent in Uzbekistan, eight families fed for twenty-seven months in Zaïre, a 279 guest wedding banquet in Nicaragua. Memorable, she decides. Almost worth it.

She hands over her American Express card, adds a tip that in some parts of the world might bring the waiter a harem.

She and Rahel are bowed out of Amandine. On the sidewalk, they solemnly vow to act as Goldstone's avenging angels.

Chapter 27: Scorpio
X'Zilancado Game Camp, Friday Evening, December 18

Blackout and a scream! Sheila's room. X'M'Bazi and the nurse rush through the infirmary's swinging doors, down the hallway to the small two-bedded room.

"Are you all right?" X'M'Bazi shouts into the darkness. He smashes against a medicine cart, bangs his thigh and knee, scatters bottles.

"No! No! Help!" Sheila shouts back.

"I'm here, I'm here," says the nurse. "It is all right. Everything is being all right."

"It's not!" wails Sheila, "The bed! Don't touch the bed!"

"Minute," says the nurse. The lights come on. The nurse re-enters the room from the corridor. "Somebody has been throwing down the master switch on the fuse box."

Sheila scrunches against her bed's steel headboard, terror in her eyes. She points to the bed's middle.

For an instant, X'M.'Bazi thinks she's having a fit or maybe gone insane. Then he sees them. "My God!"

Scorpions. Three large green ones—the species whose sting bears dread M'zu-m'zu.

The nurse is quick on her feet. From the cart the Generalissimo bumped into, she grabs two jars, one containing a brownish liquid. She moves to the sink, empties the liquid, then cautiously approaches the bed. With a quick movement, she puts the jar over two of the beasts. The third starts to scuttle away.

X'M'Bazi tears off a shoe. He bangs the heel down on the scorpion. The nurse, still holding one jar over her captives, places the other so that when the Generalissimo slowly slides his shoe away, she traps the scuttler. Furiously, the stinger in its tail jams and jams the jar's side. A white, gluey mess slides down the inner wall.

"Over there," says the nurse. With her head, she indicates a stainless steel cabinet. "You will be finding tops to these jars. Third shelf."

X'M'Bazi does as he's told and approaches with the covers. Expertly the nurse tips one jar slightly, jams the cover on. She does the same with the other. The scorpions are trapped.

"Thank God!" says Sheila. She begins gingerly and slowly to stretch out her legs and put them under the bedcover.

"No!" says the nurse. "We must be checking." She tears the cover off the bed. Nothing. She nods to Sheila.

X'M'Bazi looks under the bed and into Sheila's slippers. No more uninvited guests. He goes around the room, examines the clothes that followed Sheila to the infirmary, her red velvet sausage bag and even her Gucci toilet case standing by the sink. All clear.

Sheila trembles, hands in front of her face. "They're out to get me," she says "It's so unfair. What have I done to anybody?"

X'M'Bazi frowning, looks uncomfortable.

"There, there," says the nurse. "We will not let anyone be getting you, is that not right, Generalissmo?"

"Please," says X'M'Bazi. "Generalissimo sounds like the title for a doorman at some fancy Manhattan nightclub. "I'd appreciate your calling me Colonel."

"Well, we shall be taking good care of the lady, yes, Colonel?"

He nods agreement, tries the window, finds it half open, closes and locks it. "I'm posting a guard just outside in the hall." He turns to Sheila. "As long as you don't leave this room you're absolutely safe. You have everything you need here. I've checked the place out," he nods to a door leading to an adjoining lavatory, "I'll check in there. We'll make certain you're secure. Believe me, we're going to catch the person or persons behind all this."

From his tunic pocket, he takes out his crumpled cigarette pack. "I understand you're a smoker, like me," he holds out the pack. "*Caporales* from France. A little strong, but under the circumstances…"

"Oh, thank you," says Sheila. She takes a cigarette, he lights it for her. She inhales deeply, letting out a bluish cloud.

"Smoking is being against regulations," says the nurse, "but if it is making you feel better then I am not objecting."

"Those awful animals gave me such a turn," says Sheila between puffs.

"What'll we do with 'em?" X'M'Bazi asks the nurse.

"Oh, they will be suffocating in the jars. It is best they die, do you not think?"

"I guess we can't let 'em go back into the bush. Kind of a shame. They're not responsible for being here. But now they are, they require execution."

"More than I do," says Sheila.

"Sure thing," says X'M'Bazi. "I'll go and give orders for round-the-clock guards inside here and outside as well."

"And I will be sleeping in this other bed," says the nurse. She turns to Sheila. "You will not be alone for a minute."

"One thing," says X'M'Bazi, pausing in the doorway. "We can't blame Lincoln Goldstone, at least not directly. He's been under surveillance all day long."

"I'm glad," says Sheila. "I don't want to think he's a murderer." She frowns. "Except, I don't see how anyone else could have gotten at Helen. Or what his motivation might be for that awful letter he wrote to the Ace Corporation. I wish him well, if I can believe he and his girlfriend aren't the ones who've destroyed those I love and are doing their best to hurt the business poor Helen was building so arduously, so devotedly. I know she wasn't the easiest person in the world but...she was my sister. We loved each other. I miss her. Barry, Mike..." Her chest heaves, she puts the cigarette in a pill dish by her bed, begins to sob.

The nurse clucks and coos and pours out some medicine from a bottle. "Drink this," she says. "It will help you sleep."

Sheila looks up, her face tear stained. "Not forever, I hope." She smiles wanly.

X'M'Bazi, shaking his head, gathers up the two jars with scorpions and leaves.

Outside, Captain X'Zimbalwa accosts him. "Sir, Friend Generalissmo, I have—"

"Don't call me that!"

"What do you want me to call you?"

"I dunno. Anything but not that goddam Generalissimo stuff. 'Hey, you,' I'd prefer. "Hey, you, Sir.." X'M'Bazi sighs. "Sorry, Captain. I'm not in the best of moods."

"Well, Sir, there's a development. I carried out your orders, looked in everyone's tent. And found this." X'Zimbalwa holds up a jar. Under the infirmary's outside light, X'M'Bazi sees a scorpion. He gestures for the two of them to remain standing under the light.

The new jar has airholes punched into its metal top. Inside is a little landscape: leaves and twigs on a bed of damp soil, obviously from the hippo pond, and sprinkled with gravel. The scorpion is large, green. Definitely a local, of the *M'zu-m'zu* bearing type.

"Damn thing gives me the creeps," mutters X'M'Bazi. "So, where?"

"In the Petroff tent. On a night-table. Petroff admits he collected it. Says he's an amateur zoologist with a particular interest in poisonous arthropods." The Captain shudders.

"Damning, isn't it?" says X'M'Bazi. "Maybe we'll get our wish come true. Arrest Petroff, and for once we'll please…not M'Bowé anymore but your man, Bhulliwah. They both want, or wanted, the guy for their own reasons."

"Not only that," says the captain, "but it seems the Italian, the one with the Italian name, is involved. Petroff claims that in the States the two of them belong to some insect study organization called Arthropods.com. Monsieur Petroff kept saying, 'He's in it too, he's in it too! D'Alessandro's just as involved as I am. He helped me collect the specimens.'"

X'Zimbalwa shakes his head. "Imagine! Arthropods.com?" He looks questioningly at his superior.

"Okay," says X'M'Bazi at length. "Arrest them both, put leg bracelets on them. We've got enough, haven't we?"

X'Zimbalwa nods. "Four. Our whole consignment for X'Ziromeu City. I brought them all, just in case."

"Good. Cuff these guys and get 'em here to the infirmary. There's a second room with twin beds. We'll lock 'em in there, so the same detail of round-the-clock guards can keep an eye on both rooms. Gotta ration our personnel or we'll run out. This keeps up, you and I will be doing all-night guard duty. Anyway, take all these three jars to the lodge library and put them in a cabinet. Lock the cabinet and stick on a *DO NOT TOUCH* sign. Oh, first punch airholes in these two jars, then feed the lot before placing them in the cabinet. We can present 'em live in court as evidence when the time comes. Library door to be bolted. Place a second a sign there: *NO ENTRY: OUT OF BOUNDS! VIOLATORS SUBJECT TO IMMEDIATE ARREST!*"

Captain X.Zimbalwa clicks his heels and hastens to execute his orders.

Chapter 28: Jeffy
Cuernavaca, Mexico: Saturday, December 19

As soon as she clears customs, Suzanne sees a man in black uniform, with an equally black handlebar mustache and a black chauffeur's cap. He holds a sign: *Ms. Suzanne Carrington*. She approaches, he lifts the cap, inclines his head and takes her overnighter.

"*Non se habla español,*" she says.

"That's perfectly all right, miss." His English is only slightly accented. "Many of us speak North American."

The late afternoon sun is pleasant as they cross the parking lot: warm and dry. The air smells of jet fuel and sulfur mixed with old cooking grease, par for what some call the world's most polluted city. Coming in to land, the blue sky turned brown. Now Suzanne looks up into mustardy haze.

The man gestures towards a silver Mercedes sedan. He opens a rear door for her.

"Since we can talk, I prefer to sit in front."

The chauffeur shakes his head. "Mr. Ace would not think it proper."

Expertly, the man threads through Mexico City's horrendous traffic. At length, they are on the Acapulco highway, traveling southwest and climbing out of pollution, upward along a slope of the *Serrania del Ajusco* mountains. The driver points across a wide basin containing the city that vies with Tokyo for title of world's largest. "Those two cone peaks," he says, "our volcanoes: *Iztacihuatl* and *Popocatepetl*, each about 17,000 feet. Dormant, we hope."

Impressive sight, twin mountains standing as sentinels: blessings or curses over their city. Up and down goes the road, twisting curve after curve. Suzanne lies back in her seat, closes her eyes. A long day and now only mid-afternoon. She got up before dawn, not that she'd slept too well due to her worries and last night's heavy meal with Rahel. Over-indulgence. She's getting older, must control herself more.

Surprising how easily she'd gotten through to Ace and how positively he'd responded. By 11 A.M. it was done, the meeting set up, flight and his suggested accommodation arranged. She boarded the 1:30 P.M. *Aeromexico* plane from Kennedy and here she is.

At length, they pull off the highway into the busy streets of Cuernavaca. It seems like a mini-Mexico City but less traffic-jammed. And the blue mountain sky attests to a livable atmosphere. The chauffeur, he says his name is Carlos, drives through streets growing narrower and narrower. In a particularly small one, almost an alleyway, he stops before a modest arch. As he steps around to open the door for her, a valet appears and lifts her bag from the front seat.

"*Señor* Ace will meet you for dinner," says Carlos. He puts two fingers to the brim of his cap in salute, jumps into the car and drives away.

A sign above the archway reads *Las Mañanitas*. Suzanne passes through a front door to a modest reception area, notable for its tiled floor gleamingly polished. A uniformed man stands behind a high counter. He bows, gives her a form to fill out. To the valet he speaks in Spanish; when she is done with the paperwork, he gestures for her to follow the valet who holds her suitcase.

They step into one of the loveliest settings, at once restaurant and stage set, that Suzanne has ever seen. Restaurant tables, dressed with white cloths, stand in a semicircle of tiers forming an amphitheater that slopes downhill to a lawn. Peacocks, white doves, pink egrets strut there on manicured grass At the lawn's rear and exact middle, a mosaic basin, fed by a fountain and backed by Aztec stonework, gives the decor symmetry, as well as a reminder that civilization in these parts stretches into a past far back of the coming of Cortez and "His Most Christian Spanish" marauders.

The valet leads her down a central stairway to the grass, then left to a wall. They go through a door into a corridor with another floor of polished tiles. A second door and she enters a room paneled in dark woods, very Spanish. At its center, a canopied bed. The room opens to a small garden, walled and private.

"I guess I've landed in Paradise," murmurs Suzanne. The valet smiles, sets her suitcase on a canvas baggage rack. He hands her a slip of paper. She unfolds it, reads: *Have table for 8P. Give Maître d' Roberto your name.* The paper is initialed "J."

She spends the late afternoon exploring the grounds. They aren't extensive but with surprises: a lovely swimming-pool tucked out of sight behind another garden wall. This certainly is Mexico at its ultra-best, far from noise, dirt, street anarchy, the poverty she associates with Mexican cities and the country at large, all to be seen in her brief ride through the capital's streets and outskirts. This is Mexico as it should be, as no doubt it is for the very, very rich.

After a brief nap and long shower, she feels ready for battle.

Promptly at eight she introduces herself to Roberto, who shows her to a table on one of the restaurant-amphitheater ledges. Now that it's almost dark, discreet lighting confers an effect of self-conscious theatricality on the garden, where peacocks still strut. A managed delight for the eye. Suzanne has the impression of participating in some marvelous tableau. She only hopes she'll know her part.

A shadow crosses her vision. A tall figure takes the empty seat at her table. "Lovely, isn't it? I thought you'd enjoy *Las Mañanitas,* meaning "little tomorrows." Just being here is a celebration of sorts. During the Christmas–New Year's season someone has to die for the next person on a twenty-five page waiting list to get accommodations. Let that murderous individual or individuals in your entourage take note. A fortune to be made here, bumping off prospective guests for bribes. By the way, you should have a tequila. When in Rome...Waiter, two tequilas. Oh, I'm Ace. And you're Suzanne, unless Roberto goofed, in which circumstance I apologize for the intrusion."

He holds out a hand. Soft, pudgy. A tall man but pear-shaped. His face, rather fat with very red cheeks. Trim white beard, gold-rimmed glasses, not young. Seventy or thereabouts, she guesses.

"Yes, I'm Suzanne. Thank you for allowing me to intrude on you."

"Not at all, not at all. Always a pleasure to dine with a beautiful woman, especially here."

"Do you live in Cuernevaca?"

"Just outside, on a hill. I could have asked you up but I have a houseful of guests, a bevy of not very refined damsels; well, since you're a French-speaker, *des cocottes.* Ladies of the evening, not to mince words. Imported from Britain, Vienna and, of all places, Turkey. *Madame Claude,* the famed French and international Madam—or *Beisel Mama,* as Eastern Europeans say more colorfully—does me well. In old age one becomes more and more, how should I put it? *rococo* in one's search for amusement. Though, unlike your lovely self, I absolutely shun Los Angeles and its pleasures. Yes, I while away time before the end of time. Speaking graves reminds me of Graves, Robert. Or I should say Suetonius? The Emperor Tiberias, in any event. No stranger to murder, was he? What would

236

Tiberias have made of the goings-on in Zembeylia? He certainly became very esoteric at Capri, didn't he ever? Liked little boys and what Nabokov calls *nymphets*. Bisexual *fellatio* in his swimming pool. My tastes are more conventional, slightly more. But I take enough heed of good manners not to mix persons from different social settings."

The tequilas arrive. Suzanne wonders how, through this barrage of words, she'll get to make her case, have her questions answered. Parsing his verbiage, he's done his homework. She hadn't told him about knowing French. Or her trip to L.A.

Ace licks the salt rim off his glass. "Cheers, many happy returns," he says and drinks deeply. "Now for appetizers I suggest mini-tamales. Homegrown Mexican cuisine at its most delicious."

Two portions of small tamales are served, one with red sauce, the other with green. Indeed delicious. Good starters for a meal both tasty and refined. And Jeffrey B. Ace chatters away—most of the time salaciously—about absolutely nothing. Every now and then there's a verbal jab to show he's aware of the circumstances bringing her to him.

She opts for no dessert, no coffee or brandy. Inspired by Rahel, this is her night for de-caffeinated tea.

Ace sighs. "I feel as if I'm in the dentist's chair trying to stave off drilling by my talk. You'd better tell me what your delightful but determined invasion of my privacy is about." He gestures the waiter for another tequila.

Suzanne lays out her story. "I understand that your firm and an oil, gas and mineral exploration company called Richmond are collaborating to exploit the X'Ziloncado Basin for drilling and also uranium open-pit mining. Thus you will eliminate the area's vegetation, and starve to death all the animals living there."

Jeffrey Ace lets out a guffaw. "That's your understanding? If You're right, what would you do about it?"

"Surely you don't condone—"

"Oh, a little murder here, a little murder there. All in a good cause, my dear. That frightful harpy Helen Farrar? Do you think I wept my pillow soggy when I heard she'd kicked the bucket? Or had it kicked for her?" He shakes his head. "I'm a capitalist. I horde my tears for the great occasions, namely for occasions affecting me."

"And her death, the deaths of so many members of Eland don't affect you? Not emotionally but from a business standpoint?"

"Hardly in the way you think, honey bun."

Suzanne bristles. Overstepping there. She hopes she won't have to barricade her bedroom against him. He'd be capable of climbing over the garden wall to her patio. Then what?

"Ah," says Ace, apparently a thought-reader, "I suppose I better tell you and toddle home for my evening massage. Eloise from Birmingham, England. Quite a masseuse. What she can do with, well never mind." He looks up from his fifth tequila. "I don't suppose you give massages?"

Suzanne shakes her head vigorously. "No, not at all. Mr. Ace, if we can get back to—"

"Oh, call me Jeff. My friends do."

"All right, Jeff, but—"

"'Jeffy?' Will you call me 'Jeffy?'"

"Just Jeff."

"You're totally misguided, you know. Me finance Richmond? What a laugh! You've come on one helluva long expensive journey for absolutely nothing. And you could have talked to Harlan Fenster in New Jersey. Why didn't you? I'm retired now, Tiberius at Capri, spending his days having his private parts suckled in the swimming pool. Never mind, never mind. Not your cup of whatever. Look," behind his glasses, glittering in the restaurant's lights, he fixes her with eyes blue, bright and friendly. "I'd have gladly murdered Helen Farrar. Anytime, anywhere. But business-wise I can think of better moves. And Richmond doesn't need Ace financing. They've got all the money in the world. Besides, it so

238

happens I like lions and leopards and trees and nature. Do you want the real truth in all this, at least as far as Jeffrey B. Ace Corporation is concerned? We're takeover people. My friend Fenster's brilliant at it. We sneak in when nobody's looking and buy our way to controlling business situations that we think desirable. Zembeylia's a comer in tourism. That's the card we're playing. Tomorrow morning I'll call Fenster. I want you to go to his office, let him give you a rundown on our strategy. You'll be very surprised and you'll have an exclusive. Your trip down here won't be wasted after all. You'll be able to knock heads."

A pause for his words to have effect. Then, "One thing, though," Ace holds up an admonishing finger. "A murder investigation is okay and I'm all for you bringing the culprit or culprits to justice, since it or they ain't me nor mine. But I need your solemn promise not to mix detection with reporting. Much of what we may tell you is not for publication. We trust you, you've got to be honorable with us. Deal?"

Suzanne holds up her hands. "I hate it, but what can I do? Yes, deal."

"Just in case you think I'm a total nerd, if you ever see fit to violate our little pact of reportorial discretion, you'll find yourself in such deep doodoo you'll begin envying Helen Farrar's demise. The Ace Corporation has many investments, including many media investments. Enough said?"

Suzanne can only nod.

Ace stands up, Suzanne too. "Enjoy the rest of your evening. Everything's paid here and Carlos will drive you back to the airport for your morning flight home. Fenster's office will call. You'll learn a significant, and I think rather amusing, truth. Amusing to an old pervert like me, in any case."

With a wave of his hand, Jeffrey B. Ace strides up the restaurant's center stairway, and out of Suzanne's life.

Chapter 29: The Richmond Angle
X'Ziloncado Game Reserve and Dallas, Texas
Saturday, December 19

Another bad night. My leg bracelet prevents me from sleeping on my side, as I usually do. Have to lie on my back. Every time I doze off, I choke on saliva, jerk awake. Figure I've had about two hours real sleep from 11 P.M., when I put out the light, until I get up at 6:30.

I'm sitting at the outside table, typing my chronological diary about what lousy treatment I'm getting, how nobody believes I'm innocent and how the hell did all this happen anyway, when Colonel X'M'Bazi and the unpronounceable sergeant appear. The colonel gestures for me to stand up. I do, and the sergeant bends down, takes off my leg bracelet.

What a relief! Then the man places my hands behind my back and cuffs them.

"No! Goddammit, NO!" I shout, causing birds to twitter, monkeys to scamper from tree to tree.

"Calm down," says X'M'Bazi. "We're taking a little trip."

Visions of jail. *Madame Guillotine's* arms outstretched: *At last, lover boy. Come to the bride you were always meant for. Just lie your poor, poor head upon my lap. Don't fret. This is what we call a quickie.* "No!"

Like the French Revolutionary journalist Jacques Hébert, they'll have to drag me from the execution cart, yelling, kicking, flailing my legs and, if not tied-back, arms gesticulating while I shout my innocence to the crowd, proclaiming that I've done nothing wrong.

Had it helped Hébert? *Snick-Snack,* all done. Consolation prize: a faster, more efficient and ultimately less painful end than the electric chair or the quack lethal injections they always have so much trouble with in the good ol' U.S & A. Trouble is, I don't want to die.

"Take it easy," growls X'M'Bazi. "Just a prep."

Stone-faced bastard. How wrong I'd been to think the guy a decent human-being, man of compassion dedicated to finding truth—

"You had breakfast?"

I shake my head.

"Sergeant, phone in breakfast for three. We'll eat here. Good American breakfasts, fried eggs over easy and bacon all around, with coffee and croissants. Or," he turns to me, "do you prefer toast?"

How'm I going to eat? Put my nose in the plate?"

"Don't be surly. Just trying the cuffs for size. Wouldn't want to stop the circulation and have you go gangrenous on us, would we?" He nods to the sergeant, who unlocks them

I grunt. Still frowning, massage my wrists.

"Have to let you know who's boss," says X'M'Bazi, sitting down. "By the way, there's been a revolution. King and family fled to Beverly Hills, from what I hear. Government's all changed, new Prime Minister, even a new name for our country: New X'Zambilia, with an X before the Z, if you can beat that." He pauses, looks out at the pond. "They put an 'X' before my name, too. X'M'Bazi." He shakes his head." Oh, and I'm a Generalissimo, actually my official title is 'Friend Generalissimo'. Just think. I head the military and all police, including the elite Security Militia, or SM as we call 'em. Only problem, I don't know if I exist officially, which though you mightn't appreciate it, isn't good news for you."

"I don't see what the fucking hell I've got to do with your fucking politics," I mutter.

"Now, now. Obscenity will get you nowhere you want to be. My lad, like it or not, you have everything to do with our politics. Especially, if you're the murderer. Even if you're not, you may be our God-given sacrificial lamb who'll make us look good in the eyes of the world. Any case, what'll it matter a hundred years from now? Ya gotta be philosophical about these things."

I don't bother to answer, sit in silence until the food arrives, then gobble it down while I can. "At the seaside resort, giraffes shared our food," I say wiping my mouth. "Those were good days, before this bullshit." *The bullshit you guys concocted*, I feel like adding. But, of course, M'Bazi or X'M'Bazi, or Generalissimo X'M'Bazi, or what'd he say?–Friend Generalissimo X'M'Bazi, Sir, hadn't murdered Helen Farrar. Or the others, I guess!

"Aren't you curious about where we're going?" asks X'M'Bazi, finishing his second coffee.

I shrug. "Wherever it is, it'll be some lousy deal. I trust you for that."

X'M'Bazi shakes his head. "You don't get it, do you? I'm 'Mister Good Guy,' as far as you're concerned. Or officially 'X'Mister Friend Generalissimo Good Guy.' For the time being, anyway. Let me ask you, how many of your tour group would be willing to have breakfast with you? They'd be jumping out of their skins thinking you were pouring cyanide into their coffee or on top of the Wheaties. But me? Here I am enjoying your company, as I'm allowing you the pleasure of mine." The Generalissimo holds his hands palms up. "No handcuffs, either." He pulls his battered cigarette pack from his shirt pocket, offers one. I take it. X'M'Bazi produces a Zippo lighter, lights up mine and another for himself. "Now," he says, "we'll get to business."

He explains that, along with Captain X'Zimbalwa, we'll fly in the helicopter to X'Ziromeu City and meet Madame Briac. "She isn't dead, by the way. Just a story we decided to put out. We'll see what she has to say about you. Won't it be fun if she greets you as her long-lost *Benefactor,* who happened to poison her? Such a tender reunion. I'm sure that in her heart she'll forgive you, especially after we pickle yours and send it to her for a souvenir."

"Aw, c'mon. Leave off. I'm perfectly happy to meet this woman. I bet she says I'm innocent as the driven snow. Unless you've set her up in some way."

Again X'M'Bazi opens his hands, nods to his short-sleeve khaki shirt. "Nothing in the hands, nothing up the sleeves. No sleeves to have anything up. Okay, I'll lay off and you lay off. I won't bait you, you quit saying I'm trying to entrap you. Not true, I swear. On my kids' heads, how's that?"

"You have kids?"

"Two. Girl and boy, five and seven. Apples of my eye." X'M'Bazi pulls out a wallet, shows their photos. "Cute, 'eh?"

They are. Two nice-looking kids. "They really yours?" I ask. "You didn't buy these pictures in a store or rent the kids from somebody?"

"Now, now, now, now." X'M'Bazi shakes his head. "I'm offering you a truce. Take it, leave it, I gotta know."

"Okay, already. But no handcuffs. I'm as anxious as you to meet this Briac woman. I solemnly promise to remain in your custody without coercion, if you keep that damn ankle thing off me and forego the cuffs."

X'M'Bazi sighs "Tell you what, I won't cuff you till we get to the hospital. There I have to, since not only must I do my job but I gotta look like I'm doing it. Understand? I'll restrain you a minimum of time, best I can offer."

I acquiesce. On impulse, I stick out my hand.

X'M'Bazi hesitates. "Normally, I don't shake hands with suspected murderers, but this time I'll make an exception. Indicating that you're working your way off my list."

We shake. "Don't disappoint me," he growls.

With the sergeant, who said not a word through breakfast but plowed through his share of a generous meal, we three start for the lodge and helicopter.

Rahel is anxious to follow a lead of her own. Leaving Schulz in charge of the agency for the half day it's open Saturday, she begins a second journey. To the ranch-estate in Dallas outskirts, property of a gentleman whose interests these days are horse and cattle breeding.

Again, she has a free ticket, First Class, plus a discounted car rental, with Suzanne promising to pay all incurred expenses.

The gentleman turns out to be a silver-haired, elderly but very fit-looking fellow who dresses and talks cowboy. In the early afternoon, they sit on a patio overlooking a many-acred spread. She has an iced organic decaffeinated mint tea, while he, booted legs stretched onto a stool, nurses a Jack Daniels.

"My wife likes that stuff you're drinking," he says. "She's very health-food conscious these days. Nothing but wheatgrass, wheatgrass, wheatgrass. I prefer good ol' Texas barbecued ribs and a few shots of bourbon to wash 'em down. So, young woman, what can I do for you?"

Rahel explains.

Her host says, "I'll answer any questions, tell you everything I can that doesn't compromise confidential sources or reveal company secrets. Yes, I'm miffed at how I was treated after all that time busting my gut for Richmond. But I'm no betrayer."

Rahel knows his story. Eleven years at the helm of Richmond Oil And Mineral Explorations, Inc. Then a palace coup, engineered by a rival. An ouster, a forced retirement, with golden handshake, of course. Probably the reason for this lavish-looking place. The bone of contention over which the two fought, and he lost, was whether their company should concentrate on domestic versus foreign exploration. He argued for an Alaskan, Canadian and Sunbelt focus. The opposition felt there was more ready money in an all-out campaign focused on southeastern Africa, where nobody else was doing much and they didn't anticipate great trouble from the ecology crowd. Get ahead of the do gooders, his rival argued. And won.

She spends the better part of two hours with her host and notes that he treats her like a human-being, not in any way displaying himself as a racist of the type endemic to Texas and that she'd dreaded encountering. But then the man has traveled, knows something of Africa and its varied peoples, including, Rahel would like to imagine, the quick-minded, generally intelligent Ethiopians.

Except for some minor points, he's forthcoming about what she wants to know. When she leaves, to drive her rental car back to Dallas-Fort Worth International Airport for the flight home, she has definitely nailed down that N. Sherman Jamieson isn't merely a chain-store travel agency owner with an ancillary telephone-discount ticket business, he's also a very interested investor in Richmond, one assigned the special task of getting to Minister Zecherias M'Bowé and, through him, reserving the X'Ziloncado for Richmond's exclusive oil and mineral prospecting.

The concession rights of all finds are to be Richmond's, which it will license to the best bidder.

Jamieson and his wife Bitsy—is she afraid to let him out of her sight? A co-conspirator? Both?

In any case, they've traveled to Zembeylia three times in recent months, to set up the Richmond deal and to be onsite during secretive preliminary tests in the X'Ziloncado. These trips all occurred in the four months shortly before the Eland tour.

So, is Jamieson using the current trip as a cover? And to rid himself of Eland's hooray-for-Nature competition? Rahel stares out the plane window, while it rises into the Dallas-Fort-Worth evening and reveals early lights of Dallas that wink in the distance.

With Helen Farrar's talk of eco-tourism and promises of millions, wasn't she, plus her company, the "enemy," as far as Richmond is concerned? An enemy with whom the Zembeylians, well now the X'Zambilians of New X'Zambilia, were already doing business. Jamieson might be worried that M'Bowé and the King would think it better to deal with the White Devil you know than the White Devils you don't.

Suddenly, brutally, all of Eland's links to the country's decision-makers have been cut away. Where does this leave Richmond? Is it totally cut off from governmental backing? Or is its stake in Zembeylia intact and unchallenged?

Questions to ponder. She and Suzanne will have a lot to talk about tomorrow, when Goldstone's love gets back from Mexico.

Chapter 30: Dr. Fang
X'Fulumbane, New X'Zambilia–Saturday, Afternoon
December 19

Bhulliwah is satisfied. And not satisfied. He's in control, or at least seems to be in control. Not too much worry money-wise, despite that hyena M'Bowé stealing most of the gold reserves. Dale Uppingham III is promising another B.A.R.F. fix to see them through.

The U.S. Ambassador is making clear his government doesn't care who nominally controls New X'Zambilia, so long as power remains in the hands of those committed to free market economics, the global village and a good old-fashioned multi-national corporate approach to wealth creation: milking the poor to make the very rich, substantially richer.

"Of course," says Ambassador Hadley, a small, graying man with puffy cheeks that give his face a chipmunk look, "Of course, revolutions happening as often as they do here in Zemb…New X'Zambilia, are discouraging to foreign investment." His hands flutter. He peers nervously at his host.

Bhulliwah can practically hear the man's thoughts. A quiet post during his year and a half tenure. Until now! Couldn't the Good Lord have let it remain peaceful for just eight more months, when he, Hadley, would secure his thirty year pension and retire to Rhode Island?

Negative fellow, thinks Bhulliwah. But a guardian, if minor, of the money spigot. Putting on a broad and reassuring smile, the Friend Prime Minister says, "Friend Ambassador, let me ease your mind and your country's spirit about our revolutions. This one was practically bloodless and now all revolutions are over. Yes over! You have my word on it. So, you have witnessed the last upheaval in this land, henceforth dedicated to peace, development and prosperity. Of that you may express certainty to Washington, *mon cher collègue*."

"It is to be wished," murmurs the Ambassador. He cracks his knuckles, takes his leave.

Bhulliwah contemplates a blank space on the wall where his portrait in full Ministerial regalia is to be hung. Until now success has been almost too easy. One more maneuver and the sovereign crown could be his? Anticipation always causes a shiver to run down the spine.

Yes, yes. But how does this Chinese fellow, Fang Shi Wu, fit in? If there's a thing to be avoided like the plague it's Red China meddling in New X'Zambilia's affairs. That can jeopardize arrangements with the B.A.R.F., not to mention with corporations preparing to invest and encourage western tourism here.

This Fang person threatens a paratroop invasion. Is he promising an unwanted, unasked for influx of Chinese capital? Bhulliwah knows what Chinese capital can mean: Mao-suited bureaucrats arriving directly from Beijing. What a mess they'd make of his plans and projects!

How to avoid the Dragon's suffocating embrace? So far, he has put off Dr. Fang, but the Chinese Embassy is insisting on an audience. He'll have to grant it and play for time. Surely, the West, like John Wayne himself, will come riding out of sunrise or sunset to New X'Zambilia's rescue.

The meeting must occur over tea. Chinese are reputedly great tea-drinkers and, besides, he has always found the taking of tea in quiet surroundings a passion-dousing moment. In the British novels he has read, whenever there's a crisis, whenever the unspeakable or ineffable occurs, everyone immediately sits down to tea. Hold the bloodshed, stop the cannons, have a warming *cuppa*.

His experience of Americans, on the other hand, seems to confirm their addiction to a crisis mentality promising maximum upheaval. Nothing so American than a spirit of panicky chaos. No teatime there. As far as he can figure, they gulp coffee, then race around, shouting orders, firing guns at anyone and everyone, pushing buttons of gadgets that will blow masses of non-Americans to bits. With a guaranteed bonus of noise, noise, more noise! Act first, think later appears to Bulliwah the true American philosophy.

As for the French, well, they either try making noise *à la les Américains*–regretting they don't have as many engines of loudness, guns to fire and buttons to push. Or they retreat into argumentative, positively *Talmudic,* logicities and let disaster happen.

To Friend Prime Minister Bhulliwah's consternation, Dr. Fang refuses tea.

"This modest, unworthy person drinks only coffee," he says in English, waving a hand to indicate modest unworthiness.

Bhulliwah summons the servant who, until yesterday, was Major-Domo to the King. The ex-Major-Domo bends down, whispers into his Friend Prime Minister's ear, "Sir, no coffee."

"What?"

"The former Minister for Security, Tourism and Culture took it with him when he went on his, er, fact-finding mission." The servant's face brightens. "We have Nescafé."

"Well, bring that," hisses Bhulliwah.

The Nescafé is served on bone china that Mrs. M'Bowé neglected to abscond with.

"I have here," begins Dr. Fang, "by the way, you may call me 'Friend Delegate Dr. Fang.' I have with me a check for $1,020 U.S. This is my government's most generous contribution toward New X'Zambilia's rehabilitation. More may be forthcoming, Possibly," he pauses to take a delicate sip of Instant, "when certain conditions are met."

$1,020? As against B.A.R.F.'s millions upon millions, with almost no strings beyond the unspoken admonition to keep the rich

rich and the poor poor? Why, China's measly contribution isn't enough to siphon off preliminary bribes, little starters whetting appetites for bigger morsels to come. Bhulliwah feels like leaning over and spitting into the man's cup.

"Yes, a few conditions," murmurs Friend Delegate Dr. Fang. "We are prepared to put the sum of one billion dollars into New X'Zambilia over the next twenty-eight years. We shall open our own bank here in X'Fulumbane and supervise the distribution of monies to where we feel they are most needed. Every penny shall go to its prearranged destination and further contributions shall depend on precisely measured results, especially in the field of political re-training and re-education."

Bhulliwah shudders. His fears coming true.

"Further," says the Friend Delegate, "we are most interested in the possibilities of cultivating new and fruitful crops throughout your mountain region. Poppies, coca, hemp and related plantings have great financial potential. Factories, to refine yields, shall provide ever-increasing employment for New X'Zambilia's people. As to the final product, we shall be relying on the distribution expertise of a number of organizations well-versed in this type of international trade. You have heard of *Cosa Nostra?*" Fang pours himself more Nescafé. "Understand, our own involvement in such matters is, necessarily, deniable. At arm's length, you might say," continues the Chinese diplomat. "We would be officially shocked to learn that our generosity towards New X'Zambilia has resulted in such an abuse of funding. One thing we and the Americans agree on is Image. Image and perception are reality, as they say in the American advertising world." Dr. Fang allows himself a chuckle. "So much more significant than reality itself. Image is reality, given the power of the media in our time."

"Where does this leave my country?"

Dr. Fang draws himself up. "Together, you and my humble self shall write out a detailed protocol, to be signed only by you–in which the growing and refining of said products shall be fully legalized here. Distribution outside this country will, as I have said, be the responsibility of organizations already alluded to."

"But we'll be a pariah among nations. They'll kick us out of the U.N. We won't be eligible for foreign aid. We'll be prisoners in our land, accountable to gangsters and not allowed to travel anywhere. Maybe we'll even get invaded by a righteous force of pan-African states."

The Friend Delegate leans over. In a gesture of international fellowship and fraternity he gives the Friend Prime Minister's knee a strong collegial punch. "Not to worry. The armed might of my country shall defend little New X'Zambilia. Yes, you may find yourselves snubbed and denounced, especially by your former supporters and contributors. But you and I know just how much their citizens crave the merchandise you shall be producing and the consequent wealth these very nations shall pour—proportionate, of course, to relative sizes and needs—into both our lands."

"How is it you speak such excellent English?" Bhulliwah decides it's time for diversionary tactics. Proportionate needs indeed! It leaves New X'Zambilia with all the risk, all the opprobrium and on payday genuine trickle-down economic starvation.

"Harrow and Cambridge, King's College," Dr. Fang speaks with pride. "My parents were merchants in Hong-Kong. They valued education. Accordingly, I was sent to Harrow on scholarship and went up to King's, where I read Economics. After that, a stint at the Harvard Business School in Massachusetts, then home to China for extensive re-education in Marxism-Maoism. Thus I combine in my person the best of the capitalist-enterprise and socialist-statist outlooks." Dr. Fang leans back in his seat, a smile of satisfaction on his spare, ascetic face.

A pause. To Bhulliwah, New X'Zambilia's future looks bleak, as hitched to Red China and the drug trade. There's something so dull, so sad, so monotonous, so horribly unglamorous about everyone, including the nation's elite, such as himself, forced to wear those dreadful Mao outfits and march–singing compulsory songs?–to the fields to hoe away at coca plants. But how to unhitch from such a fate?

"The man who would be King," murmurs Dr. Fang. "Is it not true?" He gazes innocently and, yes, inscrutably, at Bhulliwah.

Bhulliwah musters his own version of an inscrutable gaze. "A question for the people to decide. Who is to be their 'Father,' the nation's guiding presence."

"This decision will be by an election?"

Bhulliwah shakes his head. "Nothing so gross. A committee of notables shall assemble to vote on the matter."

"I see." Friend Dr. Fang rubs his hands. "A committee appointed by your Parliament?"

Bhulliwah remains silent. He hasn't worked out the modality for choosing a new King, especially as he has but one candidate in mind.

"My country," says Dr. Fang as if divining Bhulliwah's thoughts, "is prepared to back the elevation of your excellent self to New X'Zambilia's highest position. As is only fitting, given your spiritual contribution to the 'People's Revolution.'"

"Such a responsibility," murmurs Bhulliwah deciding to play coy, a game favored by so many American Presidential candidates. "I don't know if I–"

"Understandable." The Friend Delegate speaks too quickly for the Friend Prime Minister's liking. "Yes, it is undoubtedly preferable that a more venerable, a more patriarchal individual such as Y. Sanjeev Sandaram be appointed to–"

"So that's it!" shouts Bhulliwah losing his cool. Sandaram! Treacherous, double-dealing, triple-dealing Sandaram. Working every angle to further his own miserable ambitions. Now all is clear! Sandaram rousing the Red Chinese! How unscrupulous can you get?

Dr. Fang doesn't appreciate the Friend Prime Minister's outburst. "Forgive the directness of this unassuming observer," he whispers in a voice so low that Bhulliwah has to bend close to hear. "I must remind you that help in sustaining your People's Revolution is already on its way. Chinese naval vessels will enter the port of X'Fulumbane at dawn in three days' time. A contingent of paratroopers is coming even sooner to restore order and uphold revolutionary principles, starting, if need be, with the extensive re-education of any and all defiant leaders. Your Disciplinary Camp One will be quite suitable for—how should I put it? A re-education campus. And the formation of newer, younger, more malleable cadres can easily be undertaken."

"We never asked for your military assistance," bellows Bhulliwah, definitively out of control.

"Ah, but you did," responds Dr. Fang. "Through Mr. Sandaram's formal request."

"Dog traitor!" Bhulliwah stands, a figure imposing in girth, if unimpressive in height. He shakes a fist at his visitor. "As Prime Minister—"

"Friend Prime Minister," interrupts Friend Delegate Dr. Fang, a slight grin on his lips.

"As Prime Minister," insists Bhulliwah, "I formally forbid the entry of any Chinese vessels, airplanes or troops into or onto New X'Zambilia's territory, extending no less than twenty-five miles at sea, as noted in Decree #22, to be published as soon as I can write it. Good day to you." He turns to stride from the room.

"You called us in, you cannot stop us now." For the first time, Dr. Fang raises his voice. "Remember *The Sorcerer's Apprentice!*"

Chapter Thirty-One: Eureka!
X'Ziromeu City, New X'Zambilia, Sunday, December 20

Fascinating to observe the X'Ziloncado Basin horizon to horizon from 3,000 feet. The helicopter travels slowly enough so that I can watch herds of antelope, wildebeest, zebras, giraffes and even elephants move across a landscape of forest and grassland. The pilot spots a lion pride sprawled by a water-hole. He flies us low. The beasts are fast asleep, the way little kids sleep dead to the world and oblivious of all. Only one lioness raises her head as our shadow flits over her. I shudder, remembering the almost-fatal but happily un-joined encounter with a concerned mother lioness. As provoked by *Moi* at the near-start of my troubles in those halcyon days when I was being accused of only one murder plus the theft of a two million dollar diamond. Oh yes, and the murder of this French farm woman we're now flying to visit in hospital. Except she's never been dead; police trick to provoke–what?–the telltale start of guilt from a suspect, namely and especially *moi* again?

Once more we lift high, to 9,000 feet to get above the Monogoros, then our whirlybird drops into the sky above a farmland and orchard valley surrounding X'Ziromeu City's southwestern perimeter. On the opposite side of X'Ziromeu, I glimpse open face mines and smoking factories.

The central area, where we're headed, has streets littered with smashed glass that glints in the sun. There's all kinds of debris from broken furniture to scatterings of upended appliances and industrial paraphernalia. Crowds of men, many in uniform, are piling things together for a massive cleanup. Our helicopter lands in the municipal hospital's rear courtyard, the pavement marked by a large red cross.

"Okay," says X'M'Bazi. "The cuffs."

Obligingly I put my hands behind my back. The cuffs click on.

We find Madame Briac sitting up in bed, knitting and watching television. She looks positively chipper.

"Are you feeling all right, *Madame*?" asks Captain X'Zimbalwa in his Zembeylian version of French, with rolling, rather than throaty, rrrr's. "You gave us a bad scare," he adds.

"I gave myself a bad scare," says Madame. "But yes, I am feeling almost well, although I seem to need lots of sleep. I am ready for your questions."

X'M'Bazi brings me forward. "Do you recognize this man?"

She gives me a careful head-to-toe look. I feel my heart beating. My God, if she...

"No," she says at length. "I have never seen him that I know of."

"Say something in French," orders X'M'Bazi.

"*Bonjour, Madame*," I say, starting to feel very relieved. "*Vous voilà en train de récupérer votre santé et j'en suis, nous en sommes tous, très soulagés*–Hello, Madame. I note that you are regaining your health and I am, we are all, very relieved."

Madame Briac nods her acknowledgment of this fine sentiment. I sound like the mayor of some small French town at the opening of a new public toilet or equivalent municipal event.

"He has an American accent, no?" puts in X'Zimbalwa. "You said the person in the car spoke like an American."

"*Monsieur* speaks like a Parisian with a slight tonic stress that could be American. I'm no linguist." Madame Briac shakes her head. "The person who came to my car spoke in a whisper, but it seems to me I heard an American intonation and a singsong accent, not Parisian. In my experience Swiss people from Geneva and Lausanne speak this way: BON-jour, comment ALLEZ vous? Instead of Bon-JOUR, COM-ment allez vous? If you see what I mean."

Whew! I smile gratefully.

X'M'Bazi proceeds to question her for a blow-by-blow version of her story. She speaks of the letters, of her trips to Fulumbane and the "sacred mission" she was being groomed to undertake.

She shakes her head. "What hurts most is not that I was a foolish dupe but that unscrupulous people should use the Church for some criminal purpose. What monsters could do such a thing? It's true heresy! I shall never, never forgive it." She takes a tissue from the night table, dabs at her eyes.

Uncomfortable silence, into which I decide to put in my two cents. "Reminds me of André Gide's novel, *Les Caves du Vatican.*

Translated into English, I believe, as 'Lafcadio's Adventures,' about a scam having to do with a supposed conspiracy against the Pope. There's a fake priest running around France raising money from gullible rich folks to keep the Holy Father safe and fight forces of evil infiltrating Mother Church."

"Yeah," grunts X'M'Bazi in English. "How does that apply here?" In French again, he addresses Madame Briac. "If I understand, Madame, you got off the train at X'Ziromeu City, walked to your pickup van in the parking lot and waited for this supposed 'Benefactor.' How long a wait would you say?"

"Eight, ten minutes. No more."

"And your walk from train to van?"

"Three or four minutes. The distance isn't far."

"This poison," asks X'Zimbalwa. "It came from a pill?"

Madame Briac describes the scene in her van, how she thought the tale of a cholera epidemic in Italy plausible, but was a little shocked at the pill's large size. She told them she'd driven home feeling fine. Then her legs started tingling. Suddenly, she felt dizzy and drowsy, lay on her bed and her stomach seized up with terrible cramps. She meant to go to the hall to her telephone stand and call for help, but everything went black. Next thing she remembers is being here in the hospital.

"You murmured something while you were unconscious, or semiconscious," says Captain X'Zimbalwa. "It sounded like '*Pierre d'Or*' which is the name of this man, Goldstone. In French word sequence."

A flush tinges Madame's cheeks. She puts a hand to her mouth. "Oh, well, I have a friend, a Monsieur Dorland, Pierre Dorland. Perhaps, in my distress, I uttered...I am embarrassed."

"Well, this is as good a time to tell you as any," says X'M'Bazi. "I'm afraid we had to inform all who inquired that you were dead."

"Dead?" Madame looks stricken. "Oh, dear. What shall I do?"

"Don't worry," says X'M'Bazi, "we'll bring you back to life as soon as the killer, who's running loose and murdering right and left, is securely locked away. Your farm is under police protection and functioning as usual. Your neighbor is taking care of the dogs."

"But, my daughter. My other friends…"

X'M'Bazi holds up a hand. "Think how delighted they will be to see you restored to life, health and happiness." He adds, "We have every hope this will be very, very soon."

Captain X'Zimbalwa leaves to check on his family. X'M'Bazi and I re-board the 'copter for the flight back to the Tented Camp. The Generalissimo removes my handcuffs.

"Hey," I ask, "should you have reassured the lady to the extent you did? You sounded as though the case was solved. Not by fingering me, I sincerely hope and pray."

"Naw," he says. "Like you've said yourself, you're the goat in all this. Suzanne too. Better tell her that."

I look at him, eyebrows raised. "You mean you've figured it out?"

"You haven't?" says X'M'Bazi? "Think, man. Reflect! Not something you Whities do easily, as my New York experience showed me. Sorry to sound racist, though I guess I am at heart. We all are, 'The Destiny of Humankind,' you could say. We're too tribal to endure over the millenia. I mean in Darwinian terms. Here today, gone as a species in a million years. Unless we wipe out everything but cockroaches by nuclear war a few years or months or days from now. Or minutes, for that matter."

"What an optimist–but I guess I agree about humanity's endurance, its inability to survive its own in-built destructiveness," I say. "Getting back to my innocence, music to my ears… are you ready to arrest the truly guilty one or ones? And prove your case, make it stick in court?"

"Not yet. I have to a lot of checking to do. Rest assured, we may have to convict you, if my hypothesis doesn't work out. A joke, ha-ha." X'M'Bazi strokes his clean-shaven, rather ascetic face. "I have to consult my people in the U.S., get confirmation on details and motivations. There are friends in the New York police and a few who owe me. They'll be a terrific help in filling gaps. Still, we both know the essentials, the basics of how it all happened and who's responsible, even if we don't yet understand the many whys and wherefores behind the situation."

"Of course, by putting me under house arrest," I mutter, "you've given me much time to ponder, which I obviously haven't done enough of."

"Well," says X'M'Bazi, "you can't hope to be as methodical, systematic and step-by-step professional as a trained detective. Don't be hard on yourself. Make allowance for your amateur status."

As we rise from the hospital, I say, "Maybe there's really one solution that explains the mechanism of events logically, coherently, inevitably. I have to think about it, review my notes, see where systematic cogitation takes me. If you and I are on the same page, and I draw the same conclusion, I'll be relieved, if hardly reassured as to my intellectual acuteness."

"From here on out," says X'M'Bazi, "it's a mop-up operation. I, or we if you're with me, need to prove it all, position ourselves…" He's silent a moment, gazing at the mountains below. Quietly he adds, "Most of all, you and I and your Suzanne too, will have to prevail." A sigh. "So let the dogwork of checking and verifications begin."

PART SIX:
J'ACCUSE!

New York City New Jersey and New X'Zambilia–
Saturday December 19 to Tuesday, December 22

"My object all sublime
I shall achieve in time
To make the punishment fit the crime,
The punishment fit the crime."
Gilbert and Sullivan, *The Mikado*

Chapter 32: Schulz Goes To Lunch
New York, NY: Saturday, December 19

At one o'clock on the nose, Heinz-Herbert Schulz shoos from the premises of Shangri-La: WorldWide Journeys of Adventure, a shrill-voiced woman who's arguing with him over the cheapest airfare to Philadelphia. From Philly to Paris she already has her ticket, bought not at Shangri-La—perish the thought!—but from one of those telephonic discounters that are putting retail travel agencies out of business.

Feeling extremely unguilty about throwing away a commission that might go as high as $1.98, he shuts the iron grill protecting the storefront. Thus was Second Avenue made aware that it won't have Shangri-La to kick around anymore, at least not until Monday at 8:30 A.M.

Using a key that I thought I'd hidden cleverly in an underpanel of the office typewriter, Schulz unlocks the door to my apartment. He has already scouted the terrain and knows that in the medicine cabinet of my bathroom he'll find a razor. He decides he doesn't have time for a full-fledged shave, hot water, cream and all. Just a few dry scrapes on his cheeks and around nose and chin. He nicks his left earlobe but finds my styptic pencil and staunches the blood. Not wanting to be late, he doesn't linger to rinse off razor or pencil before putting them back in the cabinet. What will I know? And, not knowing, what will I care?

A bottle of Yardley's Bay Rum sitting on a shelf is a pleasant surprise. He douses his face, puts liberal splotches under the arms of his shirt, nods satisfaction to his image.

Spruced and refreshed, he's gratified that the Lexington Avenue subway operates just as it should. On time, at 1:45, P.M. he enters the Grand Central Oyster Bar.

Jody Keppel is waiting in the foyer. She's a milk-complexioned blonde whom he guesses a lot of men would find attractive, except for a certain washed-out look around the eyes. This happens in the travel business.

It happens even more, he guesses, when you're off a Wisconsin farm and come to the Big Apple to make fame and fortune as an actress or model or advertising exec., then find yourself selling plane tickets to actresses, models and advertising execs.

She's dressed in her businesswoman's best. To his eye the navy blue suit and white blouse with its spread-out collar–symbolizing virginal purity?–seems dated. The 1950's June Allison look: apple-cheeked, scrubbed, wide-eyed, sexually untouched, eternally smiley: the sort of gal to whom a fine-looking pimp stationed inside the Manhattan Port Authority Bus Terminal might propose the lead in a Broadway show, if only she'll give him preliminary comfort and satisfaction.

At least her wardrobe doesn't parade the sad fact that as a "Travel Vacation Specialist;" at Eland Tours, she'll be lucky to gross $21,000 a year.

How glad he is–the thought passes through Schulz as he opens his arms and shouts "DARRR-LING"–that given his predilection, he'll never have to worry about supporting a wife or, God forbid, kids on his industry's parsimonious pay. With Hank's bouncer job at The Four Aces Bar and Grill, they're making just enough to rent a studio in Queens and live on fast food.

He hugs her, kisses her smooth cheek, suppressing a slight shudder. He thinks he feels a tremor in her too. He signals the *Maître d,* who leads them to a table.

"My dear," he tells her, once the Such-a-treat-to-see-a-pal-from-the-bad-old-days" routine is gotten through, "you can order anything you like. Oysters, lobster, wine, what your heart desires."

He peeks at the menu. My Christ! Seventeen dollars for a celery-with-mayo appetizer? Suzanne is footing the bill, so damn the torpedoes.

"I'll let you suggest," murmurs Jody. A follower not a leader, which does confer a certain charm.

Six oysters, six clams and four sea urchins for starters. A time consecrated to nostalgia. "Remember that old bag, our supervisor at Travel 'N Save? A true witch. The day she–"

A second round, he decides, should be lobster bisque. Jody sits out the soup. Then full-grown lobsters: for him broiled and stuffed, New England boiled for her. And two substantial Green Goddess salads filled with baby gray shrimp from San Francisco Bay across the Continent.

To wash it all down they work their way through two bottles of Bubbly: *Perrier-Jouët* 1969, dry in the mouth, sparkly on the tongue, fruity on the palate.

When they've rinsed lobster off fingers and started on their salads, he asks about Eland. How did she get on with Helen? Does the office mourn her death? Feel relief? What does she think of Sheila, her immediate boss? Given that Eland's principal movers and shakers are now all murdered, does it have a future?

Just as he planned, Jody's tongue wags with drink. Now she's waving her arms and tapping him on the sleeve. Her words slur.

"You think Travel 'N Save was tough? That Helen Farrar's an absolute fanatic, a Per-fec-shonisht. Always breathing down your neck, totally unforgiving for the teeniest, weeniest little mish-take." Jody takes another swallow of champagne.

"And Sheila Mondran?"

"Oh, surface-nice, if you know what I mean. But sometimes plain lazy. Just 'cause she's Vice-President of Special Events doeshn't mean she shouldn't pitch in and share the dirty work. Does it?"

"Pitch in?"

Jody shakes her head, too vigorously. "Sheila's always leaving everything to me." She starts a confused story about her boss's laziness during a travel show in Chicago, only one day prior to the Eland tour's departure to Zembeylia. "...Went off to meet a boyfriend–swearing me to she-crecshy. Well, that Barry's such a prune, I don't blame her. Mister Consht-ipay-shun himself." Jody giggles, then puts hand over her mouth. "Oops, sorry. Don't mean to talk badly of the dead. But Sheila and her colleague ride First Class to Chicago, while Ms. Southgate's helper and me, we have to sit on those narrow little seats in the back of the plane 'n hold half the exhibits on our laps."

"The Southgate woman was also on the plane?"

Jody gulps a mouthful of champagne. "Yeah, our two booths were side-by-side. And then there was the third one, run by that stuck up..." she puts her hand before her mouth again, whispers, "Bitch." She giggles. "Ooh, pardon my French."

"What stuck-up bitch?" asks Schulz. "Sounds to me like they were all snooty, making you travel Economy while they live it up in First." He shakes his head, looking sternly virtuous. "I should never tolerate that."

Jody shrugs. "What can us peons do?" Get it?" She digs him in the ribs. He flinches. "Get it?" She gives a loud laugh. "Pee-ons."

Schulz pushes back in his seat, forces a chuckle. She reaches for the champagne bottle, he puts a restraining hand on her arm. Enough, definitely enough. "So," he says, "you were joined by this third bitch. Who is she?"

"A Mrs. Jamieson from Texas, all gussied up with bangles and spangles and red store bought, or store-dyed hair. Snooty like you wouldn't believe. At least the other two were polite, like they thought we might be alive or something. She decides we're bad air."

"Okay, Elizabeth Jamieson. And you all had booths at that big Exhibition Hall by O'Hare Airport?"

Jody nods "Side by side. At the annual Travel The World show. Top-drawer event and I guess I should be grateful to have been there. Except, wait 'till I tell you what happened."

"What?" Schulz is peremptory.

"Can't I, pretty please, have more champagne?" Jody looks appealingly, if a little cross-eyed, at Schulz.

"Well," he pours her a third of a glass. "Don't overdo. So what happened?"

"That first day, Friday, December 11, we started setting up at ten, just after we arrived. About lunchtime, they all three of our bosses go! They leave! All three! Oh, not together. First, Ms. Southgate says she has to meet her partner, who's flying in. Then Mrs. Jamieson's husband—a sort of cowboy with a big hat and the craziest accent. He shows up and she declares she absolutely must get her hair done before Zembeylia. Sheila, like I told you, slips away about 12:30. Which means us two employees have to cover three booths. Can you imagine? And were we busy!" Jody's voice turns plaintive. "We stood the whole time, running back and forth, answering questions, handing out brochures, quoting prices. All the way to closing at 9 P.M. Nine hours with only coffee and a sandwich, thanks to a gentleman from the Avis Rent-A-Car booth, who was kind enough to bring them. Nine whole hours having to smile, smile, smile. No break, except once to use the ladies room. Then back at 7:30 next morning. Just not fair!" With her napkin, Jody wipes away a tear. She helps herself to a bite of salad, downs her wine and appropriates the champagne bottle, refilling her glass to the brim.

Schulz glares but keeps silent. He hopes he won't have to carry her out of the restaurant. He's looking forward to home and a good snooze on his pullout bed.

"So those three straggle in about noon on Saturday the 12ᵗʰ, after we've packed most of the stuff," Jody rattles on.

The pump is primed. He has only to eat the pie he orders, drink coffee, listen up.

"We needed to be out of the hall by 1 P.M. to make way for the next exhibition. And guess what!" Jody opens her eyes wide. "Can you imagine what I found in our trash bin?"

"Eland's trash?"

"No, no, no." Jody shakes her head emphatically. "Trash for all three booths. Anyway, there they were. Two United boarding passes in the name of Melissa Dorset: roundtrip ORD-LAX, LAX-ORD. Flight 119 on Friday, December 11, leaving Chicago at 2:25 P.M., arriving Los Angeles at 4:50 P.M. And the red eye back, Flight 124, leaving same day at 11 P.M., arriving 4:43 A.M on Saturday, the 12th. Such carelesh-ness!" Jody glares at him, slurring her words again. "Thish ish a detail-oriented bish-ness!"

"Used up passes?" says Schulz. "So what?"

"Worth mileage points, if you mail them to the airline. Poor Ms. Dorset. Whoever she is, she certainly has a right to her mileage. And one of these three, uhm, witches must've thrown them there, since this was the bin behind the counters where only staff put things. Wouldn't you want your miles if you were a traveler?" Jody looks at him accusingly. "If I hadn't rescued them, that woman would never be credited."

"So what did you do?" asks Schulz.

Jody wasn't about to follow logic's course. "As soon as we landed in New York, off the three go again, to get ready for their Zembeylia departure for that same night. Now they're being murdered over there. Listen, if Eland closes down and I get laid off," she puts a hand on Schulz's arm, "will you get me a job at your place? Will you, Schulzie, honey?"

He looks up at the light yellow tiles of a vaulted ceiling, that make him imagine a cathedral crypt, as decorated in yellow public toilet tiles. Commodore Vanderbilt, or whichever rail mogul built Grand Central as his great monument to transcontinental travel, must've been dreaming of a modern day place-of-worship celebrating swift transport allied with free enterprise. In Robber-Baron mode, no doubt, he also wanted to show off his dough.

266

Expensive material, these tiles. But they do remind him of the better sort of institutional lavatory.

Jody at Shangri-La? Not good. Wouldn't want Goldstone keeping her and firing him. In any case, since when did Shangri-La have money for more staff? Let her down easy. Especially in her present state.

He assumes an air of gravitas. "I don't think you'd wish to work there," he says slowly, as if ruminating. "Much as I'd love to have you with me, I don't know for how long I'm going to stick around. Mister Goldstone, the owner, he doesn't comprehend the travel business from a hole in the wall. He depends utterly on my expertise."

Schulz sighs. "Such a burden. I have to guide him step-by-step through the labyrinth, you might say. And is he grateful! 'HH,' he says–that's what he calls me, 'HH.' For my given names, Heinz-Herbert. Without you, I'd be positively lost. You are truly my savior."

Schulz looks smug, drinks the coffee he has ordered to offset the alcohol. He remembers his mission. "So what did you do with these boarding passes?"

"Couple of days later I posted them with a letter. But the letter came back–from a condo in Hoboken. Addressee Unknown. Can you imagine? Researching her whereabouts from airline records and writing the letter made me stay an hour and twenty minutes after closing time. Not right to burden me with so much. For nothing, as it turns out." Jody is close to weeping.

Schulz pats her hand, pours her coffee. After paying $785.43, plus bountiful tips to the waiter, the wine waiter and *Maître d.*, they stagger into Grand Central's Lower Level.

With noisy goodbyes and promises to keep in touch, they make their way replete, if worse for wear, towards their respective subways.

After a nice snooze, Schulz decides to spend the rest of his weekend composing an invoice for Suzanne. The feast and sundry expenses are all very well, but he adds a 58% surcharge for transport, ancillary disbursements and overtime costs. Plus, of course, another 27% compensation for the information he has come by.

Does it amount to anything? He shrugs. He's done his job, let Suzanne put it together. His conscience is clear.

Chapter 33:Locusts
X'Ziloncado Camp and X'Fulumbane, New X'Zambilia,
Sunday, December 20

Friend Generalissimo X'M'Bazi is playing hooky. With an armed guide for protection, he makes his way through forest and meadow, tracking birds. The morning sun is still below the treetops, a time when night predators are retiring and day predators take over. The birds trill and caw to one another: messages of protection, hunger, sex. Not necessarily, he figures, in that order.

With great stealth and care he parts bushes to watch a crimson, ebony, cobalt-blue and silvery green Schalow's Turaco take wing, its feathers fanned wide. Magnificent sight, but he's seeking a Secretary Bird. Yesterday, through binoculars, he spotted two stamping their prey to death on dry, bare ground beyond the Tented Camp's perimeter fence. X'M'Bazi wants to get a closer look at this remarkable creature with its red, stilt-like legs used to bludgeon small animals from grasshoppers to baby rats.

He comes to a rocky barren patch that elephant traffic may have stripped of vegetation. Behind a bush, he settles to wait. Reluctantly, he pulls from his pocket a faxed report from police headquarters in X'Fulumbane. It came in just as he was setting off for this walk, respite designed to help him keep sane during checking procedures that will either confirm or discredit his theory of the case. Scutwork, but vital. He doesn't want to get it wrong, arrest an innocent like the train porter or one of the Land Rover drivers. Of course, he always has Goldstone. Ha-ha Good? Ha-ha, No Good!

In any case, thank God his family and friends are safe. Bhulliwah has declared himself Prime Minister and, according to the fax, his revolution has been touted both as unbloody–and, at first, as unnoticed by the world-at-large–as any uprising could be. A few cracked heads, somebody's face gouged with a broken bottle, a van filled with looted bidets careening around a corner in X'Ziromeu City and running down a mother and child; a few volleys of shots fired mainly into the air, but also into one or two luckless individuals. That about sums up the violence. A third of a column on page fourteen of *The New York Times* had done it for world interest. By international standards, totally unremarkable.

Except, as this fax informs Friend Generalissimo X'M'Bazi, the newspeople have suddenly woken to the Chinese threatening an invasion of New X'Zambilia. Belatedly, Bhulliwah's "Glorious-Almost Bloodless Revolution" has become international hot news.

X'M'Bazi shrugs. Not to worry, so long as the media stay clear of his murder case.

Thirty minutes of waiting for the Secretary Bird? He'll have to get back. The Generalissimo gives up, heads to the far side of a hippo pond. His bodyguard raises a double-barreled shotgun, taking no chances.

X'M'Bazi has to smile. Westerners are in awe of lions, elephants, crocodiles, even scorpions. They're surprised and disbelieving to learn that hippos are Africa's deadliest beasts, so far as humans are concerned. He pauses an instant to watch big rectangular hippo heads rising-falling, rising-falling with the pond's wavelets. The tiny ears twitch expressively. One of the huge animals, cascading water, lumbers onto a muddy beach a hundred feet away. Its ungainly body, heaves along on stubby legs. It disappears into the shore's thick vegetation, no doubt to munch on acacia shoots and other underbrush delicacies.

Nobody accuses hippos of being mean, just panicky. Get between one ashore—often hidden in bushes—and its water habitat, it believes you're deliberately blocking the way home. Bellowing with fright, the huge creature barrels out at you and either runs you over like a tank, or opening its enormous jaws, snaps you in two. In both cases, it believes you're the persecutor barring the way to its beloved mud hole.

X'M'Bazi's thoughts return to politics. Understandably, after all these years of strife and city streets littered with corpses—mostly X'Zambilis, *Dieu merci*— the population now seems to be sick of real revolution. Leaving people and possessions pretty much intact during upheavals doesn't make for good drama but certainly is preferable to wholesale death and devastation.

Perhaps New X'Zambilians are demonstrating a greater dynamic for civilized behavior than their counterparts elsewhere. Compared to Albanians, Serbians, Afghanis or British soccer fans, theirs has been mild conduct indeed.

Maybe not a real trend, only momentary weariness. Given a few years and a new generation, will they return to the fray, hungry for those defining human joys of plunder, rape, torture, murder? Who can tell, X'M'Bazi asks himself, as he skirts the pond? Yes, who can—the Generalissimo freezes, puts finger to lips to signal the guide. Not six yards away, in shortish grass near the water stands a lavender Shoebill Stork shading a chick, the little one's down lighter than its mother and pink-tinged. Mom perches comfortably on one leg, the other tucked under her body, almost invisible.

X'M'Bazi signals his companion to creep far around the pair. They reach the hippo pond's edge, just in time to see pelicans feeding on the opposite shore. Near where they're standing, a huge blanket-shaped nest adorns a thorn-bush. Inside the nest's dried, interwoven grasses, huddle three fat little Weaver Birds; on the lookout for suitable prey, they watch the rest of the world go by.

The world! It's causing His Excellency Friend Prime Minister Antoine Bhulliwah X'Zilone buckets of worry, with stomach cramps too. A nice quiet revolution with no notice taken by world media, nine-tenths of whose reporters wouldn't know New X'Zambilia from Burundi or Madagascar. Such was the situation before Dr. Fang pushed the throttle of Chinese propaganda full forward.

But now! Beijing's announcement that it is forcibly coming to New X'Zambilia to set things right has galvanized newshounds from Auckland to Atlanta, Mumbai to Manchester, Nairobi to New York. These folk are descending, wave after wave, on X'Fulumbane.

Yet nobody has sighted a single Chinese plane or warship anywhere nearby. Not that they couldn't arrive in a hurry…

The maid puts a plate of American shredded wheat, his favorite breakfast cereal, in front of Bhulliwah. He shakes his head, shoos her off. Doesn't think he can choke down a cup of coffee.

His three enforced houseguests, senior media moguls, eye him as eagles would a minnow before they swoop to fight over the little creature. Bhulliwah's wife frowns but holds her tongue. For once!

Already hundreds of ace reporters, newspaper columnists, radio talk show hosts and, above all, television personalities are in town, seeming almost to outnumber the citizens, especially if you go by the decibel-level of their self-important noises. Higher-ups in the journalistic pecking order are demanding luxury housing, fine dining and a never-ending flow of drink. It's driving Bhulliwah's office frantic, with complaints pouring in from everyone local who's anyone.

The newsfolk have swept through the city's two hotels, ousting regular guests, appropriating rooms of the less prominent and dropping their own secondary lights onto lobby chairs and floorspace. like an occupying army, the reporters and back-up crews quarter themselves upon all inhabitants not living in squalor. Very Big Cheeses, TV cheeses from ABC, NBC, CBS, CNN FOX and the BBC, have taken over the empty Royal Palace, dumping electronic gear in Royal Throne Hall and griping about it having only five wall outlets for their infernal machines.

Hesitantly, the butler enters the dining room. He lays Bhulliwah's daily briefing sheet before him. The Friend Prime Minister gives it a scan. More reports of shops and markets cleaned-out, of bars running dry. And a flurry of whining–coupled with threats–from "Big Five" families about their mansions being taken over by the most brazen of these newshounds, guzzling their imported liquors and decimating their hoardings of Cuban cigars! Cursed intruders behave as if they own the place. A total pain, except, of course, for money. The media people aren't shy about spreading it around.

New X'Zambilians who heretofore had been resigned to starvation as the card life dealt them, suddenly are coming into corrupting wealth. Taxi drivers, lucky to get one job a day, scurry from client to client to client. Tips to anyone and everyone rendering a service, overflow with generosity. The foreigners, being on expenses, don't mind they're making prices rise 500% every 24 hours.

A bonanza! Last night, Bhulliwah's own Decree #51 ordering a curfew effective at 8 P.M., was totally flouted by people dancing until sunrise. In the streets! Many media representatives danced with them. Not only are they rich, they have the gall in this time of crisis to be jolly!

What, Bhulliwah asks himself, are the long-term repercussions from such a circus? He's sure they won't do the stability of his regime any good.

Still, if you don't think about the Chinese and their threats, X'Fulumbane is turning into a most delighted and delightful spot. Even now cargo planes filled with cases of Johnny Walker are winging here straight from Scotland.

All this joy and only he, Bhulliwah, remains morose. Moral constipation feeds his outrage, his indigestion, his inability to rejoice in the nation's limelight status.

With the Geneva account overflowing, money is his least concern. He's drowning in it. To him, the media are intruding upon and jeopardizing a lovely quiet not-to-be-unduly-noticed revolution, whose success he wants to celebrate at Madame Yvette's.

No chance now. She's booked every day from dawn to dawn, with sessions behind the velvet curtains limited to fifteen minutes. Not even a bribe can get you a half hour. For Yvette, as with him, money is so plentiful it has become meaningless.

His own dining room is infested by this trio of "pundits," staring at him from across breakfast. Everywhere he goes they follow, questioning and commenting, suggesting, negating, criticizing and chewing, chewing, chewing upon his utterances, his gestures, his burps, his farts. How can he possibly sneak away for private release and solace?

His wife! She's falling in love with their enforced guests: U.S. White House correspondents, on special assignment to cover the Chinese invasion. She's flirting outrageously, to the point that he's tempted to order the cook to feed them, her too, rat poison.

Dieu de Dieu! He's lucky to get into the bathroom on his own. Events are so bad they threaten to send him to *her* psychiatrist, a fate he considers worse than Chinese—damn the Chinese!—water torture.

Y. Sanjeev Sandaram's treachery! Bhulliwah lets out a snarl. His guests stare, one scribbles a note.

"Antoine! Enough!" raps out Her Excellency, Friend Madame Petrina Bhulliwah-X'Zilone.

He grunts, knowing that his noises will be analyzed at length in the global press. "I'm standing before the home of the self-appointed Prime Minister, who this morning at breakfast..."

Sandaram! Visions of carving the old man up dance in his mind. Finger by finger, toe by toe, limb by limb, marinating and

273

barbecuing the bastard, then passing him off to his media guests as "roast lamb, a so-traditional New X'Zambilian recipe." It's among the milder of his fantasies.

With the Chinese threat growing more imminent by the hour, Bhulliwah feels used, trapped, undone, his power slipping away. Every tick of the antique clock in his office and the electronic one at home seems to bring him and all his plans closer to disaster.

Chapter 34: Ace Tower
Washington D.C. area, New X'Zambilia, West Lemontree,
New Jersey, U.S.A., and In-Flight Overseas,
Sunday afternoon–evening, December 20

When Suzanne arrives at her Bethesda, Maryland apartment, she's looking forward to a long shower and a good nap. Had to get up at dawn to catch her plane back. Carlos drove her from Cuernevaca to Mexico City's airport and everything went smoothly; but with a long wait to change planes at Dallas, she's feeling the effects of her journey.

The light blinks on her telephone. Messages from Rahel and Schulz, no doubt. She's tempted not to call them until after her shower. With a sigh, she decides duty first.

Fortunately, each is at home. Rahel reports on Jamieson's involvement with Richmond Oil and its designs on the X'Ziloncado Basin. Schulz delivers scuttlebutt about life at Eland, according to Jody Keppel. He also informs her she'll find a bill for expenses in a fax at *The New Republic*.

She's just stepping out of her shower and anticipating a nap when the phone rings. She glares at it but picks up.

A Ms. Shenandoah introduces herself as Harlan Fenster's executive secretary. She says she's calling from Ace headquarters in New Jersey. "How soon can you get here?" she asks.

"As soon as you wish," replies Suzanne. Weary she may be, but always a reporter. And if this can help poor Goldstone...

"A limousine will pick you up in exactly twenty minutes. The driver will escort you to our corporate helicopter. Mr. Fenster will see that you get home safely, if you so choose."

Choose to what? Return home? Strange remark. Suzanne begins to wonder if the Ace Corporation's machinations aren't dangerous. Was it responsible for sending her on that goose chase to Califor–? No. Why should a corporate entity...?

"I'll be waiting for the driver to ring my bell three times and I'll come down," she says.

"Should you stay for dinner, do you prefer ocean salmon or free-range lamb for your main course?" asks Ms. Shenandoah. "The lamb is totally organic and comes from Mr. Fenster's ranch in Wyoming."

"Oh, salmon, if I may. A true ocean-caught fish is quite a treat these days."

"Mr. Fenster eats only deep ocean fish as well as organic meats and produce," Ms. Shenandoah's voice sounds reproving, as though anyone who doesn't eat organic isn't a respectable human-being. "Bring an overnight bag, also your passport." The phone goes dead.

A brief meeting? Possibly dinner? A bag and passport? Sold into white slavery, was that the Ace game? Small wonder Jeffrey Ace talked so salaciously at dinner last night.

Well, Ms. Shenandoah has accomplished one thing. Suzanne suspects it was the call's main purpose. The woman made the summons sound eccentric, dynamic, intriguing, in a word interesting. And if Fenster turns out to be disappointingly ordinary, or as uninformative as "Jeffy," his boss, at least she can look forward to one more damn fine meal.

Friend Generalissimo X'M'Bazi–how he loathes his new last name, even more than his new title!–decides there's no way he can get action from Fulumbane–X'Fulumbane?–police headquarters during the weekend, especially this post-revolution weekend. So he's taking time for his thorough, now confirmatory, murder investigation. Just in case he's wrong, which he doesn't think he is. But you never can be too careful…

He keeps both Petroff and D'Alessandro under guarded arrest in the infirmary, where they share a room. Despite loud complaints with threats to appeal to higher authority both New X'Zambilian and U.S., he decrees they must wear ankle bracelets.

At the Generalissimo's request, I too remain confined: in my tent and under guard. Much as I hate it, I agree to stay ankled.

"Let's not reveal the situation has changed," says X'M'Bazi. "We want the guilty party to be complacent about getting away with, well, murder. Murders plural."

"One party?" I ask. "No conspiracy?"

"Of that I'm not totally sure," answers the Generalissimo. "We need proof. You've got to reach Rahel and Suzanne in the 'States.'"

"I'd resent you making me feel like an idiot," I say, "except that I have a glimmer as to where you're head–" I punch a fist into my hand. "But of course! Finally, I get–"

He puts finger to lips. "We shouldn't even compare notes until we line up proof. But we'll work together, okay? Now, I'm gonna sit down in the library with that nice *armagnac* and those not so nice scorpions, all locked away, I trust, and do some serious cogitating as to my next actions. Everything according to 'Method Detecting,' Sherlock Holmes style. Remember how he'd squat down and examine all the ashes in a fireplace with his magnifying glass? And come up with damning evidence! That's the kind of painstaking work I admire and mean to emulate here."

Back in the lodge's library that X'M'Bazi has appropriated as his office, he gives an order for Sheila to leave the infirmary, now that the nurse considers her cured, and move back to her tent. She'll be accompanied by a bodyguard but will have free run of the camp and can take game drives too.

He decides to re-question the tour's survivors. With her talk of accents, Madame Briac has furnished a lead to consider. He has an inkling as to how the murder on the train was carried out, but at this point, no proof. A person in the group knowing French with a singsong Swiss accent would contribute to building a tight case. Then too, an indication of who visited Zembeylia, or goddamn New X'Zambilia, recently could be a second damning circumstance.

Goldstone now believes he has come up with the solution of these crimes? He's an amateur and, no doubt, has jumped to something wrong-headed. This calls for Holmesian methodology, not merely deduction but the following of a provable evidence line.

After all, the case has to be airtight for it to survive legal scrutiny; a challenge, even for a highly trained, highly experienced, top-marks graduate of John Jay, the streets of New York and the labyrinthine intrigues of politics here.

For starters, he questions distraught Ms. Southgate, pining for her D'Alessandro. And hits paydirt.

She admits to spending three years at a fancy Swiss boarding school in the French-speaking *Suisse-Romande* State or *Canton*, as the Swiss say, outside Geneva.

So who was her classmate? None other than Helen Farrar!

This may change his view of the case. The moving finger may shift again, destroying his hypothesizing. Is this is a tale of jealousy between two girls thrown together at a Swiss boarding school? The Generalissimo can conceive of a sinister business intrigue, using pliable D'Alessandro, putty in Southgate's seductive hands, for the heavy lifting.

All the more damnable since D'Alessandro actually hails from Switzerland. Born in Lugano, just across the frontier from Italy. He's still a Swiss citizen, with a passport whose crimson cover and white cross appears distinctively different from the dark blue, silver-embossed American ones.

Southgate also tells him that Sheila, born Helen's first cousin, Sheila Flohr, was, during those times, attending a Montessori school in Lausanne, also French speaking and only a few miles from Geneva.

M'Bazi–he's damned if he'll use the "X" until officialdom forces it on him–summons Sheila.

She confirms having been born Flohr. Her father, Armand Flohr, a Swiss banker from French-speaking Canton Vaud, married Helen's father's naturalized American sister. So Helen was half-Swiss, half-American. Yes, Sheila was in a day school, while Helen, along with Malvina Southgate, attended boarding school nearby. Those two spent three years at *l'Ecole-Pensionnat Schumacher,* equivalent to U.S. seventh through ninth grades. And, of course, they both speak French.

"If you started life as Sheila Flohr, how did you get to be Sheila Farrar or Helen's half-sister?" asks the Generalissimo.

Sheila grimaces. "Just after my ninth birthday, my parents were killed in an auto crash in Italy. Helen's parents brought me over to Connecticut, where they lived, and eventually adopted me. I used the name 'Flohr-Farrar' until I married. When I joined Helen's business, we found it simpler to tell the world we were sisters. We were very close." Sheila pulls a handkerchief from her purse, dabs at her eyes.

After dinner, X'M'Bazi, or simply M'Bazi as he still thinks of himself in defiance of the powers-that-be, summons the whole tour group or "remnants," as he privately calls them, to the library.

He sits Sheila, looking pale and thin, beside Malvina Southgate, flanked by Guitterez-Shaughnessy and Lazuli. The four occupy a first line of collapsible chairs brought from the lodge's auditorium/conference room used for lectures, movies and theatricals. Miho Petroff, the Jamiesons and Chandler make up a second row.

A guard, using his rifle as prod, pushes Petroff, D'Alessandro and me, the three of us handcuffed, into third row seats. X'M'Bazi signals the guard to remove our cuffs.

Miho Petroff and Ms. Southgate turn around, blow kisses at their men. Sheila turns to give me a stare.

X'M'Bazi clears his throat. All heads swivel back to him. He stands silent for a moment, shifting his gaze to each person. They look questioningly back.

The library door squeaks slightly as it opens. In comes a man who quietly takes a chair facing the group. A white fellow with gray hair. He wears tan trousers and a matching open-necked shirt. I've seen him here and there in camp.

"Folks," says X'M'Bazi in English, "this is Monsieur Marc Gaudin, the camp's accountant. He is originally from France, from the city of Orléans where people are reputed to speak a particularly pure form of French." He turns to Gaudin and, still in English, asks, "Can you distinguish between French regional accents?"

The accountant nods. "I've been in the hotel business for eighteen years. Both in northern and southern France where local accents are very different. Also in the Valais, a Canton of French-speaking Switzerland. And then in Lebanon, which has its own version of French. I have served in several countries of West Africa, former French colonies, as well as here. So I've heard my share of accents."

"Yes, but how's your ear?" asks X'M'Bazi. "Some people are tone deaf, just as others are color blind and no matter how many accents they've been exposed to they can't identify them."

Monsieur Gaudin smiles. "When I was a child my mother forced me to take violin lessons. I hated them and the teacher told her I had no talent; except I did have what he called 'the gift of perfect pitch.' The teacher demonstrated this by playing a note on his fiddle and having me sing it. I always got it right, no sharps or flats or half tones off. That, it seems, is perfect pitch."

"So you consider yourself good at identifying accents?" the Generalissimo insists.

The accountant nods.

"Do you know any of these people personally?"

279

Gaudin shakes his head.

"All right," says X'M'Bazi, "We'll begin. First, those of you who speak, read and write fluent French raise your hands."

No response. Everyone just gazes at the detective.

"C'mon, people. You think we aren't in the process of checking you out? Refuse to cooperate and you may drag things on another day or two. But let me give you my personal guarantee. You do that, you refuse to help us, and when we find the guilty party or parties—believe me, we will!—I personally promise to make it my business, my crusade you might say, to go as hard with you as I can. That'll be damned hard! Most of you haven't heard of 'Disciplinary Camp One' but you have of 'Sing-Sing' and 'San Quentin.' Well, our little camp makes those places look like luxury holiday resorts. 'Kay?"

A stir among the group.

"I'll ask again. How many speak, read and write French fluently?"

I raise my hand. So does Sheila. Malvina Southgate, heaving a huge sigh, raises hers, and then D'Alessandro. Both the Petroffs and Guitterez-Shaughnessy put up their hands, as does Lazuli. Even Chandler tentatively puts up his.

"*Kee-rryyst!*" X'M'Bazi shakes his head in irritation. The whole damn lot, except for the Jamiesons. Well, forward march! He gives each of us a sheet of paper. "When I ask you one by one, I want you to read out what I've typed. It's in French. The English translation is: 'Hello. How are you? I'm an American. Do you think it will rain today?' Read in a natural tone." He looks at Bitsy Jamieson. "It doesn't matter if you know the words or not. When I point to you, just read."

He starts with me. I read out: *"Bon-JOUR. COM-ment allez-vous? Je suis Améri-CAIN. Pensez vous qu'il va pleu-VOIR aujourd'hui?"*

X'M'Bazi turns to the accountant.

"Oh, definitely an accent from Paris or some not too distant urban area in north-central France. Like my hometown. It's what we call standard French. However," the man pauses, "the speaker is a foreigner whose native tongue is probably American English. He must have lived a long time in France, the accent being relatively slight. Except," Monsieur Gaudin raises a finger, "except for a problem with our glottal 'r,' so difficult for foreigners to master. Funny thing, no American I've encountered can get our French 'r' in the word *Américain* quite right when speaking a full sentence. Paradoxically, it's one of the hardest words for foreigners, especially English speakers of American provenance, to pronounce, no matter how good they are in French."

"Okay," says X'M'Bazi. "An American who lived in Paris and learned French there. That certainly jibes with what we know. Next." He points at D'Alessandro.

"BON-jourr. Comment ALLEZ vous? Je suis A-MERR-icain.Pensez vous qu'il va PLEU-voirr *aujouRRRd*'hui, NON?"

"Definitely Swiss-Italian. That is, he must come from the part of Switzerland where they speak Italian but learn French in school. He rolls his r's and has a Swiss tonic accent."

"Yup," says M.Bazi nodding. He points at Sheila.

"BON-jour. Comment ALLEZ vous? Je suis A-MER-icaine.Pensez vous qu'il va PLEU-voir aujourd'hui?"

"An urban Swiss accent from the French-speaking area," says Gaudin. "Could you have her say one thing more? *Bonne année?* That is, Happy New Year,' or more literally, 'Have a good year.'"

Sheila says *"Bonne A-NNEEEE,"* drawing out the é.

When the Generalissimo points back at to me, I say "Bonne Ann-EE," with the last syllable much shorter.

Malvina Southgate is next and pronounces exactly as Sheila. Guittererz-Shaughnessy is as like them both as peas in a pod.

"And where did you learn your French?" asks X'M'Bazi.

It seems Guitterez attended a French school run by Swiss in Bogotà and then two years of engineering school at the University of Neufchâtel, before getting into The U.S. Air Force Academy in

Colorado. "In Switzerland I passed all my exams. And they were in French."

Silently, X'M'Bazi points to Miho Petroff.

Monsieur Gaudin applauds her accent. "Excellent, my dear, excellent. Of course, a bit guttural and you roll your r's because that is the operatic style, even for some native French singers. But you are very clear, a pleasure to listen to."

Miho bows her head slightly. "Most honored," she says softly. "We had to learn French at the conservatory in Tokyo."

"Well," says Gaudin. "I hope you shall sing for us. A selection from *Carmen*? Or is *Faust* more your style?"

"I will certainly not sing so long as my dear husband is a prisoner," says Miho Petroff, blushing deeply but tossing her head.

"Let us hope, then, he is soon rel–"

"That'll do!" X'M'Bazi raps out the words.

Silence.

The other tour members have American accents, according to the accountant. Chandler and Petroff read fluently, while both Jamiesons stumble over the phrases and don't seem to know French at all. Predictably, Lazuli is competent in French but rolls his r's, New X'Zambilian style.

"Thank you, Monsieur Gaudin," says X'M'Bazi. He shakes hands with the man, dismisses him. The accountant leaves the library.

"Now," says the Generalissimo, "we'll explore French connections I don't know about you, Mr. Chandler. Where did you learn French?"

"A couple of years in high school and then college. I've worked in French-speaking countries setting up air charters. I've often had to negotiate agreements in the language."

Roughly the same story of learning French in school and later using it for business from Petroff. X'M'Bazi doesn't feel he's getting anywhere further with this than he already is. His theory of the case? Still intact.

"Okay," he says. "I have what I need. You can go. Guard?" He indicates that D'Alessandro, Petroff and I should be recuffed. "When you get 'em back to the infirmary and tent, don't forget the ankle-bracelets."

"Look here," says Petroff in his aggressive whine. "That damn thing is most uncomfortable. I'm not going anywhere. Where could I go if I wanted to? Sleep in the jungle with lions?"

"Yes, yes," echoes D'Alessandro. "We can go nowhere and you know it so."

"'Lead us not unto temptation,'" says X'M'Bazi. "Someone put scorpions on Ms. Mondran's infirmary bed. *M'zu-m'zu's* a helluva lot more uncomfortable than an ankle-guard. Gentlemen–if such you are and that ain't proven by me–learn to love 'em is all I can suggest."

As the group rises to leave, the Generalissimo shouts, "One more thing." Everyone freezes. He lets the silence stretch. Then, "How many of you have been in Zembeylia, or whatever we call it now, sometime in the last six to ten weeks?"

A show of hands: Sheila Mondran, Miho Petroff, Ms. Southgate, Gordon Chandler, D'Alessandro, and Petroff, indicate they have. As have the Jamiesons. Lazuli and I are the only ones who keep our hands down. Our guide, of course, lives here.

"Well, well," says X'M'Bazi. "So what's this tour about, I wonder?" He shakes his head. "Very strange. Mrs. Mondran, why were you here?"

"I came for ten days in September and early October on my sister's orders to arrange our journey."

"Where did you travel?"

"I took our exact itinerary, making reservations, inspecting accommodations and contracting for excursions and events along the way. You can check it out."

"Oh, I have and I shall. Recheck, that is. Mr. Chandler?"

"Here in late September, early October to discuss air charters with Mr. Sandaram of X'Zambili-Africa Tours. I'd hoped to negotiate with the government, but it was tied to Eland."

"Ms. Southgate and Mr. D'Alessandro?"

She answers. "Same time-frame: September and early October. As a major tour-packaging firm specializing in African safaris, we, like Mr Chandler, were working with X'Zambili-Africa Tours as in-country manager. We have backing from Olympia International, a large hotel conglomerate that wishes to invest in Zembeylian resorts through Mr. Sandaram's organization, not through his rival, Zemba Royal, and certainly not through Eland."

"Then why," asks X'M'Bazi, "are you on a tour organized by Eland?"

Ms. Southgate smiles grimly. "The opposition invited us, hoping to win us as subordinate suppliers. We thought it an ideal time to check on how they were doing, and to keep contact with our New X'Zambilian friends, one of whom has just become Prime Minister." Her smile grows broader. "Besides, it's a freebie, more or less."

Jamieson and Petroff are less forthcoming. They merely say that business, legitimate business, brought them briefly to Zembeylia during late September, early October.

Bitsy Jamieson announces, "I accompanied my husband because I'm fascinated by gems, especially your tsavorites."

At last X'M'Bazi lets them go, except for me. "In my book, you're still chief suspect," he says loudly. "And I've got some unanswered questions just for you! Guard, wait outside for your prisoner."

When the others have left and he has locked the library door, the Generalissimo asks, "Was this enlightening? Are we further along?"

"Accent-wise we sure know I'm innocent, which makes me feel further along." I nod. "But we're missing information and substance. I bet you'll find both in the U.S. Not here."

"You believe, as do I, that it's someone with a Swiss accent in French and who was in this country during September and October of this year?"

"Let's see, that limits us to only Malvina Southgate and her something-or-other Giorgio D'Alessandro, Guitterez-Shaughnessy, the Petroffs, Chandler, the Jamiesons and Sheila Mondran. So we're down to nine souls, the whole lot of 'em, except for Lazuli and me. By the way," I go on, "Petroff's wife, Miho, with her excellent ear, how do we know she can't do a perfect Swiss-type accent? Remember, whoever accosted Madame Briac wore a mask and spoke in a whisper."

"At least," says X'M'Bazi, "with my French accent test, we've eliminated the Jamiesons and Lazuli. Three down."

"What about faking? What if the Jamiesons both know French and can imitate all kinds of accents? After all, Jamieson keeps trying mightily to talk Texan, except the Bronx pokes through. You're not getting too far with this line."

"A confirming line, remember. One of those essential tasks a trained detective has to do."

"Well, I haven't heard anything yet to contradict my own idea of what happened. I did reach my friend and colleague Rahel in New York and she gave me interesting information on the Jamieson guy. The wife has red hair and could certainly play a 'ditzy' redhead,to quote those postal people in Los Angeles who received and delivered the poison package that killed Barry Mondran from the person imitating Suzanne Carrington. My, I think and hope, significant other. Yeah, *ditz* might describe Bitsy Jamieson under certain circumstances, although she probably has a steel-trap mind. She also dropped out of the Chicago travel show in time to catch a two-something flight the same afternoon to L.A. It got in around 4P.M. local time, according to Rahel. This would give Bitsy ample opportunity to rent a car, get over to the Valley and waltz into that mailing office at 6:25, putting on her act so the two men there would be sure to remember her. She didn't show up in Chicago again until next morning, so could easily have taken the 'Red-Eye' back. My agent, Schulz, found out about some boarding passes that exactly fit this scenario."

I ruminate a bit. "The Jamiesons seem so damn fake. What's their game, I wonder?"

"Your whole group all seem pretty fake to me," mutters X'M'Bazi. "Present company possibly excepted.

"Well, thanks for that sliver of acceptance. From what Schulz reported to Rahel," I continue, "the Eland staff are very worried about their company's future. Who's left for them? Only Sheila. Has she got the iron hand, the negotiating skills, the willpower to carry the company through rocky times, as it's sure to face now? She's so much softer than Helen Farrar, whom everybody disliked but who really personified her business. In any case, Eland's people are feeling very leaderless."

I pace the width of the room behind the chairs, wheel to face the Generalissimo. "I bet Suzanne has the glue to put everything together. I can't reach her. She seems to be out of circulation." I frown. "Very worrying."

A marvelous ride, Suzanne decides as the helicopter wings toward Ace Industrial Park near West Lemontree, New Jersey. Lights of towns and cities sparkle like diamonds, with here and there the ruby red and sapphire blue of a neon sign. They pass over Philadelphia's carpet of lights, then turn from a northern heading to go west.

Suddenly, ahead, looms a tower. More lights stud a flat diamond-shaped roof. As they draw closer, she sees an illuminated emblem adorning the tower's face: the Ace of Spades.

"Ace Tower," says the pilot, pride in his voice. "We land on the roof."

They hover and slowly let down. As power is cut to the rotors, two mechanics, doubling over for safety, run out to secure the craft. A woman in a blue uniform opens the door on the passenger side, helps Suzanne alight. The woman leads the way to an elevator. It descends one floor to a level marked *Penthouse*. The door opens and Suzanne steps into a large lounge at the center of which stands an empty reception desk.

"Please sit," says her guide, motioning to a couch. "Someone will be with you." She disappears behind mahogany double doors.

Suzanne picks up a copy of *Forbes*. She hasn't started to thumb through it when a gray-haired African-American woman appears.

"Ms. Carrington, I'm Nora Shenandoah. You've brought your overnight case and passport? Excellent. Right this way."

She leads Suzanne through the mahogany doors and along a corridor, thick-carpeted, softly lit, decorated in muted colors. At its end, she knocks on an unmarked door. It swings open. An angular, white-haired man, Caucasian, rises from behind a huge mahogany desk. Suzanne notes that it is bare of papers.

"Suzanne Carrington," announces Ms. Shenandoah. "Shall I get the document?"

"When I ring," says the man. He gestures for Suzanne to sit in a comfortable-looking mahogany chair with black leather cushions. "Harlan Fenster. Good of you to come at such short notice." He takes his seat.

Striking features, Suzanne decides. Far from ordinary. A long face set off by a large, curved nose giving a hawkish look. Sixty-five or so. Very distinguished, if somewhat grim. Not a man, she guesses, who smiles easily. His suit is as black as the night beyond a large wraparound window that gives a view of moon, stars, and in the distance, the shadow of hills. Despite a slight note of color lent by his maroon necktie, unfashionably narrow, she could be in the presence of a high class mortician. The tie merely accentuates the suit's—and the man's—austerity.

"Now then," he says, "I understand you suspect us of all manner of foul deeds and plots when nothing could be further from the truth. The truth, in fact, is rather amusing *An-one has the eye to see it*, as Shakespeare remarks in *Hamlet*." He pauses, takes a deep breath. "I am prepared to tell all and to back up my words with documents." He reaches into a desk drawer, pulls out a black folder, which he waves at her before setting it down on the desk. "However," he goes on, "this brief is totally confidential, a table of our current investment projects. You must sign a paper swearing to keep everything I tell you and everything you read here," he taps the folder with his forefinger, "entirely secret, unless I authorize release. You must also certify your understanding of what might happen to you and yours were you not to do so. As a newswoman—I call news-gathering a kiss-and-tell-all pastime—are you willing to undertake such an obligation?"

Almost not hesitating, Suzanne says, "I'm not here for any story. I'm here to get at the bottom of a tangled affair that is threatening a very close friend and has almost ensnared me. I want this over with. I want the truth."

Fenster allows himself the embryo of a smile. "Had you objected, I was prepared to have you flown home immediately. But if it is truth you seek, then you are knocking at the right door. Together we shall make common cause to serve our common interest."

He presses a buzzer. Ms. Shenandoah enters bearing a silver tray on which lies a single folded paper. She unfolds it, hands it to Suzanne. A typed statement: her promise to reveal nothing of what she sees or is told that pertains to the Ace Corporation, its plans, projects or current investments.

Quickly, Suzanne signs. Fenster signs as witness as does Ms. Shenandoah.

"I will put this in the safe," she says and exits the office.

Fenster looks at his watch. "We'd better start." He rises. Ms. Shenandoah re-enters, bearing a black raincoat, which she puts around his shoulders like a cloak. He nods acknowledgment.

"Come, my dear," he says to Suzanne, as he lopes off down the corridor. *"Miles to go before we sleep…"*

They return to the helicopter. Again it crosses Philadelphia's lights, to land at the international airport near a line of private hangars.

Men in white coveralls are hovering around a sleek business jet, its tailfin decorated with the ace of spades. Suzanne notes torpedo-like extra fuel tanks at the wingtips.

Fenster scrambles out of the whirlybird, gesturing for her to follow. They climb aboard the jet, where a woman in a business suit, but with gold ace emblems on her lapels, shows them to facing seats.

Across the aisle are drawn curtains. A delicious odor, something simmering in wine, makes Suzanne realize how hungry she is. The only meal she's had all day is an Economy Class breakfast on the flight from Mexico to Texas.

Almost before she has caught her breath, they're underway. After a long takeoff, Philadelphia is there for the third time sparkling and spread beneath them. They bank eastward, heading for the ocean.

"Now may I ask where we're going?"

"To Zembeylia, where else?" says her host. "In nine hours we'll land at Cape Verde to refuel. Then another seven hours to M'Bukusa, an airfield half in South Africa, half in Zembeylia, with separate Customs stations for each country." Fenster gestures towards the curtains. "Two private cubicles containing bunks. You'll be able to sleep quite comfortably. But now," he rubs his hands, "sustenance."

The meal, brought by the flight attendant, a lavender-housecoat over her blouse, is spare, servings small but every bite delicious. A white *Puligny-Montrachet, 1961*, perfectly complements souffléd sea-urchins and an exquisitely prepared salmon in the lightest of cream sauces touched with *anisette*. A mushroom salad follows and a beautifully presented platter of goat cheeses.

"*Montrachet*," says Fenster. "My favorite white. For its finesse on the palate, its cool elegance, its wonderful bouquet with just a hint of almonds. Didn't Alexandre Dumas say that *one should drink Montrachet while on one's knees, head bowed and bared in thankfulness for such a marvelous gift?*"

"I believe so," says Suzanne. "I really don't know."

Fenster chats about this and that, avoiding mention of business until the clearing away of dessert: a frozen orange filled with sorbet—and the serving of coffee accompanied by snifters of Alsatian raspberry brandy. Raising his glass, he pushes the black folder toward her. "Use our time in limbo here and read this through. At breakfast, ask me any questions you want. But get rest because tomorrow promises to be strenuous." He stands. "There are two lavatories aft. I'll leave you now." He moves to one set of curtains, brushes them aside to reveal a bed and narrow standup space facing a bulkhead. The space holds a closet. "Just enough room to hang your clothes and get into pajamas," he says. "We'll meet again after the fuel stop at Cape Verde. That will give us plenty of time to brief one another." He bows slightly, and as the curtains came together, says, "I bid you good night."

Chapter 35: Into Battle
X'Ziloncado Tented Camp, Monday, December 21

I keep trying to reach Suzanne. No luck! Making holes in my stomach. Finally I decide that I'll have to act on my hunch without her. I telephone the front desk, get X'M'Bazi and request that certain New York inquiries be made.

The Generalissimo is amenable. He indicates he'll contact some colleagues. "Shouldn't be too hard," he says. "As I told you, there are those in the police department and district attorney's office who owe me."

X'M'Bazi can't put off reporting to Bhulliwah. On the phone he waits and waits. While he has receiver to ear, the hotel manager, face bearing a worried expression, bustles into the library, hands over a paper: *PARTY OF TWO: HARLAN FENSTER AND SUZANNE CARRINGTON ARRIVE THIS EVENING STOP. NEED SEPARATE ACCOMMODATIONS FOR BOTH STOP.*

"Can you house them?" asks X'M'Bazi.

"These are VVIPs. We just have to." The manager pauses, cocking his head and looking up at the detective. "Friend Generalissimo X'M'Bazi Sir, could you please arrest another person or persons and put them in the infirmary? We are short one tent."

"Well...I can move Goldstone. He'll cooperate."

The manager, looking relieved, hurries away.

When X'M'Bazi finally gets through to Bhulliwah, the Prime Minister says, "Friend Major—you are a Major now. There are no longer funds for a colonel in your slot, sacrifices having to be made.

"Friend Major X'M'Bazi, I am not delighted by the slowness of your investigation. You have your mastermind criminal, Eugene Petroff, and your robot-executioner, this Goldstone. Why haven't you checked them into 'Disciplinary Camp One' in preparation for their trial and sure condemnation to the guillotine? Why delays and prevarications?"

"Excellency," says X'M'Bazi, "it is not—"

"Friend Excellency, if you please," interrupts Bhulliwah. "We must be scrupulous in observing niceties, if they are to be adopted by the population-at-large."

"Sir, Friend Excellency, it is not at all clear that the two you mention are our culprits."

"Of course they are." X'M'Bazi hears the irritated snap-snap of the Friend Prime Minister's fingers.

"I see there's nothing for it," Bhulliwah heaves a huge sigh, "nothing for it but for me to come there personally. In any case one must get away from the international press which, thanks to the Chinese, are infesting X'Fulumbane like rats. Bubonic rats!"

"Friend Major, you may prepare for my arrival this evening."

When the manager hears the news he almost faints.

291

Fenster and Suzanne in the Ace jet touch down at M'Bukusa airfield just after 9 P.M. Its southern side belongs to South Africa, the northern one to New X'Zambilia. The plane taxies to the southern terminal.

Two men wait on the tarmac. Fenster shakes hands warmly with one of them. "My dear," he turns to Suzanne, "meet Security Minister Zecherias M'Bowé, an old friend."

M'Bowé bows and kisses the air above Suzanne's hand in perfect French etiquette for rendering homage to an unmarried lady of social standing. "Ex-Minister," he murmurs. "At least for now." He gestures towards the other man, spare, gray-haired, Caucasian. Despite the 95 degree Fahrenheit heat, he's wearing a trenchcoat. "This–uhm–is Mr. Green from the town of Langley in your state of Virginia."

The man gives a nod.

"Thanks to Mr. Green, that jeep," M'Bowé indicates an open vehicle standing nearby, "has been generously loaned to us by our South African friends. He also has arranged our crossing without hindrance into the land that I shall ever think of as Zembeylia." The ex-Minister shakes his head. "To change the name after all the trouble I took over our national anthem and associated poetries...Well," he gathers himself. Shall we proceed?"

With Green at the wheel, they're about to drive off when a flurry of motion catapults from a nearby hedge; a figure hurls itself at the jeep.

"Wait!" it cries in English. "Hold on there!" The figure grabs the vehicle's door trying to hoist aboard.

Mr. Green guns the engine, jerks the jeep forward ,throwing the would-be intruder onto the pavement. Quickly it stands and, running after them, yells, "You've got to take me. I'm NBC!"

"Up yours!" roars Mr. Green as they speed away. "Sorry, M'am," he adds.

The jeep follows a perimeter road around the runway and through an open gate in a chain fence separating the airport from the world. A two hundred yard drive takes them past a large, well-lighted gas station to a red-and-white barrier, South Africa's frontier post. On the opposite side of a hut housing border police, a car is crossing into South Africa.

"Fuel is so much cheaper this side of the frontier," says M'Bowé. "Our local vehicles come here to gas up. That station supplies the Tented Camp. Had I been allowed to continue my 'Modernization and Self-Sufficiency Program,' we would have had our own fuel no more than eighteen months from now."

"Thanks to Richmond Oil?" asks Fenster dryly.

The ex-Minister doesn't answer.

A South African officer emerges from the hut. Mr. Green mutters a few words, shows a paper. The officer nods, pulls a lever that raises the red-and-white barrier. They drive through.

A hundred yards more brings them to a similar station. The barrier is already up but, dutifully, they stop. Nothing happens. Mr. Green taps his horn, flashes the jeep's lights. A languid hand appears out the hut's window, shoos them on. They're in New X'Zambilia.

Only a quarter of a mile down the highway they see a sign saying *X'Ziloncado Camp.* An arrow appears to point straight into the bush. Headlights pick up a narrow dirt track over which they bounce and bump for half a mile before the camp lights appear.

As they arrive at the main lodge, Suzanne notes two helicopters standing in a parking area, along with several jeeps and open Land Rovers.

"Ah, Generalissimo," exclams M'Bowé as he alights from the vehicle and goes to X'M'Bazi, who stands waiting with the manager on the lodge steps. "How good to see a friend and loyal subordinate."

X'M'Bazi's greeting is less effusive, but to Suzanne he's particularly warm. "I'm truly glad you've come," he tells her. "We need to talk." He turns to the sergeant-with-the-unpronounceable-name. "Escort the lady to Mr. Goldstone in the infirmary and remove his ankle-bracelet. After that, report to me here."

"Yes, Major." The sergeant clicks his heels.

M'Bowé raises his eyebrows. "Major? Is that where exemplary loyalty and sense of duty have brought you?"

"I'm damned lucky to be anything at all in this New X'Zambilia of ours."

The ex-minister shudders to hear the name. "Horrible," he murmurs, putting a handkerchief to his lips.

X'M'Bazi escorts the arriving males to the library. There, installed behind the desk, that the former Generalissimo had thought his personal appropriation, is Prime Minister Bhulliwah. Sitting next to him is none other than Dale Uppingham III of the Bank for African Restructuring and Funding. (B.A.R.F.).

Mr. Green and Uppingham exchange nods. Uppingham even cracks his predator's grin. Bhulliwah doesn't stand, waves the newcomers to the folding seats that X'M'Bazi had ordered brought in for his linguistic investigation.

"You may summon my prisoner," says the prime minister.

Handcuffed, looking rumpled, Y. Sanjeev Sandaram is hustled into the room by two SM guards. They shove him onto a seat.

Bhulliwah points at the octogenarian. "You see before you a traitor. This individual has caused the possible imminent invasion of our glorious land by Red China. As I speak, parachutists prepare to alight upon our soil and a naval task force is heading for X'Fulumbane. In our hour of crisis we must put aside personal differences and tribal considerations and look to New X'Zambilia's survival."

"My, my," says Ex-Minister M'Bowé. "Exalted rank has certainly made you pompous."

A vein bulges on Bhulliwah's forehead. "Pompous? That godawful doggerel you wrote when you were in power wasn't pompous? Yes, Parliament has left me with an oratorical turn of speech but I don't inflict dreadful ditties on the people!"

Ex-Minister M'Bowé jumps to his feet. "One more of your gratuitous insults and I'll break your nose again." He turns to the others. "See that bump on his nose? I did that. Bled like a stuck pig, he did. And I'll do it again!"

"Gentlemen!" Dale Uppingham rises. "We have much to discuss and the Chinese won't wait. I suggest we do as Prime Minister Bhulliwah says, forget our differences long enough to solve our many problems." He reaches into his bush jacket's inner pocket, pulls out a yellow note paper. "Now here's an agenda: #1. We need a coherent and stable government in this country. B.A.R.F. will not back fly-by-night régimes. We want continuity and peace. Right in this room, for instance, we can settle the politics of whatever you choose to name your nation once and for all. #2. We must determine investment priorities. That's why Mr. Fenster has come from so far. #3. It's important to get this murder business resolved. We can't have our budding tourist industry jeopardized by private investors and backers running around killing each other. I understand that Friend Colonel, sorry, Friend Major X'M'Bazi, has the investigation well in hand and that sometime after breakfast tomorrow he expects to wrap things up. Am I right?"

X'M'Bazi nods. "I expect, yes," he murmurs. "I certainly hope so."

"So do we," says Uppingham. "A pity if from Colonel to Friend Major you're demoted to Friend Corporal. Or worse!" He pauses. "Any case," he continues, in the context of these three agenda points, we have the fourth and most urgent one of dealing with our Chinese friends." Again he stops, looks at them all. "I warn you, if we can't get joy on points one, two and three, the B.A.R.F. will let the Chinese have you for all the good you'll do us. Or them."

Fenster speaks up. "I suggest we adjourn for two hours. We'll go to our quarters, bathe and change, rest. Then we'll gather again in the dining room. Over dinner and a bottle or two of wine, I'm sure there'll be a meeting of minds. In fact, we'll sit until we damn well have a meeting of minds. Okay?"

After more palaver everyone gives a grudging nod.

"And," says Fenster, "let's treat Mr. Sandaram like the venerable and elderly gentleman he is. Take the handcuffs off, let him come freely to our meeting. I'm sure his contribution will not be negligible."

After they all file out the library door, the sergeant, two helicopter pilots and X'Zimbalwa enter. Along with X'M'Bazi, they'll sleep here tonight, since the VVIP's have taken all tent accommodations.

X'Zimbalwa sidles in looking embarrassed. Friend Prime Minister Bhulliwah has given the captain a "field promotion," to Lieutenant-Colonel on grounds of his X'Zambili ethnicity.

X'Zimbalwa expected to feel deliriously happy at his good fortune. On the contrary, he's ashamed that his promotion has absolutely nothing to do with merit.

X'M'Bazi, on the other hand, is supportive. "You deserve it, after all the years you've put in. Take it with joy. Don't look a gift horse in the mouth."

For the lack of rancor and jealousy, X'Zimbalwa is grateful to the man he still thinks of as his chief. He hopes they can keep working together.

"May I suggest," says X'M'Bazi to his nominal superior, "that at first light you take the helicopter and get Madame Briac? She should be here by 9 A.M. latest." He lights a cigarette. "We'll leave the politicos to jaw-jaw in the dining room. I trust they'll keep on course, though you never can tell. Right now, I'm going to join Goldstone and his lady. With luck, our part in this will be over before tomorrow noon."

Chapter 36: Elephant
X'Ziloncado Tented Camp, Monday, December 21

As sea waves thunder upon a beach, then recede before they return in thunder, so from midnight to sunrise voices behind the closed doors of X'Ziloncado Camp's dining room rise to fury, fall to mumbles, rise furiously again.

At 4:23 A.M., Friend Prime Minister Bhulliwah storms from the room, shaking his head. He wrenches open the door to the library. "How can I work with traitors and criminals?" he shouts. "Even Dale Uppingham is stabbing me in the back!"

He stops peers into the room's darkness, making out four lumpy forms in sleeping bags on the floor. He hears snores, switches on a light. Friend Major-Detective X'M'Bazi and Friend Lieutenant-Colonel-Detective X'Zimbalwa sit up. The friend sergeant-with-the-unpronounceable-name and the friend helicopter pilots merely groan, put hands over eyes and shift away from the light.

Bhulliwah makes an irritable gesture. *"Voyons,"* he says to X'Zimbalwa, "I hate to disturb your beauty sleep; be so good as to follow me."

Hastily, the newly-minted light colonel scrambles to his feet, trails his patron out of the lodge and onto the verandah.

Tables there are already set for a breakfast that the camp schedules before dawn game-drives. The friend prime minister paces up and down, his city shoes clicking on the area's imported Italian tiles. He puffs at a cigarette making it glow furiously. He doesn't offer one to his subordinate. "They are insisting we eliminate the courtesy title of 'Friend.' Too evocative of the Soviet 'Comrade' is what they're telling me. Struck down! My first innovation! *Et tu, Uppingham?*"

Bhulliwah glowers at the detective. "Bah! I'll have to accept."

As if unaware of this momentous decision, stars continue to sparkle in a black satin sky. A gibbous moon follows its course without deviation, a hyena coughs, a hippopotamus burbles, a lioness calls to her mate.

At length Bhulliwah grinds his third smoke underfoot, re-enters the lodge and knocks on the dining room door. It opens just enough to let in his bulk. Quickly, the door closes, locks.

X'Zimbalwa, relieved that he might no longer be a "Friend," goes back to his library sleeping bag.

At 5:48 A.M., as the East is lighting up with sunrise and waiters are bringing pots of coffee plus trays of croissants to the verandah's serving sideboard, a shout, "HURRAH!" rises from the dining room.

The four in the library, already awake, sipping coffee and preparing for a long day, look at each other significantly.

They disperse: X'Zimbalwa and a pilot to fetch Madame Briac from her hospital, the sergeant to check on those lodged in the infirmary, and Major X'M'Bazi to stand outside the dining room awaiting the pleasure of the high-and-mighty. The other pilot, personal aerial chauffeur to the Head of State—whoever that might be at any given moment—decides to go back to sleep.

X'M'Bazi hears loud voices and the slap-slap of enthusiastic men pounding each other on the back. "How like monkeys we humans are," the ex-colonel murmurs to himself. "Our rituals, our hierarchies, our petty upheavals. Except, we're more destructive and probably a lot less canny. After all, zoologically speaking, our species is classified as a 'Great Ape,' one of a sizeable collection of big apes. And what a calamity the homo-sapiens ape is, both for all other species on Earth and for itself! What a blessing in Nature when we become extinct, which'll be none too soon."

Cheered by such thoughts, the Major looks on as a beaming group spills from dining room into lobby, Those in suits have shirt collars open, neckties askew. All look disheveled but relieved.

Bhulliwah takes X'M'Bazi aside. They confer in whispers. Slowly, the major's face breaks into a smile.

Eagerly, the others make for the verandah where they fall upon croissants and coffee.

The prime minister and major join them, as the Tented Camp's regular guests, the surviving, disgruntled, members of Eland's American travel group, arrive from their tents. The staff hurries to bring extra food, juice, coffee and tea as everyone mingles.

"Now what?" demands Ms. Southgate.

Bhulliwah puts finger to lips. "In due course, Madame, in due course."

"Haven't got time for due courses," she grumbles. "Business back home is waiting for me."

"Ah," says Bhulliwah. "*Pazienza*–Patience, as they say in Italy. Much business awaits here. That is if the author, or authoress, of these unfortunate killings isn't..." He shoots her a suspicious glance. "You must try these croissants. Quite delicious because baked with real butter, not those awful oils or margarines they're using nowadays, even in Paris."

We prisoners, handcuffed and ankled, Suzanne's arm around my shoulders, limp escorted onto the terrace. X'M'Bazi, eyebrows raised, looks at the two of us. We look back, grinning.

"People," the major shouts, clapping his hands. "No game drive this morning but we do have a little wait. Meanwhile, nobody in the travel group leaves this verandah. Guards, place yourselves accordingly. Sergeant, you may uncuff and unankle our suspects. If you need anything from your tents or from your belongings in the infirmary, the staff will bring them. Our distinguished visitors are, of course, free to come and go as they please."

X'M'Bazi joins Suzanne and me at a small table away from the others. We drink coffee and confer in whispers.

At length, he rises to approach Bhulliwah. The two walk up and down in the garden beyond the verandah that contains a small pool with multi-colored fish. The pool and green space is bordered by a low gated fence leading to the parking driveway.

299

Suzanne and I watch five Nyala antelope–milk chocolate brown with white pinstripes across their backs–drink at a pond in the forest uphill beyond parking lot and the camp's fenced outer perimeter. Another pint-sized antelope, a gerenuk, stands on hind legs to browse a thorn bush. In a garden tree, weaver birds hover on olive-and-yellow wings before entering a cluster of sphere-shaped dwellings woven into branches.

"It is very exotic," says Suzanne. "I can understand why you were so excited about coming."

I squeeze her hand.

The sky grows bright, the sun warmer, the other tour people become restless.

At Sheila's request, a staff member brings her red carpet bag. She fishes in it for sunglasses, turns her gaze toward me. I return the look but her silvery lenses flash back my own image, make her expression inscrutable.

At long last, about nine o'clock, we hear a rumble in the sky. A helicopter appears. Slowly, it lets down onto the parking area. Lieutenant-Colonel X'Zimbalwa climbs out and holds the door for Madame Briac. He leads her to the verandah.

"Ah," says Bhulliwah standing up. He speaks in French. "Now that we are all assembled, I shall make some important announcements and then," he frowns, "others shall deliver themselves of statements and make certain inquiries."

Madame Briac sits at a table. A waiter serves her coffee and croissants.

Bhulliwah clears his throat. "Let all those present take note. I, Antoine Bhulliwah-X'Zilone, hereby announce that I have, by the unanimous wish of an official 'Advisory Council' convened this night on these premises, I have, I say, been consecrated by unanimous acclaim the reigning monarch of our country." He acknowledges a scattering of applause from the notables present and a few tour members. Suzanne and I don't stop holding hands. "Our nation's name now and forever more shall be…" He pauses to let suspense build, "Zambeylia." He spells it out: Z-A-M-B-E-Y-L-I-A. Note," he continues, "the presence of an 'A' and absence of an 'X.' In fact, to promote the end to destructive tribal rivalries, all 'X' and 'M' prefixes to all names have as of this moment been abolished. After my coronation, on January 1, 1988, to which you are all invited, I shall be known as 'Bhulliwah-The-First.' As of now, my family name of Zilone begins only with a 'Z.' Our new Prime Minister, formerly Zecherias M'Bowé is henceforth simply Zecherias Bowé. So it is for Lieutenant-Colonel Zimbalwa, promoted to full colonel, and Major Bazi, promoted to full General and head of our *Sûreté Nationale,* or 'Criminal Detective Force.' Colonel Zimbalwa is seconded to the capital as General Bazi's chief assistant. This in recognition–as you shall see–of having solved the mysteries surrounding the foul and pernicious murders undermining our American tour mission and sparking unrest in our country." He gestures to now Prime Minister Bowé and sits down.

Bowé rises, walks to the front of the tables. "Our country has embarked on a number of new policies. The reign of King M'Zumba I–or rather, plain King Zumba, has been annulled. His assets have been impounded and turned over to the Zambilian National Treasury. Mr. Zumba and his wives are presently residing at the Beverly Hills Hotel, Los Angeles, California. It is doubtful they will be able to pay their bill, the U.S. authorities, by our cabled request, having seized the money on their persons plus, as collateral, their baggage." A moment to regard his audience. "For the good of the nation," he continues, "and at the insistence of the Bank for African Restructuring and Funding (B.A.R.F.), King Bhuilliwah and I have agreed to reduce our personal budgets! Somewhat. From now on our expenditures will be supervised by an 'Advisory Board,' consisting of three appointed parliamentarians, a local representative of the B.A.R.F. and the Minister of Finance. He is returning from the Cayman Islands, where he has been persuaded by the forceful offices of Mr. Green, here present, to keep the national gold in his custody safe, sound, and restorable to the last ounce. Mr. Fenster, would you like to add a word?"

Dressed in a lightweight version of the black suit he wore in New Jersey, Harlan Fenster gets up from his table. "I have several announcements," he says "First, a number of you have been laboring under some serious misapprehensions and I want to set matters straight." He points his finger at Malvina Southgate. "You, Madam, are a rabble-rouser and bear a certain responsibility for the troubles we now face with the Chinese. Ace Incorporated has never contemplated investing in the international drug trade. We are also firmly opposed," he looks pointedly at Jamieson, who draws back in his seat, "to the rape of the Ziloncado region for the exploitation of oil, mineral and natural gas reserves possibly in this area. Even to undertake large-scale prospecting for such resources means destroying vast tracts of vegetation and the killing off of animals dependent on their current environment. To the contrary, Ace Incorporated is committed to tourism and eco-tourism through our Silent-Partner holdings in Olympia International, the resort development entity that Ms. Southgate and Mr. D'Alessandro depend upon for financial backing, as does Mr. Chandler's air charter company and Mr. Sandaram's corporation, now to be merged with and renamed, I believe, 'Royal Consolidated Eland-Zambili Africa Tours,' or along those lines. In any event, Ace has always been there for you. To hedge our bets, we also have an investment in Eland, instigator of your former competition. Our philosophy is, as it ever shall be: let the best company win, so long as we profit." Fenster rubs his hands together, a dry sound. "And so we have," a chuckle equally dry. "So we have indeed! Now, about the Chinese. Mr. Green, will you comment?"

The Ace man sits down as Green rises. He speaks in gruff tones, as near to monosyllables as he can get. "A fighter squadron from South Africa is patrolling the skies of Zambeylia. The French have dispatched an aircraft carrier from Djibouti and the U. S. Navy is diverting a nuclear missile cruiser from near the Persian Gulf."

302

The American's lips curve into the caricature of a grin. "Under the circumstances, Zambeylia shouldn't expect any uninvited Chinese visitors. In fact, Dr. Fang Shi Wu, the author of this drama, left Zambeylia last night for France, with ongoing reservations to Beijing." Green sits down.

A moment of silence. King Bhulliwah rises again. "As your Monarch," he regards Sandaram who, pokerfaced, looks back at him, "as your King, I say, I hereby pardon Mr. Y. Sanjeev Sandaram for his foolish, foolish, most foolish but possibly not totally malicious mistake of involving Dr. Fang in our little internal difficulties. "However, I also banish Mr. Sandaram from Zambeylia for one year beginning at midnight tonight. His cousin, three times removed, Mr. Gowinda Lazuli, shall represent Sandaram family interests within our nation. He has been acting as Mr. Sandarm's informant and go-between throughout the ill-fated tour of our American travel group. Is this not true?"

Bhulliwah gazes at Lazuli, who nods.

"In any case, as Mr. Fenster has indicated," continues Zambeylia's new ruler, "Zambili-Africa Tours and Zemba Royal, Inc., shall combine into a single company, to be known officially as: Royal Consolidated Zambeylia Tourism, Inc. This is now its name. It shall be what the French call a 'Mixed Corporation,' with fifty-nine percent of shares held by the government, the rest by Royal Consolidated Zambeylia Tourism, Inc., under the stewardship of Mr. Lazuli acting for Mr. Sandaram. That is," Bhulliwah stops short, "if and when Mr. Lazuli is cleared of all complicity in the foul murders, thefts and crimes that have occurred during his less than untroubled guidance of our most valued tour and travel agents."

Lazuli squirms, wipes his face with a handkerchief.

"And now," Bhulliwah continues, "last but certainly not least, we come to said horrendous crimes and criminal happenings. I turn to General Bazi, our newly appointed Chief of Criminal Detection."

"Thank you, Your Royal Highness." Bazi bows to his King. "We've had the following crimes involving the American travel agent-tour group, whose surviving members are present: the murder of Mrs. Helen Farrar-Mahoney aboard the now Royal Zamba SilverSpear Express; the murder of Michael Mahoney, husband of Helen Farrar; the murder of Mr. Barry Mondran in Manhattan; and two attempts, both abortive, on the life of Ms. Sheila Mondran. There is also the theft of a large diamond belonging to Mrs. Farrar-Mahoney and named by her Eland Diamond. This makes five felony crimes. However, we have reason to add a sixth crime, a murder attempt upon the person of Madame Félicité Briac, residing on a farm near Ziromeu City and having no apparent connection to the tour group. This failed murder initiative was also perpetrated by the same person or persons responsible for the aforementioned crimes. Madame Briac has joined us this morning. Madame, would you please stand up?"

She rises from her chair. The group inspects her with curiosity. With equal curiosity, she surveys the group.

"Madame," says General Bazi, "We are grateful that you are with us this day. And we salute your courage in coming here to face a group sheltering one or more of your potential killers. We also are mindful of the difficult, the very near lethal times you have had to go through." The General stops talking. He seems to marshal his ideas before going on. "We're all here together to answer the question: who did these deeds? One person? Two people? Every member of the group acting together? Who?" He sees he has his audience's attention: the attention a cornered field mouse gives to a rattlesnake. "Well," he says, after another pause, "when we started our investigation, the answer seemed to jump at us. All evidence pointed to one individual. In fact, there was such an abundance of evidence implicating Mr. Lincoln Goldstone that for a time we felt we were dealing with the most incompetent murderer alive. Mr. Goldstone's close friend, Ms. Suzanne Carrington, who joins us today, seemed also to be involved in New York, because of the death of Mr. Barry Mondran, acting as Eland's anchor-man while Helen Farrar-Mahoney was in what's now Zambeylia. At first

304

glance–and I believe the true criminal was counting on it being our only glance–we seemed to have our multiple murderer and jewel thief dead to rights." The General walks over to the verandah sideboard, pours himself coffee. Everyone's gaze follows him. "Certain questions kept coming up in my mind to which I saw no answers. If Mr. Goldstone was the culprit, what had he done with the diamond? Believe me, we took him and his belongings apart. Also, what other motive could he have? Was he acting as a straw man for some takeover group like the Jeffrey B. Ace Corporation? But why him, especially given that Mr. Eugene Petroff is the nephew of Mr. Harlan Fenster who currently runs Ace?

"Ms. Carrington's involvement seemed to us even more improbable, after I conferred with colleagues on the New York police force. She had nothing conceivable to gain from murdering a man she didn't know and in whose business she had no interest." The General takes a sip of coffee, sits down straddling a chair backwards to face his audience. "I'm as lazy as the next guy, but the more I considered Goldstone as the criminal, the more I felt I was coming up with two-and-two making three, not even five. So, I shifted gears and suddenly there was a whole range of interesting, more plausible possibilities. But, since Mr. Goldstone was cast as villain and since he and I know what really happened, why it happened and how, I'm going to let him continue this session." He pulls his chair frontward.

I rise to face the group. "Magic," I say. "It's all a glorified magic trick and the key is the crime, or I should say crimes, on the train. I mean, of course, Helen Farrar's murder and the theft of her diamond. This was the toughest bit of illusion to set up and to unravel but its unraveling created an arrow pointing the way to everything else. Like most elaborate tricks, it was carefully prepared. Nothing spontaneous here. The occasion for the crimes was our trip to this country with a group of people who were rivals and antagonists of Helen Farrar and her Eland Corporation. Every one of you, Sheila excepted," I look at each member of the group, "had plausible reasons to want Helen out of the way and her company destroyed. The Petroffs, Ms. Southgate, Mr. D'Alessandro, Mr. Jamieson and spouse, Mr. Chandler and, presumably, his son-in-law, the chief pilot of his airline, Mr. Guitterez-Shaughnessy. You all had connections with the X'Zambeli-Africa Tour group shunned by Eland in its cultivation of rival Zemba Royal Africa Tours, now joined with the former competition as Royal Consolidated Zambeylia Tourism, Inc. Mr. Gowinda Lazuli, too, had such a connection with, through his relative, Mr. Y. Sanjeev Sandaram. How convenient for every one of you if Eland disappeared. And Helen was Eland's driver, its force personified. Mr. Jamieson especially was anxious to persuade the then Zembeylian government to do away with ecological tourism here in the Ziloncado Basin, in favor of oil drilling and open-pit mining. Helen Farrar's plans were blocking him." I stop to wipe my sweaty face. Sun getting hotter and hotter. "So there were plenty of motives all around. And who wouldn't like a diamond that might fetch up to two million? A group trip like ours to, well, Zambeylia, has to be planned a long time ahead. And lo and behold! In late September, early October, several weeks before our tour, Chandler, the Jamiesons, the Petroffs, Ms. Southgate and Mr. D'Alessandro all show up here. So does Sheila Mondran with her assignment to prepare our journey. Any one or any combination of you all could have evolved a plan to murder Helen Farrar in her locked and sealed cabin aboard what is now the Royal Zamba SilverSpear Express. For the present, let's not worry about *Whodunit* but *Howdunit.*" I signal a waiter for more coffee, gulp a mouthful before going on. "Here's a theory that fits the facts: The would-be murderer needed a dupe, some local innocent bystander to maneuver as required. But how do you do that? You can't go up to a law-abiding person and say, *I want you to help me commit murder.* No, you have to engage the individual's good will, get that person psychologically and unsuspectingly on your side. Our criminal had an ingenious notion. The French settlers here in Zambeylia are

306

mainly from Brittany, one of France's more remote regions. Bretons are not known for urban street-smarts but for sincere devotion to their Catholic faith. "Suppose our plotter went to some country town or village, say Nouveau-Locronon, a community near Ziromeu City, where the Breton-French ethnic group predominates. This person might attend Sunday services in the modest chapel there. Let's assume that he or she kept eyes and ears open, perhaps talked to the local priest, to some villagers and discovered there was a particularly pious woman, elderly, a widow, hard-pressed for money and living on a farm that she was struggling to run by herself. And suppose our unscrupulous individual wrote a letter to that widow enclosing a substantial money order, promising more money but most especially promising a great mission in aid of Mother Church."

Eyes turn to Madame Briac.

"So,"I resume, "for the noblest of causes here were welcome funds and a mission to prepare. What does the preparation consist of? Oh, nothing strenuous, in fact very agreeable. Every other Tuesday, this person would ride in a luxury sleeping compartment aboard the SilverSpear from Ziromeu City to the capital. There, she would pray at the cathedral, spend the night at a hotel, all accommodation and meals paid for, and Wednesday, next day, go home, again aboard the SilverSpear. What an easy, agreeable mission. *N'est-ce pas,* Madame Briac? Is this not what happened to you?" I ask as gently as I can.

She nods. "I am so ashamed of being duped." Her voice is low.

"Do not be, Madame, you shouldn't be. There was no way you could possibly know." After a pause, I go on, "So every second week, always on a Tuesday and Wednesday, back and forth, back and forth, Madame Briac travels aboard the SilverSpear. To the train staff, she becomes a known entity, a fixture, one of the regulars. So no one pays particular attention to her and here is the murderer's purpose. All this, of course, is easy enough to arrange through anonymous contact with a local legal office, paid handsomely to dispatch a series of envelopes at regular intervals and forward used ticket stubs, to a private mail service address in New York City indicating that the subject, Madame Briac, is following instructions received. Each envelope bearing her money order and instruction letter has been stuffed in advance by the criminal. A series of hotel nights are also paid for in advance, as are the train reservations. The police in Fulumbane and Ziromeu City have confirmed all this. Am I correct, General?"

Bazi nods. "The law firm of M'Fune and Bertillon—now Fune and Bertillon—made arrangements per instructions of a Mr. Pierre Morin of Brooklyn, New York. To the best of the New York City Police's knowledge, no such person exists, except that a private mail receiving company in Manhattan takes in mail for Mr. Morin. To that extent he does exist, but only as a mail drop."

"On her last journey," I continue, "Madame Briac's instructions change. Madame, did you return on the SilverSpear as usual?"

"No," answers the Frenchwoman. "That time I took the local. Instead of leaving at three in the afternoon, it left at 1 P.M. and arrived at Ziromeu Station at 6:55."

"Of course," I say, "examining the timeline of your arrival in Ziromeu City and your meeting with the killer, you couldn't have been on the SilverSpear. But a Madame Briac *was* on the SilverSpear. She occupied the compartment that adjoined Helen Farrar's with a locked communicating partition. How could Madame Briac be on both the one o'clock train and the 3 P.M.SilverSpear?"

Murmurs, everybody looking at everybody else. I sip coffee. "If we believe Madame Briac, it had to be an impersonator. Someone in a wig, dressed like her and of approximately the same size. A person whom the train staff accepted as their usual passenger and didn't look at closely. Let's say this individual, he or she, gets into Cabin Three, Madame Briac's assigned space, and, using a special copy of the train porter's key, unlocks the partition to Cabin Two that Helen Farrar is due to occupy forty minutes after the train leaves the capital when it stops to pick up our group."

I signal the waiter for still another coffee. "Remember, Helen comes aboard ill, having been deliberately dosed with the emetic Ipecac. She lies down on Cabin Two's couch. The train gets underway. Enter fake Madame Briac who, with an accomplice to do the unpleasant part, strangles Helen. The killers then carry the body to the adjoining cabin, that is Cabin Three. They place it in the hollow space under the sofa that ingeniously allows for passengers to sit on a couch by day and turns upside-down with a mattress attached on its underside to become a bed by night. There's a large space underneath the mattress strapped to the couch. This area is used for storage of sheets, blankets, pillows, all the elements needed, mattress aside, to make up a bed. Fake Madame Briac then does a quick change of wig and clothes and takes Helen's place back in Cabin Two. The partition is now closed, locked, the porter called and asked to make the bed in Cabin Two because Helen is ill and won't be going to dinner This he does.

"While he's in that cabin, fake Helen appears in the observation lounge so that all can attest to their leader being alive at 6:25 P.M., when in fact she's lying dead under the sofa-bed in Cabin Three, the one supposedly occupied by Madame Briac, who isn't aboard the train. Remember, fake Helen talks only to Mike Farrar and stands near the lounge's bar far forward of the group, all clustered together toward the car's rear. You group members see a figure you assume to be Helen because you're prepared to assume it. Mike, obviously the accomplice, then follows fake Helen back to Cabin Two. She gets into the made-up bed. And the charade with the waiter bringing food from the dining car is carried out. As soon as the waiter and Mike leave and she has re-locked the corridor door, fake Helen jumps up and with her special key unlocks the partition to Cabin Three. She drags real, very dead Helen out of that cabin's sofa-and-bed's hollow space, coolly smashes her skull, cuts her wrists, smears a blood figure on the mirror and does all the

309

other things to make the crime look like a violent act following a struggle.

"Then, as the train starts to slow for Ziromeu City, the killer dumps Helen's wallet and personal effects through the sinkhole onto the tracks. This individual also smashes Helen's watch, so time of death appears to be around 7:20 P.M., instead of much earlier. Which helps to point the finger at me, since at 7:20 Helen and I are supposedly alone in the sleeping car, except for Madame Briac, who has no known connection with us, or we with her. The perpetrator removes Helen's uncut diamond, hurries back into the cabin reserved for Madame Briac, locks the partition one last time, does a quick change and, as Madame, steps out at Ziromeu City station. This person goes to the parking lot, in a dark, unlighted corner, where the farm lady has been instructed to park her pickup van and wait for 'Benefactor.' The murderer dons a mask and covering cloak, has a session with real Madame Briac in her vehicle, during which Madame is given a poison pill so the police won't find her alive." I spread my hands. "*Et voilà.* That's how the first murder happens."

"So you're telling us," says Eugene Petroff, "that Mike Farrar was an accomplice?"

I nod. "You saw his sleight-of-hand tricks on the plane. During our lunch in the M'Bélé—now plain Bélé—hut he came around and talked to each of us one by one. Perfect occasion to slip Ipecac into my beer and into Helen's. Nothing to it, for a magician. He also typed a compromising letter that had me plotting to destroy Eland on behalf of Ace. While I was away from my tent, he slipped a carbon copy of that letter into a cut he made in the lining of my suitcase. He then sewed the lining up again in a deliberately clumsy way so the police would discover it and extract the letter. Mike had typed it back in New York before our group left for then Zembeylia, now Zambeylia. Just to reinforce the evidence against me, he put some cyanide-tipped cigarettes in my dresser drawer. He easily got into the tent because I'd been summoned away and he knew it."

"But the diamond. Where is it?" asks Ms. Southgate. "You haven't accounted for the diamond."

"Sheila, dear," I say, "I'm dying for a smoke. Do you think I could have a cigarette?"

For several seconds she gazes at me, then reaches into her red bag and whips out…Not her cigarette case but a Beretta pistol. She throws herself at Madame Briac, puts the weapon to the ex-Frenchwoman's head. Two guards raise AK-47 assault rifles.

"No!" shouts General Bazi. "Don't shoot!"

"I want that," Sheila gestures towards one of the guard's weapon. "Give it to me and nobody gets hurt. I have no cause to kill anyone here. So I count to five, otherwise I blow the woman's head off. One, two–"

"Okay," Bazi orders the guard. "Hand it to me, I'll hand it to her."

"No!" shouts Sheila. "Lay it on the front table. " Three, four–"

At the General's nod, the guard does so.

She grabs the weapon and, locking Madame Briac's chin and neck in the crook of an elbow, drags her through the garden to the parking lot.

All Land Rovers have keys in their ignitions, ready for game drives. The two pile into the nearest vehicle. Sheila starts the engine. A squeal of tires and the car charges up the driveway's hill leading to the South Africa road. Only three-quarters of a mile and she'll be safe over the frontier: no extradition treaty and a valuable uncut diamond in her pocket. At the Zambeylia border post she'll say she's going for gas, or maybe speed straight through onto friendly soil.

Ahead is the camp's tall steel fence. Sheila tumbles out of the vehicle, dragging Madame Briac along in the same grip. The murderess pushes the gate open, then giving the old woman a shove into thorn bushes, sprints back to the Land Rover and speeds away towards freedom.

Shots ring out. Wild shots, the bullets fall short. She glances back. Her pursuers have piled into another Land Rover but they're well behind and need to stop to untangle and rescue her hostage.

Less than half a mile now. Brushing trees and bushes, her Land Rover hurtles along the narrow track, careens around a bend.

M'Kawi-X'Zamba–to be known evermore as plain Kawi-Zamba–is standing smack in the roadway chewing acacia leaves. Hearing the jeep the elephant's ears twitch. He goes on tearing branches from the tree to get at its delicious leaves.

Sheila screeches to a stop, leans on the horn. Stupid, old beast!

The bull turns, lowering his head, his sail-like ears stand straight out. More shots, the cops are gaining. Sheila keeps the horn honking, guns the engine, starts forward. Head down, uttering a fearful trumpet, Kawi-Zamba charges. A flip of his trunk sends the vehicle crashing onto its side. He pushes against it, turning the Land Rover completely over. Sheila starts to crawl from underneath.

The elephant's forefoot comes down on her head, crushing it like an eggshell.

Chapter 37: Mop-Up
Zambeylia: Monday, December 21

"I suppose I can see Sheila, and Mike too, wanting to rid themselves of Helen," says Malvina Southgate. After a pause, she adds, "Who wouldn't? Though I'll miss her, our ongoing battles. So you're saying Sheila does a black-widow spider act, murdering both Mike and Barry?"

"Now, now," says Giorgio D'Alessandro. "Mustn't speak that way of the dead." With his right hand he pretends to brush dust off his bush-jacket, quickly crosses himself. "Let's remember what good we can of them."

We're still sitting at a verandah table, Suzanne, myself, and General Bazi, who frowns occasionally, trying to get used to his stripped-down name. He's awaiting a call to the helicopter, which will carry him to the capital. On the way, it will stop to deposit Madame Briac and Colonel Zimbalwa at Ziromeu City.

"What I don't get," Southgate eyes both the General and me, sitting on the table's same side, "is how you guys figure Sheila for the culprit. And I still don't understand about the diamond. Also, how the hell did she enter Helen's locked cabin? Even if she'd knocked and Helen had wanted to open the partition, she couldn't have, not without calling the porter with his one and only key."

"In New York," I answer, "thanks to General Bazi's former police colleagues, we discovered a few things about Sheila and Mike. They were lovers, for one. It wasn't that either was nuts about the other; both were pretty calculating characters. Mike used his easy charm to get a grip on what he saw as his main chance. He and Sheila were due to inherit from Helen; but her lawyers in New York confirm that Sheila was getting the Eland shares. Mike figured he could control her; she seemed so soft and pliable, personality-wise the opposite of his bossy wife. If Sheila and he married, he was sure he would eventually get his mitts on her Eland inheritance. Then a 'tragic' accident could be in store for her. Little did good ol' Mike realize—"

"Yes, yes," interrupts Malvina Southgate. "That still doesn't get the cabin partition open."

"In a way it does," General Bazi takes up the story. "Mike was fascinated by magic from the time he was a kid. He'd read, of course, about the great Harry Houdini and his famous escapes from chains, locks and locked chests. In high school and after graduation, he apprenticed to a locksmith, spent time fooling around with locks. He did his research, learned that the SilverSpear's sleeping cars all came from U.S. rolling stock, with these particular cars manufactured by only two companies. This led him to figure the train as the right place to stage Helen's murder. You see, locks and

313

keys opening sleeper car doors and inner wall partitions were built by one U.S. sub-contracting firm, now out of business. So they're uniform. The manufacturer's idea was that no matter which car or train a porter was assigned to, he'd be able to lock and unlock what was required with his own permanently issued key. He'd never have to worry about getting different keys for different trips or different passenger rolling stock. A small but practical inducement for U.S. railroad passenger car manufacturers to keep buying locks made by this same outfit." He stops to drink ice water.

Like the General, our group is waiting to leave the Ziloncado: we're going via Land Rover to Bukusa Airport for a flight to Fulumbane with a final hotel night there, prior to emplaning for New York, Wednesday evening, December 23rd. Wednesday morning will be devoted to funeral services for the four deceased tour members: Helen, Sheila, Mike and *in absentia*, Barry. Then with sunset, farewell Zambeylia and First Class home. Helen and Mike, too, have reservations on our flight: in the baggage hold. Sheila will be cremated, as specified in her Will. Once at rest, in a tasteful urn to be selected by no less than King Bhulliwah I himself, she too will be repatriated on a subsequent flight.

His Majesty and all dignitaries present at this morning's confrontation will attend the funeral–Mr. Green excepted; he has pressing business in Afghanistan. King Bhulliwah has promised a long, long speech, while Prime Minister Bowé is busy composing an even longer "Ode To The Tribulations Of Nationhood And Human Destiny."

"As one familiar with the locksmith trade," I take up where the General left off, "it was pretty easy for Mike to get hold of a sample standard lock made by the defunct Ellerby Lock Corporation of Green Bay, Wisconsin. He probably pulled it from the wall partition of a junked sleeper. Taking the lock apart and using calipers to measure, very precisely, both top and bottom pins, he was able to bring these specs to a locksmith, get a key made. He was a touch careless there, not going off his beaten path. Thanks to the

General's connections, we've confirmed that Breitman's Elite Locks on Broadway, near Zabar's Delicatessen in Manhattan, was the outfit. I bet Mike stopped for a pastrami on rye while waiting to get his murder key."

I look at the cloudless sky and Bazi continues. "When Sheila was on her trip here to set things up for the tour, she rode the SilverSpear overnight. We now know that she went to the expense of reserving *two* communicating cabins, though she was traveling alone. She needed a partition to test her key on. Obviously, it worked."

"*Hmph!*" says Ms. Southgate.

Madame Briac emerges from the lodge. The cuts and bruises from Sheila's rough treatment have been disinfected and bandaged at the infirmary. She has showered, and a chambermaid mended a tear in her skirt. She's smiling as we all stand to greet her. The General pulls a chair for her from the next table.

"I am ready to go home," she says. "I particularly want to thank you, *Mon Générale*, for your generosity on my behalf."

"Richly deserved, Madame," says Bazi. I did nothing, only ran a little interference, as they say in American football."

At his insistence, King Bhulliwah has announced a special government annuity, the first installment to be paid this week, to ease Madame Briac's financial burden.

Then, too, she has just finished a long telephone talk with Pierre Dorland. He will meet her upon arrival at Ziromeu City and drive her home. After that, who knows?

"I always liked Sheila and felt sorry for her having a stepsister and boss like Helen," Malvina Southgate never drops the thread of her thoughts for long. "But she and Barry are among the few people whom Helen was good to, in her obnoxious way."

"Not good enough," says Suzanne. "Through Schulz and his gossipy friend at Eland, I learned that Barry Mondran had been a rising star in the accounting business. When Sheila married him, he was making a high six figure income. Then something happened, he

315

got too smart trying to save his clients–and himself–tax money. There was a scandal, he lost credibility, became entangled in a ruinous lawsuit. The only person who would give him a job was his sister-in-law, at wages that he and Sheila considered near-starvation compared to what they were used to."

D'Alessandro asks, "Why did Sheila, attractive as she was, choose such an unpleasant husband?"

"Since Barry doesn't seem to have gone for females," I get into the conversation again, "we can assume a marriage of convenience. For him, respectability, with freedom to pursue other pleasures. For her, in early days, the promise of wealth. When that didn't transpire he became a burden." I squint to see hippopotamuses rising and sinking in their pond beyond the garden. "Sheila came on very sexy, very feminine, yet I don't think sex meant anything to her, except as leverage. Money and power were her thing. Helen, a true power maven, was constantly outdoing her in both areas. Sheila, summing it up, was only a power wannabe who never made it, maybe never could have even if she'd gotten away with her crimes and taken on Eland. Anyway, I have the feeling it started when they were kids and Sheila came to live with the Farrar family. I'm sure everyone tried to be kind, but compared to Helen, true daughter and heir, Sheila, as adoptee, must've felt second class."

A waiter comes by with a plate of iced mangos peeled and cut. He places a pot of tea on the table. A second waiter brings delicious looking chocolate truffles. We all fall silent, eating fruit, drinking tea, devouring rich candy.

"Okay, but," says Malvina Southgate dipping chocolaty fingers into a finger-bowl and wiping them on a paper napkin, "Sheila was a victim too. All psychological crap aside, I'm still not sure you guys fingered the right criminal."

The General gestures for me to answer, "What better way to divert suspicion," I say, "than to become a victim? She paints her lips with a bluish substance, swallows some almond oil and a slug of Ipecac to give herself genuine symptoms of distress. No problem

316

there. But the nurse was getting suspicious. Sheila sensed it. In that bag of hers, she had insurance: a jar of three *M'zu, m'zu* scorpions that she or Mike must have dug up outside one of the tents. So when she overhears the nurse beginning to talk to the colonel–I mean General–here and together they walk outside the infirmary, she scatters the scorpions at the foot of her bedspread, runs into the hallway, pulls the main electricity switch, curls up on the bed as far from the critters as she can get and screams her head off."

"You still haven't told us how she came to be a suspect," persists Malvina Southgate.

"Pretty simple, really," I answer. "Let's give credit to General Bazi for solving the case while I was still lost in my notes and chronology of what had happened directly to me. The General got suspicious because whenever Sheila drew my attention, disaster involving me happened; always somewhere else than I was. So it had to be with help and only Mike could have done all the things she needed done by an accomplice. For instance, that person alone was allowed to get close in the train's observation lounge when she was disguised as Helen. If Mike had been innocent, he would have exposed her right there." I stroke my chin. "When the General sat me down and led me through the situation step-by-step, I recalled that at the beach resort, when I joined Sheila for early breakfast, she quickly left our table for a few minutes to go into the hotel lobby. We believe she was phoning Mike that the coast was clear and he could enter my room, plant a small bottle of Ipecac with my toilet articles. It was there for the police to discover when, they searched my train cabin after the murder. And when Sheila summoned me, during our first afternoon here at camp, Mike planted his letter and put other compromising material in my tent. What a pair!"

"Sheila summoned you?" asks Suzanne. She withdraws her hand from mine, folds arms against chest, leans back in her chair. "Why did you go?"

I knew this was coming, had prepared a nice lie about suspecting her and trying to find out information. I look at

Suzanne, redden. "I, uh…I was attracted. You called me 'Thursday's' man. I figured Sheila for Tuesdays, maybe Saturdays…"

Suzanne says nothing, just nods.

I help myself to a mango slice. When in trouble, eat!

Silence all around.

"Okay, okay," says *La Southgate* breaking it. "I persist in not seeing how you've made the case against her airtight. Sheila, that is. Why not Bitsy Jamieson? She could have done most of the things you said. She's almost attractive enough, in a chorus-girl-gone-to-seed way, for Mike to have been her lover, not Sheila's."

I shake my head. "Everybody, except me, who was on that train had all the others to alibi them. It had to be somebody in our group supposedly off the train—or, rather, supposedly off the train and working with Mike when the murder occurred. In other words, one of our group with the perfect cover of not being present at all." I reach for a truffle.

Suzanne grabs my wrist. "That's two you've had, lover boy. Gonna get fat on me as well as faithless?"

"You nagging like a wife?"

"Oh, well," she drops her hand. I reach for the chocolate, hesitate, take my hand away.

"So?" says Southgate.

General Bazi continues where I've stopped. "This person off the train. An individual who had to be capable of impersonating Madame Briac. Can you imagine Guitterez-Shaughnessy, built like a ten ton truck and sporting his black mustache pretending to be you, Madame? Unless that mustache is fake. If he wasn't a foreigner with connections, I'd have pulled it to see. Believe me, I've been tempted." The General shakes his head. "Neither he nor his tall companion, Chandler, make a very convincing you, Madame Briac," he nods to the Frenchwoman. "That leaves the only other absentee: female and, yes, a bit taller and slimmer. With the right bulky clothes and wig, the porter or other train people wouldn't remark such details, as long as your impersonator kept her distance. Sheila, both as you and as Helen, locked herself in the cabin once the train started. She stayed far from the porter, also from the group in the observation car."

"How did she manage the timetable?" asks D'Alessandro.

"Oh, says the General, "she showed up at Dr. Hermann's clinic, all right. Early on our police checked this as part of investigating everyone's movements. Unfortunately that's all we checked, first time around.

"Yesterday, I had our people go back, probe deeper. Seems Ms. Mondran arrived an hour and a half earlier than scheduled, at about 9:30 A.M. She declined both a full tour and the lunch the good doctor had laid on. Said she had an emergency. Sort of galloped in, galloped out. Then she must've raced to the train station at Ziromeu City, a seventy mile trip on a pretty good highway, parked her rental car there, then grabbed a taxi to the airport for the 1 P.M. flight back to Fulumbane. It arrived at 1:55. As Madame Briac, she boards the SilverSpear for its 3 P.M. departure. When the train got to Ziromeu City, she met real Madame Briac, fed her poison, threw the car papers onto the station's AfriCar rental desk–closed for the night–and barely managed to get back aboard the train. She excused her lateness, her failure to show up for drinks with Chandler and Guitterez on grounds she'd had a flat tire along the way."

"But how did she do all the quick changes, the wigs and mask and disguises?" asks Suzanne.

Tentatively, D'Alessandro raises his hand. "I know that one. The bag. It's a genuine Di Fortuna carry-all. In Florence I have an uncle in the luggage business. A beautiful bag, really a work of art. Almost worth the $1,479 it costs in New York. Handmade, you see. You get them only by special order at the Italia Boutique on Fifth Avenue. Anyway, one surface is red, uhm, not velvet, not satin," he snaps his fingers, "how do you say? Plush? Yes, red plush. But thanks to clever tooling, you can turn the bag inside-out and presto,

319

it becomes green, but not plush. Canvas. A lovely piece. Sheila carried all her equipment in the bag's big interior and, when she wanted to be Madame Briac, she simply reversed colors: Sheila Mondran had a red plush bag, Madame a plainer green canvas one." He looks expectantly at the General. "Am I right, Dick Tracy?"

"Absolutely, my dear Hawkshaw. Couldn't have said it better myself."

"I'll acknowledge the evidence against poor Sheila," says Southgate. "Now, the diamond. This morning, when it was mentioned, Linc here asked for a cigarette and she bolted. The connection?"

Before anyone can answer, Colonel Zimbalwa and the sergeant with-the-still-unpronounceable-name come to the table. They both salute. "We leave now," says the newly-minted colonel. He smiles happily.

The general smiles back. The two of them are delighted, not only with their promotions but by further glad tidings. Shortly, they, with their wives, will leave for Paris to attend a six month training course in "Investigative Bureaucracy" by France's Judiciary Police. "For a little diplomatic polishing," as Prime Minister Bowé put it.

We all stand to shake hands. I even shake the sergeant's hand. "No hard feelings I hope, *Monsieur Le Non-Assassin*," says the policeman-detective, looking slightly embarrassed. "Nothing personal. Only duty."

"Yeah," I say. "You sure were enthusiastic about your duty. But all's well that ends well." I'm surprised at the pang I feel, saying goodbye to my three pursuers, whom I doubt I will see again, except to nod to at the funeral. To General Bazi, I say, "If you ever get to New York... "

"I'll certainly look you up. And leave the ankle guard home, okay?"

"You better!"

"Anyway," says Bazi, "I've enjoyed our conversations, even when I figured you were guilty as hell. Philosophically, we both belong to the Pessimist persuasion. Very un-reassuring, yes? So keep in touch. Who knows, you may get back here someday, to whatever our country is called when you do."

All of us embrace Madame Briac, kissing her on both cheeks in the French style.

"*Bonne chance, Madame*–good luck," I murmur.

"*Je vous remercie de tout coeur, jeune homme*–I thank you with all my heart, young man," she responds.

I beam. "Nobody's called me young man in a long, long time."

The three go to their whirlybird. Soon it roars into the sky. We on the ground wave until the craft disappears above the trees.

"The diamond," insists Ms. Southgate.

"Look," I say, "Diamonds can be colorless, right? The best diamonds are."

"Right."

"Because," I continue, "you have colorless and near-transparent ones, they take on the color of whatever they're up against. There was a famous pinkish diamond belonging to the Russian Tsar: 'The Paul I Diamond,' named after Tsar Paul, Catherine the Great's son. He reputedly paid a fortune for the stone, considered unique and priceless. Then some expert claimed the striking color was due to it being mounted on red foil. Today it's thought to be just a more or less colorless diamond taking its tinge from the foil." I decide, after all, to eat the last truffle. Being for once a co-detective and even a target of admiration is famishing work. "Back at Kennedy airport," I go on, "I first saw Sheila's cigarette case. Again thanks to General Bazi's connections in New York, we found she only began smoking eight months ago. Helen probably thought it was in imitation of her. She may have been flattered. But Sheila really was kicking-off her whole scheme. She knew Helen was to lead the group tour coming here and would buy a diamond. So suddenly the cigarette case appears and Sheila becomes 'Ms. Nicotine Two.'" Her image springs to mind. So sexy, so ruthless. Such a damned good actress, as well. And what resourcefulness! A pity she hadn't put her brilliance to positive use. Probably it would have taken a saint to resist the lure of wealth and the power flaunted, as Helen flaunted it every hour of every day. "The cigarette case, now in police custody, is gold color," I continue. "With a few cheap jewels stuck to its cover. The biggest is a teardrop-shape golden beryl, so she told me in New York. I have no reason to doubt the truth of her statement then. Remember 'The Purloined Letter?' She pulled an Edgar Allen Poe trick. You know, hiding the sought-after object in plain sight. We all saw her help Helen choose a diamond whose shape and size were teardrop, very much like the cigarette case's beryl. On the train, after she or Mike strangled Helen, Sheila pried the beryl loose from her cigarette case, glued the diamond in its place. It reflected the case's gold, as diamonds do. So it was under our noses all the time."

"Wow," says Malvina Southgate. "Tricky, tricky. And she seemed such a straightforward gal."

"The Honest Iago type," says Suzanne.

"When we get to the hotel," Southgate goes on, "let's the four of us go out to dinner away from the others. There's something quite different that Giorgio and I would like to discuss."

Suzanne and I nod our assent.

"That afternoon when Mike planted stuff in your tent wasn't the only time you went to Sheila," says Suzanne. We're in the plane, winging towards Fulumbane. "You really were lovers?"

"One evening we danced together and I escorted her to her bedroom door. I think we would have been if I'd insisted. Something held me back."

"Her basic frigidity?"

"No, and not even your recent coolness. I admit to being a somewhat flighty person but I've never actually been unfaithful to you. You damn well know it too!"

"You came very, very close. She calls you in the small hours and you run to her tent hoping for 'L-U-V.' You gonna deny?

Gonna tell me you were just wanting to get more framed for murder?"

Don't know how to answer. I stare out the window. Then turn to her. "You've treated me damn bad. For months. Yes, I was attracted and I would have been attracted even if you'd treated me good. I'm attracted to attractive woman, that's kinda built in. But," I lean over, grip Suzanne by the shoulders, turn her towards me," if you hadn't been so bitchy, I'd have controlled the attraction a helluva lot better. I was wrestling with it the whole time; and wrestling against a voice saying 'What does Suzanne care? Take it while you can get it!' If I'd known you really cared, I'd have—"

"Done it anyway," says Suzanne, with sparkle in her eyes.

"Ms. Cynic. Can't resist having the last word."

"Why you love me, Goldstone. Imagine spending the years we've piled up together with a compliant, adoring, ever-agreeable nymph."

"Sounds damn good to me."

"Ah, you'd be bored. Listen, suppose you'd made it with Sheila. How do you think she'd've done for you, I mean if casting you in the role of killer didn't work? Scorpions? Cyanide? Where'd she get her poisons, anyway?"

"She was on a hospital board. I imagine she had connections. A little flirting with the hospital pharmacist. In college she majored in biochem, had an M.S. And also made a name for herself in amateur theatrics, noted especially for tragic rôles. Wonderful at turning on tears. A regular gusher."

"Mike. You never said how she murdered him."

"Too simple. She sends him on a game tour that first evening, after he plants the fake evidence on me. We all, except her, leave for the bush, she sneaks into his tent, substitutes a pill bottle loaded with cyanide for the open anti-Malaria-*M'zu-m'zu* tablets Mike was faithfully taking his medicine from. Like a good traveler, he pops his pill before bedtime. Whammo, he's out of the picture."

"Mmm," murmurs Suzanne. "I wonder what that Southgate woman wants with us at dinner. Don't you dare be seduced by her."

"There's seduction and seduction," say I. "Be good to me and you have nothing to worry about."

We dine *Chez X'Zantu*, Fulumbane's most sophisticated restaurant for genuine French and local cuisine. Have to wait an hour because all tables are occupied by press people, desperate second-stringers hanging here despite the world's news hurrying to other climes. Henceforth, of course, *X'Zantu* will become just *Zantu*, necessitating purchase of a large new outdoor neon sign for the front. The M'Bélé, now a denuded Bélé, proprietor spends this evening visiting his guests table-by-table to complain about the unfairness of putting him to such extra expense.

Our main course is charcoal-roasted baby lamb over couscous, the meat tender and delicious. The talk is even more delicious: I'm being offered a two-fer: a buy-out and a job.

"You see," says Giorgo D'Alessandro, "we require an editor for our new initiative: a deluxe, glossy magazine with a big budget. To be called *Romantic Africa*. It will run not only in English but also in German, French and Japanese, sparking tourist interest in the African countries where Olympia International, Inc. is building hotels, and to which Chandler's airline will fly. In conjunction with Zambili-Africa Tours, when it consolidates with Zamba Royal's air routes. Olympia is planning a super golf course at a Zambeylia beach resort. And there's *the SilverSpear* train, an attraction in its own right. The tented camp too will spawn a number of satellite vacation camps." He chews his meat meditatively. "For starters, aside from Zambeylia, the company wants to promote tourism in Zambia, Botswana, Namibia, Kenya, Tanzania, Morocco, the Ivory Coast, Senegal, Ghana, Mauritius, The Seychelles and Madagascar. You'll have to travel to these places as a writer-editor, as well as commissioning and overseeing articles from freelancers. Until, that is, the magazine gains enough momentum to justify your hiring

324

permanent staff for the various regions. Strenuous work and a strenuous life."

"Sounds like what I was born to do." I can hardly contain my excitement. "Unifying travel and journalism."

"Up to you to create and coordinate everything," says D'Alessandro. "We are hoping, if the magazine has the success we anticipate, to add more countries and spin off a radio talk show. The show itself, we'll call *Sophisticated Africa*. You might be hosting the radio too. I hear you did some radio newscasting during your Paris years. In any event the advertisers for both magazine and radio will be high end. Offering all kinds of services from the airline to Olympia International's hotels, as well as independent restaurants, boutiques and so on. Then there's the countries themselves. For instance, something like *Come see the lemurs of Madagascar. Visit them in luxury and style.* The magazine, radio show, and maybe someday a TV program, will promote scenic beauty, as well as cultural and natural curiosities. Get it?"

"Startup money is coming from Olympia?" I ask.

"Not exclusively. The B.A.R.F. has promised a contribution, as have several of the African countries named. We even hope to get a State Department grant, for generating mutual good will between the U.S. and African nations. It's really quite a project."

I bow my head. "I'm honored you thought of me."

"I'll never, ever get to see you," murmurs Suzanne.

"I'll make time for you Thursdays." Can't resist the jab.

Suzanne looks genuinely unhappy.

"Look," I say. "Come and join me. We'll make a reportorial-editorial team. Time you ditched that damn TV show. And you're pretty much in a typecast slot at *The New Republic*. No upward advancement for you there, unless you want to forsake journalism to become an executive, which I don't think you do. Why not quit while your ahead? A quicker way to Johnny Carson, once we're a known entity."

"I should resent what you're saying," she says, "but it's sort of true. Oh, and I got a cable from the Carson people. Not like the call that Sheila put Mike up to when they had me off on their wild goose chase so she'd be sure I was in L.A. while she was impersonating me with a red wig in the San Fernando Valley. No, this was forwarded by Rahel, saying that Carson may consider having us both on to tell of our adventure. Anyway, we'll see."

I turn to Southgate-D'Alessandro. "I don't understand how my agency enters into the mix."

"We've studied it," says Southgate, "just as we've studied you. For a long time. In fact, we were instrumental in getting you on the tour."

"You?" At last the answer to a persistent mystery. "I knew you wanted something from me but I figured Sheila was the mover-shaker getting me aboard. She needed her sacrificial lamb to blame the crimes on."

Ms. Southgate smiles mysteriously. "No! We insisted on your presence as a condition to our going. Sheila and Mike merely took advantage of a guy they figured for a sucker."

I grimace. "Thanks a lot. Oh, it's true. But it still hurts."

"If not you, they'd have found somebody else. Even Lazuli would have served in a pinch. But you, traveling alone and with no major business clout, seemed ideal. Your resources and reach were limited, they figured. And you couldn't have afforded a high-powered lawyer or pulled strings to make an international fuss. Quick and easy." Southgate nods in Suzanne's direction. "They hadn't made allowance for you, my dear, your resourcefulness. Nor for the devotion and energy of Shangri-La's staff."

"Okay," I say, "so you picked me for the trip, not knowing," I look hard at the two of them, "there were machinations-to-be. I still don't understand why."

Southgate chuckles. "Machinations." She turns to her paramour-partner. "I told you we had the right guy." Back to me. "No, those machinations, as you say, were strictly Sheila doing her

Scorpion-Queen thing. Our machination is far different." She pours herself a glass of *Château La Tour M'Loulou*, Zambeylia's best white wine, looks over at Suzanne, who shakes her head. "Mmm," Southgate drinks, gargles a bit, smacks her lips. "Lousy, but drinkable. Yes, well, first we spotted your agency. You don't realize it but you're sitting on a treasure trove. Given its location and a bit of travel know-how. You're surrounded by fancy condos, a crowd of businesses and a cluster of world-class teaching hospitals down the block. You have literally thousands of possible clients whom you've never really tried for."

"I know that," My voice is surly. "Where the hell do I get the money to promote us properly?"

"Poor little agency," Southgate shakes her head. "Neither you nor the previous owner have handled it right. We're prepared to buy you out: $10,000 cash, no conditions."

Negotiations last several hours. The four of us move from the restaurant back to the hotel lobby. We men consume several glasses of *cognac*, the ladies stick to *crème de cacao* topped with a layer of goat's cream.

I manage to get Shangri-La's price up to $14,700, soon to be renamed The Sav-Rite Travel Store. Schulz will stay on as manager with a two year contract, renewable. Rahel is to come to the magazine as my personal executive assistant. She will get a salary two-thirds higher than what I've been paying her, plus health and 401K retirement benefits and, of course, all travel expenses.

The money and terms I wrangle for myself will allow me to rent a decent apartment in Manhattan with enough left to for me to live like a human being. Long-distance travel will always be in Business Class or better, with the far-flung hotels, where I'll have to stay much of the time, guaranteed to be best available, or at least designated First Class in the bigger cities.

Suzanne, too, if she decides to join me as a freelance reporter, designated eventually to become my first hire, will be paid

327

reasonably. And she needn't give up her current job at *The New Republic* until the new magazine shows itself as a success.

Suddenly I, who for years have been nobody, am back to being a potential somebody. This time I'll make it stick! But, beyond the agency, I still can't figure out...I decide to look a gift horse in the mouth. "I need to know why me for the editing job."

"We like you," says D'Alessandro. "We know your work in journalism before you jumped into travel. Maybe reporters, given their training as sideline kibbitzers, shouldn't try to run businesses. It's like the guy who watches a chess game and thinks he knows exactly how to win. When he sits down at the board he loses in ten moves. As a reporter you made a name for yourself with that kidnap-murder case you covered in France. It happens your former colleague, Dimitri Speer, is a longtime client of ours. I've been with him on several trips and we're friends. He mentioned you, gave you high marks as a newsman. Said you'd done radio reporting on his show. Besides, not everyone wants to live hopping from one country to the next, chasing stories promoting tourism. You seem ready to enjoy the challenge."

"With all my heart," I answer. Good old Dimitri, a friend of many years. I'll have to get him a case of champagne or something special.

"By the way," D'Alessandro looks grave, "since we'll be socializing back in New York and you'll meet our respective spouses. We count on your discretion."

"But of course," I speak in my most suave Continental manner. "It goes without saying." I want to ask what it is that requires discretion, since I find it hard to imagine that Mrs. D'Alessandro and Mr. Southgate haven't by this time heard from multiple sources how their loved ones spend time *en voyage*. In any case, I'll not be one to bring enlightenment.

When at last my new employers have gone off to their room, I take Suzanne into the hotel garden. The air is redolent with tropical flowers emitting spicy night perfumes. A fountain plashes near the baobab tree, where so long ago it seems, our group, jet-weary but in its plenitude, posed for photos.

"Now that I'm reborn as a journalist-editor," I ask Suzanne, "will you marry me?"

"While you chase every skirt you cross in your far-flung travels? You're still only a publicity journalist, not a really real one. And for dubious causes. Let's see." Pursing her lips she looks at the star-studded sky. "For a first issue lead, how about: *Meet the West's great friend, Central Africa's exiled Emperor Jean-Bedel Bokassa. Watch him occasionally dine on roasted babies deliciously dipped in honey, smuggled to him by 'Friends In High Places.' He'll most generously share the recipe for a supplementary fee.* Or," she's on a roll, "*Witness Sacred Leader Mobutu of Zaïre personally poking the eyes out of dissidents. Like to try your hand at eye-poking? He graciously consents to allow. Cost: $5,000 per eye, no local currency accepted.*" She rants on, "*Dear Mobutu, Zaïre isn't The Belgian Congo anymore but re-named 'Zaïre.' Nothing else has changed it's still a charnel house licking the boots of its European exploiters.*"

A righteous pause, then "For your back-of-the-book section, I suggest: *Observe Zimbabwe's permanent President arrange for his beloved people to die of cholera, while he sticks his hand in the National Treasury to pull out mountains of gold. Unfortunately, we cannot let you personally take away some lingots as 'souvenirs.' B.A.R.F. rules don't permit.* Then two or three issues along you could get a Pulitzer for: *Calling all sadists. Unique opportunity! Participate in genuine genocide. Visit Sudan and help massacre the citizenry. Torture sessions on arrestees guaranteed.* That's enough to get you started. You run outta ideas, just come to me."

"Goddamn!" I exclaim, exasperated. "First of all, there are promising nations in Africa. Botswana is a democracy, I think. Namibia's, well run. South Africa is struggling with Apartheid problems and overcoming them. There's Ghana, Kenya, Tanzania. So don't just cite the bad apples. Anyway, if you're with me as my first freelance reporter, you'll be bound to the travel magazine and its policies just as I am." I take a breath. "You want me to turn away and say, 'No, I cannot compromise my soul by taking on a job

I'd love and that I'll do extremely well? Thank you very much but I will just go back to selling ferry tickets for Hoboken.' Is this what you want m'dear? Because in that case, you're outta luck."

Silence from my maybe Significant Other.

C'mon, Suzanne," I say. "Lighten up. Anyway, I'm going to stick to lions, elephants, golf and waves plashing on golden shores, or golden-red shores as the case may be. Bokasa, Mugabe and even B.A.R.F. can go to hell, as probably they will in time."

"Lifestyle?" bounces back Suzanne. "You gonna make D'Alessandro-Southgate your role models?"

I shake my head. "Despite all your baloney I've been faithful, more or less. I'm ready to make a commitment to you. I'll even help produce some *bambini* of our very own."

Suzanne's turn to shake her head. "No more *bambini*. I'm too old."

"Good," I feel relieved. "Only trying to be nice. So why can't we regularize, I mean consecrate, our relationship?"

"We'll see how things work out. I'm willing to consider it. Provided..."

"Provided?"

"Provided you do a helluva good job as editor and I fit in more or less contentedly as your freelancer; and I gain trust that you're making this a stepping stone to something more settled, more truly, objectively journalistic, more bookworthy. So you can sit down to serious long-term truly significant work, writing work, and we can build a life together, an anchored life." She pauses. Then, "Understand, everything between us is finished forever if you suddenly buy into the zipper biz, or a Burger King franchise, or dabble in any profession but the writing profession. Or if you chase after some *zoftig* floozie with a thrust-out behind who just wants to murder her way to the top of whatever dung hill holds her ambition. Stay on the straight-and-narrow and we'll work a three year plan, okay?"

"Deal," I say. "You're the only floozie for me. Now turn off your judgmentalism and enjoy our being together in this romantic garden, sort of like Adam and Eve, no?"

"Adam and Eve came to grief. But for as long as you hold true, I'll soften."

Under a full African moon the size of a medicine ball, and burnished as beaten gold, we share a long kiss.

Chapter 38: The Proposition
Dallas, Texas: Many Months Later in July 1988

King Bhulliwah is tired after his two week state visit to the U.S.A. He has dined with the President, been given keys to Chicago by its Mayor, thrown a baseball to start a game in Kansas City, ascended the St. Louis arch and in New Orleans overindulged in delicious, spicy creole-Cajun food, causing a night of heartburn.

He hasn't neglected to pay his respects to California's Knott's Berry Farm, since it is now twinned with Zambeylia's Diamantville. The Farm threw him a lavish Western style chuck-wagon barbecue, resulting in horrendous heartburn that inspired the visit to a spa outside of Phoenix. There he'd been starved, rolled in hot sand, Rolfed, steamed and generally made miserable.

Now he has come to the world of J. R. Ewing, of *Dallas* fame. In a hotel penthouse suite, he looks out over the Texas metropolis's flat cityscape dotted with skyscrapers.

His visitor wears boots, a string tie with silver clasp and a ten gallon hat that—so Bhulliwah imagines—is taken off only to shower. He speaks in the courtly, if difficult to decipher, tones of a West Texas cattle millionaire. Only a diphthong or two reveal Bronx origins.

They rise from a conference table. On its polished surface lies a large ordnance map of the Ziloncado Basin and Game Preserve.

N. Sherman Jamieson bows. "Waal, youah Haaghness, ah think ouwah leetle playynn won't cause no bothah to nobody. Leastwise, not immeejutly. Ahh'll give ouwah Richmond folks strict oahdahs to stick to duh toity-toid quadrant, jes' confine theirselves to thet taahny space feh drillin' n' them othah minin' ineetiateeves. Only in due time, Haagh-ness, in due time ah sey, we'all will allow ouwahselves some variances and spreadouts until we get a real good profitable operation goin'. Nah, we won't staht distoibin. them animules awhile yet."

Bhulliwah rubs his hands nervously. "I myself am an animal lover. On my royal estate I have over thirty civet cats in cages. Their musk is coveted by French perfume-makers, quite a profitable operation. Not friendly creatures, but I often stroll by to bid them hello and listen to their snarls." Worry shines in his bulgy eyes. "These travel people, Ms. Southgate with her ecological hang-ups, the Goldstone fellow but especially this General Bazi, our own General of Police. He is forever organizing protests and demonstrations, always inciting our population to riot in favor of animal, as allied to human, rights. I can't fire him; I'd be run out of the country, probably guillotined. Even if I arrange for him to have a fatal accident, that will cause a revolution, leading to my own, er, liquidation. Communism, sheer utter Communism! That's what I'm up against. Or at least the Socialist democracy of Denmark and those other Scandinavian countries in Europe."

Bhulliwah gives his interlocutor a look that brims with self-compassion. "Both Zambilis and those we used to call M'Bélés consider Bazi their champion: defender not merely of our damn wildlife but of human life too. He says it's all one: no Nature, no human survival. All the people, even the poorest, idolize him." Bhulliwah's tone turns confidential. "He's likely to try and be my successor, though I intend to hang on to the Crown, by my teeth, if need be. I take inspiration from that Mugabe fellow in Zimbabwe, who seems to be living forever. If he can conquer eternity, so can I!"

His diatribe leaves King Bhulliwah both breathless and bilious with indignation. Nevertheless, Zembeylia's monarch, ex-Parliamentarian that he is, soldiers on excoriating Bazi. "The man is writing articles and editorials both in our national newspaper and *The New York Times*. His subversive pronouncements extol Zambeylia's natural riches. Bazi's even agitating for MORE protected land than we've already given his environmentalists. What a howl the General will raise, along with *La Southgate* and Goldstone, the Olympia and Ace Corporations backing them too."

Bhulliwah wipes his face with a handkerchief, takes several deep breaths, proceeds in calmer mode, more reflective mode. "Bazi isn't even hopeful of success in the broadest terms. The man's a dyed-in-the-wool Pessimist, who ultimately despairs of the human race's survival from its own greed and genius for destructiveness. He believes we humans will wipe ourselves and all life off our planet within a relatively short time. He actually thinks this a good thing, given what he says is/was our, and I quote, 'lousy, stinking stewardship of what has been entrusted to us.' He wrote that in a leftist U.S. magazine called *The Nation*."

Zambeylia's ruler pauses once more, gazing out at Dallas. "I prefer to look on life's brighter side, especially my own success both as Monarch and contributer to my family's prosperity. Also, to Zambeylia's, of course. As you point out, only the thirty-third quadrant of the Ziloncado is to be affected. For now. Let's see," the King bends over the ordnance map, as far as his ever-expanding waistline allows. "A mere three hundred square miles. And in eight months, an expansion of eighty further square miles. And then, five months after that, a second 'Improvement-Development' of six hundred square miles. 'Improvement-Development,' that sounds most positive. I think I may be able to–how do you say?–swing approval with Parliament. Especially if Richmond hits immediate oil, gas, or valuable mineral deposits. All three? Bazi and his cohorts will have to quiet down. We could sell this as a great boon to the public good." He smiles. "Money always talks; I thank you for your generous gift to my Royal charity fund at Pfister Bank, Geneva."

"Allus a playysure to do bidness wid a true bidnessman," says Jamieson. He makes another bow, then sticks out his hand. After only the slightest hesitation, remembering where he is and joining the spirit of egalitarian democracy in social situations with a not-quite-up-to-snuff citizen, His Royal Highness reaches out his own hand and gives his guest's a soft squeeze.

The Bronx boy-turned-Texan takes his leave, warm in the knowledge of having served not only his pocketbook but also the international marketplace: triumph of human-created industrial development for the sake of *The Global Village* over ever weaker Mother Nature.

Safely alone in the penthouse's private elevator, his thoughts stray back to that fateful evening in the X'Ziloncado Camp, when monkeys savaged his tent. Bitsy standing like Biblical Ruth in fields of alien corn amidst smashed bottles of her creams, perfumes and hand lotions, jewelry scattered all around, dresses bespattered and torn...

How she'd looked at him; her tearful, reproach-filled eyes, those almost girlish cheeks black with running mascara. Accusing him of incompetence plus deliberate mental cruelty.

Well, now he can taste revenge. Glancing around to make sure no spies lurk, he mutters in native Bronxian, unbesmirched by Texan, "Dat'll loin dem damn baboons!"

END

Characters, places, and institutions in alphabetical order:

ACE, Jeffery B. – Chairman of the Jeffrey B. Ace Corporation, known for raids and takeovers. Currently he resides in Cuernavaca, Mexico.

AMAHDI, Gerhardt – A Germano-Turkish rug importer.

BANK FOR AFRICAN RESTRUCTURING AND FUNDING (B.A.R.F.) – A private international monetary fund operating in Southeastern Africa.

BHARASTRI, Mr. S. K. – A postman.

BHULLIWAH-X'ZILONE (Bully-wah-Zee-lone), Antoine– Minority leader in the Zembeylian Parliament.

BHULLIWAH-X'ZILONE, Petrina–Antoine Bhulliwah X'Zilone's wife.

BRIAC (Bree-yac), Félicité, 64–Widow. Runs an ostrich farm near the Zembeylian village of Nouveau-Locronan.

CARRINGTON, Suzanne–U. S. newswoman.

CENTRAL SERVICES DIVISION (C.S.D.)–Zembeylian national police agency equivalent to the F.B.I., France's *Police Judiciaire* or Scotland Yard of Great Britain.

CHANDLER, Gordon–Wall Street travel executive and owner of a charter airline.

COUNCIL OF UNITY AND GOVERNANCE–Zembeylian governing authority under the King.

D'ALESSANDRO, Giorgio–Co-owner, with Malvina SOUTHGATE, of an agency specializing in African safari tours.

DORLAND, Pierre–a farmer at Nouveau Locronon, Zembeylia.

ELAND TOURS–A travel company owned by Helen FARRAR.

FANG, Dr. Shi Wu–an official of the Chinese embassy in Zembeylia.

FARRAR, Helen–Organizer of a tour to Zembeylia.

FENSTER, Harlan–Executive Vice President of the Jeffery B. ACE CORPORATION.

FULUMBANE (Foo-lum-bah-nee)–Capital of ZEMBEYLIA.

GAUDIN, Marc–An accountant at the X'Ziloncado Tented Camp Resort.

GOLDSTONE, Lincoln–Owner of a Manhattan travel agency.

GREEN, Mr.–Envoy from Langley, Virginia. An implied agent of the CIA.

GUITTEREZ- SHAUGHNESSY, Alvaro Maldonado y–Travel companion to Gordon CHANDLER.

JAMIESON, Elizabeth "Bitsy"–Wife of N. Sherman JAMEISON.

JAMIESON, N. Sherman–Owner of a chain of travel agencies in Texas and U.S. Sunbelt.

KEPPEL, Jody–Employee of ELAND TOURS, INC., Manhattan.

LAZULI, Gowinda–Tour guide. Member of Zembeylia's Indian-Tamil minority.

LAWRENCE, Clive–Owner of PINK HORIZONS, a travel agency in the San Fernando Valley, Southern California.

MAHONEY, Michael–Helen FARRAR's husband.

MADAME YVETTE– Proprietress of one of Africa's finest Houses of Pleasure, located in Fulumbane.

M'BAZI (M'Bah-zee), Detective-Colonel Félix–Senior investigator for CENTRAL SERVICES, based in FULUMBANE.

M'BELE (M'Bee-Lee)–Zembeylia's politically dominant tribe.

M'BOWE (M'Bow-ayy, H.E. Zecherias–Zembeylian Minister holding the portfolios of Internal Security, Tourism and Culture.

M'KAWI-X'ZAMBA (M'Kawee-Zamba)–an elephant.

MONDRAN, Barry–Sheila MONDRAN's husband.

MONDRAN, Sheila Flohr-Farrar–Helen FARRAR'S stepsister, a Vice-President of Eland, Inc., and Barry MONDRAN's wife.

MONOGOROS–Zembeylia's highest mountain range. MT. ADRIENNE (6,732 feet) is its highest peak.

MUL–Unit of Zembeylian currency–$1U.S. = MUL 50.

M'ZEKE, Known to Tour Group as **"ZEKE"**–driver-guide at Zembeylia's X'Ziloncado Resort and Game Preserve

M'ZUMBA I–Zembeylia's reigning monarch.

PETROFF, Eugene–Owns a company specializing in world golf tours.

PETROFF, Miho–Eugene's wife. Japanese. An opera singer.

PINK HORIZONS–A travel agency specializing in gay and lesbian travel.

RICHMOND OIL AND MINERAL EXPLORATIONS,INC.–
A Dallas-based petroleum prospecting company.

SECURITY MILITIA (SM)–An elite police-military unit. The only
Zembeylia military unit paid regularly by the government.

SANDARAM, Y. Sanjeev–Distinguished spokesman for Zemebylia's
Indian-Tamil community and CEO of X'ZAMBILI-AFRICA
TOURS.

SCHULZ, Heinz-Herbert–Employee of Lincoln GOLDSTONE's
travel agency.

**SHANGRI-LA: WORLDWIDE JOURNEYS OF
ADVENTURE**–Manhattan travel agency owned by Lincoln
GOLDSTONE.

SOUTHGATE, Malvina–Business partner of Giorgio
D'ALESSANDRO.

TEFURI, Rahel–Lincoln GOLDSTONE's office manager.

UPPINGHAM, Dale III–A banker with the B.A.R.F.

X'ZAMBILI (Zam-bee-lee)–Largest ethnic group in Zembeylia.

X'ZAMBILI AFRICA TOURS–Rival to *ZEMBA ROYAL TOURS*
in Zembeylia.

X'ZILONCADO (Zilon-kah-do) NATIONAL GAME AREA and
ZEMBEYLIA'S main animal preserve.

X'ZIMBALWA (Zim-bal-wah), Captain-Detective Matthias–A police
detective from Central Services, based in X'ZIROMEU CITY.

X'ZINTUXZ'XIMBULU (Zintux-Zim-boo-loo)–Sgt. X'Zvinanda
(Zee-vee-nanda) Capt.X'ZIMBALWA's assistant. Known to the
U.S. tour group as "The-Sergeant-With-The-Unpronounceable-
Name."

X'ZIROMEU CITY–Zembeylia's second city, located in the
country's mining area producing tsavorites and diamonds, at the
northern base of the MONOGORO MOUNTAINS.

ZEMBA ROYAL TOURS, INC.–A Zembeylian tour company.

ZEMBEYLIA–Southeast African nation bordered by South Africa,
Mozambique and the Indian Ocean. Until 1973, a French colony.

Acknowledgements:

Many grateful thanks to the members of The Bedford Wordsmiths of Bedford, MA and to Read, Write and Publish of Cambridge, MA., two groups of writers whose meetings I have attended and who have consistently given me insightful critiques plus suggestions on how I might approach and construct the present novel.

By the same token, I give special gratitude to the author Rebecca Leo-Nichols for her devoted proof-reading and editing suggestions for the novel in its intermediate state. Without her insightful help the manuscript would be far less than it is.

Heartfelt thanks to Don and Pat Sweeney for loyal friendship and fellow-writer Don's editing suggestions.

I owe deep gratitude to Nancy E. Phillips for a friendship that has kept me sane through writing anguish, as well as, once again, her editorial remarks and copy-editing while work was in progress.

Finally, not last and least but first and foremost, thanks to Robin Stratton, my publisher. Robin is an author in her own right plus a discoverer of others' writing talent. Big Table Publishing is becoming a force to be reckoned with as producer of distinguished works by authors from New England and beyond. May my modest effort add to her growing reputation as a serious editor/publisher/creator of memorable manuscripts.

Thomas R. Bransten, Somerville, MA
April, 2016

www.ingramcontent.com/pod-product-compliance
Lightning Source LLC
Chambersburg PA
CBHW032137270626
47172CB00008B/135